Never Again, No More 6:

Karma's Payback

Never Again, No More 6:

Karma's Payback

Untamed

www.urbanbooks.net

Urban Books, LLC
300 Farmingdale Road, NY-Route 109
Farmingdale, NY 11735

Never Again, No More 6: Karma's Payback

ISBN 10: 978-1-64556-461-4

First Mass Market Printing September 2023
First Trade Paperback Printing June 2022
Printed in the United States of America

10 9 8 7 6 5 4 3 2 1

*This is a work of fiction. Any references or similar-
ities to actual events, real people, living or dead, or
to real locales are intended to give the novel a sense
of reality. Any similarity in other names, characters,
places, and incidents is entirely coincidental.*

Distributed by Kensington Publishing Corp.
Submit Orders to:
Customer Service
400 Hahn Road
Westminster, MD 21157-4627
Phone: 1-800-733-3000
Fax: 1-800-659-2436

Never Again, No More 6:

Karma's Payback

by

Untamed

Dedication

To all the readers who stayed with me on this
journey. This is for you!

Acknowledgments

God first, forever, and always. There is no creativity without the Creator. Thank you for allowing me to borrow this gift while I grace your Earthly plane.

To my hubby and kids, my original and forever riders, y'all keep me grounded, and your support means the entire world. This vessel doesn't run without the moving parts. Thank you all for fueling me every day. I love you.

To N'Tyse and Urban Books, thank you for giving my book baby series a home.

To Robert White, Royaltea Book Club, Book Club Bosses, J. Sapphire, My Luv of Books, Sip and Flip Book Club, Kaybee's Bookshelf, Diamond's Literary World, Sip then Read, and the numerous book clubs, reviewers, and bloggers who got behind this series, my thanks are limitless!

To the countless small and Black-owned bookstores who house the series, thank you! Thank you! Thank you! I must give special love to two bookstores that have been instrumental to me.

Acknowledgments

Urban Reads Books in Baltimore, you all show out with selling my books! And Source of Knowledge in New Jersey, the cornerstone bookstore to get Untamed out there to the world of urban book readers, I'm forever grateful to you, Patrice and Dexter.

To the readers who journeyed with these crazy-ass characters and my loopy self throughout this series, bless your hearts! They end here, but we all know nothing this good ever really ends, right? Ha! Thank you for the ride. Join me one mo' time!

Last, but never least, to my mother. You spoke this over my life. I wasn't ready when you tried to push me, but I'm ready now. Thank you for giving life and speaking life. Rest well, my beautiful angel.

Chapter 1

Gavin

"LaMeka! LaMeka! Baby, I know you hear me! LaMeka! LA-ME-KA!" Standing outside on her front steps, I took a swig of my Hennessy straight out of the bottle, then wiped the remnants of the liquor from my mouth with the back of my hand before recapping the bottle. "LaMeka! Open this door. Talk to me!"

"Gavin?" I heard a voice by the side of the house.

It was her nosy-ass neighbor, Mr. Jim.

"Yeah, it's me, Mr. Jim. Just trying to talk to my girlfriend. You can go back inside."

Mr. Jim looked at his watch. "You do realize the hour, don't you, son?"

I looked at my watch. Twelve thirty in the morning. "Yes, I do. You do realize I'm not talking to you or knocking at your door, don't you, Mr. Jim?"

"Listen to me. You're drunk. Nothing is going to get resolved today and definitely not at this godforsaken hour that doesn't have disaster written all over it. Why don't you come inside with me and let me fix you a hot cup of coffee? You can sober up, and we can talk. Then you can start fresh again in the morning with Meka."

"No. She's gonna answer the door. You just wait and see."

"Gavin, she hasn't answered in the full two weeks you've been coming over here. Now, son, come on over for some coffee before someone calls the police on you."

"If they call the police, she'll probably *open the door*." I kicked the front door with my foot.

Suddenly, the door swung open, and LaMeka walked out wrapped in her robe and bedroom shoes. "Hi, Mr. Jim. It's okay. I'm going to let him in. You can go back inside. I'm sorry for the disruption."

"It's not your fault. Are you sure you'll be okay?" he asked, eyeing me closely.

"She'll be fine. I'm not gonna hurt her. I just wanna see her. Talk to her." My eyes never left LaMeka as I caressed her face. "I've missed you so much. Don't you miss me?"

She sucked her teeth and swatted my hand away. "I'll be all right. Goodnight, Mr. Jim." She waved at him as he nodded and went inside. "Get your ass inside this house and shut up before I call the police on you my damn self."

I staggered inside as she closed and locked the door. Her mom and sister were standing there in their robes, too, one with a baseball bat and the other with a frying pan.

"Heeeeyyyyy!" I put my hands up. "What the hell?"

"Oh, we're here just in case you get outta hand," Misha said, holding the frying pan. "I love you like a brother, Gavin, but this is my blood sister, and ain't nobody putting a hand on her again."

"And I second that," her mother concurred.

"Ms. Barbara. Come on, Mama. You know I'd never do anything to any of you all. I just want to see Meka."

"Well, Hennessy makes people do strange things. Makes them act out of character. I'm just here to make sure that you don't get out of character because if you do, I *will* get out of hand," Ms. Barbara said. "Do you understand me?"

"Understood." I put my hands up to let her know there wouldn't be any problems from me.

LaMeka walked in front of me, turning her attention toward them. "We're going to go to the family room and talk. You guys can fall back."

They looked at each other. "We'll be in my room, which ain't far from the family room. If I hear one thing that sounds remotely like a cry of distress—"

"I promise you won't." I interrupted Ms. Barbara's rant.

"I better not," she said before turning away. "Come on, Misha," she ordered as they both walked away, eyeing me closely.

LaMeka turned around, rolled her eyes at me, folded her arms, and proceeded to walk to the family room. I followed behind her. Watching her ass swish side to side in that silk robe made me want to grab her and make love to her right there on the floor like I never had before. She flipped her hair, which made me take notice. She'd gotten her hair done and added some long tresses to it. Long hair looked very good on her. She was a goddess no matter how long or short it was, though. I just wanted to run my fingers through it and kiss her.

It wasn't just about the sex with LaMeka either. For as many sexual fantasies that were going through my mind, I had just as many family fantasies. As we reached the family room, I peered at the dining room and smiled as I thought of all the Sunday dinners we'd shared in that room. Pictures of the boys were everywhere. To me, they weren't just LaMeka's boys. They were my sons.

My eyes fell on a picture that LaMeka and I had taken with them at Six Flags. Our first family photo, so to speak. I thought of all the times we'd sat on the floor in this room by the fireplace and held each other, talking about our dreams and aspirations. I missed everything from Saturday morning breakfasts to joking with Misha, helping

Ms. Barbara deep clean, playing Transformers with the boys, and hell, even running to pay bills. I missed Meka and everything about her like crazy.

"What the hell is your problem coming over every day causing drama for me with my neighbors?" LaMeka sounded off, breaking my thoughts.

I sat on the sofa and put my bottle of Hennessy on the table. "Baby, I'm sorry for that, but I had to see you. You've been avoiding me."

LaMeka put her hand on her forehead in frustration. "Gavin, I haven't been avoiding you. I broke up with you. I don't need to see you because we need to go our separate ways."

Leaning forward, I shook my head. "I didn't break up with you."

"Ugh!" she bellowed. "This is ridiculous. It doesn't matter who broke up with whom. It only matters that we are no longer together, but you already know that. You're not dumb by any stretch of the imagination. So, let me be clear. Do not come by here anymore. Stop calling, stop texting, stop emailing, stop leaving me gifts, and stop trying to corner me at the workplace. Just stop. We're done."

"I can't!" The words bounced out of me as I jumped up from the sofa. "Meka, I can't let you go. How can you just let us go like that? Didn't I mean anything to you?"

The question lingered in the air for a while, then I attempted to walk up to her. I needed to be in her space, but she put her hand up as a signal to thwart my attempt to enter her closeness.

"No, don't come near me."

"Why not?" I kept approaching her. "Are you afraid to be close to me? Afraid that if you're close, you'll be weak? Your feelings will take over?"

"You reek of alcohol, and it stinks," she said plainly.

A smirk spread across my face at her comeback. "You're playing hard. I know that's your MO." She waved off my words, but I continued despite her dismissiveness. "I know everything about you. I know that you really don't want to let me go." Still reaching out for her, I pulled her to me by the waist. "I love you, baby. Don't let us go."

Clamping down on her bottom lip, she began to blink back the tears that had begun to form in the corners of her eyes. "God, Gavin! Why can't you just leave me alone? You keep bringing up emotions that I am trying so hard to let go of. I don't want to let you go. I want to be with you, but I can't. Your family would never allow it to happen, and I owe it to my family not to put them through that. We have no choice but to end this, so just stop."

There it was again. The source of my forever headache, my family. Scratch that. My father and my brother were no family of mine. Their racist views had driven a wedge the size of Texas between LaMeka and me, and while I didn't give a damn about their opinions and threats, LaMeka did. With all that had happened in her life, I couldn't blame her for not wanting to engage in this fight, but I'd be damned if I wouldn't. I had enough fight built inside for the both of us. If only she'd allow me to be her fighter.

Gently, she pulled away from me and took a seat in the recliner. My recliner. I had deemed it as my favorite seat months ago. I kneeled in front of her.

"I don't care about my family, and I would never let them do anything to hurt *our* family."

Her sad eyes lifted in shock from the words I'd spoken. Simultaneously, a small gasp escaped her lips, and her hand moved to her heart. "You said *our* family."

Leaning forward, I caressed her face. "Yes. Ours. You, the boys, your mom, and Misha. You all are my *real* family. My loyalty is to you, and I will protect you all at all costs."

Briefly she took in my words and then slowly shook her head. "I love and appreciate the fact that you want to be with us, but that is your father and your brother. They are your blood. If things don't work out between us, then who will you turn to?"

"Things will work out between us. I know this. I can't explain it to you, but in my gut, when I think about living my life with you, it just feels right. You're my soulmate, Meka. I may not do all I'm supposed to do in my Christian faith, but I believe in God, and I believe He made you just for me."

She wiped the tears that had finally managed to escape, then stared at me for a few moments as if searching deep within my soul before she spoke again. "Gavin, I'm scared, and I can't feel secure in what you're saying because I sense your fear, too. It's best if we just end things. We can be friends. You know I'd do anything for you as a friend."

She could not be serious. The realization of her words was beginning to take root, and I needed her to understand that the only fear she saw was the fear I had of losing her. My emotions got the best of me, and it was like a knot was lodged in my chest. Tears welled up in my eyes, and I jumped up.

"*Friends?* I don't want to be your fucking friend! I want to be your man. *Your man,* Meka! *Fuck* friendship. *Fuck* Gerald Randall. *Fuck* Gary Randall. *Fuck* Tony. *Fuck* every *fucking* body who tries to come between us!"

Before I could turn around, Ms. Barbara was already in the family room. "Everything all right in here?" she asked with the bat planted firmly in her hands.

"We're fine, Mama," Meka said with exasperation.

"I think it's time for you to leave, Gavin. It's after one o'clock in the morning, and the boys are trying to sleep. Now, you've said your piece, and Meka has said hers. It's time to end this mess tonight, so we can all get some rest," Ms. Barbara said definitively.

"Mama, please don't push me out right now. I need to talk to Meka a little longer. I just have to get her to understand—"

Meka stood and threw her hands up. "Enough! I've heard enough. No more talking. I have to rest for my exams tomorrow, so I'm going to bed. Gavin, you're drunk, and you're not driving anywhere in your condition. I will bring you some blankets and a pillow to sleep on the sofa. In the morning, I want you to be gone before the boys see you like this," she demanded before walking out of the family room and taking my bottle of Hennessy with her.

As I sat on the sofa, I knew there was no use in arguing with her. I didn't want her mom to call the police on me or have the police called on her for beating me to death with that bat, so I decided to chill. I could try to explain again the next day that I had called my father and told him to buy me out. I wanted out of the family business, the family money, and the family. My father hadn't been pleased with me at all. In fact, all he had said to me was that he'd look into it and then he hung up in my face.

Oh, well. He could feel how he wanted to feel about it. At the end of the day, I was sticking by LaMeka. She was my sole concern, but I needed her to know how committed I was to her and our life.

"Here," I heard Meka say to me. I opened my eyes and saw her standing over me with blankets and a pillow.

"Why can't I just sleep in our bedroom?"

"Because it's not *our* bedroom. It's mine." She shook her head. "You are a piece of work."

"I'm a man in love with a woman."

Ignoring my words, she said, "Set your watch for seven in the morning. Junior has a therapy session at eight thirty, so you need to be gone before he wakes up. Here are two ibuprofen and a small cup of coffee to fight off that hangover you'll have in the morning."

As she slipped the pills in my hand, I grabbed her hand. "I love you, baby." My voice dripped with deep sincerity.

"I know," she said, turning to walk away.

"Please say that you still love me, too," I begged just before she walked out. My voice was thick with emotion as I pleaded. "Please."

She stopped, and I could sense the internal debate she was having. Slowly, she turned around, let out a deep sigh, and told me the one thing I needed so desperately to know. "I love you, too, Gavin."

Before she could move to leave, I got up and walked to her. Without warning, I kneeled on one knee and pulled out a small box that contained a three-carat diamond solitaire engagement ring. I opened it for her. She gasped as I held her hand.

"This is how ready I am to prove to you and the world that you are the only woman for me. I'm selling my shares back to my dad. I've already set that in motion. I'm out of the family business and money. You are my family now. I gave it all up for you because you're meant to be my wife. I love you, LaMeka Shantel Roberts. Please do me the honor of allowing me to be your husband. Will you marry me?"

Emotion had overcome her as she stared at the ring and took in my words, and the tears that she'd once successfully withheld spilled down her face in waves. "I don't . . . I don't know what . . . I don't know what to say."

"Say yes. Please. Say yes."

She put her head down and bit her lip but still didn't answer.

"I've done *everything*. I've given back the business. I've given up those two Randall men, and I've sworn them off. I promise, on my life, that I will never leave you. I want to be your husband, Meka. Please say you'll be my wife. My life is with you and the boys. I want us to get married, have a little girl or boy of our own. Raise the kids. Grow old together. I can't see my life without you in it, Meka. Say you'll stay in my life and be my wife. *Please*."

Meka fanned her tears away with one hand as I held her other trembling hand. "Gavin," she said barely above a whisper. "I don't know."

"What can I do to show you? Tell me, and I'll do it." Standing, I took the ring out of the box. Bringing my left hand to her face, I gently wiped away her tears as I held the ring in my right hand. I drew her eyes into mine and held her gaze until she could see to the depths of my soul. "I promise you. I will never let you go. Never."

Her brow furrowed as I saw her resolve beginning to dissipate. "Are you sure that you want to marry me?"

"Yes, woman! Only you. No regrets. *Not one*."

"And your family?" she asked again.

"Not a problem or one regret."

She bit her bottom lip and nodded. "Yes! Yes, I'll marry you."

I slipped the ring on her finger and picked her up, holding her tightly in an embrace. Once I put her down, she wrapped her arms around my neck and brought my face toward her for the softest, sweetest kiss we'd ever shared.

"I love you," I whispered through bated breath as we touched foreheads.

She smiled giddily as she looked at her ring. "I love you, too. I'm getting married! I'm so happy."

Hugging her tightly again, I declared, "That's right, Mrs. Gavin Randall. You are. So, what do you say we go and celebrate?" I took her hand to led her to the bedroom.

She stopped me. "Ugh, no." She removed her hand from mine and then crossed her arms, looking at me defiantly. "You're still on sofa duty tonight, chief. You reek of alcohol, and you're not getting that smell in my new pillowtop mattress," she said before strolling up to me sexily. "Besides, I want you to go home in the morning and sober up. We'll take the family out for dinner tomorrow to announce our engagement, and then we can do whatever we want to do." She placed her arms around my shoulders in a loose embrace.

"Hmmm. Whatever we want?"

"Anything," she answered, her voice dripping with seduction.

Bending down, I kissed her plump lips. "Ask Mama to keep the kids for us tomorrow night. I have a big date to plan."

"I will." She smiled giddily. "Goodnight, hubby."

"Goodnight, wifey." I smiled at her as she sauntered out of the family room.

I made my pallet on the sofa then took off my leather jacket, my Polo boots, and my long-sleeve shirt. I lay down with just my T-shirt, jeans, and socks on, with nothing but good dreams planned as I smiled down on the inside. Meka was going to be my wife. There is no greater joy in the world than being with the one you love and having that love magnified tenfold.

As soon as I dozed off, my cell phone buzzed. I reached in my pocket and answered without checking who it was.

"Yeah," I answered sleepily.

"Glad to hear you're up, s—."

"Actually, I am asl—."

"If you answered, then you're awake. And stop cutting me off," he interrupted. "I'm emailing you some paperwork in the morning. It's about your shares."

Groggily, I asked, "What's my buyout?"

"Nothing."

That was enough to jerk me out of my alcohol-induced slumber. "Huh?"

"Your lack of business skills amazes me sometimes, son. If I hadn't had a blood test done on you myself, I'd wonder if you were really mine," he said, sounding disappointed.

"Son of a bitch," I mumbled. "I can't believe you."

"I don't see why you shouldn't. I had all my children tested. Of the seven that were blamed on me, only you, your brother, and your half-sister Veronica were mine."

"Huh? I was talking about the shares. Wait a minute. I have a half-sister?" I asked. This was just like my dad to say something like that without regard to a person's feelings. Just plain uncouth.

He heaved a sigh. "Yes, you do. I forget your brother is the only child of mine who actually talks to me to know these things. Veronica is like you, stubborn as a mule and mean as a rattlesnake. She refuses to talk to me."

"I wonder why," I said sarcastically. "Anyway, back to the subject so that I can go back to sleep, please."

"Ah, yes. The reason your buyout is nothing is because you didn't adhere to the clause about interracial dating restrictions. Seeing as how dating a *black girl* is the reason you want to give up your ownership rights, you get nothing. Not even the right to say it was yours. Hell, I gave it to you anyway. It was never yours."

I shrugged. "Whatever. It doesn't matter to me. Goodnight."

"Wait, son. Not so fast. However, I will need the interest produced from the shares that you've lived heftily off of. My accountant estimates that to be around five hundred thousand. You'll need to give that back to me."

Now he had my undivided attention as I sat up straight. "Wait a minute. You know I don't have that kind of money."

My mom's policy was only two-hundred-fifty thousand, and I had that in an escrow account. It had only made about a hundred thousand. I was planning on using part of that for the wedding, then flipping it into a higher yield interest-bearing account to set us up for a nice savings and retirement plan. My pay at work was only about a hundred grand a year. It was decent, but nowhere near close enough to pay off that kind of debt.

"Yes, I do know this, son. You think I don't?" my dad said snidely. "And it will need to be paid in full in sixty days."

"*Sixty days?* That's two months."

"You can do math. That's refreshing."

"You can't be serious."

"Oh, I'm very serious. Oh, and I pulled my funding for the hospital today. Thanks to you, they will no longer receive their annual million-dollar contribution. Oh yeah, and I've pulled my support of their cancer research project, which is a multi-million-dollar deal. After that went down, the head of the hospital administration called me, and I explained to him why I was doing all of this, which is the fractured relationship with their employee, my son. In the morning, you have a meeting with your boss and the administration. I might as well tell you this because I hate surprises, so I won't surprise you. Your job is on the line. If you don't figure out a way to get them those funds back, you can kiss your career goodbye—and Meka's, because I fully intend to go after her job, too. I'm so glad I got that off my chest," he said with a sigh of relief. "*Now* . . . you can go back to sleep, son. Goodnight and sweet dreams. Tell LaMeka I said hello."

I was so mad, my entire body started trembling. "You leave her out of this, or I swear—"

"Doesn't she have a baby with autism that currently receives treatment from the hospital? The biggest financial contributor to that program is my good friend Hans Johannesburg. Do I need to make a call to have that program discontinued?" he asked snidely.

"Wait! No. Don't."

He laughed. "I think you get my point. Keep your idle threats to yourself before you ruin any more of your life or LaMeka's."

"Dad, can we just talk about this?"

"Sure we can. I can talk, and you can listen," he said firmly. "I'm done playing games with you, Gavin. You're *my* son. Mine! And I will not sit idly by while you ruin my family name. So, either you leave that . . . that . . . *jig* alone, or I will not stop until I have single-handedly annihilated everything you hold near and dear to your heart. And that can only be five things: LaMeka, Tony Jr., LaMichael, Barbara, and Misha."

"How'd you—"

"Know about her entire family?" he finished for me. "The same way I know everything I know. I have the money and the power to find out anything. And you won't have the money to help her live out of a cardboard box by the time I'm done. Just how long do you think she'll stay, knowing you're the cause for all the problems in her life? She's a good woman. She's just not the woman for you. Hell, I don't care if she *is* the woman for you. She's not the right woman by my standards, and my standards are the only standards that matter. Checkmate, son. Game over."

I swallowed the lump in my throat. I was so hot I thought I was about to have a heat stroke. How could he do this to his child? All I wanted was to marry Meka, and now, everything was messed up after I had promised her that I could protect her. Not only could I not protect her, but I also couldn't protect myself. I had just convinced her to marry me. If I told her what was going on, she'd throw that ring back in my face and never speak to me again.

I needed time to think. I couldn't let him ruin LaMeka's life.

"I swear you are nothing but pure evil."

"I've been told that the devil is afraid of me." He chuckled as if it didn't faze him at all.

I rubbed my forehead, hoping to buy myself some time. "Please don't cut the funding to the hospital programs or mess with Meka's career. I'll think of something. Just please don't do that."

He sighed. "I must be getting soft hearted. Fine. Since you're my son, I'll give you thirty days to be rid of this woman. I won't cut the funding. I'll call back and let them know it was a misunderstanding and not to say anything to you or LaMeka. But thirty days is all you have. Please don't test me. You don't want to go toe to toe with me. Believe me."

As bad as I wanted to cuss his ass out, I tucked my tail. "Okay."

"Thirty days, Gavin," he said with finality and hung up in my face.

I deleted his call and slid my cell phone on the coffee table. Running my hands down my face in frustration, I picked up her engagement ring box.

Without realizing it, I squeezed the box until I crushed it. Deep down, I wished it was my father's head. One day, that bitch karma was going to serve his ass the justice that I couldn't. I prayed that I lived long enough to witness it. For now, the only thing going through my mind was the seven-thou-sand-dollar price tag of that damn ring, which was purchased through the interest of the money I now had to pay back.

I was so distraught I didn't know what to do. So, I did the one thing I had gotten away from that always helped me calm down and use sound judgment. I got down on my knees, and I prayed.

Chapter 2

Charice

I was not a hater. I wasn't. I swear to God above I wasn't a hater. But sitting there in my little sitting room, reading a book and trying to keep my mind off the state of my relationship with Lincoln while being interrupted by my best friend screaming—at the top of her lungs, no less—that she was getting married to the love of her life was not putting me in the best of fucking moods. Yes, I was miserable, and even though I really was happy for LaMeka, I kinda wanted some of that company that misery attracts, or at the very least, to wallow in my own self-pity in peace.

"Girl, I can't believe it. I simply can't believe it!" she squealed in my ear.

"Me either. I thought you broke up with him." I managed to get a word in after five minutes of her yelling and screaming on the phone.

"You are such a killjoy. Why do you have to bring up old stuff?"

Smacking my lips, I sucked my teeth. "Hell, it ain't old. You just called me last week and told me you broke up with him the week before, and now a week later, you're getting married. How the hell is that old?"

"I would've thought your first response would be 'Congratulations, Meka. When is the date?' or 'I'm so happy for you.' Not 'I thought you two broke up.'" She fussed, irritation laced in her tone.

"You're right. I'm sorry. Congratulations, Meka. I'm so happy for you. When is the date?" I rattled off, trying to muster up true glee.

"You know what? Fuck you, Charice. When things are going bad in your life you shut down and kill everyone's spirit around you," LaMeka spewed.

She was right, but I wasn't going to give her the satisfaction of knowing it. "I'm sorry. I really am. I promise I wasn't trying to kill your spirit. I'm happy for you and Gavin. Honestly. He's a great guy, and he only anted up his stock by choosing an awesome lady to be his wife. I'ma have me a little mixed god-baby with long hair and blue eyes."

LaMeka laughed. "Shut up! You are so stupid. Mixed god-baby with blue eyes. Only your silly ass would think of some shit like that to say."

"No, actually, Lucinda and Misha would say the same thing," I countered with a snicker.

"You've got a point there."

"So, when is the date? Oh, and I want to pick out my own maid of honor dress if you don't mind."

"We haven't set a date. In fact, we haven't even talked about it since he proposed last night. He left early this morning, and I'm on my way to take an exam. We're supposed to be having a family dinner to announce the engagement tonight, but I just couldn't hold it in any longer. I had to tell somebody before I burst open," she exclaimed. "I'm so freaking excited, Charice. And yes, you can pick your own *matron* of honor dress as long as I approve. Speaking of, let's get that straight now. You're a *matron,* not a *maid,* darling."

"Well, that depends on how fast you plan on getting married." I got quiet after those words came out.

"Huh? What the hell? What's going on, Charice?"

Although Ryan wasn't home, I had to be careful. Peeping out the door to ensure the coast was clear, I said, "I'm filing for a divorce."

"*What*? Why? How?"

All I could offer was, "It was inevitable."

"Tell me this is not because of Lincoln. You're not honestly giving up on your marriage to go run off with that man, are you?" The disbelief was evident through the phone.

The groan that followed was intended to display my disdain of speaking on the matter. "I can't help how I feel or who I love."

"No, but you can help your actions. Come on, Charice. You chose to marry Ryan. *You* chose that. You could've remained single, but you got married trying to run from the pain of losing Charity and losing Lincoln. Now you want to disrupt the boys' lives and break Ryan's heart because you think you made a mistake," LaMeka preached.

"Well, I'm sorry that you have it going on now and are making wise and confident decisions about your life, but I'm not happy, and I'm not going to live my life hoping and wishing. Or at least I hope not."

She let out a heavy breath. "I'm sorry, girl. I shouldn't have judged you. How can I? Not too long ago, I was contemplating getting back into a relationship with my HIV-positive ex-boyfriend who beat on me and slept with my sister, so I apologize. And honestly, for as excited as I am, I still fear Gavin's family's reaction to our engagement," she admitted. "Do what you need to do to make yourself happy, but I do have a question. If divorcing Ryan might not give you the happiness you need, then why do it?"

"It's not the divorce I'm worried about. It's whether I'll still have Lincoln. He's gotten tired of waiting mainly because he thinks it's not going to happen. He won't call me or answer my calls unless it's about Lexi, and I was informed the last time he dropped London off to dance class that I'm no longer allowed to pop up at his house to visit. I'm in the dark because he's being so cryptic with me. He won't just come out and say that it's over, but that's exactly how he acts."

"I've learned that you always trust how a person acts, not what they say or don't say. If their words are truthful, then their actions will line up with that. I think he's telling you that it's over, but he doesn't know how to tell you that," LaMeka counseled.

"But what if he's just guarding his heart until the divorce is final? Maybe he feels that if he acts as if he doesn't care, then he won't be disappointed if I don't follow through with it, even though I am."

LaMeka let out a small grunt. "Hell, I don't know. Men guard their feelings a lot more than women, so you may have a point. I can't really say. You know him better than I do. I say use your best judgment, or better yet, find a way to actually talk about it before shit hits the fan for real."

"Yeah, I know," I said dejectedly. "Look, I'm sorry. You called with all this good news, and I'm flooding you with my issues. Tell me about this proposal."

Without skipping a beat, she filled me in on everything about the past two weeks of visits, gifts,

all the way through last night and the proposal. I
could tell that she truly wanted to be his wife, and
I smiled, feeling her happiness burst through the
line. Thank God somebody had a silver lining in
the clouds.

"Wow. He gave it all up for you? Girl, that's some
powerful love to go against family and give up a
huge fortune just to be somebody's husband. What
kind of hood-girl moves have you thrown on this
white boy to make him snap like that? You've got
him so loco for you that he's gonna be dressed up
like Louis Farrakhan, selling bean pies and singing
Negro spirituals."

"My side. It hurts. Stop it." LaMeka struggled,
crying in laughter.

"Girl, you and the kids gonna be dressed up
like Black Panthers, and he's gonna be the ring-
leader. Fight the damn power, Gavin! I hear ya,
my brotha!" I joked some more and made the
legendary symbolic fist with my hand.

"Oh em to the freaking geeee! I'm gonna piss my
pants if you don't shut the hell up. As a matter of
fact, I have to go. I'm sitting in this car on campus
with people looking at me as if I'm crazy listening
to your ass. I'm so glad I wasn't driving. I would've
wrecked." She laughed. "Listen, I'ma call you
tomorrow so we can discuss these wedding plans.
By then, I should have a date, and you just clear
your damn calendar because as my matron or

maid of honor, I'm gonna need you, like *need* you for real down here in the ATL."

"I've got you covered. Go, do great on that exam, and put it down hood-girl style on your fiancé tonight. I'll talk with you tomorrow."

Though I wanted to be at home enjoying a good book, I was becoming restless. Perhaps I'd settle for my old fallback and go shopping. Don's wife was always asking to hang out, so I figured I could hit her up and put some damage on the Amex card. It was one of the rare days when I had the house to myself. Johanna was off, the boys were at football practice, Lexi was with Lincoln's parents, and Ryan was at football practice as well.

But I knew what my biggest issue was. I wanted to talk to Lincoln. I went inside and poured myself a glass of wine and decided to call him. He couldn't avoid me forever. Maybe they were on a break or something where I could finagle him into agreeing to meet with me.

Maybe not. It went straight to his voicemail. "You've reached Linc. At the tone, you know what to do. Have a good one."

"Linc. It's me. I know you're at practice. I just wanted to call you and see how you were doing." I paused before releasing a distressed sigh. "Lincoln, please call me so we can talk, and not about Lexi. About us. I need to know where your head and your heart are with me right now. Mine have been in the same place they've always been—with you. I miss you. Call me. *Please*."

The greatest thing about the season was that I got to see Ryan less, but the worst part was that when he was home, he wanted to tear my back out, getting sex after bouts of absence. I tried to withhold sex from him, but it was hard living in the house with a man like Ryan. Not to mention, it was hard having urges for sex and not being able to get it from the person I wanted.

Being without Lincoln these past couple of weeks had me thinking a lot about the hardships in my life. The most pressing hardship of all was that it was hard—damn near unbearable—loving someone else and living a lie. I had to file for divorce. Forget my past mistakes, bad decisions, or even the effect it had on everyone's lives. I was just tired of living a lie. I loved Lincoln, and I wanted to be his wife. If I had taken the time to come to this realization sooner, I might not have been sitting there wishing I had Lincoln in my life again.

"Hey, girl. Are you ready?" Felicia asked me as I answered my cell phone.

"Yes. I need a good relaxing day at the spa and a trip to the nail salon. I'm getting my purse now."

"Well, I am like five minutes away. I'm just ready to blow up some of Don's money. That new contract was fat!" She laughed.

"You are a mess."

"I don't know why you're playing like you don't know where I'm coming from, *Mrs. Westmore*. You are the boss with the most. The baddest boss bitch in town. The lady beside *the prodigy*—the fifty-million-dollar powerhouse feet. Those of us who are in your position crave to be like you, and those who aren't would die to trade places with you. You are not the equivalent to the ish. You *are* the ish!"

"Wow. Here I thought I was just plain ol' Charice from a little city called Atlanta who married her high school sweetheart. You guys sure know how to make people feel superhuman."

"Honey, please. You stopped being regular the moment Ryan signed that NFL contract," she said. "But I guess that's why he's Mr. Faithful, unlike Don. You're so down to damn Earth that you keep him grounded. Tell me, how do you have access to all that you have and still manage to act as if you don't?"

"Trust me. If you had a history with Ryan as I do, it'd be easy. In life, I guess I've learned to expect less out of most people. That way, if they give me more, I'm pleasantly surprised, and if I get less, then I didn't get any more out of them than I expected in the first place. That way, I'm never disappointed."

"Oh, I get it. Men. Honey, we all expect less out of a man. Just like next week, I *expect* Don will be in some titty bar or with some exotic model. Just as long as I can *expect* that money to stay in our house, I'm not trying to put a noose on that man. If he's faithful, then score one for Felicia. If not, score one for that Amex," she joked.

I just shook my head as my line beeped. "Girl, I'll see you when you get here. I have to take this call."

"All right, girl."

She hung up, and I clicked over. "Hello?"

"Hi, Charice. How are you?" my attorney asked.

"I'm doing pretty good considering."

She sighed. "You poor thing. I understand, honey. Is now a good time?"

"I have a few minutes. I'm actually going out with one of my girlfriends for a girls' day."

"Well, that's great. You probably need that," she encouraged. "If it's not too much trouble, can you stop by my office to pick up some paperwork? I just need you to go through it and make sure all of the terms we decided to ask for are what you want. Let me know if I need to make any changes or adjustments."

"Umm, well, I'll probably be out for at least three hours. I can cut the day short after the spa and nail salon."

"Oh, the simple pleasures that I must rush to enjoy. I can't remember the last time I had time for a spa treatment," she said, sounding starry eyed about my day of fun.

An idea came to me. "Why don't you come with us? Felicia doesn't have to know that you're *my* attorney. She can just think you're my friend who *happens* to be an attorney."

"Girl, I'm not sure about that. I need to finish up so much stuff."

She reminded me so much of myself, making time for everything and everyone except for self.

"Nonsense. You can do that stuff later. Why don't you just meet us there? You can leave the paperwork in the car, and when we get ready to leave, I'll ride with you back to your office. You know you want a massage. Relax those tired muscles. Pamper those aching feet. Smell that aromatherapy."

"Okay, okay! You sure know how to sell a girl. Maybe you missed your calling. You seem more like a salesperson or advertiser to me."

"A true lady is a jack of all trades and a master of a couple."

"Amen to that, sister!" she said. "All right. Give me the address, and I will meet you all there," she agreed, then I rattled it off to her.

Felicia and I were busy drinking our tea as we sat in the waiting area in our white robes, gabbing it up. This was the best decision. I was ready for my deep tissue massage, aromatherapy treatment, and herbal foot soak. All the toxins in my body were just screaming to get out. I needed to de-stress.

After I put the final touches in place, it would be time to break the news to Ryan. I was serving him with a divorce. Whether or not I ended up with Lincoln didn't matter. I couldn't stay married to him anymore. He'd had me under his thumb since high school, and it was time to spread my wings and fly solo. For once in my life, I could truly say I was not in love with Ryan Westmore anymore.

"How much longer is it going to be before your friend gets here?" Felicia asked, picking up a magazine. "I'm so ready to get this show on the road. I'm a month overdue for this."

Before I could respond, I spotted Mona coming around the corner. "Here she comes now." I waved at her as she approached us, already in her robe.

"Hello, ladies!"

"Hey, girl." I stood up and hugged her. Then we turned to Felicia. "Felicia, this is my friend, Mona Sims. Mona, this is Felicia."

Felicia shook her hand. "It's a pleasure to meet you." She stood up and we walked toward the aromatherapy room. "Charice tells me you're an attorney. What type of law do you practice?"

"Yes, I am. I'm a family court attorney."

Felicia nodded. "Divorces, wills, settlements, child support, and alimony, right?"

Mona laughed. "I see you know my role *very* well."

"Being married to an NFL player, you better." Felicia laughed, as did we. Even though she had a sick sense of humor, she was mostly right.

"Oh, so you're married to an athlete, too?" Mona asked.

"Yes, Don Peterson of the New York Giants. That's how I know Charice."

"What are you smiling for?" Mona asked, playfully pushing on me.

"It's just that you referred to our husbands as athletes. Mostly everyone else says ball players. It's just funny to me that you described them like that," I said, thinking of Lincoln.

She laughed. "From what I know, some athletes get offended when you call them ball players, as if their career is a joke. I understand that. It is their profession, and they work just as hard at it as any other professional. Besides, the word *athlete* has a certain finesse to it. Just like I'd rather be referred to as an attorney than a lawyer. Finesse. It's all about finesse."

I laughed to myself. She sounded like Lincoln to the tee.

"Well, enough athlete-slash-ball-player and attorney-slash-lawyer talk. You say tomato. She says to-mah-toe. I say aromatherapy, ladies!" Felicia belted as we laughed and went into the room to start our treatments.

The next couple of hours were nothing but pure spa bliss. We talked about current events and of course, laughed about some of the other patrons. It was as if Felicia, Mona, and I were long lost sisters. We each had very different and distinct personalities, but we all meshed well together. Mona even decided to hang with us as we went to the nail salon. It was the most female bonding I'd had since I moved from Georgia and left my girls. I never knew how much I missed and needed this. I vowed that all three of us would have to do this again. Maybe just after my divorce.

"So, ladies, now that we are all dolled up, let's get some shopping in," Felicia said excitedly.

Mona declined. "Actually, I need to get back to work, so I won't be able to join, but I promise I will next time."

"Life for the working-class woman sucks," Felicia said. "Well, I guess it's just me and you."

"Actually, I got a call from my dance studio. I need to go there. Mona, do you think you have time to drop me off there?"

"Sure, I can."

I looked at Felicia and asked, "How about I meet back up with you in say, forty-five minutes?"

She shrugged. "Suit yourself. By then, I should be a couple grand or more into my next month's Amex bill," she joked. "Hit me up, and I will tell you where I'm at. You working-class women go and handle your business. You guys are my *sheros*."

We said our goodbyes, and I followed Mona to her beamer. "Nice ride."

"Thanks, honey. Before I forget, here is your paperwork. We can stop by my office and go over them, and then I can take you home so you can meet up with Felicia if you'd like."

"I'd like that," I agreed, holding the manila envelope in my hands. This made it official. Divorce.

Mona put her hand on top of mine. "It's okay. You'll be fine," she encouraged, noticing the worried expression on my face.

"Thanks for the encouragement." I breathed a sigh of relief.

She winked at me. "I'm not just your attorney. I'm your friend now."

I settled back in her car, and a familiar scent hit my nose. I began to sniff.

"Are you catching a cold?" Mona asked.

"No. The fragrance. It just smells really familiar to me."

She giggled. "My boyfriend and I went out last night. He smells so good that it lingers for a while."

I looked at her as if she were crazy. "I thought you were gay."

"I'm bisexual, actually. I was with a woman for many years, but after meeting my man, I must say that he brought the hetero back into my sexual." She laughed.

"Dang, girl. He must be something else."

"He is," she said confidently.

"So, does he know you're bi?"

She nodded. "Yes, he does. He wasn't thrilled at first, but he was more elated that I was honest and forthcoming. I am not trying to share him or anything, but I swear I keep wanting to have a threesome with him and another woman. That's every man's fantasy. Shit, mine too." Both of us laughed as she pulled up to her office building.

Shrugging my shoulders, I agreed. "Hey, if he accepts it and you're willing, then I say go for it. Life is short. Make all your dreams come true. Real talk."

Once inside her office, I settled into one of the chairs in front of her desk and went over the paperwork carefully. The only thing I needed to do was notate some changes, and then we left.

On the way to my house, I felt the weight of the world on my shoulders as I tried to think of ways to break this to Ryan and ways to get Lincoln to talk to me.

"Are you all right?" Mona asked sincerely.

"Just a little bummed out."

"Well, don't you worry, okay? He's the one missing out on a great woman. You'll feel so much better when you're out and on your own, doing your own thing," she said as we approached my neighborhood. "In fact, once this is over and you've gotten some alone time and made peace with yourself, maybe you might decide to check out the other side of the fence. It's not so bad on my side of the grass." She winked at me.

I laughed aloud. "I know you're not hitting on me."

"Only if it's working," Mona said as she pulled into my driveway. She brushed her index finger along my chin, then she turned to face me and sighed. "Forgive my unprofessionalism, but I have to put on my friendship hat for a moment and get this off my chest. Men don't fully know how to take care of us or pleasure us the way we can do it for ourselves. So, if you are ever interested, just know that I am *hella* interested. Real talk, you are hands down the finest woman I've ever laid eyes on, and I'm ashamed to say, but it is the number one reason I accepted your case."

Oh em to the fucking gee! I had just had my first lesbian experience, and at the hands of my attorney, no less! Where they do that at? As "flattering" as her offer was, I wasn't gay, and I wasn't going to start being gay or bisexual. I didn't give a damn how many men broke my heart.

"Hmm. I don't know what to say right now to that, Mona."

She smiled at me. "Just say, 'Mona, I'm straight, and this is uncomfortable.' I'll understand. I'll be disappointed, but I'll understand."

She was right. It was better to nip it in the bud now, attorney or not. "Mona . . ." I paused because something caught my attention in her back seat. I reached back and grabbed it. A jersey. Lincoln's jersey number. "Oh, you're a fan of Lincoln Harper, huh?"

Looking confused, she stared down at the jersey in my hands, then a giddy smile spread across her face. "Yes, I am. My brother adores him, too. He always has. I guess that's what kinda drew us to each other."

My stomach plunged into my toes, and my hands got sweaty instantly. My mind began reeling, and the palpitations in my heart couldn't be denied. I didn't want to ask for fear of being on the cusp of a bombshell of news, but I had to know. I had to be sure.

"Drew you to each other?" I reiterated to get clarification. Something told me I wasn't at all prepared for what I was about to hear.

She blushed and bit her lip. "We're quiet about it because it's new and fresh, so please keep it between you and me. Lincoln is my boyfriend. We met a little over a month ago at this club. I swear I was just asking for his autograph. Who knew it was going to turn into so much more?" She gushed.

Suddenly, my ears started ringing, and heat spread to my core. It was as if my breath was leaving my body, and it felt as though I was hovering over myself, a true out-of-body experience. It made so much sense now. Her comment about the athletes, the scent of the cologne—YSL, his favorite brand—the arrogant attitude he had, and the flagrant disregard for my feelings. He'd hooked up with this bisexual heifer, not knowing she was my fucking attorney!

I jumped out of the car, trying to catch my breath.

"Charice, honey, are you okay?" she asked, jumping out and running to my side. "Do I need to call a doctor?"

As much as I wanted to haul off and beat her like she stole something—because technically, she did—I held in the ATL hood chick side of myself. If not, I would've beaten her prissy Connecticut ass. I couldn't believe this. All this effort, and he was out prowling around, scoping for a new woman. Attorney or friend, I had never told Mona I was dating Lincoln on the side. Just like I didn't mention Lexi. She wasn't a concern in this divorce, and neither was Lincoln. Nor was I damn foolish enough to mention it. Maybe I *should've* said something. No. Maybe he should've waited on me. *Son of a bitch!*

I shook my head. "It's just an anxiety attack. I get those every now and then," I lied. I fanned myself and stood up. "See. I'm better."

Mona patted my back, and when she was satisfied that I was all right, she continued changing the subject back to business. "Well, at any rate, I'm going to have the changes drawn up, and I'll call you tomorrow with the details. Then we'll be ready to file this thing."

The only thing on my mind was Lincoln's deceit. I couldn't care less about what she was saying. If Lincoln wanted to play that game, I was all for it. I was not going to be made a fool of. I'd make sure to have the last laugh on this shit.

I reached up and rubbed my finger across her cheek. "Thank you, Mona." I winked at her. "For everything."

She blushed. "Maybe I was wrong about my assumption in the car."

A coy gaze crossed my face as I bit my bottom lip. "Maybe you were. Something about that threesome sounds very tempting. We'll talk about it, though," I teased.

Yuck! Yuck! Yuck! Operation scrub down of my hands would be in effect as soon as she pulled off.

"That we will." She winked at me. "Think about it, Charice," she said and hopped into her car. "Real talk. I can make Lincoln and *you* very happy," she said, looking at me seductively, and I swear it took everything in me not to vomit.

"Just so long as my divorce and this discussion stays strictly between you and me, I'll think on it. With Lincoln being on the same team and all, I don't want any mishaps with my case. You understand, don't you?" I asked her to be sure she didn't mention a word of this to Lincoln.

"You know I'm bound by strict legal confidentiality restraints. I'm not risking my reputation or license for anyone, including Lincoln," she confirmed. Then she leaned her head out of the window toward me and said in a hushed voice, "Besides, I would never do anything to jeopardize *any* opportunity I could possibly have with you."

"Can I ask you a question, though?"

"Anything."

Leaning my head in close hers, I stared her directly in the eyes to gauge her honesty. "If Lincoln is your boyfriend, why risk it for me?"

Mona exhaled, her facial expression turning serious. "Honestly, he knows how I feel and how I am. I don't have to hide from Lincoln. Until or unless we're committed to settling, why shouldn't I enjoy myself? And in the process, he gets to reap the benefits, too. All in all, he'll still have me, and we can both have the best of both worlds."

I nodded in agreement, content with her answer. I winked at her and patted her car door. "I'll talk with you later, Mona." With that, I bid her goodbye before I blew my own cover.

The look of ease and contentment on her face was enough to make me vomit as she started her vehicle and waved goodbye. "Talk with you later, sweetie." She winked at me and then left.

Oh, you bet your ass you are talking with me later, sweetie. And when I am done with your little playboy-ass boyfriend, you'll hate his guts and possibly mine, too. But not before you get me divorced with a hefty-ass alimony and child support settlement.

Hopefully, I could hold my anger in long enough not to fuck Lincoln up. Once I got that, I was contemplating taking my kids and moving to another state somewhere free from Ryan and Lincoln and most of all these damn ball players.

Chapter 3

Mike

Sitting on the bench in the park, I noticed a young interracial couple—the woman Filipino and the man black—with three children. I'd guess they were in their mid-thirties or so. The kids were beautiful. There was an older little girl who I'd guess was about seven, and two smaller kids, a boy and a girl that were obviously twins, who appeared to be about three years old. It was apparent to anyone who paid close attention that the oldest girl was not the man's biological child. Not because she was being rude or said the classic catch phrase—*you ain't my daddy*—or some foul shit like that, but the oldest daughter was straight Filipino just like the woman, while the younger siblings were biracial.

The older child not being the man's wasn't the thing that stuck out the most to me. It wasn't even the thing that had me staring at them like some kind of stalker. What intrigued me about them was the very thing that was missing in my life. Love. The love the man had for the child who obviously wasn't his, the love that the child had for the man who obviously wasn't her biological dad, and most of all, the love the couple had for each other. It spoke volumes without them even having to say anything at all. The *love* was what was missing between Lucinda and me, or rather from Lucinda toward me, and there was no love between Nadia and me because of that. And for that reason, I was stuck at a crossroads.

"Sorry I'm late," Jennifer said, sitting down beside me on the park bench. "What's up?"

I looked at her and threw up my hands. "What's up? What's up is that you were supposed to keep Aldris away from Lucinda. Remember when I convinced you to try again after Lu forgave me for the whole disastrous dinner date? You said you would, but apparently, you haven't."

She took off her shades and laughed at me. "How do you figure that?"

"Because the last time Lu even talked to me, she told me she loved Aldris. Ever since then, I haven't been able to see her. She won't answer my calls. She won't stop by, and she won't answer her door."

The look on Jennifer's face was unapologetic, and I didn't appreciate the smirk that followed. "If you're having girl problems, I feel bad for you, son.

I've got ninety-nine problems, and a . . . *bitch* . . . ain't one," she sang, patting me on my shoulder as she put her shades back on. "Your issue isn't with me. It's with Lucinda."

"If you'd tried harder to get Aldris back, I wouldn't be in this predicament. I know you were pissed because he chased after Lucinda, but you started this shit, and I want you to end it. I want Lucinda!"

Jennifer stood then turned to face me. "Then that is a battle you have to fight on your own because the shoe is on the other foot. Instead of it being Aldris this time, it's Lucinda. Mike, I don't know how to tell you this without bringing you down off that cloud you're stuck on, but Lucinda is in love with Aldris, not the other way around. I know because I did my part. I played the nonchalant, sweet, innocent baby's mother and gave him his space. And you know what happened? The precious Lu hung herself. Aldris got pissed about a little tirade she had and swore off Lucinda a little over a month ago. Since then, he's been up my ass every day. As a matter of fact, in about three weeks, I plan on accepting the marriage proposal that he gave me last weekend. I played this one to a tee. I didn't want him to reflect and get suspicious that I accepted his proposal so quickly. No, I played hard to get. It makes it appear more *real*. In three weeks, I will be Aldris's fiancée.

"So, I'm sorry if Lu is avoiding you and that you are no longer an option for her, but it has absolutely nothing to do with me. Aldris is my man now. What I thoroughly suggest you do at this point is figure out a way to get Lu back and keep her away from my future husband," Jennifer threw at me, and with that, she walked away. Her stilettos gracefully stabbed the pavement with each determined stride.

Wow. I had no idea. Now, this was definitely karma. Lucinda was in love with the man I took her from. Of course, it made perfect sense that she was crazy about him now that he didn't want her. That's how it always works. The thrill of the chase was gone. Now that she had to evaluate her true feelings, it was *sayonara, Mike*, and *hello, Aldris*.

It wasn't going down like that. If Lucinda wasn't going to come back willingly, I was going to make her have an epiphany. I hadn't put everything on the line to lose her now. With that thought, I made a couple of phone calls, and then I drove to Lu's house.

"Hi," I greeted Lu once she answered the door. My eyes were cast downward as I tried to quell the nervous energy coursing through my body.

She released an elongated sigh and waved. "Hello."

Mustering courage, I complimented her. "You're looking great."

Refusing to engage in conversation, she breathed deeply and skipped to the point of my visit. "What is it that you want, Mike? You said on my answering machine that you had something important to give me. I shouldn't have to remind you that we broke up after my fuck up. I own up to that, but ever since then, you have been hounding me like the plague. All I want to do is find peace within myself, be one with me. Get to the point where I can smile and be content."

It was true. Lucinda and I were no longer together. After she called me Aldris by mistake, I flipped out. I called her like ten times, and she wouldn't answer the phone, so I left work. When I got home, she wasn't there, and I almost went over to Aldris's house, but I knew Lucinda would never have my babies over there like that. At least I was praying she wouldn't.

When I didn't find her at home, I went to her mother's, where I found her and all the kids. She was shocked to see me, but not surprised, and her mother told us to go home and talk. We went to my house, and I cursed her out from A to Z. She didn't flinch or retaliate, which was the weirdest thing to me, especially knowing Lucinda's attitude. It was so awkward that eventually I sat down and shut up.

There was an uneasy silence for damn near five minutes, and that's when I finally noticed it. I could see it in her face. I knew that conversation was the beginning of the end for us. For the next heartbreaking five minutes, I listened to Lucinda apologize and explain why we wouldn't work and how she had to get her own emotions together. Then she broke up with me, gathered all her things that were at my house, gave me my key back, and left. The saddest part was that I had to go and pick up my kids from her mother's house, looking like an even bigger ass than I already felt I was.

"I understand, and I don't want to press you. I just came by because I have a graduation gift for you."

"Graduation gift? You know I'm not walking until December. Granted, that's only a few months away, but still not close enough for graduation gifts."

"I actually got it the day you received your grade from your last class. I was going to wait until December, but seeing as though we didn't make it, I thought I'd give it to you now." I reached inside my pocket and gave her an envelope.

She eyed me suspiciously and then took the envelope.

"You can open it now."

She opened it and slowly read it. Soon, her eyes grew as wide as saucers, and she gasped, covering her mouth. "Are you serious? Is this for real?"

I nodded. "Yes. It is."

"An all-expense paid five-day, four-night vacation package for two to Puerto Rico. You've got to be shittin' me?"

"No. No shit here. I know that you said that you've never been anywhere outside of Georgia, so I figured you deserved to go out of the country. Surprise and congratulations on your graduation." Turning away, I prayed that she would stop me before I left.

"Wait, Mike." She gripped my arm.

Bingo. I smiled on the inside as I turned around. I knew this would be the clincher. To my surprise, however, she handed the envelope back to me.

"I know why you did this, but I can't accept it, especially given the circumstances. It was for you and me, and I just can't go on the trip knowing where we stand."

There was no way I would allow her to refuse that gift, so I put on my best protest. "Nonsense. I got it for you. Yes, it was originally supposed to be for us, but you can take whomever you want. Maybe Trinity. I'm sure she needs to get away for a while. But the trip is paid for, and it is for you, so take it. I insist."

She stared back and forth between the envelope and me, unsure of what to say, then reluctantly placed the envelope in her back pocket. "You never cease to amaze me. Even with all that's happened, you still want to be right there for me."

Grateful that she'd taken the bait, I shrugged, offering a cliché response that I both meant yet knew it was bullshit. "Love makes me do crazy and unexplainable things. What can I say?" I let out a nervous chuckle. "But on the humble, regardless of the fact that things didn't work out for us, I'm always going to be there for you, Lu. I'll always be your friend."

The light in her eyes sparked, and I felt the warm glow of her affection radiate onto me. That was the Lu that I remembered and loved. Slowly, she reached up and palmed my cheek. Her touch emitted the same fire in her eyes, and her caress felt like a soothing balm on my lonely soul.

"That's so sweet," she cooed as she caressed me.

Swallowing the lump in my throat, I pointed behind me. "Well, I guess I'll be going." No lie, the moment had me emotional, and I wanted to rein it in so as to not appear overly fazed by her attention.

"Hmm. Well, at least let me cook you dinner or something."

"Ah, no. I think it's best if I just go."

By the time I got inside my SUV, Lucinda jogged up to the car. This was the moment I'd been waiting for. I rolled down my window.

"What's up, Lu?"

"Look, Mike, I know that things between us have not gone as we would've hoped, but I just want you to know that I care about you. I really do. Without you, I would probably still be a hot mess. Not that I'm much better now, but at least I'm not as bad as I was," she joked, causing us both to chuckle slightly. "Anyway, there are just some things I think I need to figure out for myself and work out before I can try to devote myself to another relationship."

Mission failed. Those were definitely not the words that I thought or hoped would fall from her lips. I'd pulled my best stop, and still she pushed me away. It was in that moment that I realized we would truly be over if I couldn't pull this off.

"Like the fact that you're still in love with Aldris." The words oozed out with sadness.

Putting her head down, she nodded. "Yeah. Like that. I thought I was over him, but I'm not. It's like deep down on the inside, I know that we're meant to be together. Now that my anger is gone and my head is clear, I just have this overwhelming urge to work things out."

There it was. Her truth. Defeat threatened to consume me, but I refused to be weighed down with the thought. It was hard as hell to hear that, but I'd also known that fighting for her heart was an uphill battle. She loved Aldris through and through. Still, it never stopped me from fighting for her or loving her. Yet, at this moment, I won't lie. That shit hurt.

I reached out and tilted her chin up to look into her eyes. "Then you do what you have to do." I ran my finger down her cheek. "I don't regret any of our time together, but I'm man enough to step away from this situation just to see that you are happy."

She reached inside the SUV and hugged me. "Thank you so much for understanding. I wish so much that things between us could've worked out. You're a great man. A great, *great* man."

"And you are one helluva woman," I added, starting my SUV. "Listen, maybe I'll take you up on the dinner thing tonight. But what do you say we go out just for old time's sake? As friends."

She smiled demurely. "Actually, I'd like that. Where'd you have in mind? I sure hope not Nikolai's," she joked.

I laughed and pointed at her. "Funny," I quipped sarcastically. "How about that little dinner and jazz spot downtown we never got to try? Casual dress, zesty food, and soft neo-soul music. A nice little celebratory end to our relationship."

She burst out in laughter. "You are so silly. Who celebrates breaking up?"

"Two very good, *great* friends."

Holding up her pointer finger, she agreed. "Touché."

"It's five o'clock now. What do you say I swing back by here at say seven thirty?"

She nodded. "I'll be ready," she promised and kissed me on the cheek. Looking at me with sincere eyes, she breathed out. "Thanks, Mike." With that, she walked back inside of her condo.

After she was safely inside her place, I backed out of her driveway, picked up my cell, and made the call. "Hey, Jen."

"Hey, so did your plan work?" she inquired.

"All I'm gonna say is this. Make sure you and Aldris are at the spot at eight o'clock tonight. I told you not to worry. I was not to be deterred."

She giggled. "All right then. I'm feeling a little jazzy tonight anyway. See you at eight for a night to remember," she said and hung up.

Screw Aldris. I knew I was wrong, but I was already knee deep in the shit as it was. I might as well dive in headfirst. Wasn't no sense in half-steppin' at this point in the game. Besides, if I was gonna go down as a trifling-ass nigga, well, I was gonna go down as the best and end up with the ultimate consolation prize, Lucinda.

After arriving home, I jumped in the shower then put on my favorite lotion and sprayed a few shots of my Giorgio Armani cologne. Yep, nothing but the good shit that night! Determined to make a lasting impression, I decided on my black button-down dress shirt topped off with my Levi's dark denim relaxed fit jeans and my black ALDO dress boots. I finished the look with my black-brim hat and big-faced watch. I admired myself in the mirror. My cut was fresh and my style superb.

Tonight was the night that I would get my woman back. I even stopped by a florist stand and grabbed Lu a bouquet of flowers. I would've done roses, but that would've come off too strong. An assorted arrangement was sentimental enough to keep her hooked yet not clingy enough to throw up red flags. Your boy was smooth now. Operation "eliminate Aldris" was in full effect.

When Lucinda opened the door, I nearly passed out. Her soft shoulders were highlighted by a multicolored halter top with black silk pants and super high-heeled stilettos. The long, loose curls of her hair hung beautifully yet haphazardly, and she smelled divine. I had to hold my chest to catch my breath. This woman was exquisite. It was as if I were watching her in slow motion as she tossed her silky hair over her shoulder and she smiled at me. Her smile set off a twinkle in her gorgeous hazel brown eyes, and I had to resist the urge to pull her into my arms then and there.

"Earth to Mike." She waved her beautifully manicured hand in front of my face. "I asked if those were for me."

I nodded. "I'm sorry. I was just admiring your beauty," I admitted before I knew it.

She looked at me closely. "Oh, okay," she said slowly.

I chuckled. "You look good. Hell, what am I supposed to think, Lu? Do you wanna look bad?" I tried to play off my reaction and response.

She thought about what I'd said and behind a giggle, assessed, "I guess you're right. So again, are those for me?"

"Oh, yes." I handed them to her. "Just a little something to cheer you up. I know you're going through it, so I just wanted to be thoughtful."

"And you are," she concurred, sniffing the flowers. "They're gorgeous. I'll put them in water when I get home and put them on the dining room table."

She placed the flowers on the foyer table then grabbed her leather jacket and locked up the house. As we got in the SUV, she grabbed my hand and laughed. "I've never been given flowers just for going out on a date."

"What? Aldris didn't do that for you?" A definite plus on my part.

She looked as if she were in deep contemplation. "No. Let's see, a few times for make-up flowers, birthday, anniversary, Valentine's Day, and the night of the proposal, but never date night flowers."

I snapped my fingers. "I should've trained him a bit better," I joked, making her giggle. "Well, nobody can be perfect."

"You said a mouthful then," she said as I turned up the satellite radio to put us in the mood with a little Jill Scott.

Once we got to the restaurant, there was a nice-sized crowd. The dimly lit atmosphere with candlelit tables, soft jazz and neo-soul music, spacious settings, and a dance floor off to the side gave the place a romantic ambiance. We found a table near the back and ordered a couple of drinks and our food.

The food was delicious, and the drinks were on point. Whoever was mixing up those cranberry and vodkas was handling their business. Lucinda and I talked a lot about work, her upcoming graduation, and our kids, and then she finally told me why she felt she was still in love with Aldris. It hurt like hell to sit there and listen to that, but I had to endure. And endure I did, until I got my cue.

"I don't mean to interrupt, but this is my song. I love Babyface. Would you care to dance?" I asked.

"Sure," Lucinda agreed, and we walked hand in hand onto the dance floor.

I held her close as the saxophonist bellowed the panty-dropping classic, "Soon As I Get Home." I wanted her to feel the connection with me on that song. I wanted her to know that I gave good love, too. In fact, *better* love than her beloved Aldris.

She leaned her head on my shoulder, and I wanted to jump for joy. The spark was still there, but the mission wasn't complete yet. After the song ended, we walked hand in hand back to our table, and lo and behold, whom did we see? Jennifer and Aldris.

"Aldris? *Jennifer*?" Lucinda said, looking back and forth between them in confusion. "Wow. Fancy seeing you two here," she said uneasily.

Aldris nodded. "Hello, Lu and *Mike*. Out enjoying yourselves, I see," he said, pointing toward the dance floor, giving us the message that he had seen us dancing.

"Yeah, just a little bit," I said, noticing that Lucinda was eyeing Jennifer.

Lucinda nodded, looking toward Aldris. "It's good to see that you and Jennifer can hang out like this. Not everybody has that relationship with their baby's mother or daddy."

Jennifer tossed her a lazy smile before looping her arm with Aldris's arm. "I guess getting along would have to be a big part of the equation when you're getting married." She cast her smiling eyes up at Aldris as he stared back down at her.

Lucinda coughed and directed her attention to Jennifer. "Excuse me?"

Aldris put his hand on Jennifer's hand. "Sweetie, just let it go for now."

Jennifer pretended like she hadn't heard him. She smiled at Lu. "Aldris and I are getting married."

Lu blinked several times as if someone had punched her in the face. "Oh. Um. Wow. Really? Damn. Okay. Um. Oh. Wooow. I . . . uh . . . I guess this is uh . . . umm . . . congratulations."

Aldris sighed and looked at Lu. "Lu, I didn't want you to find out like this—"

She put her hand up. "No. It's cool. We're not together. I would've eventually found out anyway, though I doubt I would've gotten a wedding invitation," she said, and I could tell she was trying to keep her composure.

Aldris rubbed his fingers about his forehead before shrugging. "Yeah, I guess." He gestured his hand toward Lucinda and me. "I mean, but you and Mike are together and probably headed down that path yourselves."

Thank you, Jesus! He just sealed the deal for me. I started to speak. "Uh. Actually, Lu and I aren't—"

Without warning, Lu pulled me close to her and patted my chest. "We aren't sure what day is good to set a wedding date. You see, Mike wants it to be a summer wedding, and I'm looking more toward maybe Valentine's Day. Isn't that right, baby?" she lied, caressing my cheek.

Playing along, I looked down at her and smiled lovingly. "Uh, yeah. That's right. I'm trying to convince her not to do the Valentine's Day thing. The anniversary would have to be killer on that day." My joke let off a series of giggles from Jennifer.

Aldris held an awkward smirk plastered on his face. "So, I take it congratulations are in order for you, too?" Aldris commented, looking directly at Lucinda.

She nodded. "It's like you said, move on and be happy, right?" she quoted with a slight air of arrogance in her tone.

Aldris huffed and grabbed Jennifer's hand. "You are exactly right, and I'm very happy." He smiled at Jennifer.

"And I'm super happy," Lu said, smiling at me.

"Well, I guess we're just a set of happy-go-lucky people, huh?" Jennifer giggled as she caressed Aldris's hand.

"All day," Lucinda answered.

Pretending to be tired of the strained exchange, I offered, "We shouldn't hold you guys up—"

Lucinda lightly tapped her forehead. "You're right. We're being rude. We're just going to go back to our table and finish enjoying this date. And that is a beautiful rock, Jennifer."

"Thank you. Where's yours?" she asked.

"Getting sized," Lucinda lied again. "It's gorgeous. You'll see it one day. You all have a good night," Lucinda said as she wrapped her arms around my waist.

"Good night, you guys," I said, and we walked back to our table.

As soon as we sat down, the waiter came over. "Would you like anything else to drink or eat? Perhaps dessert."

"No dessert. Give me a shot of Patron silver. Two actually," Lucinda said quickly.

"And for you, sir?" he asked.

As I looked up at the waiter, I held up my hand. "I'm good."

When the waiter walked away, I refocused on Lucinda, who was fidgeting with her purse, and I reached out and grabbed her hands. "Are you okay?"

"Who, me? I'm fine." She shrugged then continued rambling. "It doesn't matter. We're not together, and they do have a child together. Thank you for playing along with me. I just . . . I couldn't give him the satisfaction." Lucinda huffed.

The waiter came back, and she downed the two shots almost before he could walk away.

"Can you call him back over here? I think I need another shot."

I placed my hand atop hers before she could lift it to signal the waiter. "I think maybe I should take you home. I'm not gonna let you have an emotional breakdown in front of him."

She didn't readily agree, but she didn't protest either. After a few moments of contemplation, she acknowledged that I was correct. "Thanks. I think that would be best."

After she conceded, I called for the waiter and paid the bill. On our way out, we waved goodbye to Aldris and Jennifer. Lucinda held me by the waist all the way to my SUV. Once inside, she broke down.

"I can't believe he's marrying her," she cried into my arms. "I thought we were meant to be together. Why can't I just get over him?"

Rather than address her questions, I focused my attention on comforting her. "Just let it all out." I rubbed my hand up and down her back as she cried on me until her cries became whimpers.

When I arrived at her house, I helped her to the door and opened it up for her. She threw her heels to the side and plopped down on the sofa.

"I'm sorry for using you. I know you want to go, so you can," she said with the pillow covering her face.

Easing in front of her, I removed the pillow and tossed it to the side. "I'm going to make you a cup of coffee and watch some television with you. Or we can talk. But what I will not do is leave you like this." With that, I walked in the kitchen and put on some coffee.

Once it brewed, I made her a cup just the way she liked it, then brought it to her and began massaging her feet as we sat on the sofa in silence. After a few minutes, she sat up and drank some of the coffee. Then she got up and put the bouquet I had bought in a vase with water and placed it on her dining room table.

"It's beautiful," she commented, staring at the floral arrangement.

"Not as beautiful as the owner."

She turned to face me. "You're such a good man."

"I try." I shrugged then stood and walked over to the dining table that she was leaning against. "If you're feeling better, I guess I should go."

In a move that shocked me, she wrapped her arms around my neck. "You don't have to go."

My head fell forward as I released a small sigh. "Lu, you're hurting. I understand. But we can't keep doing this to ourselves. You love Aldris."

"He's marrying Jennifer."

"And what does that have to do with us or your feelings?"

"Nothing and everything. I've allowed him to come between us. I should've been focused on you and not on Aldris. I messed up again. *You* are the man who brings me flowers just because, or listens as I tell you I love someone else knowing that you love me. You've sacrificed your own happiness just so I could have mine, and for that, I am ashamed. I'm ashamed because while I was chasing a broken dream that I should've had the sense to let go of, I was hurting the only man who has truly been there for me through thick and thin. I'm sorry, Mike."

Pretending to be taken aback, I smiled softly. "It's okay. Like I said, I'm always gonna be here for you no matter what. Love makes me do crazy and unexplainable things."

A beat passed before she flashed her beautiful eyes at me, and I swear I got lost in them. "I want to learn how to fall in love with you."

I won't lie. Even though this was the result I'd hoped for, her statement caught me off guard. "You're just heartbroken over Aldris."

She looked away. "You're right." She groaned in frustration. "I'm such a mess."

I held her in my arms, giving her a while to sort through whatever was dancing around in her head. When she seemed to gather herself, I turned her face back to mine.

"You're right. You are a mess, but I don't mind helping you pick up the pieces. *I love you*." My words came out with conviction. Seizing the moment, I kissed her passionately, so passionately she swooned.

She gasped as we pulled apart. "Mike. I . . . uh . . . don't think you've ever kissed me like that before." She fanned herself.

"I have," I replied, staring deep into her eyes. "You just weren't paying attention."

The realization passed over her face, and she hugged me tight. "Can you just hold me tonight?"

"And I'll never let you go," I whispered, gripping her just as tightly. "And we can work on finding our way back to each other later. How's that?"

"Perfect." Without another word, Lucinda pulled away from me and led me to her bedroom, where we slept holding each other all night.

Oh yes, Aldris was officially out of the picture, and I was on my way to etching my name in Lucinda's heart forever. I loved it when a good plan came together. And soon, Lucinda would have an engagement ring of her own. Yep, it was going to be nothing but sweet, sweet dreams for me from this night forward.

Chapter 4

Ryan

"No," I bellowed, jumping from my sleep.

Charice turned to face me. "Are you all right?" she asked groggily.

I swallowed hard and nodded. "Yes. I'm fine. Just go back to sleep."

She settled back into the bed and immediately fell back into a deep slumber. Instead of attempting to join her, I got up and went downstairs to grab a bottle of water.

For the past two weeks, I'd been having the same recurring dream. Charice and I were on this great vacation, wining, dining, and having the best sex of our lives. Then the next day, I'd walk into our hotel room and see her with a man. He had no face, but I wasn't focused on that. I was focused on Charice's lips telling me that she was leaving me and taking the boys and Lexi with her. We'd argue, and she'd leave with this man with no face.

Suddenly, I'd be standing in my bedroom, and her side of the bed was empty. I'd run to our closet to find all her clothes gone, all her personal items gone, everything gone. Then, I'd make a mad dash down the hall to Lexi's empty room and quickly make a left turn and head to the boys' room only to find a picture of all of us left on their computer desk. At that point, I'd scream, and that's where I woke up. Every night. For two weeks.

As I sat at the island in the kitchen, I tried to piece everything together. The dream seemed so real, except nothing Charice had been doing was out of order. By that, I meant she was always where she said she was when she said it. No mysterious phone calls or secret early-morning or late-night meetings. Nothing. It was like my mind was playing tricks on me. Usually, whenever I had a dream about something, especially a recurring dream, it was dead on, but not this time.

I figured that maybe the information I'd been given was driving me insane. You see, my teammate and friend, Don, told me before Charice and I went on our honeymoon vacation that he thought that Charice was cheating on me with Lincoln. He swore he heard Rico bring up Charice's name to him in the parking lot, and it sounded like he was asking if she'd left me for him yet.

At first, I thought Don had his facts screwed up. I mean, my wife and I were about to take a romantic getaway. Also, Charice would never do that to me. Even if she did, she wouldn't be trifling enough to sleep with both of us at the same time.

I had to admit I got worried the more Charice avoided sex with me, but I refused to believe it. Then, when she told me about not wanting to get pregnant, I was relieved. I was even more so relieved when I explained to Lincoln that we were having a baby when we returned from our romantic getaway and he didn't seem fazed because, come on, I'd never buy him a T-shirt on my vacation for the reason I gave him. Everything I did had either a good intention or a very bad motive. I figured if he wasn't fazed and Charice gave up the sex, then Don had his facts wrong. Rico worked closely with Charice at the community center, so there was no telling what Don heard.

That was until I saw the name Mona Sims on our caller ID one day. It wouldn't have stood out to me except I knew all Charice's female friends, and none of them were named Mona. I figured she was a new dance instructor or staff member at the studio, so one day when I went up there to meet Charice for lunch, I asked the receptionists, none of whom had heard of her. I wanted to let it go, but something about it just got the best of me, so I called the number from my cell phone on the way to training camp, and when I heard the receptionist say, "The Law Offices of Berchman, Reynolds, and Sims," I nearly choked.

I asked her what type of law office it was, and she promptly told me family law. My mind immediately went back to what Don had told me. I couldn't admit that shit to anybody that Charice was possibly thinking of divorcing me. I psyched myself up to believe that maybe she was getting a new child support attorney, or maybe Mona was Lincoln's new child support attorney. There was no way I could question Charice about it without looking suspicious myself, nor could I question the attorney for confidentiality reasons. I just prayed for the best and tried to do whatever I could to show a good face in front of Ricey.

That's when I noticed she was always wound up extra tight, reserved, and at times, completely shut down from me. I had to figure something out to stop this damn divorce. Then I saw the woman who I now knew as Mona Sims hugged up with Lincoln at that restaurant, and none of this shit made sense anymore. Maybe Lincoln had simply called Charice from his girlfriend's office. Maybe Mona was representing Lincoln because she was his girlfriend and was giving Charice a hard time. All I knew was that none of this shit made a lick of sense, even down to that damn dream.

It bothered me to think that Charice may want to leave me. I knew I'd done some ill shit to her, but I didn't want my marriage to fail. If it failed, then I'd be a failure, and I had never failed at anything in my life. That meant I'd stay married to Charice even if I ever fell out of love with her. Even if I had to get sex on the side, I'd never give up on my wife because I was Ryan Chad Westmore, the Prodigy, and I *never* failed.

"Are you sure you're all right?" I heard Charice say from beside me while my head was down on the island.

I jumped slightly before answering. "Yeah."

"You've been having a lot of bad dreams lately."

"Yeah."

"Ryan," she spoke and then paused.

The way she spoke my name stirred my deepest fears. I could sense the pending words looming over us like a thick cloud of smog threatening to suffocate me. I couldn't allow her to complete her thoughts. Emotions welled up inside of me, and tears began to fall from my face. I turned to face her, and my voice filled with emotion.

"Charice."

My outcry threw her off kilter, and her mouth snapped shut. She stared at me, shocked and confused. "Ryan?" she asked with worry as I pulled her to me by the waist and leaned my head on her chest. She slowly embraced me. "What's going on, Ryan?"

"I just love you so fucking much," I cried. "I don't want to lose you. Please tell me that we'll be together forever. Please tell me that you love me, too."

"Ryan, I love you. What's this about? What has gotten you so upset?"

I lifted my head to peer at her and wiped my tears. "I keep having a dream that you are leaving me and taking the kids with you. It just seems so real."

Her expression was blank, but I could tell that it shook her. Her eyes blinked rapidly after a few moments, and I couldn't read whether it was because it was true. "Wow. What would make you have a dream like that?" she asked.

"I don't know." I decided to give her a little bait to see if she would bite. "I guess I'm still a little apprehensive of you and Lincoln. I mean, things have been going so well between us lately that sometimes I wonder if it's real. But then, I saw Lincoln with his girlfriend Mona down in Tampa Bay, so I figured that it's just me."

She sighed deeply and folded her arms. "When it comes to Lincoln and me, you don't have to worry. We're only tied together for Lexi's sake. He's living his life with Mona, and they are happy."

I was shocked. "So, you knew about Mona?"

She nodded nonchalantly. "Yes. I don't broadcast it or anything because that's their business, which I have nothing to do with." She shrugged. "His life outside of Lexi is a moot point for me. Lincoln Harper is the least of our troubles."

Talk about ecstatic! I was overjoyed to know that Don had been wrong. I was overjoyed to know that the phone number meant that she only knew of Mona through Lincoln and not about a divorce. Woo! I could breathe a sigh of relief and get back to loving my wife instead of having restless dreams. Now that I knew that Lincoln officially had a woman, I might even let go of the notion to have another child.

"Wow. I guess that fool really doesn't brag."

Her eyebrows scrunched, and her eyes flittered upward to me. "What's that supposed to mean?"

"Umm. I was just thinking out loud," I said, trying to save face. Damn. I couldn't tell my wife that I was really thinking that if I were Lincoln, I'd brag to the whole world that fine-ass woman was my lady. I loved my wife and trust she was the whole package, but so was Mona. And that sexy-ass dimple gave her an inch more sex appeal. An *inch*. It's not much, but enough to make me stray if Charice wasn't giving up the booty. I'm just saying, if you're gonna cheat, upgrade, even if it's only a notch.

Charice eyed me suspiciously. "You find her attractive, don't you?" she asked, crossing her arms and rolling her eyes.

Oh, shit. Here we go. This was not how this conversation was supposed to go. I pointed to myself. "Who, me? What are you talking about?

Babe, please. Shit. Now *you* . . . you are attractive."
I stood, hoping to end this conversation quickly.

"And you never said she wasn't." Charice rolled
her eyes and walked off.

I was right behind her. "You're my wife. I only
have eyes for you. Besides, if I were interested in
light-skinned women, don't you think I would've
married a light-skinned woman?"

Charice turned to face me. "Briana Abrams."

Confusion etched my brow, and I asked, "Briana
Abrams?"

"The first chick you ever cheated on me with."
She smirked. "As if I didn't know you cheated with
her. The point: Light skinned," she said sarcastically, throwing her hands on her hips.

"I was seventeen! We were in high school. You
knew about that?" I was honestly shocked that
she knew.

She pursed her lips. "Mm-hmm. And Shameka
Turner. Light skinned."

"My old college girlfriend?" I asked, shrugging
my shoulders.

She nodded. "And after her, Livia Logan. Also,
light skinned."

I fanned her off. "Okay, so two college girlfriends. So what? They weren't special to me. Just
females to pass my time, just like Briana."

Charice folded her arms, rolled her neck, and
smacked her lips. "All right then. What about Iris,
the supermodel? The lightest of them all."

She got me there. That cut deep. Iris was the only woman I'd ever loved outside of Charice, and she was extremely fair skinned. Okay, so I had a thing for light-skinned women. But what mattered most was that I loved every inch of my wife's beautiful brown skin. And you know she had to be super fine if she made me go against my "thing" I had for light-skinned chicks.

"What's your point, Charice?"

"My point is you find light-skinned women like Mona attractive. I am the exception. Therefore, you felt Lincoln should brag about his *light-bright* girl," she said with an attitude.

I sighed and shrugged. "Okay. Okay. You got me. She's attractive, but the only reason I made the comment is because most of us on the team are always bragging about our wives or girlfriends or jump-offs. The fact that he doesn't just seems strange to me."

"Strange because she's too fine not to brag about, right?" Charice huffed.

"Strange because that's what men do, baby!" It wasn't a lie, but it also wasn't exactly the truth. I hated how well Charice knew me and could read me. It messed with me that I couldn't do the same with her.

I rubbed my neck and walked over to her, pulling her by the waist. "Come on, baby. Why are we getting worked up at three o'clock in the morning over this?"

"You started it."

"Okay, well now, I'm finishing it." Grasping her waist, I pulled her close to me. "I brag about you all the time. *You* are my wife. I love you."

She cocked a half smile, eyeing me suspiciously. "You do?"

"Yes, I do," I said, lifting her face to meet mine. "I love you, and I love making love to you." I bent down and kissed her. "How about we go upstairs and make up for lost time? It's been damn near a month."

Charice stared at me for a few moments, then kissed my cheek and caressed it in the palm of her hand before patting my chest with two light taps. "I need to try to get back to sleep because I have to get up early in the morning, and you have practice tomorrow, so you need your strength. Let's go to bed."

Feeling dejected, I shook my head. "You go on up. I'll be up there in a minute." I kissed her on the forehead. "Goodnight. Love you."

She smiled at me and went upstairs. I went into my study and plopped down in my chair. I was so sick of begging for sex. I missed the spontaneous Charice that would meet me at the door in a thong and heels. The one that would be ready whenever I even hinted at sex. The one who would wake me up at three o'clock in the morning with a head job. Now, it was always something. Work. The kids. Tired. Sick. Period. Headache. Not in the mood. *Always* something. And when I finally could manage to spread those legs, it was over and done with so fast it was hardly memorable. She'd nut. I'd nut. Then she'd wash off and doze off. Foreplay consisted of me kissing her until she gave in, and then it was "hurry up and let's do this." Forget caressing or oral sex, and if I thought I was gonna hold her all night, then I was mistaken.

I went to my bar and poured myself a shot of bourbon. It had become apparent to me that my marriage had turned mundane, every day taken for granted. I had to think of something to bring the life back into this before I lost my mind and my wife. But for now, I needed some "get right with Ryan" time. I sat down, unlocked my desk drawer, pulled out my cell phone, and powered it on. Three voicemails and one text. Damn.

"You have three voice messages sent today. Message one, 'Hi, Ryan. This is Diamond. I was just calling to see how you were doing. If you want to see me, just let me know. I can clear my schedule of Rico. I've been dying to hook up.'"

Delete. That was trouble. Now that I knew Mona was Lincoln's girl, I couldn't fuck with her. I already knew that Diamond and Mona were good friends. She wasn't about to trap me. And I ain't talking about with no babies, because the only thing I had wanted her to do was wrap those lips

around this missile. She wasn't going to trap me
with proof of an affair. Lincoln's girlfriend being
a divorce attorney was too close for comfort, especially since I knew that Diamond was her friend.

"Message two. "Yo, Ryan. It's me, Randy. I'm
going out to the titty bar. Let me know if you're in.
I'm feeling like a private show tonight. Ya feel me?
Holla at your boy!"

Delete. Too late for that.

"Message three. "Hi, Chad. I know you hate that
name, but I still adore it. I really need to see you
again. If you're up tonight, send me a chat. Talk
with you later, love."

I pulled up my chat app. I had one message sent
an hour ago.

Beauty: Waiting

I smiled to myself and typed.

Prodigy: I'm here.

Beauty: Took you long enough.

Prodigy: My bad. I had wife issues to straighten
out.

Beauty: Hmph. Whatever.

Prodigy: Don't get mad. It is what it is, remember?

Beauty: Yes, I remember.

Prodigy: You have me now.

Beauty: All right. Log on.

Prodigy: That's my girl.

I turned on my laptop computer and my web cam. Then I reached in my other drawer and pulled out my hand towel and Vaseline. Suddenly, Iris appeared on the screen.

"Hi, baby," she said, sitting on her bed stark naked.

"Hey, sexy."

She picked up one of her sex toys. "Let's get this show on the road. I'm about ready to bust all over myself."

I chuckled quietly. "Me too." I began massaging my man below as I watched her play with herself. "That's it, baby. Show daddy what you got."

"I'll be in New York next week. We should hook up and make it official. I'm growing tired of our web cam episodes over these past couple of months. I need to feel the real thing, Chad," she pleaded.

I licked my lips and closed my eyes. "We'll see. I must be careful. You understand?"

She sighed. "Yes. I understand that I let you slip away, and now *Ricey* has you. Chad, she's beneath us, honey. We're the elite. We'd make an awesome power couple. You don't need some little backwoods high-school girlfriend. Together, we are unstoppable, and you know our sex was not like the 'hurry up and finish' routine that you get now."

My brows furrowed at her assessment. Masturbation aside, she wasn't going to disrespect Ricey.

"Let that go. She's my wife. We have what we have, and that's it, so stop that. You don't get to talk about my wife or my marriage like that."

She huffed. "Well, I get it from you. You're the one who talks to me, remember?"

"Yes, I do, and if you want me to continue talking to you, you'll stop that."

Her look was incredulous, but she knew I was being truthful. "Fine. I'll be there next week. I expect to see you," she ordered as we jumped full-fledged into our voyeurism session.

By the time we were done, thirty minutes had gone by, and I'd nutted twice. The sad part was that I was ready to tear her pussy out of the frame. I was horny as hell and immediately agreed to see her the next week. Once I was logged out and everything was locked up nice and tight, I marched upstairs and eased in bed with Charice.

"What the hell?" she asked groggily.

"I need you." I kissed her on the neck.

"Ryan."

I eased her panties down and rubbed my throbbing manhood on her ass. "*Please*. Come on."

After a few more nibbles on her neck and stroking myself against her backside, she finally consented. Thank God! No arguments. If only I could have my cake and eat it too. The thought of fucking Iris on the side and making love to my wife danced in my mind as I made passionate love to my wife. In fact, having her and Iris at the same time would be a dream come true. Thinking about that brought me to a completion quickly, and soon I was stress free.

"Are you good?" Charice asked as she rolled on her side.

"Good and satisfied." I smiled at her. "Goodnight, Ricey. I love you." I snuggled into my pillow.

I did love her. If she would do this all the time, I wouldn't be out searching for the Diamonds and the Irises of the world, and if she kept it up, I wouldn't see Iris next week. But I knew she wouldn't, so I prepared myself for some mind-blowing sex with Iris. I'd promised myself to keep it to oral sex like with the maid, but with Iris, I'd have to make an exception. This was like a *deep* carpet cleaning. One deep scrub should last a lifetime.

Just this once. I swear it. Besides, my marriage can't fail, remember? I'm not a failure, not Ryan Chad Westmore.

Chapter 5

LaMeka

I was the happiest woman on Earth. As I sat there staring at my rock of an engagement ring, I felt elated all over again. I was getting married to the man of my dreams. We were going to be a family and live happily ever after. It was a true fairytale. Nothing would stop this dream from coming true. Or so I hoped.

Despite my elation, I was still skeptical about Gavin's father and brother. I knew they despised interracial relationships, but that's not what troubled me. I was bothered by what I didn't know, such as their reaction to our engagement and subsequent marriage. And let's not forget, I had to tell Tony, too. I didn't have time for his attitude, but I'd rather see his reaction than not see it. In fact, I was shocked that he'd been as quiet and nuisance free as he had been the past few months. All three of them scared me with these acts of silence.

Emotions I could handle because they showed
their playing hand when they let their emotions
out, but silence usually meant schemes and plots,
the things I wasn't prepared for. I prayed for the
best, although it was hard as hell not to expect
the worst.

However, I forced myself not to worry about
that because I had a wedding to plan. Gavin and
I decided to get married on the anniversary of
our first date, May sixteenth. That meant I had
less than eight months to get this thing together,
and so did my friends. The only people I could
depend on for my wedding party were Trinity
and Terrence. Hell, I didn't know whether to ask
Ryan or Lincoln to escort Charice in the wedding,
and the same was true for Lucinda. Was it going
to be Mike or Aldris? If Trinity called me talking
about her and Terrence were falling apart, then
fuck it, I was gonna just elope and have a wedding
reception. My day was not gonna be tainted with
fighting couples and their side affairs, baby daddy
drama, and the KKK. No, thank you. Hell, eloping
might be the better option anyway.

I looked up from the bridal dress book to see
Gavin saunter into the living room and plop down
in his favorite chair. "Hello to you, too, baby."

He waved. "Hey, babe," he grunted out, grabbing the remote and turning on the television.

Okay. That was unusual. Gavin had just gotten home from work, and instead of my usual romantic greeting with a kiss and tight hug, he barely acknowledged me. In fact, over the past week, it had been the same routine—just like him drinking every day was becoming routine. I watched him get up and go to the bar to pour himself a glass of brandy. A beer or drink every now and then was cool, but every day?

Then, the night we announced to my mom and sister that we were getting married, the sex was off. As promised, the kids stayed with my mom, and we headed to a hotel room. The room held a sensual ambiance, but even that couldn't spark the romance in the room. Gavin was distant and curt. Even with a couple of drinks in his system, he was wound up so tight that he needed a pull string to deflate him. He was so out of character that I hurriedly tried to get sex from him. Hell, I was horny from the past couple of weeks without him and high off my engagement announcement. I needed some, so I tried to get it before he killed the entire mood. Even then, he was only working half-staff, and when I finally managed to get off, I felt like I had put in a double shift at the hospital just to get a little relief. He didn't even complete. He just rolled over and went to sleep.

It was the first time since we'd been together that I had to pleasure myself just to get satisfied.

Me, the whirlpool tub with the jets, and my fake man had a wonderful time blasting off while Gavin slept away. Thank goodness I had the fake one, which I had only brought to enhance our experience. That was also strange because Gavin was a man who wanted to go at least three times, and he hadn't even tried to do anything since the night he proposed. With this day five repeat action, I concluded that something was not right, and I was about to get to the bottom of it.

I walked over and bent down in front of him as he sat in the recliner. "Kiss me," I whispered sexily. The glance he gave me was less than enthusiastic, but he gave me a quick peck on the lips. I waved my index finger in his face. "That's not a kiss. That's a peck. I want a kiss." I straddled his lap, lifted his chin, and planted a nice juicy kiss on him.

He didn't even hold onto me, and when I pulled up, he just licked his lips and drank a swig of his brandy.

I stared at him as he put the glass down. "What?" he asked.

"You tell me."

"I have nothing to tell. You're the one looking at me crazy and blocking the television."

What? Did he really just come at me like that? I picked up the remote and turned the television off. "Now it's off. Do you want to explain to me what the hell your problem is?"

"Besides you turning off the television?"

Calm down, Meka. "I'm gonna be patient despite the fact that you're trying to take me there. Baby, something is wrong, and all I'm asking you is to tell me what it is."

"Again, besides the fact that you turned off the television, nothing," he said snidely.

I stood up and clasped my hands together. "Gavin, stop playing games with me."

He huffed and hunched up his shoulders. "I'm not."

"Okay, so why haven't we had sex since the night we announced our engagement? Why do you come home and not acknowledge me, pour yourself some alcohol, plop in the seat, and watch television until you pass out? All week it's been the same routine, and now, you give me that lame-ass kiss. What is bothering you? Just tell me. Did I make you upset? Is something going on at the job? Whatever it is, let's talk about it."

Gavin cupped his chin and then rubbed his hand across his mouth. "Can I just watch television?" His annoyance was on full display.

"No, you can't. Not here. Not until you tell me what's going on."

He shook his head and drank another swig. "What's going on is that I have a woman who is pissing me off because she wants to create a problem instead of letting me watch the fucking TV."

Caught off guard, all I could do was gasp in utter shock. Gavin had never talked to me like that. Never. "You know what? You can leave. Go to your house if you're gonna act like this, but you better get it together. I'm not entering a marriage if it's going to be like this every day. That's not what I signed up for."

He rolled his eyes and got up. "Fine. Whatever. I'm out. I don't have time for this stupid shit anyway. Every time I turn around, it's always a battle with you."

"Really? Really, Gavin?" I followed him to the door. "If it's always stupid shit, then why ask me to marry you? If you don't want to do this anymore, just tell me."

"Man, I ain't got time for this. *You* want me to be out, so let me be out."

"Be out *how*, Gavin? Out for now? Or out for good?" I asked, turning him to face me.

Gavin gave me the angriest glare that I'd ever seen on him in my life. He stared at me for what seemed like forever. Then, he closed his eyes and shook his head. I didn't know what to say, so I just stood there anxiously waiting on his decision. I felt like the weight of the world was on my shoulders except I had no clue as to why. I didn't know whether to be upset or worried. Most of all, I didn't know why he was pausing so long to answer my damn question.

He licked his lips and swallowed. "I'ma just go to my house and chill out. I'll talk with you later, okay?" he said and kissed me on my cheek.

"Gavin, please. What's wrong?"

He caressed my face. "I just need to clear my head. Okay?"

"Gavin—" Before I could finish, he interrupted me.

"Okay, baby? Please?"

Reluctantly, I nodded my head. His only response was to kiss my forehead and leave. After returning to the family room, I put away my bridal books and anything else concerning this wedding. There was no way I could concentrate on planning a wedding when I wasn't even sure I was getting married. I'd been engaged for a week before there was trouble. Was that a bad omen? I didn't know. But one thing was for sure, it was a sign for something.

Before I had a chance to digest what had just happened with Gavin, Tony popped up with the boys. I had planned for Gavin and me to sit down as adults and explain to Tony that we were getting married. Not that I owed him anything, but I always tried to be right and just. He needed to know if for no other reason than he would need to come to peaceful terms with Gavin if he wanted to continue to see his children. Kids' father or not, he didn't run my life, and he wasn't going to stop me from getting married either—if there was going to be a wedding, or a marriage for that matter. But Gavin wasn't here now, so I guess it would have to wait.

"Hi, boys!" Nothing made my heart dance more than seeing Tony Jr. and LaMichael come through the door in front of Tony.

They both hugged me tight. "Hi, Mommy."

"Do you guys want some cookies?" They nodded. "Good. Go to the kitchen and ask Grandma to give you some," I instructed them, and they took off toward the kitchen.

"Li'l Tony is doing so much better now. He's really improving," Tony said.

"He's a smart kid. He just needed a little help. That's all. Thanks for dropping them off for me."

"It's no problem. I enjoy my time with them."

"Good."

We stood there staring awkwardly at each other. It was odd that I'd been with him for all those years, and now, we could barely formulate two sentences to engage each other. The truth was that so much more bad blood had been spread between us that it was tough to bother with pointless conversation. However, I mistook his reason for quietness, until he spoke up.

He pointed to my hand. "I see that congratulations are in order."

My eyes grew wide, and I glanced down at my engagement ring. Damn, I had forgotten to take it off. There was no hiding the information until the right time at this point.

Deciding to keep it simple, I offered, "Yeah. I guess."

Tony eyed me intently. "You guess?"

"You should be going—"

"Meka, he's not going to marry you," Tony blurted out. He quickly put up his hands to stop me from cussing him out. "Just hear me out, please, before you kick me out," he asked sincerely.

What could it hurt to hear him out? Fanning my hand, I motioned him into the living room. Once we settled, I addressed his comment straight on. "So, do you want to give me Tony's take on my engagement?"

"You know at first I was very raw about you and Gavin. In a lot of ways, I still am. I admit that. But when I say that Gavin isn't going to marry you, I'm not saying that to be mean. I'm saying it because it's the truth. I may not give a damn about Gavin, but I do care a lot about you. Having said that, I don't want you to get your hopes up on this. The only reason I say that is because the day that Gavin's brother found out you were black, I overheard him in the hospital parking lot telling Gavin that he couldn't get out of the family business.

Basically, he told him that his only option was to get rid of you," Tony advised.

Just as I suspected, he held a little cup of hat-erade for my situation still. Then he tried to use this as the perfect opportunity to pour it out. Not this time. I wouldn't allow his misery to spill over onto my life.

"I hate to bust your bubble, chief, but Gavin proposed to me *after* that day. He gave up his portion of the business, the money, and swore off his folks, so that blows your little theory out of the water. Nice try, though. If I didn't know any better, I would've almost believed that you were trying to be the good guy for a change." I rolled my eyes. He thought he was slick. Wanna come over like the concerned babies' daddy. Please.

He shook his head, fired up. "I *am* the good guy for a change, Meka." His words came out strained with emotion. "I'm not saying that Gavin is playing you, but you're playing yourself if you believe those white folks are gonna sit by while you marry that dude and give him two black babies to raise and possibly some more little half-breed children. If you were so secure in your pending nuptials, why did you say, *'I guess'* when I said that congratula-tions were in order?"

Now, I was piping hot. Not only did I not appre-ciate his bold assessment about my engagement, but I was fuming over his questioning the stability of my relationship, none of which was any of his concern. "That is none of your business. It has nothing to do with you."

Tony hadn't been a good guy in so long that I didn't know if any goodness was left in him. So, he could miss me with all that.

He leaned forward. "Well, I'll tell you what does," he hissed, pointing into the kitchen. "Those two little boys in there. Now, I may not have been the father I was supposed to be, but I am still *their* father. As far as I'm concerned, you can keep your problems with Gavin a secret from me, but the moment— and I mean *the moment*—they begin to affect my children, there's gonna be smoke in the fucking city. You can take that check to the bank and cash it for damn sure."

Did this fool just threaten me? Seriously. Did he just threaten me?

"I would never do anything to hurt my children. You know that goes without saying."

"I know you wouldn't *intentionally* hurt them, but you've got your head so far in the clouds, or rather so far up Gavin's asshole, that you can't see what's in plain view. You're having issues with him because somehow, some way his family is involved. That father of his is far too influential to say he doesn't get what he wants. Nine times outta ten I can pretty much guess that what he wants is a LaMeka-free life for his son."

That was it! I had taken all that I was going to
tolerate from him. He wasn't gonna sit up in my
house and disrespect me like that, not after all the
shit he had put me through. Hell no. I furrowed
my brow.

"How dare you have the audacity to say that I'm
too far up Gavin's ass to worry about the safety
and welfare of my children? Are you insane? You
are the one who got addicted to drugs and alcohol,
abused me, then slept with that disease-infested
Kwanzie, giving yourself the package and damn
near infecting me with it, too. Don't you ever talk
to me about intentional or non-intentional hurts!"

Yeah, it was a low blow, and I regretted the
words as soon as they left my mouth, but fuck that.
Tony ran around wreaking havoc on my life for
years, so he was far from the savior he was trying
to portray. Besides, my man had promised me that
it was handled, and I believed him. No one, and
especially not Tony's grimy ass, would make me
disbelieve in my Gavin.

Tony's eyes bulged as my harsh words hit him
like a sack of bricks. I saw his face contort before
he inhaled a sharp breath, flicked the tip of his
nose, and stood up. "On that note, it's best that I
leave. Like I said, I know my past mistakes, and
I'm man enough to own up to them, but what you
won't do is keep tearing me down because of them
just because you don't want to hear the truth about

your fiancé. One day you'll realize that for once, I was trying to have your back," he snarled, walking to the door, and I followed him.

"If you really want to have my back, then be happy for me and trust my decisions."

He huffed as he opened the door. "I want to see you happy. I really do. But the verdict is still out on whether or not that happiness is going to be with Gavin. As for your decisions, it's not *you* that I don't trust. All I am saying is you better get to the truth first this time, because Gavin is gonna be all right. Nobody is gonna pick you or our boys up if Gavin fails you," he warned me and left.

As much as I wanted to argue him down, this time, he had a valid point. I hated that he, of all people, had a point, especially when I knew deep down in the pit of my stomach that something was terribly wrong with Gavin. He was not himself, and my best judgment told me that Gerald and Gary Randall were behind it.

As his future wife, I deserved to know what was going on, but I'd already had my experience with taking matters into my own hands. Until Gavin decided to tell me truthfully what the hell was going on, this engagement was gonna be an extended one.

Chapter 6

Trinity

All I was trying to do was protect my family. That's it. How'd things get so fucked up? If I had known that Terrence's freedom would be in jeopardy, I never would've agreed to help Pooch. Never. Now look at the mess I was in. Terrence damn near hated me. I wished he could see that I wasn't trying to hurt him, but rather help us. But damn that. I had to do what I had to do for my husband.

Ever since he'd found out about my agreement to help get Pooch released in the case of Aaron's kidnapping and murder plot, he hasn't said two words to me. Forget intimacy or anything like it, not that that wasn't the norm these days anyway. All he did was sulk and take pain pills all day. His business was suffering, and he had become mean and impatient with the kids. I barely knew Terrence anymore. Therefore, I put some things in motion. I'd held his business together by making a few deals for him, and I'd sold some of my artwork to major bidders in local auctions. We weren't hurting by any means, but that didn't mean I was going to sit by and watch everything that we'd built together crumble. I was Dread's wife, no matter how he saw me. Nobody had his back like I did, and nobody ever would.

I decided to meet up with Stein at his satellite office in Illinois while he prepared for Pooch's case. He needed to hear my final decision face to face, so there would be no denying my position. I wasn't going to testify for Pooch, not at the risk of losing Terrence.

"Come in," I heard Attorney Stein say. I opened the door.

Floating inside the room like new money, I peeled my designer shades off my face and strolled deeper inside his office with the confidence and looks of a runway model. It appeared that I wasn't the only blast from the past that had blown into Stein's office.

"I'll be damned. So, it's true," Flava said as I walked inside the room. "What the hell did Terrence do to you to make you testify on Pooch's behalf?"

Disgust filled me as I thought about all the times she'd tried to replace me. "I should've figured you were behind this. You've always wanted to be me."

"No, I've always been *me*. Not a scared little girl like you," Flava shot back.

"Ladies! Ladies! We have the same goal here. Let's not argue," Stein intervened.

Flava and I gave each other the stare down before Flava disengaged with me. "Is that Trinity?" Some chick asked Flava.

Not waiting for Flava's response, I chimed in. "Who wants to know?"

"My name is Adrienne, and I'm one of Pooch's women," she replied with an air of arrogance that she definitely should not have had.

I couldn't help the chuckle that escaped my mouth. She was assuredly his type. "I hope you're not as dumb as that sounded."

"You don't know me like that—"

"And you don't know Pooch. None of you do. Not like me." I intercepted whatever unimportant tirade she was set to deliver.

Flava wagged her finger at me with her lips curled into a scowl. "What he saw in you, I'll never know. The only person you ride for is yourself," Flava said, shaking her head.

"And that's all I need to ride for."

Standing, Attorney Stein put his hands up to stop the continuous back and forth. "Trinity, what can I do for you? We have a meeting next week," Stein asked, walking around the table to address me.

Getting to the point as he wished, I said, "Meeting's off. Testimony is off."

"What? You can't be serious," he said, folding his arms.

"As a heart attack," I said, putting my hands on my hips. "You're going to have to find another way to get Pooch off. I'm sticking to my original story."

Flava rolled her eyes. "I knew we couldn't trust that flip-flopping bitch," Flava said.

"Isn't it enough that you kept his child from him? That's why he got out in the first place. To find his children," Adrienne yelled.

Had I been this naïve? Of course I had. Seemed like I was on my way to being dumb again, listening to Stein, which I was sure was powered by Pooch's demands. Pooch had really done a number on these broads. It was amazing how he could flip a story to make it fit for each individual. I was beginning to think that Terrence was right. This had been Pooch's plan all along, to make me think he was making a deal with me just to get out and send Terrence back to prison.

"You know what? If you believe that, then you're about as stupid as I was to believe that Pooch would leave me and my husband alone to raise our daughter without interference from him. Pooch was in on that deal to kill me or Terrence or both of us, until he realized he was getting double crossed by Aaron. All of you can go to hell. I'm not testifying, and that's that." Turning on my heels, I waltzed to the same door that I'd just entered.

"You know I can still make you testify," Stein called out to me.

Letting out a chortle, I turned to face him. "Go ahead. Tell me, Stein. Did you forget that I'm married? You can't make a spouse implicate their spouse. Speaking of the law, what's the going rate for bribery, conspiracy, and coercion? All of which I have you and Pooch on, if you try to make me testify on his behalf."

"You don't have anything," Stein sneered.

"Try me," I barked daringly. "I did my homework, Stein. It's mighty strange that the day I got that phone call from Pooch—from a cell phone inside the prison yard, no less—that he'd received a visit from a woman named Adrienne, who I assume is the same one here today, especially since she's probably the same one who tried to bribe the judge for Pooch." When I saw their mouths drop, I knew I had them. "Oh, yes, I research and *listen* very well." That tidbit was my hint that I had been given inside information. "I will have all of you so caught up in a shit storm that it will take twenty years to find out what the truth is. I'm not testifying, and that's that. Have a great day and tell Pooch I said don't drop the soap."

Opening the door, I blew out the same way I blew in, fast and furious. It felt good walking out of that building and telling Stein and Pooch what I thought of their little plot. In fact, I'd already contacted the District Attorney about the coercion and bribery from Pooch and informed them of Stein's knowledge of it. I was going to show my husband whose side I was on.

"*Thomas*!" I shrieked when I got in my car. "What the hell are you doing in my car?"

"Trying to find out why the hell you're going to see Jacob Stein," he said as more of a question as he eyed me angrily.

"I . . . uh . . . had to deliver a message to him." I went to put my key in the ignition. Thomas swatted my hand away. "Look, it was nothing. Have you been drinking?"

He laughed. "Maybe I have a little bit, but you are one piece of work. You're here to testify on Pooch's behalf? After all my family and I have done for you," he yelled, hitting the dashboard.

His outburst caused me to flinch. Gulping in air to calm my resolve, I turned to face him. "No! I told Stein I wasn't going to do it. I promise."

Thomas glared at me with fire in his eyes. "I don't believe you."

"I *did*. You can go ask him if you want. I'll even go with you."

Thomas searched my eyes for any sign of untruth. When he found none, his glare lost some of the steam, but only a little. "But you were."

"Only because I thought he would leave my family alone. That's it." My eyes pleaded with him to understand.

Thomas grimaced and pointed his finger in my face. "I told T back when he was trying to find a way to get you back from Pooch that you were probably damaged goods. Let me be clear. Your loyalty is shaky, and I don't trust you as far as I can see you."

Matching his tone, I barked, "I don't give a damn what you think about me. *I love Dreads*."

"Testifying for your ex-lover despite what he's done to your husband and my brother is how you show it?" he asked, sucking his teeth. "I honestly thought that I had been wrong about you. I began to like you even. Now you better pray you're telling me the truth."

Sneering, I gave him the hard side-eye. "I am, but even so, Dreads wouldn't let you hurt me. Don't ever think you can threaten me."

He sat there for a minute before he let out a grunt. He opened my car door and got out. "You know my cousin, so you tell me, what's his greatest pet peeve?"

"That no one messes with his family." I directed that toward him.

"That's one. No one messes with his family, not even a member of the family. And above all else, he hates to be made a fool of. You remember that, Trinity," he said and walked away.

No lie, Thomas's impromptu appearance shook me. He'd gone off the deep end ever since his brother's death. It was no surprise that he gunned for any and everybody who he felt was against the family. I'd only heard of this side of him. I'd never witnessed it until now. Before I left, I took a deep breath, then called Terrence as I pulled away.

"Yeah," he answered the phone.

"You have to talk to Thomas. He must've found out about my deal and followed me to Stein's office."

"Oh, yeah?" he asked.

"Yes! Your cousin is crazy. I don't like the way he was talking to me as if he were threatening me."

"What did you tell Stein?" Terrence asked dismissively.

Pulling the phone away from my ear, I was baffled that he failed to address anything I'd said about Thomas. Still, I answered his question before turning the attention back on his cousin. "I told him I wasn't testifying, of course. Did you hear me about Thomas?"

"I heard you." He paused before releasing a deep sigh. "I'll talk to him."

For the second time, I stared at my phone in disbelief. I didn't want to believe that he had sent Thomas to follow me, but that's exactly how he was acting. Given his recent attitude shift, I wouldn't put anything past him either. He treated me as if I were a stranger to him.

"Do you love me, Dreads?"

"I think the bigger question is, do you love me?"

"It goes without saying."

His voice held no emotion when he rattled off, "We'll see. Talk with you later." With that, he hung up.

What the hell? I didn't know what was going on, but it was time to get to the bottom of this. I didn't need Thomas's half-cocked ass putting ideas about me in Terrence's head just to get next to Pooch, especially since Terrence's head wasn't in a good place these days. I had to show him that I wasn't the enemy. When would this shit with Pooch ever end? All I wanted was to be a family with Dreads and raise our children. Was that too much to ask? Now his family was flipping out on me, and he was not too far behind them. I had to make everything right because I didn't trust Thomas, and as much as I hated to think it at this point, Terrence was questionable, too.

Tears rolled down my face as I thought of how I had gotten to this point in my life. It seemed like every time I tried to be a good wife to Dreads, it blew up in my face. I felt like such a failure to him. He always had my back, and even when I tried to have his, it looked as if I didn't. I couldn't take losing him again. I couldn't take going back to that empty space in my life that consumed me when he wasn't in it. That emptiness allowed me to fall for a bastard like Pooch and even brought me close to taking my own life. I shuddered to think what would happen if Dreads walked out of my life for good. Yet, that's exactly how I felt at this very moment. Alone.

This was the first time since we'd moved to Illinois that I regretted it. I realized that we had done what we had to do at the time, and the regret wasn't about that. It was about this feeling I was experiencing right now—the fear of being alone. I needed someone to talk to and keep my spirits high. An outlet. A brief getaway. That job had always belonged to my girls, but being separated from them the way I was, with all the things going on in our individual lives, made life that much harder. With Dreads trippin', I was damn sure ready to hop on the first thing smokin' back to the ATL or up to New Yitty, even if it was only for a day. Hell, I'd take an hour. Right now, though, I'd have to settle for yet another long-distance phone call.

I pressed speed dial number 3 on my cell and willed Lu to answer her phone. "Come on. Pick up."

"Trinity?" she answered.

"Lu," I exhaled into the phone.

"I need you so much right now," we both said at the same time.

"You first," she said.

Just then, it dawned on me that she'd wanted to speak to me just as bad as I wanted to speak to her.

"If you needed me, why didn't you just call? You've been my girl for longer than I can remember. You know I'm always here for you."

"You have enough on your plate with nursing Terrence back to good health. I didn't want to worry you. Besides, I have LaMeka. If anything, I should've been calling you to make sure you were all right, which obviously you aren't, mamí. So, what's up?"

I exhaled heavily and began telling her the entire story about Pooch getting arrested for the attempted murder of my husband, from the unfaithful night at the warehouse to him having his attorney, Jacob Stein, offer me a deal. Stein wanted me to testify on Pooch's behalf that he didn't intentionally shoot my husband. In exchange, Pooch would promise to never bother me or my family again. I'd initially agreed out of fear, and then reneged once my common sense resurfaced. I even explained how Dreads had found out about it and how livid he was now. Lu sat there patiently and listened, even when I know it boiled her to be quiet.

"Ay, chica. What were you thinking?" she asked once I finished. "Don't answer that. I know you were only trying to make sure your family was safe. I get it."

"I know it was dumb, but I was just so afraid, Lu. I've been living in fear of Pooch for so many years, and it seems that no matter what I do, I can't escape him. I feel so trapped."

"Aww, sweetie, I know. I could kick his ass myself. He knew you would go for that deal. Ugh. I'm tired of this shit for you, and with everything you're going through, you do not need this," she vented for me. "But listen to me. Feel me on this for real, Trin. Everything is gonna be cool. I promise. I don't know how or when, but it will be. I know Terrence, and you know him too. He's just hurt right now, and that anger is coming from a lot of built-up frustration. You have to remember that for all the shit that Pooch has put you through, he's been going through it with you in some form or fashion. All I know is Dreads loves you, and he's not gonna let you go unless you let him go. Once he's had some time to clear his head and marinate on it, he'll come around. That man almost lost his life for you. He ain't going nowhere." Lucinda comforted me.

Tears dropped from my eyes at her words, and for the first time since this debacle had begun, I breathed a sigh of relief. She always knew exactly what to say. Now it was my turn to be there for her.

"I needed that so much, Lu. I swear I did. Even though I feel like hell, I know you're right."

"Of course I am. I always am," she joked, making me laugh for the first time in a long time.

"Now, what has Mike or Aldris done that has you in a funk?"

"Aldris asked Jennifer to marry him," she blurted out plainly.

"*What?*" I was glad I had pulled over because leave it to Lu to just spring news on me with no warning or buildup. Just boom, there it is.

"You heard me right," she huffed. "I'm just trying to cut my losses and pick up the pieces. I was so sure I was over him, Trin, but when I heard that I just—Ugh, chica. I can't even describe it."

"Well, it's his loss. We both know you were the best thing for him, so if he doesn't realize that, then fuck it. Give your heart and time to someone who does realize it."

"I wonder what Raul is doing," she joked.

"Get the fuck outta here!" I laughed. "If you were to ever—"

"I get my monthly checks, and that's all I care about. I haven't seen him in forever, and I don't care if I never do. Hell, I don't think Nadia cares anymore."

"What about Mike?"

"I don't know, Trin—"

"Give it a chance." I cut her off. "Or hell, be good to yourself. Sometimes that's the best medicine."

"I'm doing that now. I just wish I could find a real relationship and real love."

"Then look in a *real* place for it. Or at least try. I'm not saying that Mike is the one. I'm just saying if Aldris has moved on, then you've gotta let it go, and if you can't, then get off your ass and fight for him, Lu. It's gotta be one or the other. You just have to figure out which."

Lu sat there and took in what I said. "I love you, chica," she said, signaling that she appreciated the advice and wanted to end that part of the discussion.

"I love you, too," I said, respecting her unspoken wish and not delving further. I switched to my Bluetooth and pulled back onto the highway.

We talked until I reached my house about things going on in Atlanta and the latest on LaMeka and Charice. By the time I arrived back at my house, I felt so much better. Not only better, but able to handle what was going on in my household. And for now, that was all the comfort I needed.

Chapter 7

Aldris

"What's on your mind?" Jennifer asked as we sat at the table eating dinner.

I looked up at her. "Oh, nothing." I continued picking over my food.

She looked at me intently then sighed deeply. "It's something. You barely touched your plate, and even Jessica has finished eating before you."

Forcing a smile, my gaze turned back to her. "I just had a long day at work today, baby." I eased out of my chair and placed my plate inside the microwave. Then I kissed her on the top of the head. "I promise it's nothing."

She grabbed my hand as I began to walk off. "You know you can talk to me about anything, right?"

"Yeah. I know. I'm just gonna take a shower."

She stood up and wrapped her arms around my neck. "All right, baby. I love you."

I bent down and kissed her lips. "I love you, too," I seconded before walking to her bedroom.

As the water flowed down my back, I pressed my palms against the shower wall. My mind replayed for the millionth time the look on Lucinda's face when she found out that I was marrying Jennifer. I knew her all too well, and I knew she wasn't marrying Mike. At least not then, maybe later down the line. It was the same expression she'd had on her face when I admitted I'd slept with Jennifer. Her reaction bothered me because I just wanted to move on from that situation, not break her down. That wasn't my MO. At the end of the day, I knew Lucinda was a good woman who'd just made some bad decisions.

Hell, so had I. I blamed her for choosing Mike, but on the real, if I'd been a man in the way I handled Jennifer, then I wouldn't have pushed her over to him. While I was busy ignoring her and trying to please Jennifer for the sake of Jessica, I was allowing a doorway of closeness between her and Mike. If you really want to get down to it, had I not cheated at all, there would be no such thing as Mike and Lucinda. It's one of the laws of physics: every action has an equal and opposite reaction. Or as my mother would say, what goes around comes around.

The whole thing left me wondering. The thought came to me about whether I was marrying Jennifer to try to one-up Lucinda and Mike. At the time, I swore it was because I wanted to marry her, but when Lucinda told me that she was marrying Mike, it did something to me. Even though I knew she was lying, it fucked with me down on the inside because what if she *wasn't* lying? That's why I took my little snipe at her about being happy in my situation. I *was* happy, but that was more so a comment to piss her off for saying that she was happy and marrying Mike.

What if she *was* marrying Mike? The thought of that made my nose flare and my blood boil. But why? I was marrying Jennifer, and I loved her. What Lucinda did or didn't do should not bother me. Right? Of course.

I got out of the shower and put on my favorite apparel, basketball shorts and a white tee. It was the perfect outfit to relax in while I cleared my head and got some sound and much-needed advice.

"Hi, Mama." I breathed out, happy she'd answered her phone.

"Hey, baby," she said giddily. "To what do I owe the pleasure of this phone call?"

Her excitement warmed my soul. "You always sound so excited to talk to me."

"You're my baby. I'll always be excited to talk to you."

"Are you busy?"

"Nope. Just fiddling around the house. Why? What's up?"

"Is it cool if I come over for a bit?"

"Yes, of course. You and the family can come."

"Not Jen and Jess. Just me."

"Oh, it's one of *those* kinds of visits. Sure, Al. Come on over. We can have some tea and chop it up."

Her newfound lingo made me chuckle. "All right, Mama. I'll be there in a bit. And stop watching BET."

"My bad. I love today's music. Never thought I'd say that, but I taught myself how to do the Nay-Nay, and that little Trey Songz reminds me of a modern-day Bobby Brown! Heyyyy!"

"A little too much information, Mama!" I shook my head. "Bye. See you soon." I hung up the phone before I heard any more.

After putting on my socks and Nike slides, I grabbed my wallet and keys and walked to the living room, where Jennifer was sitting combing Jessica's hair. Standing in the doorway, I took them in. They were my little family. More importantly, Jessica was my everything. I had to be sure when it came to this relationship between her mother and me. I couldn't put any more undue stress on Jessica. I owed her that much.

Jennifer looked up at me in shock. "Where are you going?"

"Just over to my mom's house for a little bit." I walked over and kissed her on the cheek.

Jessica jumped up and down. "Can I go to Grandma's house? Please. Please."

"No, doodlebug. You're getting your hair all dolled up, and you have school in the morning."

Jennifer stood up and followed me to the door. "Are you sure you're okay?"

"I'm fine. I just want to go and check on my mom. That's it." I rubbed her arms reassuringly. "I'll be back shortly."

"It's just that you rarely go over there, and now, you're going over at night in the middle of the work week, no less," Jennifer said suspiciously.

I hugged her close to dispel her doubtful thoughts. "Baby, stop worrying. I'm just going to check on my mom. Okay?"

Though she still didn't seem convinced, she nodded her consent.

The ride to my mom's house was one of great turmoil for me. One radio station was blasting all the songs that reminded me of my time with Lucinda, and another was blasting all the ones that reminded me of Jennifer. Finally, I just turned it off and drove in silence. Even my silent thoughts were mentally disturbing. By the time I got to my mom's house, I felt like I had been fighting in a war with myself, and my head was throbbing.

When I walked in the house, I was damn near in tears with laughter. Instead of the sounds of gospel music blaring on her cleaning day as it normally would be, she was blasting her new favorite artist—well, many women's favorite artist—Ariana Grande and one of her new hit singles that was sweeping the across the nation, "The Way." I would never admit this to any of my boys and break the man laws, but hell, I liked the damn song, too, though I'm certain I wasn't alone.

"I like the way," my mom was singing as she watered the plants in the house.

"Mama," I called out over the radio as I laughed at her grooving and dancing in her own little world.

She jumped. "Ooh, I forgot you had a key. Lawd have mercy, you scared me." She laughed and turned down the radio.

"Please don't let me interrupt your singing session."

She fanned me off, walked over, and hugged me. "Shut up, boy. I'm doing her a favor by closing my mouth, 'cause Lawd knows if I keep singing, I'm gonna be the one that kills it," she joked along with me.

"Mama, you're a mess. It's good to see you happy."

She turned around and watered the plant in the windowsill. "Thank you, baby. So, what brings you by?"

Although I heard her, my attention turned to the plant she was watering. "Is that . . . is that Daddy's plant? All big and blossoming like that?"

Her smile told the story. "Yes, it is. It was so beautiful I had to bring it inside the house to be admired by my guests."

"I guess he's still looking out for it from Heaven."

Her eyes lit up at my comment, and she smiled brightly. "I'd like to think so. I guess this old plant just feeds off undying love. At least I'd like to believe that this plant is not only symbolic of our love, but also that it grows because of it. Real love is something that you can never shake. We can move on, and you can even love again, but the *real love* never dies," she explained. "So, what do you want to discuss, or did I somehow answer your question?" she asked, looking back over her shoulder and eyeing me knowingly.

I couldn't help but smile. What she said made sense, but my question was who was my real love, Jennifer or Lucinda?

"Mama, how did you know that Daddy was the one?"

She turned to face me and heaved a deep sigh. "I knew that he was the one because when he asked me, I had no hesitations. To me, if you have to second guess if that person is right for you, then they aren't."

"But what if it's not doubt but rather insecurities?"

"Insecurities and doubt are totally different. Trust me on that one. I had insecurities about getting married, but there was never a doubt in my mind who my husband should be."

Standing in deep contemplation, I folded my arms across my chest. "So, if I'm doubtful, then how do I clear that up?"

"Then you ask God to show you the way. Only He can give you your soulmate, and only He can help you find her. They say women have intuition, so I'd say men have gut instincts. If down on the inside you know that you can't live your life without that person, that if you were to move on you wouldn't be complete, that if they were to move on you would be devastated, that you'd pledge to love them, honor them, care for them, be faithful to them through the good and the bad, through richer or poorer, through sickness and in health, until death, then *that* person is meant to be your spouse."

I plopped down on her sofa and put my head in my hands. "You're right, Mama. I know it. It's just that I don't know when things got so complicated."

She sat down beside me and rubbed my back. "Sometimes we cause complications for ourselves, Al. Maybe you should go back to the source of your complication. Find the moment in time when everything went wrong for you and start searching from there."

Grateful for her words of wisdom, I reached over and hugged her. "Thanks, Mama. I don't know what I'd do or where I'd be without you."

"I'm glad to hear you admit that." She giggled.

"Yeah. I knew you'd eat that up." I stood up. "Well, I better get back before Jennifer gets more suspicious than she already is."

"She has to learn to trust you if you're going to be together."

"Given my track record with her and Lucinda, I can understand why she doubts me."

"But she chose to come back. If she chose that, then she must learn to believe in that. But then so do you. Don't marry her if you're unsure, Aldris. Listen to me for once. You make sure before you make a promise to God and to that woman because in ten years, you don't want to look back and wonder what the hell you were thinking. There's no pain like old pain," my mother warned.

As I was driving home, I thought a lot about what my mother had said. One thing stuck out to me at that moment, going back to the source of my complications. Everything got complicated for me back when I began allowing Jennifer and my feelings for Jessica to separate Lucinda and me. It all exploded when I slept with Jennifer. Why *did* I sleep with Jennifer? Because I was drunk as hell. My unfaithfulness had nothing to do with my feelings. At the time, I loved Lucinda. So maybe I just needed to speak with Lucinda again. Apologize for my behavior and forgive myself for it so that I could get over this feeling. This uncertain feeling.

"Hello?" Lucinda answered.

"Hi, Lu. It's me, Aldris."

"Humph. Okay. What is it that you need, Aldris?" she asked dryly.

"Are you busy?"

"Not at the moment."

"I wanted to . . . well . . . apologize for the other night. It came off kind of harsh—"

"She's your fiancée. What's there to apologize for? It is what it is, right?"

"I mean, yeah, but I just didn't like the way it went down." I exhaled. "Listen, we've both done and said some harsh and regrettable things to each other over the past few months, and I just want to apologize for my part in that. You know? I was wrong when I first cheated with Jennifer, and from that point to any other that I've hurt you, I'm sorry," I said sincerely.

It was truly time to bury the hatchet and try to live our lives as best we could, and I couldn't do that carrying around any more burdens about Lucinda. I was hoping that this would go over smoothly, but I wasn't so sure at this point because Lucinda was so quiet you could hear a pin drop from ten miles away. I just wanted to get back to the point where we were cool with each other and possibly salvage our friendship.

"Wow. Okay then. I'm not sure why you felt the need to say that, but I guess you had to get it off your chest. Look, Dri, you're marrying Jennifer. You have your family now. That's cool, and I wish you well, so please lose my number. At this point, there's no need for us to talk to any further. It only complicates things. Have a nice life with your family. As for me, I have to go and finish up dinner for my fiancé and Nadia."

I stared at the phone in shock. "Are you serious?"

"Yes, I am. We don't need to talk."

"No, about the marriage."

"Yes, I am. Just as serious as you."

I paused. "Umm, Lucinda—"

"Aldris, there is a certain point where it's just not cool for us to be involved with each other anymore. That point was a week ago when Jennifer announced your engagement. Out of respect for both of our relationships, this conversation, this friendship, or whatever you want to call it, is over. Have a great life." And with that, she hung up in my face.

I swear it took another minute or so for me to hang up the phone. I couldn't believe what had just happened. Wow. Her tone was so definitive, so final. Either I had thoroughly pissed her off, or she was really gonna marry that fool. How could she actually marry him? Mike? Really? Wow. And then there was that damn word again—*complicate*. I guess that's where the complications lay. We were complicating each other's lives.

It was safe to say it was official. Lucinda hated me. There was not going to be a mutual understanding or happy ending between us. I couldn't say that I blamed her. I had made it perfectly clear that I wanted a Lucinda-free life, and that's what she was giving me. The facts were that without Lucinda in my life, I was engaged to the mother of my child, back in church, doing great on my job, and I was happy. So *please* tell me why I felt like I was the loneliest man on earth.

I willed myself to accept what she had stated on the phone. I didn't need Lucinda Rojas in my life. Not at all. That's what I kept telling myself over and over again.

Chapter 8

Charice

"Hi, Ms. Charice," London screeched, running up to Lexi and me.

"Hi, sweetheart. How've you been?"

Tucking her hair behind her ear, she scrunched her face. "I'm okay. I miss you."

"I miss you, too." What I really wanted to say was, "If your dumb-ass daddy hadn't moved you from my dance academy, you'd see me all the time."

Yes, that's right. Lincoln had moved London to one of my competitors' dance schools so he didn't have to deal with me. I knew that was what it was all about. The less he had to face me, the less he'd have to risk telling me about Mona.

Mona. Mona. Mona. I'd never despised a woman so much in my life. She had what belonged to me, and the sad part about it was on the one hand, I didn't even want Lincoln anymore. Here I was risking it all for him, and his ungrateful ass was doing me dirty. Claiming he loved me. Hmph. He didn't love me enough not to go searching for someone else. He could've just believed in me. Trusted me. But no, he had to go find ol' light bright.

I couldn't wait to burst his fucking bubble. If I didn't have so much at stake, I would've confronted him on the spot and told him to go straight to hell. On the other hand, I wanted what belonged to me, what he promised me—a life with Lincoln. That was why it hurt me to my core.

He had tried to be overly slick about not seeing me, so he'd asked if Lexi could spend the night with him just so I wouldn't know about his parents' big family gathering that day. It wasn't all that big. It was just his parents, Lincoln and the girls, and his brother and Krista. They were celebrating Krista's first pregnancy, twin boys. In fact, Krista was how I found out. She'd called me and asked if I was coming because she wanted to talk to me about caring for twins. She said she'd asked Lincoln to invite me. Funny thing was, I never got the invite, so I put two and two together. He didn't want me to know about it so he wouldn't have to face me. You see, ever since Mona came into the picture, Lincoln would only pick up Lexi when Ryan was home, but mostly, he'd have me drop Lexi off at his parents' house and pick her up from there.

Thanks to Mona's infatuation with me, I knew all their business. They didn't know where each other stayed, and Mona had no idea what his baby girl looked like, let alone who his baby's mother was. No wonder that fool had the nerve to drop me off and hit on me in front of my house. She didn't know her man lived exactly three doors down.

I used her ass to bait all kinds of information. I knew every time they talked and even down to every time she fucked *my* dick. She was like an open book with me, not only because she was my friend, but because she desperately wanted to fuck me. With the phone sex I'd been dropping on her ass, I knew she'd do anything to try to get to the real deal.

Trust me, the phone sex was for her enjoyment. Wasn't nothing sexy about listening to that bitch moan and groan in my damn ear. Believe me, she was never gonna get any closer to my good stuff than what she could imagine over the phone. If anyone knew the lengths that I went to with all this, they'd probably think I had lost it, but I had a plan. Oh yes, being with Ryan all this time had paid off tremendously. I controlled all of the strings to all of my little puppets, and when the time came, I was gonna snip every last one of them—one by one.

I kind of felt sorry for Mona because in hindsight, she was the innocent party in all of this, but even fake wars had casualties. She became a casualty the moment she slept with *my* dick. The moral of the story was: Do your homework before you lay it down with a man or woman. Do your homework.

Back to the subject at hand. I told Lincoln that Lexi couldn't spend the night after Krista, Lincoln's sister-in-law, informed me of the family gathering. I made up some lame-ass story about taking the kids to visit one of my relatives. He was upset, but rather than invite me, he claimed to understand. So here I was, front and center at their old home in Queens, with Lexi in tow. Surprise. Surprise. Surprise.

Checkmate, Charice.

"It is so good to see you, Ms. Charice. I didn't know you were coming. Can I help you with anything?" London asked.

"If you could grab Lexi's baby bag for me, that would be great, London. You're such a sweetheart. Is everyone in the house?"

"Yes, ma'am. I was just out here listening to music on my iPhone."

Great. This was gonna be fun, especially since I knew Mona was out of town working on a case. Besides, Lincoln wouldn't have her around his family until she knew the truth about Lexi. It was too risky for her to find out the truth by coming here. In fact, she hadn't even known about the cookout, and she still didn't know. How did I know that? Why, of course, because I meddled in their business. Like I said, do your homework.

"What's up, family?" My announcement came as London and I walked into the house with Lexi.

Krista was the first one out into the foyer. "Charice!" she belted, waddling over to hug me. "Oh em gee! I didn't think you were coming." She hugged me tightly. "And let me see my niece."

"Sure thing, honey." I handed over the baby. "You are simply glowing, Krista. You wear pregnancy well."

"Thank you, honey." She blushed as she held Lexi. "She's beautiful."

By this time, everyone was in the foyer. "Hey, Charice," Lincoln's brother Leo said, coming over to hug me.

"Leo." I hugged him back.

"Well, Charice, I didn't expect to see you here," Mr. Harper, Lincoln's father, said, embracing me after Leo.

"Hey, Leonard. I didn't think I was coming, but I couldn't let Leo and Krista miss a chance to see Lexi."

"Hi, sweetie," Mrs. Harper, Lincoln's mother, said, taking her turn to hug me. "Thank you for coming."

I hugged her back tightly. "It's no problem, Eleanora. You know I love you guys."

"We're all in the kitchen talking and getting the food prepared. Why don't you come on back?" Eleanora invited.

"I don't mind if I do. I just have to get Lexi's bouncer out of the car."

"What the fuck are you doing here?" I heard Lincoln's voice behind me as I opened the trunk of my car.

I shifted so that we were face to face. "Bringing Lexi to the family gathering."

"How'd you know about it?"

"Apparently, I was invited."

"Krista," he mumbled.

"Yeah, Krista," I shot back. "So why didn't I get my invite?"

Lincoln's jaw twitched. "It's a *family* gathering. The only member of the Harper family that lives in your household is Lexi."

"So, you were going to bring my child all the way to Queens and not have the decency to tell me?"

"*Our* child. And no, I wasn't. I was going to tell you when we got here," Lincoln said with an attitude. "Now that you've brought her here, you can leave her with me and go."

"Are you crazy? I did not drive all the way to Queens just to drop *our* baby off. Krista wants to see me, so I'm staying whether you like it or not."

He stood with his hands about his waistline and huffed. "Why do you want to be here?"

I refused to offer an answer immediately, so instead I turned and pulled the bouncer out of the trunk and shut it. Once it was out, that's when I addressed his question. "I think the bigger question here is why don't you want me to be here?"

"Simple. You're not in the family. You're a Westmore, remember?"

"Is that what all of this is about?"

"All of what, Charice?"

"Attitude, lack of communication, you not wanting to see me or talk to me, that's what. What about our relationship, Linc?"

He rubbed his face with a chortle. "You mean our affair?"

"If that's what you want to call it, yes."

Lincoln went to speak and then stopped, putting his hand up at me. "You know what? I'm not doing this at my parents' house."

Sexily, I walked up on him, closing the space between us. "Why not?" I ran my finger down the middle of his chest. "We *do* each other so well at this house."

He pushed my hand away. "Stop it."

"Don't flatter yourself. I'm not the same stupid and desperate Charice that was crawling around your kitchen floor, begging you not to leave me, Lincoln. And I won't be ever again. Not for you or anybody else."

Just then, his brother walked outside. "Hey! What's the hold up?" he asked, running over to the car where we were. "You guys can talk inside. Everything all right?" he asked, looking back and forth between Lincoln and me.

"I'm good," Lincoln said, plainly staring at me.

"Great," I sneered, eyeing him back.

"Okay then. Linc, stop being rude. Grab that bouncer from Charice, and let's go. Mama is wondering what's going on," Leo ordered.

Lincoln grabbed the bouncer from me and said roughly, "Let's go inside, Charice."

"Let's." I marched ahead of him straight for the house.

Lincoln leaned over to whisper to me. "This discussion is finished."

I chuckled. "Whatever."

Once inside, I had a blast, laughing and talking with Eleanora and Krista. London was busy on her cell phone and practicing her dancing in the back yard, and the men were watching sports in the family room. Then Lincoln and Leo got on the grill to hook up the barbecue, while Krista and I played with Lexi, and I gave her some pointers with the twins.

The dinner was a BBQ bonanza. Hamburgers, hot dogs, ribs, BBQ chicken, macaroni and cheese, potato salad, baked beans, salad, corn on the cob, and Mrs. Eleanora's special red velvet cake. I completely hurt myself trying to eat a little of everything. We were all stuffed and miserable. We all decided to go out in the backyard and play some Spades while we digested the large meal.

"So, bro, you haven't had two words to say to your baby's mama all day. What's that about?" Leo asked as we all sat there playing Spades.

"Leo," Krista said warningly.

"I'm just asking." Leo shrugged.

Lincoln eyed me. "Everything is cool. We just prefer it this way. Don't we, Charice?" he asked, drinking a swig of his beer.

"Yep, we do." I pointed at Lincoln. "You reneged."

"No, I didn't," he yelled.

My eyebrow raised at his tone, so I gave him back the same energy. "Yes, you did. You cut my clubs with a spade three books ago. Now you just threw out a club."

"Oooh, brother, you sure did," Krista laughed.

"Give up those books, Lincoln," Eleanora laughed as she sat holding her husband's hand at the other table.

"I did not renege," he continued to argue.

"Hold up your books, bro," Leo said.

Lincoln rolled his eyes and threw his book over to me. "Fine. You caught me."

Leo, Krista, and I laughed and high-fived each other. "All of them, baby. Give them all up." I continued laughing as he handed over all his books.

"I've known for years that fool was a cheater. I'm so glad he finally got caught. Good job, Charice," Leo thanked me with a high-five to boot.

Smirking, I quipped, "If you're gonna play the game, you have to learn to be the best. Do your homework. Ain't that right, Lincoln?"

His only response was the sulking expression that he threw toward me.

"Stop being a sore loser," Leonard fussed. "She caught you fair and square."

"I know this, Dad," Lincoln grumbled, causing everyone to erupt again at his babyish behavior.

We continued to play, but Lincoln got up and went inside the house. Once everyone's attention was back on the card game or listening to the radio, I decided to go inside the house, too.

"I'm gonna go check on Lexi," I whispered to Krista before easing inside.

When I went to the bedroom, Lincoln was standing there watching over her.

"She's beautiful when she sleeps, isn't she?"

He looked back at me and nodded. "Yeah, she is."

I walked up beside him, and we stood there staring at her in silence.

"Sometimes, it's hard to believe that we made this beautiful baby," he said.

Gazing up at him, I touched his arm. "But we did. *We* made our beautiful daughter. She is so reminiscent of all the beautiful things that we could've been."

His head fell back in agony. "Charice, don't go there."

My eyes watered at his instant rejection. I'd thought we were finally having a breakthrough as we doted over our baby, the one thing we got right and shared together. Still, even in the sweetest and purest moment we'd had in forever, he showed his utter disdain for me. Damn. He despised me that much? Apparently so, and it hurt like hell. The frustration I felt about his constant rejection of me with no explanation finally got the better of me. If he didn't want me here, then we would go.

"Fine. We're leaving in a few."

"You can leave her with me."

"You've been drinking. I think not."

He turned, facing me with an incredulous look on his face, and held up his finger. "I had one beer."

"One too many for me." I walked out, and he followed, so I told him how I really felt about the situation. "I care about the welfare of our daughter, and whether you believe me or not, I care about your welfare, too."

He smacked his teeth. "Do you?" he asked with an attitude.

"*Yes*." I gave him back the same attitude he'd given me.

Lincoln stood there for a second looking as if he was in turmoil as to what to say next. For a moment, it seemed as if he'd finally engage me, but a split second later, he shook his head, and the stone wall that he'd placed around his heart had returned.

He was about to walk past me, and I reached for him, falling into his arms.

"Charice, I can't keep—"

I put my finger to his lips. Staring into his eyes, I held his gaze for a second, trying to silently convey what he wouldn't allow me to explain. Our sexual synergy was too far off the Richter Scale. I could sense it, so I went for broke.

"Kiss me. You know you want to."

The next thing I knew, we were kissing madly inside the hall bathroom. Lincoln picked me up and put me on the sink.

"I'm going to hell," he said huskily.

"In a handbasket."

We giggled and continued kissing each other.

"In some pussy is more like it," he whispered as he lifted my skirt up. "You know what this outfit does to me."

Indeed, I did. Although the temperature had dropped, it was one of the last few decent days left before the freezing winter weather hit, so I threw on one of Lincoln's favorite outfits to make him salivate over what he'd been missing. I had nearly frozen my ass off outside playing cards, but this bathroom romp was so worth it. Because this . . . this right here was called homework. Watch and learn.

"Oh, Linc!" I moaned. "I need you. I've missed you so much."

"Oh gawd. *Fuck me.*" He bellowed his annoyance with himself as I continued unbuckling his jeans. They dropped to the floor, and I put his hand between my legs. "Shiiit. No panties." He swallowed hard.

I whispered in his ear. "This kitty has been purring and pouring all day for you, baby. Handle that, Linc."

I knew he couldn't resist. One of his greatest fantasies was to come home to me in one of his favorite outfits with no panties on and to fuck me in the first place in the house we ended up. Yes, I was giving him one of his greatest sexual fantasies, and he didn't even know it until it was too late.

The next thing I knew, he was deep inside of me, banging the hell of out of me on the sink in the bathroom.

"Shit. I can't help myself," he said as he fucked me. "It's so good."

"It's yours, baby." It had been so long and felt so good that my body began to cave early against my will. "Come with me."

He gripped my legs tightly as he shoved all of himself deeply in and out of me. It was like he was going for the gusto, etching his name inside of me. I had to struggle to maintain my focus—and not just my eyesight, but my foresight. Deep down, I still loved Lincoln, and I had to force that out of my system.

"Oh *gawd,*" he moaned. "I've missed my sweet pussy. Fuck, I'm not gonna last."

"That's it, baby. *Come.*"

"*Charice,*" he moaned deeply as every vein in his neck and arms began to bulge.

"*Coooome,*" I moaned.

Just then, the bathroom door flew open, and Mr. Harper stood there in shock, blinking his eyes and looking back and forth at Lincoln and me.

"Dad," Lincoln said and instantly stopped pumping, trying to cover himself and me.

"Shit," I mumbled.

My disappointment was great. I'd stopped taking those damn birth control pills just for Leonard Harper to fuck up my grand moment. Shit. Shit. Shit. No babies today. Oh, well. It was back to plan A. Damn.

"What the fuck are you two doing?" he asked.

"Leonard, I'm so sorry—" I hurriedly tried to deliver my Oscar-worthy apology.

"Dad . . . we . . . uh . . . we just got carried away," Lincoln intervened, finally managing to pull up his boxer briefs.

"I'm gonna pretend I didn't even see this, and I refuse to tell your mother. She'd stroke out. Get yourselves together and get out of here before London catches you. Jesus Christ, Lincoln. She's married," his dad said, shaking his head, and shut the door.

I eased off the sink as Lincoln pulled up his pants. "He's right," he said.

"Oh, please, Lincoln."

"Oh, please, hell. You're married, and I can't believe I fucked up again." He shook his head in disbelief. "Stay away from me, Charice. Just *please* stay away from me," he said and walked out of the bathroom.

Sorry, Lincoln. That's just not possible.

After I finished getting myself together, I walked out to bid everybody goodnight and take Lexi home. Enough of the mission had been accomplished today anyway, pregnancy or not.

Chapter 9

Gavin

I was a man living on the edge of insanity. Day in and day out, I went through the motions of life without actually living it. If I was lucky, slow death would come and take me away, so that I could be removed as the common denominator causing strife in everybody's lives.

When I thought of my life as a family man, I imagined the life that my mother had practically embedded in us from as young as I could remember. I saw myself one day having a family of my own and growing old with my wife; teaching my boys how to play baseball, basketball, football, or whatever sport they wanted to play; sitting on the front row of my little girl's ballet or piano recitals, filming her extra special rendition of "Old McDonald." I looked forward to changing the oil in the car in my garage and firing up the grill in the backyard, watching my wife in her bathing suit whip up some fresh batches of ice-cold lemonade as the kids dove in and out of the pool. I imagined Saturday night date nights to dinner and a movie while the next-door neighbors watched the kids. I could even smell the Sunday morning breakfast that was being prepared while we all laid out our Sunday dress clothes for worship service. I figured our kids would be in the choir, and we'd participate in the different church functions. I had all these dreams that I saw for myself once I got married. Never, not once, did I foresee blackmail and coercion into marrying a person I did not want or love.

I couldn't keep going like this. LaMeka's patience was growing thin, and I was running out of time. This had to be the longest thirty days of my life. I didn't know what to do. If I did what I wanted, I'd risk losing everything—not just my career, but Meka, too. If she found out that I had put her or her family at risk to the kind of devastating blows my father was threatening, she wouldn't give a shit why I did what I did. I'd never marry her, and I'd never see her again. The truly fucked up part about it was, if I did what my dad wanted, I'd have the same outcome. That's why I was so frustrated these days. No matter which chess move I made, my queen was in jeopardy.

My attitude had gotten so bad that for the past couple of days, I just stopped going over to Meka's house. She was already suspicious and pissed with me because of my actions. It's not like I could blame her. Hell, I couldn't even bring myself to tell her why I was acting like an ass. If I did, our breakup would beat the deadline that Gerald Randall had already set for us. I figured the best thing to do was to face the situation head on. I needed to have a sit-down, one-on-one talk with both my dad and my brother as men. Maybe if they genuinely saw my pain and love for LaMeka, it would melt the coldness in their hearts. There would be no outside interference, just three grown men discussing a grown man's issue. I promised myself to keep a level head regardless of what was said. That promise still took a lot of prayer.

Here goes nothing, I thought as I opened my front door to allow Gerald and Gary inside. After everything, I was unable to refer to them as my father and brother, although I decided to keep that tidbit of information to myself for the purpose of this meeting.

"Hello. Come inside." I stepped aside and allowed them inside my home. "Thank you for meeting me."

They both nodded. "Gavin," they said in unison as if they were joined at the same central nervous system.

Above my father, my brother, Gary, was simply sickening to me. The power of the almighty dollar stole too many souls and put others in financial ruin, and he'd cashed in his soul years ago. I'd thought I'd always have him as an ally, but my name wasn't Benjamin, so there was that.

"Please come in and have a seat." I led them to the living area.

"For such meager means, your house is spotless, and you do actually have some taste like your old man," Gerald said, sitting on the sofa beside Gary as I sat on the loveseat.

I bit my lip to quell the smart remark that threatened to spew from my mouth. *You promised yourself not to go off*, I mentally reminded myself.

Just because I chose a house to fit my standards in a nice upper-middle-class neighborhood and not a mansion on the top of some hill away from the rest of civilization did not make my means meager. That was the problem with those two. They considered the *best* of everything to be bigger, better, exclusive, and more exquisite than other people. To me, the *best* was what made an individual happy. If I chose to live in a damn cardboard box because it made me happy, then that was what was *best* to me, a concept they would probably never understand. And another thing, just because I didn't have maids and butlers at my beck and call didn't mean my spot wasn't clean, or that I didn't have nice things. Unlike them, I knew how to use my own elbow grease, and I wasn't afraid of a little thing called work. If they tried it sometime, they might not be the self-centered bastards that they were.

Woosah, Gavin. Just hold it together.

"Well, thank you. I think."

Gary crossed his legs in his tailored Armani suit. "To what do we owe this pleasant invitation to your home, brother? I haven't stepped foot in here in years, so this is quite the honor. Pray tell. What is this joyous occasion all about?" he asked with a smirk on his face.

I took a deep breath and leaned forward. "I wanted to speak with you both face to face, man to man. We're family, and there's no reason we shouldn't be able to air out our concerns and grievances amongst each other, together as men and father and sons."

Gerald nodded. "Fair enough."

Gary nodded. "We're listening."

"I know that I'm not like you two, and I understand that disappoints you. It would make all our lives easier if I were, and I get that, but I'm not. I don't agree with most of the things that both of you do or say, but I endure and respect it because you're my family, and I love you. All I'm asking is for the same in return. As a man, allow me to make my own decisions concerning my life and respect those decisions. If you choose not to be a part of my life, then I can respect that, too. It would be sad, but it would be your choice and not

mine. Just know that if you ever change your mind
and wanted to be a part of my life, that I would
willingly accept you both with open arms." There.
I'd successfully pled my case to them.

Gary sighed and switched legs to cross. "Little
brother, it's like this. I personally don't give a
flying fuck what you do with your life. You burned
your bridge long ago with me, and while I love you
as my brother, I don't need you in my life either. I
have a beautiful wife, a handsome son, a wonderful
father, a respectable career, a ton of friends, a shit-
load of money, and a bad bitch on the side named
Yolanda to fuck me just right, so I'm just fine. You
have always been a nonfactor for me. Honestly, I
don't know why father wastes his time on you or
our trash sister, Veronica. It's obvious that you all
like mingling in the pigsty, so he should let you
wallow where you like and be done with the both of
you," he said matter-of-factly. "I mean, since we're
being honest and all."

I put my head down to keep from jumping up
and whipping his ass. As many times as I saved
him from getting his ass whipped when we grew
up and looked out for him, giving him my last food
or money when Mama didn't have it, and this fool
says something like that to me? What was sad was
that I honestly didn't believe Gary felt the way he
did, but he'd always been easily swayed by the
promise of a better life. Any opportunity he had to

come up, he took it, no matter how he achieved it.
He'd been that way since we were kids. I just never
knew that he'd allow it to drive a wedge between
him and me. Yet here we were. He'd burned a
bridge with me, too, and if he didn't watch his
mouth, I was going to light his ass on fire to match
the burn in the bridge.

I also didn't want to make a move on him because I knew Gary was Gerald's golden child.
Anyone or anything that attempted to harm precious Gary was met with grave consequences.
Therefore, I knew he was talking shit more so
because Gerald was there and not because he felt
he could actually whip my ass. He knew he
couldn't. Punk muthafucka.

I laughed sinisterly. "Well, bro, I'm glad to know
how you really feel. I respect that, too."

Gary matched my laughter. "Oh? So, you're not
going to go all *'hood'* on me? How do they say it?
West Side," he said, attempting to throw up gang
signs.

I wished I did live in the hood at that very moment and let somebody pull up on his scary ass. I
shook my head at that idiot.

"We live on the East Coast, Gary. Why would we
rep West Side?" I asked sarcastically, just to take a
dig at him.

He rolled his eyes. "Oh, you know what I mean.
You hang in more ghettos than I ever have or will,"
he said smartly.

Gerald touched Gary's arm. "Enough, son. Let's not get into a tit for tat. That's not what we're here for."

Gary rubbed his eyebrow. "Sorry, Father. You're right as always."

Seriously, did he have an electronic chip stored in my brother? That shit was just foolish to me. He had straightened up as if he were programmed to do so. Shit. It was either that or my dad needed to be the next Super Nanny.

Gerald unbuttoned his blazer and placed his index finger to his lips. "Gavin, you've said all of that to ask what?"

"I'm asking that you please leave Meka and her family alone. I'm asking if you would leave us alone and allow me to marry her and build a family with her. She's gone through so much—too much—and she doesn't deserve to be hurt through any of this. I pursued her, I dated her, and I want to marry her. It's all on me. Can't you just take your shares back, call it even, and let me be at peace with my own life? No damaging anybody's career or healthcare coverage."

Gerald stood up and paced with his hands in his pockets for a few moments. Then he turned to face me. "You are so weak, just like your mother."

Now, that was it. All bets were off when it came to my mama. I stood up. "Do not disrespect my mama. Don't do it."

"I figured something would break the camel's back." Gary laughed sinisterly.

"Shut up, Gary." The words came out before I could stop them.

"Or else you'll do *what*, Gavin? Hmm? What are you going to do if I disrespect your *mama*?" Gerald taunted me.

My jaw twitched, and it took everything in me and the grace of God not to fuck him up. So, I just stood there quietly.

"Exactly. Nothing. You know better than to try me," Gerald said. "You know your mother left me for some damn black man? He made her happy, she said. Well, tearing his career down and forcing him to leave your mother made me happy, too. There is a lot that you do not know or understand, Gavin. A lot. Now, whether LaMeka stays or goes doesn't matter, but blood family is forever. You cannot get another father or brother, but you can get another LaMeka. We would just prefer to call her Susie or Trisha." He and Gary laughed.

"I refuse to give up on you as my son, and I refuse to hand you over to some low-rent ghetto bitch just because she's got a big butt and sweet pussy. Now, I've told you to let it go, and I mean it. Marry a Trisha, a Becky, or Susie or some shit, and if you absolutely must have LaMeka to get your rocks off, then double strap and handle your manly business. Real Randall men know how to keep the wife happy and the bitch on the side pleased. Nobody oversteps their boundaries, and everyone is cool with playing their fucking positions. Just ask Gary's wife, Diana, and his bitch, Yolanda. They understand. Or you can ask my girlfriend, Carly, and my bitch, Tasha. They understand.

"So, having said that, let me break it down in the simplest of ghetto terminology so you understand me. All LaMeka can or ever will be for you is your cum catcher. Get used to it and get the fuck over it."

I had never wanted to kill someone in my life until that very moment. No, seriously. I wanted to go to my lockbox, pull out my 9mm Glock, load it, and unload it right in Gerald's dome—and Gary's if he got in the way. Then reload and unload it again just to be sure it was done right. The rage burgeoning inside of me was like an inferno waiting to explode, so I had to hurry up and get them the fuck away from me before we all made the six o'clock evening news.

"I think your son is upset, father," Gary said, standing up. "His nose is doing that flare-up thing it does when he's on edge."

Gerald turned to face me. "Listen, son, don't be mad. I love you, and I'll never give up on you. I'll tell you what. You can do what you would like with any money I've provided for you. It doesn't matter to me because you're my flesh and blood. Just give up on this crazy notion of marrying LaMeka.

I never said you couldn't have your way with her. You just can't have her as your wife. Life is about choices and sacrifices. LaMeka and you can both have the life you deserve if you just do what I say."

"So, it's like that, huh? Just fuck what I want? Although I am your son and I'm damn near begging you?"

Gerald sighed. "It's because you're my son that you've even been given these many chances. My subordinates only get one warning. This is your third. But it is also your final. Now, I'm done with this whole marrying the jig. You know the deal. Handle it."

"That's what I get for assuming I could appeal to the humane side of either one of you. No such side even exists."

Gerald looked at me, and I could tell he was just as pissed as I was. "You know, my *humanity* is in taking care of what's mine. That would be you and your siblings. That's it. Everything else I do is a courtesy. How dare you speak to me in that tone? After all I've done for your ungrateful ass. The first time I can even get a decent invitation to your home is so you can beg me to marry some black bitch. That piece of ass didn't pay your way through college. She didn't allow you to live off any interest of her money. So, you be clear about one thing: *I* am the hand that feeds you, and *I* am the same hand that will rock the fuck out of your cradle. You just better be glad that I have enough *humanity* to endure you and your temper tantrums," he said, then motioned for Gary to follow him to the door.

"Is that all?" I asked as they passed me.

"You've got two weeks, Gavin." Gerald rolled his eyes and walked out of my house.

"Tick tock, baby brother." Gary laughed as he patted my shoulder. "You sure can piss Dad off. You'll be fine. If you want to marry her, do like we used to do back in the day—pretend. Buy the bitch a Cracker Jack ring and have her check the yes or no box," he joked.

"Get the fuck outta my house."

He shook his head. "You'll never learn. So sad," he said as he walked out.

I slammed the door so hard it hit him on the ass as he walked out. He was so fucking lucky that was all that hit him.

I was so fucking pissed off I couldn't do anything but pace the damn floor. I wanted to get in my car and ride on them. It wasn't so much their demands that pissed me off, but they tried me on my manhood, talking to me in my house out of the side of their necks and disrespecting my lady. At the moment, I was trapped because there wasn't shit I could do about it without jeopardizing LaMeka's wellbeing. It was either allow them to disrespect her or be the cause of them shutting down her life. That was a hell of a decision, but it was one I had to choose carefully. LaMeka's welfare was of far greater importance than defending her honor, but trust me, as God was my witness, there would come a day when they would both severely pay for trying my manhood. Bet that.

I had to get out of the house and clear my head. As soon as I put my hand on the knob, the doorbell rang, and I flung the door open.

"*What?*" I screamed, thinking it was Gerald and Gary again.

"Damn, bruh, you are really on edge," Tony said.

"Man, today ain't the day, dude. I promise this is so not what you want. And why are you even at my fucking house?"

"Whoa, white boy. Pipe your tone down, 'cause trust me, you don't want it with me either. Don't get all twisted with me because you can't handle your pops and his sidekick," Tony spewed.

That caught me off guard, and I eyed him for a moment.

"Yeah, you just stuck right now, huh?" Tony spouted.

Not wanting to let on that he was correct, I feigned confusion. "What are you talking about?"

His laughter let me know he wasn't buying into it. "Don't play dumb with me. I've been out here for the past ten minutes. I was coming to see you, but imagine my surprise when I heard all the commotion going on about you and Meka. Truth is, it took everything in me not to run up in here on your punk-ass people about disrespecting my babies' mother like that, but it's not my battle to fight. It was yours, and I must say, you lost miserably."

I waved him off with a level of confidence that I didn't have. Gerald and Gary had not only tested my manhood but exposed it to the one man in this world that hated me just as much as I hated them. That shit was embarrassing.

"Miss me with that shit, Tony. What do you even care about Meka for anyway? It's not like you're concerned about her welfare."

"See, that's where you're wrong and you under-estimate me. If it wasn't for you, she'd be back by my side despite my situation. I have no doubt of that. I love Meka just like you do. I haven't always done right by her, and, yes, I've not always had her best intentions at heart, but I've grown up, and her and my boys are the single most important people to me. So, don't get it twisted, muthafucka. The only reason I even endure you is because I love her enough to back the fuck up," Tony said sternly.

Tony's bravado did nothing for me. I'd just endured Gerald and Gary Randall. Tony's idle threats were nothing more than child's play after dealing with the likes of them.

"Whatever. What the fuck were you coming to see me for? Let's just get to that point so I can get the fuck out of here," I said.

"Aren't you going to invite me in?"

"Did you ask for an invitation the last time you came to my house?" I asked, taking a jab at him about breaking in and trashing my house.

He chuckled. "Well, since we're being honest and all, no, I didn't. Just like you didn't get my permission to tell my job about my HIV status or my college about my living arrangements."

"Whatever you think is fine with me. If you feel like I did, then go with that."

"Cut the crap—"

"No, you cut the fucking crap. What do you want?"

"Look, I don't like you—"

"Please tell me you didn't waste your time and mine to tell me something that we both already knew."

"If you shut the fuck up! I swear you white folks—"

Stepping into his space, I interrupted whatever snide comment he was about to make. "I've had just about enough racial slurs today from you or anybody else. Kill the white boy and white folks' analogies. I'm not disrespecting you as a black man, so don't do it to me. *Especially* not today."

Tony's eyes lifted in surprise. I was positive it was from the shock that I didn't fear him and would step to him if need be. Unlike Gerald and Gary, I owed him nothing. They got a pass off the strength of who they were to me. I had zero fucks to give when it came to Tony.

With a smirk on his face, he raised his hands and eased back, reinserting the space between us. "Fair enough. Listen, I'll be brief. You have to be honest with Meka about your family situation. As much as I hate to admit this shit, she loves the hell out of you. I've never seen her so happy, even when we were together, not even at our best. If being with you is what makes her happy, then I'm all for it, regardless of my feelings towards you. My boys adore you, and I know that you don't treat them ill, so I can fall back for the sake of your relationship. But what's not gonna happen is me allowing your family to tear her or my boys down because they don't want you with her.

"I tried to tell her that they would be an issue, but she won't listen to me. She doesn't trust me, so I came to talk to you. You have to find a way to make your people cool with this whole marriage thing or walk away from her, 'cause I'm not going to allow you to get her hurt just to spare your heart." Tony put it out there on the line.

Damn. I was getting my ass handed to me by everybody today. And again, the fucked-up part of it was that Tony was absolutely justified in what he was saying. He was the boys' father, and he owed it to them to protect them just as much as I did. I couldn't even be mad at that. I wanted to, oh, I wanted to, but man to man, he was right.

"I'm trying. I'm trying to think of any and everything I can to do that. I feel you one hundred percent on where you're coming from because I feel the same way. And on the humble, I can respect you for what you're doing and saying, especially as the boys' father. You have every right to be concerned and take the necessary action if needed."

We paused for a long time, not really knowing what to say or do. Finally, Tony asked, "So what is your plan?"

"If you have any suggestions, I'm all ears."

"I know you're in a truly fucked-up situation if you're asking me for help."

"Yeah. I am. I never would've proposed if I'd known all this shit was gonna backfire on me. I just want to marry Meka and be a family."

"Yeah, well, as lovely as that sounds, I don't care to listen to you talk about marrying her. There's only so much I can deal with here."

"I feel you. Listen, I'm going to think of something, but man to man, I'm asking you to put everything aside between you and me while I do this. Promise me you won't tell Meka about today while I try to get this worked out."

"Only if you promise to walk away from her if you can't."

I huffed, nodded my head in agreement, and put my hand out to him. We gave each other pound and a head nod.

"All right, bet. Truce for now," he said.

"Truce for now."

"But I'm serious. You're not such a bad cat really, and we'd probably be cool if you wasn't kicking it with my babies' mother. Cool-ass cat or not, I will bring it to your ass and your family's asses if they try Meka or my boys. Real talk," Tony warned.

"I can respect that, and I appreciate you looking out for me on this. Real talk."

"You sure you're that man's son?"

"By 99.9998 percent."

"That thousandth of a percent must belong to a black man," he joked.

"Get the fuck outta here." I laughed. "Tony Light, you're all right."

"You ain't so bad yourself, Gavin Randall." Tony chuckled.

Tony and I chopped it up for a few more minutes before he left. I wasn't too far behind. I had to get some fresh air. As I left to clear my mind and think of something to fix my situation, I was glad that at least I'd made peace with Tony, for the meantime, which gave me a little comfort. And at this point, even that little bit of comfort was encouraging.

No matter how much I tried to clear my head, there was only one place where I had true solace. With Meka. It had been a couple of days since I'd seen her. We'd texted and spoken briefly at work, but today, I had to see her. I needed to hold her and tell her that I loved her, especially if our time together was coming to an end.

"What brings you by tonight, stranger?" Meka asked with a slight attitude as she answered the door.

Without a word, I gripped her by the waist, brought her to me, and kissed her deeply. "I love the absolute shit out of you, woman," I said as we finally pulled up for air.

She took a deep breath. "Damn. I love you, too." She smiled.

"Get a room," Misha said as she trotted by, and we both laughed.

We stared into each other's eyes for a few moments as I held her close in my arms.

"Can I come inside? Please."

Without hesitation, she said, "Always," as she held my hand and led me in.

Chapter 10

Pooch

"Dear Lord, God the Father, Jesus Christ, and Holy Spirit, I don't know how to address you because it's been a long time since I said a prayer or talked to you even. I hope I got all of them names in there. Why *do* you have so many names? Oh yeah, I forgot Emmanuel. But that might not be cool. Maybe I should call you Mr. Emmanuel. Anyway, I'm gettin' off the subject.

"Listen, my dude, Jesus Christ, I mean. I need a favor. That slick-ass bitch of a baby mama of mine, I mean Trinity. Trinity. She has reneged on her promise to me, and you know I don't do well with shit—stuff . . . like that. I'm asking you to touch my heart because if you don't, when I get out of this mutha—place, I will kill her damn a—her behind. She screwed me over in all of this. Okay, maybe I left her no choice, but I was gonna keep my word. We both know that, but I know who changed her

mind. That maggot-ass—my bad, her so-called
husband and his cousin, Thomas. Now they got a
chip on their shoulder wit' me, but Aaron got
his own ass—self killed. It was either him or me.
That wasn't even a decision. Anyway, I need you
to keep me from going after all three of them dirty
muth—people.

"First, I need you to find a way for me to get out
of this hellhole. The way I feel, no matter what I
say or do with you, I got one foot in the fiery pit
anyway, so if I'm gonna burn, hell, let me burn
once not twice. To break it down, ya know, just in
case you got lost in all my babbling, I need help to
get outta this place and, uh, I need to not wanna
kill the niggas who was supposed to help me get
out of this place. And, uh, I guess thank you. My
grandma said to always thank you, so yeah, thanks.
Amen and hallelujah." I remained kneeling beside
my cot as the ramblings of my prayer bounced
around the four walls.

Talk about mad. I thought *I* could blow up,
but Stein must've been around too many thugs,
gangstas, and outlaws because that fuckin' white
boy damn near ripped me a new asshole when he
came to tell me the news. See, I kinda hadn't told
him that Adrienne was sneaking contraband into
the prison and that was how I was able to per-
suade—or as the law likes to say, *coerce*—Trinity
into testifying for me.

I didn't believe in that coercion shit. I mean, if a person makes an offer and the other person doesn't refuse it, is that my fault? I mean, she could have taken a chance on my threats, but she chose not to. How was that coercion or even my fault?

Coercion and bribery were at the cornerstone of the American way of life. These damn lawmakers just changed the terminology to fit their law records so they could pin a prison sentence on a nigga. Coercion and bribery were nothing more than sales pitching at its highest level. What was the difference between me offering to leave Trinity alone in exchange for her testimony and a car salesman offering to give you cash back, rebates, and a free DVD entertainment system upgrade if you purchased the vehicle? Nothing. The outcome was the same. If the person took the deal, everybody got something out of it. So, how was my shit illegal?

Hell, at least my deal was straight up and straightforward. I was positive those car salesmen screwed over everybody to make their money. Crooked wasn't nothing but crooked. But if you got a raw deal with them, you still had to make them damn car payments, didn't you? You couldn't go back and say, "Oh, he *coerced* me into this by bribing me with this DVD system, and now, I don't feel I should pay this high-ass car note." As if the loan people were gonna say, "Of course, we'll just write it off and you can keep the car for your inconvenience." Hell no. Those fuckers were gonna tell you pay that note or risk repossession, and if you did get repo'd, most places still made you liable for the loan. Ain't that a bitch? You still had to pay for something you couldn't afford anyway, and you still didn't have shit to show for it, and *that* shit was legal?

I'm telling you; America is fucked up. It was built to keep certain people up, certain people down, and the rest of us were locked the fuck up because we were hip to the deception. Like me. They bet' not neva let me have a chance to run for a political office. It'd be a real New World order. But that, just like the fucking testimony from Trinity, wasn't never gonna happen.

Anyway, I ain't never seen Stein so outraged. That fool actually threatened to walk out on my case. Me! Pooch! If I wasn't already behind bars, I woulda chin-checked his ass for threatening me. He knew I couldn't afford to get nobody else, and when I was pulling that paper, his pockets stayed laced big time. How dare he come at me with some ol' bullshit like that? Talking about I put his career on the line. Man, Trinity wasn't gonna say shit about that. He was too paranoid.

At the end of it all, he promised he'd stay on my case, but I had to promise to stay out of it and allow him to do all the preparation and leg work.

Whatever. Fine with me. I just wanted to get out of there, and I prayed that when I did, God would touch me so I wouldn't touch Trinity's ass. Real talk.

On to some good news. My baby, Flava, got off. As a bonus, Adrienne had convinced her to give me another chance. I'll never forget when I waltzed into the visiting area and saw her and Adrienne sitting there. I couldn't do nothing but grab her and kiss her. Adrienne got a little jealous, but I had to explain to her that I was just happy to see Flava. She was with me no matter who came or went, but I was hoping like hell that Adrienne went, 'cause Flava rode hard for me.

That visit was all about observation for me. I had to see where Flava's head was at. Was she really in this for me or because Adrienne wanted her to be? By the end of the visit, I was convinced that she'd gotten over her anger about nearly going to prison for helping me move weight and that she was still that ride or die chick she'd always been.

One thing was extremely apparent. It was gonna be harder than I thought getting rid of Adrienne. As much as Adrienne loved Flava, Flava loved her back. They held hands the entire time they were visiting me, and it wasn't just that. It was their *way*. I mean, they completed each other's sentences, and they were constantly giggling when the other made a joke. It was like watching teenagers in love for the first time. Honestly, this was the most feminine I'd seen Flava, other than on the pole in Club Moet. She was always so hood, but with Adrienne, she was so gentle and sexy. She even pushed Adrienne's hair out of her face for her. Now, that move was on some real love shit, the kind of stuff you do after you finish making love to your woman and you wanna hold and caress her.

Yeah, it was like *that*. She wasn't like that with her before. I guess Adrienne being there for her through her lockup and trial really brought them together, and I knew that it was gonna take some fancy slick talk to separate those two.

I was beginning to feel like the third wheel that would be there strictly for dickly purposes. You know, whenever they grew tired of sucking and licking on each other and wanted the real deal, then they'd call me. Fat chance. I was not about to be their man whore for hire. I wanted Flava to myself, and that heifer Adrienne could be the damn sidekick. Therefore, I had to tread lightly because this was gonna take a little finesse. I'd have to keep Adrienne around for a little while in order to be able to get rid of her. Otherwise, that crazy bitch Flava may just choose her over me.

"Inmate," the CO called into my cell. I sat up. "You've got a visitor." I looked at him with confusion.

He nodded. "Yes, you. Your government name is still Vernon Smalls, right?"

Smart-mouthed bastard. "Yep."

"My bad. It did change to Inmate 612541 for DOC," he joked.

"Well, like a wise man once said, it ain't what they call you. It's what you answer to."

He immediately stopped laughing and huffed. "Well, *inmate*, you have a visitor."

As if his little quip was supposed to fuck wit' me. I knew I was an inmate. That wasn't no fuckin' new news. Like I said, it was what I answered to that mattered, and the fact that I just ignored his ass when he said that ignorant shit meant I didn't answer to "inmate." I answered to Vernon Pooch Smalls. Remember that shit. He could miss me all day with that fake-ass authoritative tone. Wasn't nothing separating me and him from the inside of these cells except gettin' caught. I knew for a fact that the majority of the COs, including him, were nothing but one snitch away from being Inmate 612542.

As he handcuffed me, I asked, "Is it my lawyer?"

"You'll see when you get there. I have better things to do with my time than keep track of your visitor's list."

Man, I really couldn't deal with a hundred and one years of this bullshit right here. Really. I exhaled loudly as we walked.

"You know you drug dealers are all alike. You swear you own the world and are the toughest people on the planet. If you'd put that knowledge and power to some good, then you wouldn't have to go around trying to prove shit to the world. You'd be somebody who was genuinely respected," the CO preached.

"Miss me with that 'We are the World' speech. You can't group me with nobody else 'cause you don't know me. And it's some people who use their knowledge and power for good and still can't get respect."

"That's where you're wrong, inmate," he said, pulling on my cuffs. "Respect is earned, not given."

"Well, you have to give it first to get it."

He pointed a finger in my face. "That attitude is why you're gonna fail. Not because you have a different way of thinking, but because you don't respect anybody else's way of thinking," he said as we stopped at a private visiting room.

Ignoring him, I focused on who was visiting me and deduced that it had to be Stein. He opened the door, let me in, and closed it. I was shocked as hell to see who I was seeing.

Plopping down in the chair in front of me, I was almost at a loss for words. "Terrence?"

"Yeah, not who you expected, huh?" he asked coolly.

Furrowing my brow, I asked, "How did you get in here to see me? You're not on my visitor's list. And how the hell did you get a private room?"

He put his hand up to silence me. "Don't worry about any of that. The mere fact that I can do it is all you need to be concerned with."

Who the fuck? "What the fuck does that mean?"

He eyed me for a moment, and I knew his thoughts were running through his mind like calculations. The one-up he had on me was that he had always been a thinker. Sometimes I allowed my anger to consume me and rushed into things, but not him. Even in his highest level of anger, he remained calm, only exerting force when direly necessary. If I was a bitch-ass nigga, I might admire that quality, but because I wasn't, it only pissed me off.

He licked his lips and breathed out. "It means that as much as you can touch me, I can touch you, too, nigga. Feel me on that first and foremost. Now, I don't know what you said to my shorty to make her agree to that shit in the first place, but it ain't going down. Since I know your attorney has already hipped you to that information, let me hip you to some more."

He paused and leaned forward, never breaking eye contact with me.

See! Do you see? This right here was exactly why I couldn't turn over this Christian leaf. This nigga did *not* just come to prison to let me know he could get at me. I *know* he didn't do that. Kind of made me wish I'd saved a couple of bullets for his ass the same way his cousin did. No sense of muthafuckin' loyalty. If I had shot off on him, he'd surely be dead. The fucked-up part was this nigga actually shot me, and he was still breathing. Not just because he pulled through his surgery, but because I vowed not to fuck with him. I didn't need to die because being locked up in here and not being able to "touch" this nigga, as he could put it, was a slow enough death.

My jaw locked tight, and I pursed my lips. "What other information are you gonna so-called hip me to?"

"If you come near me or my family, whether you're in or out of prison, you're gonna wish you would've died up in that hospital. In your words, I need you to uh, how does it go? *Remember that shit,*" he sneered with an air of cockiness about him.

Flicking the tip of my nose, I asked, "Oh yeah, my nigga?"

His eyebrow raised, and I took the opportunity to let my feelings be known.

"Well, listen to this and be clear," I said. "I don't give a fuck about you the same way you don't give a fuck about me. It is what it is. If you gon' do something, do it. Don't talk about it. Be about it. But this is the shit I want *you* to remember. I gave you and my baby's mama a free pass back at that storage. I gave you life, even though you tried to take mine. Playtime and passes are up, muthafucka. Do what you gotta do, and I'll do what I gotta do. But *mark my fuckin' words*. I will get out of here whether your bitch helps me or not, and when I do, we'll finish this conversation then."

Terrence rubbed his goatee, smiling sinisterly. "Indeed, we will." He stood up and called for the guard. "You can take your inmate back. I'm done."

As the CO was coming to cuff me, Terrence limped out of the door.

"Later." I chucked up the deuces at him.

He chuckled. "Later."

"Ready, inmate?" the CO asked.

I simply glared at the CO, who shrugged and prepared to take me back.

"Are you going to bible study tonight?" he asked as we prepared to leave.

I shook my head. "Nah. I'm too much of a sinner to be a fucking saint."

Chapter 11

Aldris

Ever felt like you were just going through the motions? Like you were living your life, the life you've always wanted, but it still just didn't feel like enough? Or you didn't feel like you were doing all that you wanted or needed to be doing? That's how I felt these days. My life was good. I'd venture to say great even, but at times I just—I don't know—felt like it wasn't enough. I prayed to God every night for that feeling to go away and to renew a vibrant spirit within me.

The night before, Jennifer had spent the night with me. My mother watched Jessica, so we could enjoy some alone time together. Dinner and a movie at the house were the perfect ways to end the evening.

Deep down, I knew the real reason Jennifer wanted to stay with me. She wanted me to help her with some wedding plans, which was exactly why I

was procrastinating with getting dressed the next
day. I didn't feel like going out. I wanted to lounge
in my bed and chill out. However, I finally dressed
so I wouldn't have to hear Jennifer's fussing.

Every time I turned around, Jennifer had me
looking at this or choosing that. The wedding was
the woman's deal, and I didn't mind picking some
things, like my tuxes or my groom's cake, but she
was treating me like I was her mother or matron of
honor. Where the hell were those two at? Shouldn't
they be the ones cackling and helping her with this
wedding-day bliss? Hell, I'd even appreciate it if
she'd ask my mother. And, as I thought about it, it
rubbed me the wrong way that she didn't include
my mother in any of the plans. Lucinda had included my mom and her mom along with her girls.
She had made the planning special for both of us.

*Wow. Did I really just think that? Fuck. I've got
to stop doing that.*

Jennifer was not Lucinda, and Lucinda was
not Jennifer. I wasn't trying to compare the two.
I'm just saying that I believe the manner in which
Lucinda handled the planning was better than
Jennifer. She really was wrong not to include my
mother, though. I didn't give a damn how she
sliced it.

"Are you ready yet?" Jennifer asked as she walked
into my bedroom. "I've paced a hole in the carpet
waiting on you. We have an appointment to keep."

"Would you stop stressing? I just finished getting dressed. A couple of sprays of cologne and I'm all good. I don't see what the big deal is. We're just tasting some wedding cake. Hell, I thought all wedding cake tasted the same anyway."

Jennifer rolled her eyes. "No, it doesn't. Does all pound cake taste the same?"

"It does if it's made right," I mumbled.

"I heard that."

"I'm just saying."

She huffed. "I mean, it's *our* cake for *our* day. We should taste it to see if we want different flavors like strawberry or lemon, and the type of icing we should get. That's what this is all about. It's supposed to be fun and special."

By the time she finished her rant, I'd finished up, and we were heading out the door.

"I just don't see how special it's gonna be when we are probably only gonna get to taste a forkful when we feed each other. By the time we get back from our honeymoon, that cake is gonna be as good as gone."

Ignoring me, she continued to walk ahead toward the car. "Well, I want to make sure my forkful is exactly what I want."

"You didn't water the plant?"

"Huh?" She stopped in her tracks and turned to look at me.

I pointed to the plant that Lucinda and I had begun growing. "It's dry. You didn't water it yesterday like I asked you to."

She hit her forehead. "No, I forgot, but we don't have time for that. Besides, you know I don't have a green thumb. I leave that shit for you and your mother."

"Hold up. It'll only take a second. Go ahead and get in the car."

She stomped. "Really, Al? For a damn plant? We really don't have the time."

"Hey, you want me to make time for cake tasting. I'm going to make time to water a plant." I turned on the hose and began watering.

After I finished watering the plant, I headed to the car, where she stood leaning against my vehicle.

"Can we go now, or do you need to feed the birds and the bees, too?" she asked, sliding into the driver's seat.

I got in the car. "Woman, drive to this place."

Our drive was a silent one. It would be an accurate guess to say that I'd never told Jennifer that Lucinda purchased that plant. I don't know why I kept it. It was the last reminder of Lu at my house. I liked plants, just like my mom did, so I figured I'd keep watch over it until Lucinda decided to come and get it. I could not tell Jennifer whose plant it was, or it'd be chopped up and trashed. Why do that to the plant? It wasn't its fault. Besides, it was really blossoming, and if push came to shove, I'd take it over my mom's house so she could continue giving it the love and care that it needed. I hated to admit it, but it just reminded me so much of my mom and dad, so I held onto it as if it were a rare piece of fine jewelry.

"You didn't say anything about my outfit," Jennifer said, breaking into my silent thoughts as we got out of the car.

My focus turned to her. "Huh?"

She huffed. "You always said that you like to see women in skinny jeans. You know I've never been a fan of them, but since you said you liked how they look, I went and bought these jeans with this nice wrap sweater shirt, and you didn't even notice."

Taking in her words, I looked her up and down. Damn. She did look hot to death in that outfit. Here was where a man had to learn to fudge the truth. I really didn't pay her any attention because I was used to Lucinda wearing them. Actually, Lucinda was the reason I liked to see women wear them. Of course, I couldn't tell Jennifer that I wasn't paying attention because I was used to another woman wearing that style and not her, so I fudged.

"I'm sorry, baby. I did notice it, but you were rushing me so hard about making this appointment that I didn't say anything. You really do look hot, and they become you. Maybe later on I can see what it feels like to slide you out of those jeans."

We linked arms, and she giggled. "Maybe you *can* talk me into that later on, Mr. Sharper," she said with a sexy smile.

I breathed a sigh of relief that I'd dodged a bullet. A little fudging never hurt, especially when trying to prevent an argument. If I'd admitted that I really didn't notice it, then I'd have been accused of not paying her any attention, and the snowball effect would've begun. The lesson of today was fudge.

"Hello, we have an appointment with LeAnn," Jennifer said to the receptionist as I picked up a brochure.

The cakes in there were extraordinary, exquisite, and fucking expensive. *Who in the hell spends two grand on some damn cake?* And that was a base price for one of the low-budget ones. My cousin Debra worked in the bakery at Wal-Mart and could've gotten us a nice three- or four-tier cake for two-hundred and fifty, no more than five hundred dollars tops, and it would've been all to the good and sent everybody into a diabetic coma.

I leaned over to Jennifer and whispered, "Do you see these fucking prices?"

She nudged me with her elbow just as a lady walked up to us.

"Hi! Welcome to Uniquely Tastes Cake. You must be the future Mr. and Mrs. Sharper. I'm LeAnn, and I'm going to be showcasing our work here for you today. I'm positive by the end of your experience, you'll taste a cake that is uniquely right for you," she said, all bubbly.

Jennifer smiled. "We look forward to it. I'm excited."

LeAnn turned to me. "And don't worry. We have some delicious groom's cakes that are to die for. You'll be excited, too."

"Do the groom's cakes start at two grand, too?" I asked before I knew it.

Jennifer gasped, and LeAnn chuckled. She touched Jennifer's arm. "Don't be upset. The men are always the skeptics. Money is always their first motivating factor, but once they taste our cakes, it goes out the window," she jokingly reassured her.

"Really? What do you put in it to make me lose my mind? Crack?"

By this time, Jennifer looked mortified, and I was beyond ready to go. Two thousand dollars. Shittin' me.

LeAnn was a good sport and only grinned at my comment. "No, but we have been known to dabble in cocaine."

Jennifer and I both looked at each other.

LeAnn burst out laughing. "I'm just kidding! You should've seen the looks on your faces. Oh my goodness. I just had to throw that out there because that crack comment was hilarious."

That loosened us up, and even I couldn't help but burst into hysterics with the ladies. LeAnn showed us different groom's cakes first. I had to admit those were some of the best cakes I'd ever tasted. All types of flavors and shapes of one- and two-tier cakes. However, I am basic. A simple chocolate groom's cake would've served me just fine. At five hundred to one thousand dollars a pop, I would've baked my own damn cake. A three-dollar box of Duncan Hines and a two-dollar jar of chocolate frosting weren't looking too bad to me. The thought made me chuckle inwardly. Lucinda had rubbed off on me. I had become frugal.

Next, we went on to the actual wedding cakes. It was like being in a cake extravaganza. There were so many different styles, colors, assortments, tiers, designs, and flavors that it was making me want to set a dentist appointment on the spot. As we sat there tasting cake after cake, I began to forget which ones I liked and which ones I didn't.

"Wait! Wait!" Jennifer chuckled as we sipped on wine. "I'm starting to lose count here, girl."

LeAnn waved her hand. "That's why I'm here, to keep count. However, we can take a break if you like."

I was the first to agree. "Yes, I need to digest some of this and look over what we've already tasted. These Uniquely Taste cakes are just that, unique and tasty."

LeAnn winked at Jennifer. "Converted another non-believer. I told you just to wait," she said as they shared a laugh.

Scooting back my chair, I stood, stretched, and then asked, "LeAnn, where is your restroom?"

"Just around the corner to the right. You can't miss it."

Bending, I kissed Jennifer on the forehead. "I'll be right back."

Taking the path that LeAnn had explained, I turned the corner to the right and the sign that said RESTROOMS wasn't the only thing that stuck out to me. I knew that bodacious booty in skinny jeans anywhere. All I could see was her booty down to her boots, but I knew it was her—Lucinda.

I moved to the left and peeped down the aisle, and lo and behold, she and Mike were standing there sipping wine and talking to a consultant.

They're doing a cake tasting, too?

That made it official. That bastard really was planning on marrying Lu. Damn, she looked good. Real damn good. I had to lick my lips to keep from salivating, looking at her in those jeans. Jennifer looked hot in her outfit, she really did, but it was as if skinny jeans were built, cut, and tailored to fit Lucinda. She wore those things as if she created the design herself. Seeing her ass in them made my heart skip a couple of beats. I may not have been with Lu anymore, but there were some things a man never forgot, and the bodacious body of Spanish Fly was one of them.

"What's taking you so long?" Jennifer asked from behind me.

Jumping out of my skin, I nervously replied, "I . . . uh . . . was just about to go to the restroom."

She pointed to the sign to the right of us. "Baby, the restroom is right here. You haven't been in yet?"

"Uh, no. I was just uh—"

She peered down the aisle. "You were just spying on Mike and Lucinda, right?" she said with a slight attitude.

"I was just shocked to see them. That's all."

She rolled her eyes and folded her arms, anger oozing out of her pores. "I don't know why. They are getting married, too. Why are you so concerned with them? We have to finish our own appointment."

"I just saw them, and I was shocked, that's it. I mean, Lu is just a little more practical with her spending. I never would've expected to see her here."

"Oh, so now I'm high maintenance because I want the best for my wedding? Is that what you're saying?"

Shit. Here we go. Why didn't I just carry my ass up in that restroom?

Now, I still had to piss while I stood there and fussed with Jennifer.

"No, baby, I'm not saying that at all."

"You may as well. You've been fussing about the prices since we got here."

"Let's not do this here. Let me take a leak so we can finish."

"If you would've taken a leak instead of worrying about your ex, then we could've been on the road to completion," Jennifer shot back.

"Is everything okay?" Lucinda's voice wafted through the air, cutting into our argument.

Damn. We'd been so engrossed in our little rift that we didn't even notice that Lucinda had walked up on us.

We turned to face her. "Yes," we said with fake smiles.

Lucinda gave us questioning stares before she turned her attention to Jennifer. "The cakes taste amazing, don't they?"

"Yep. They do," Jennifer said tensely. Anyone listening could tell she was pissed.

I intervened. "Fancy seeing you guys here."

As if on cue, Mike waltzed up and kissed Lucinda on the forehead, causing her to giggle and blush. "Well, you know we have a wedding to plan. We just wanted to get an idea of what kind of cake we wanted."

Whatever. They were so sickening. I prayed my true feelings weren't expressed on my face.

"We were doing the same thing, actually," Jennifer said, linking her arm with mine.

"How did you like the cream cheese groom's cake?" Mike asked me.

"I didn't. I like chocolate. I'm simple. If you ask me, the shit is overrated and overpriced." The words came out before I could stop myself because everything that came out of Mike's mouth irked the hell out of me.

Lucinda smirked at me. "Wow. I never thought I'd see the day that you were frugal, Aldris."

"Well, I guess I rubbed off on you and you rubbed off on me."

"Well, whatever my baby wants, she gets. I told her to spare no expense," Mike said as he caressed her face, and they smiled lovingly at each other.

Jennifer sighed and let my arm go. "Great. Well, we really need to get back to *our* appointment."

"Oh, don't let us hold you. We're done. The lemon-filled cake, cream cheese, and strawberry extravaganza cakes are to die for. You should try those," Lucinda said. "Let's get our samples and get out of here. I'm starved, and you promised me lunch at Chops Lobster Bar."

"That I did." He hugged her and placed his hand on her booty. I wanted to chop the muthafucka off.

"Cute outfit," Lucinda said to Jennifer. "I may have to cop those skinny jeans."

"Please do, baby, because you can rock the fuck out of them," Mike complimented, standing back and admiring her ass in the jeans she had on.

Unintentionally, my eyes followed Mike's to her ass, and I swallowed hard and licked my lips. Hell yeah! She did wear them well. My dick jumped, and I hurriedly looked away.

"See you all later," Mike and Lucinda said in unison as they walked away.

"See ya. I'm going to the restroom." I darted off before Jennifer could speak.

It took a minute for me to drain the lizard. My dick had rocked up eyeing Lu in those jeans, and I had to calm down just to piss. Finally, the pressure subsided. I drained, washed my hands, and walked out of the restroom. The moment I did I was met with a slap to the face.

I held my face. "What the fuck was that for?"

"I've canceled the remainder of the appointment, Aldris. I told her you weren't feeling well. You must not be feeling well to stand up here and blatantly disrespect me," she mumbled angrily.

"What are you talking about?"

She folded her arms. "Don't play dumb with me. Do you think I didn't see you watching Lucinda's ass in her jeans, and I couldn't even get a damn compliment on my outfit?"

"I wasn't," I lied.

She gave me the evil eye. "Do not patronize me. I'm not stupid, Al. I know what I saw."

I threw my hands up. "Well, what do you want me to say, Jennifer? Damn."

"*I'm sorry* would be a nice start," she spewed.

Walking up close to her, I'd offer anything to put an end to this argument. "Okay." I rubbed her arms and closed my eyes. "Lucinda, I am so sorry."

She gasped and put her hand up to her heart. "Oh my God! Did you just call me Lucinda?"

I kept my eyes closed. Yes, I did just say that bullshit. Damn me straight to hell. I wanted to keep my eyes closed as long as possible because I had no idea what would happen when I opened them. Jennifer didn't make that possible because she slapped me so hard my eyes not only opened, but they also rolled around like a pair of dice in a craps game.

"Go to hell," she yelled, storming out of the store.

I stood there for a moment, and then I walked around the corner to LeAnn. "Um, I'll just take the samples."

She eyed me and shook her head. "I have them here for you. Just so you know, I overheard, and I may be out of place, but if you're not ready for this marriage, Mr. Sharper, then don't do it. This should be a happy time for the both of you. I didn't get into this business to watch people make mistakes. I want to help happy couples who are meant for each other create a special day. I don't turn business away from anybody, but if you insist on getting married to Jennifer, then perhaps Wal-Mart might be a better option. That way, you won't be out of so much money on a marriage that may not last," she said callously, then handed me the samples and walked away.

I couldn't even argue with her. I took the samples and walked out of the store.

When I walked to the parking lot, I saw that Jennifer had left me. *I knew I should've driven.*

I called her on her cell phone and didn't get an answer. It figured. I had fucked up completely, and I had to make it right with her, but at that moment, I just didn't feel up to the battle.

I scheduled an Uber and gave the driver my mom's address. As he drove, I saw Lu and Mike down the road, holding hands and laughing. They looked happy together. It pained my heart to see it because I knew that was what I didn't have with Jennifer. I was satisfied and safe with her, but not happy. Not like them. In fact, there was only one time in my life that I'd known that type of raw happiness, and it was when I was with Lucinda. Now, as I passed by those two, I realized Mike had everything I ever wanted. I sat back and sulked. He'd won. I'd lost. And it was all my fault.

Chapter 12

Ryan

I was clearly losing my mind. Clearly. I had to get a grip on reality and fast. This was the second time in the past three weeks that Iris had been in town. Our first meeting was three days of non-stop bedroom romps in her room at the Waldorf Astoria. I'd been lucky on that. Charice's all-star girls hip hop team had a competition that week, so she was gone the day Iris arrived and didn't arrive back until the day after Iris left.

My mother had come into town that week and stayed with the boys and Lexi the majority of the time, so everything had worked out. She didn't question my going and coming because she'd become used to the trivial demands of my celebrity status career. Not a bone in her sanctified body tipped her to the fact that her prized and precious son was creeping on his wife with his mother as an alibi. In fact, she scolded me for devoting so much time to my "brand name," telling me that I was giving too much of myself for the sake of The Prodigy and not enough of myself for the sake of Ryan Westmore. If she only knew. I was giving too much, but I don't think breaking my back for a nut was quite what she meant.

I ain't gonna lie. I struggled with it; the cheating, I mean. I swear I did. I loved Charice. When I married her, I was dead set on making my marriage work. I owed it to her. I wanted to be a family man. I wanted to be a good husband and father, fidelity included. I still wanted those things, but it was easier said than done.

I was also dealing with raising a daughter that wasn't mine on top of getting satisfied at the mercy of Charice. I didn't sign up for that shit. Okay, well, I did sign up for the out-of-wedlock baby, but I always assumed that Ricey's undying love and affection would more than make up for that. The Ricey I knew in high school and pretty much all our adult lives had taken a back seat, and now, I was dealing with *Charice*, the angry, bitchy woman, all the time. You know *that* type of woman, the snapping-back, popping-off, me-first, kiss-my-ass type of shit. *That* I wasn't used to.

I didn't expect Charice to be a doormat. I just liked to lead, not be led, because I damn sure wasn't a follower. All these "yes sir"-ass Negros in the world that let their wives wear the pants and the skirts were ridiculous. Ricey was my partner, true enough, but I was the owner and CEO. Her role was the presidency. I'd let her slip in and out of the CEO position a few too many times. Now, I had to stop that before she tried to be in the owner's box.

While I took some of the blame for my cheating ways, I had to blame some of it on Charice. Marriage is, as they say, fifty-fifty. That's fair enough.

My current issue was that this thing with Iris was cool over web cam, text, and the one-time romp we had, but now, she was back in town, and like a moth to a flame, I was back in the saddle again, trying to make up for what I wasn't getting at my house. I had to stop this. I didn't want to get caught, and more importantly, I didn't want to confuse Iris's feelings. This was just sex, a means to an end.

"Why are you so quiet?" Iris asked, rubbing my shoulders as we lay in her hotel room bed.

Glancing over at her, I shrugged. "I'm not quiet. I'm just watching television while you were sleeping. That's all."

She looked back and forth between the television and me. "National Geographic? You may be the king of the jungle or just a basic dog on the hunt, but you've never watched those types of shows, Chad. You forget. I know you, too."

"A lot about me has changed since we were together, Iris," I said through clenched teeth.

She kissed my neck. "And a lot hasn't, my dear." She stroked my nature.

"Now, why you wanna stir him up? You know I gotta get outta here in the next thirty minutes or so. Weren't two rounds good enough?"

She laughed aloud. "Two rounds were plentiful. However, I never grow tired of you, and the Chad I know doesn't grow tired of me either."

"Not tired. Just cautious. My situation is different now, and you know that." I pushed her hands away.

"Your situation was different when you came here the last time. What's the real problem?" she asked, throwing her hands up in the air.

"I guess it's my *situation*." I looked back at her.

"Then fix it," she said with an air of arrogance.

"You may be right." I stood up. "Maybe I should be *fixing it* rather than creating another issue."

Iris gasped. "I'm not an issue. I'm a problem solver."

"A *situation* resolver is more like it," I mumbled, grabbing my clothes.

"Chad, come on. It is what it is. I leave tomorrow. Don't leave like this. Just once more for the road, and I promise you'll be all Charice's again." She stood up and placed the palms of her hands on my chest. "I just have to have you once more before

I leave. Is that too much to ask?" she pleaded seductively as she opened her robe and revealed her smoking hot body.

Everything inside of me screamed, "Go 'head, playa", but that little nagging voice in my ear that I swear sounded like Charice was softly whispering, "Is she worth it?" I stood there for a moment, contemplating whether to hit it one time for the road or leave well enough alone.

Iris tossed her golden-brown hair over her delectable shoulders and giggled. "That Charice has really put a number on you this time. I remember when you first went pro. She begged you to show her even the slightest bit of attention while you and I were jet-setting around the globe." She laughed and spread her arms out for emphasis. "Now, you can't even make a decision without wondering what she will think or do. I must give the girl some credit. Once she hooked you, she *hooked* you."

My jaw tightened. "What are you trying to say?"

"You're a punk. A pussy. Scared of your own shadow, Chad. Face it. You're pussy whipped, and the sad part of it is you're whipped over rationed pussy. If she told you she was giving it to you on Tuesday at eight p.m., you'd cancel every appointment and show up with wine and flowers just to know you were getting some ass," she joked.

"She's my wife! And that shit ain't funny." Iris had my blood boiling. I added to soothe my bruised ego, "I run shit! Not her! If I was so whipped, would I be here? Huh? All I'm trying to do is be a good man for change. That's it. I do what I want when I feel. Be clear!"

She dropped her robe and exposed all her splendor. "What do you feel like doing with this?"

Without hesitation, I pulled off my boxers and charged full steam ahead to Iris. I picked her up and put her on her back in less than five seconds flat.

"That's it, baby! Take me," she moaned.

I reached on the nightstand and grabbed a condom, ripped it open, sheathed my missile, and slid inside of Iris for takeoff. Our sex was hard and fierce. I tried to tear the bottom out of her frame, so she would know that Ryan Chad Westmore was the man.

Acting as if I can't make a decision as a man. Hell, I do.

As a man, I made a decision to get my kicks off Route 66 because I wasn't getting shit on Murray Hill. I stretched Iris's legs far behind her head and power-drove deep inside of her sweetness.

"Whose pussy is this?" I asked, almost animal like.

"Yours, baby! Oh gawd, Chad! Take control, baby," she moaned as sweat poured down the sides of her face.

"That's right. I am the man." I lifted her hips to meet my thrusts. "This is some good shit. Damn, your pussy feels so good."

"And you are the best I ever had. Fuck Tobias," she yelled. "I'm coming so fucking hard, Chad!"

"Give it to Ryan, baby. Give it to me," I huffed as sweat beaded down my arms and back. I couldn't contain myself as I gripped her and emptied my sac inside the condom as her cream covered the matted condom.

"Shit!" We chuckled at the same time as we struggled to gain our composure.

Just then, there was a knock at the door. "Housekeeping!"

"Come back! We're busy." Iris laughed.

Before we could regroup, the door opened, and the woman barged into Iris's room. "Oh, this will only take a minute."

"What the hell?" We hid under the covers.

As soon as I focused, my heart plunged to my feet. My heart raced a mile a minute, and my breathing got so labored I thought I was having a heart attack.

"Charice!"

She smiled and nodded. "Yes, *Charice*."

I went to get up, and Charice pushed me back down.

"Baby, let me explain."

She put her hands up. "There's no need to explain. Please lie down and rest up from your festivities because from the sounds of it, I know you're tired. This will only take a quick second."

"Pl—please don't hurt me. I'm light-skinned, and I can't fight," Iris whimpered. "You'll mess up my modeling contract if you get scars on me."

Even in the midst of this debacle, Charice laughed out loud at Iris. "You two deserve each other. The Prodigy and Iris the Model. Your brand names mean more to you than respecting your family name. Honey, don't worry. I'm not here to mess up your brand. You actually made this a hell of a lot easier for me than I thought it would be, so I guess in a way I should thank you."

"What? What are you saying?" I asked, sitting up but being careful to keep my jewels covered by the sheets.

She rolled her eyes. "Oh, Ryan, please. You haven't been faithful since high school. It was only a matter of time before the old you found its way back into our lives again, so spare me."

"Well, if you had been giving me sex the way we used to—"

She cut me off with a hard slap to the face. "This is the point where you shut up, I talk, and you listen."

I swallowed hard. How'd she know where I was? I had been careful. Could Iris have set me up? I looked over at her, and from her panicky, squirmy, and trembling body, I knew there was no way she knew Charice was coming. Had Charice had the dime on me this whole time? But how?

She handed me a package. "I was going to send a courier, but I think it's more appropriate that it comes from me. You've been served, Ryan. I've filed for divorce. Everything is in order. But to briefly break it down for you, I want the house, my Maybach, and the Camaro. Joint custody of the boys with physical custody being with me. I want my dance studio free and clear as sole owner and all profits—past, present, and future. Child support, my one-time lump sum payment, and the details about our other homes and matters are outlined in the paperwork. I'm being very generous. I didn't even ask for an ounce of money from your endorsement deals. This is what they call an airtight-and-I'm-out-of-your-hair deal. I think you'd want to agree to all the terms unless you want me to change the reason for divorce from irreconcilable differences to extramarital affair," she said snidely, handing me the envelope.

"This way, you can keep Iris, any hoes you met on the road, and even the housekeeper in the Grand Cayman Islands whose tuition you paid for, if you want. What was her name? Claudia, right? You can have all of that, and I didn't even leave you close to being broke. I've also taken the liberty of having a moving van move your clothes and personal items to the West Side apartment. The locks on the house have been changed, so you can contact me when you want to get the moving van to get anything else."

My mind was reeling. She knew about Iris and Claudia? How the hell could this be? This was fucking insane. Wasn't no way she tracked me like that. No way. My shit had been moved under my nose and everything. I had to get to the bottom of it, but for now, it was too late. My only option was to reason with her. I wanted Charice. I wanted my wife back.

I wrapped the sheet around my nakedness and jumped up. "What? Wait, Charice. Come on. This was a mistake. That's it. You don't want to do this. We need each other. We love each other. We've been through too much to give up because of this."

Furrowing her brow and biting her lip, she huffed. "Are you really gonna stand there with the stench of another woman dripping off your nuts and tell me you love me and that we shouldn't give up? You are beyond low. And how in the hell you, Iris, have the gall to sit there like a bump on a log while the man you're boning begs for another woman in front of your face after you just blew your back out giving him your gushy stuff is beyond me. Y'all are sick."

"All she was *was* sex! Let me wash off and I'm cool," I pleaded, grabbing her hand. "Then we can leave and talk."

Charice stifled a giggle as Iris rose and popped the shit out of the back of my head. "You low-down, dirty dog. All I am is sex to you? I mean nothing?"

"Come on, Iris. Just knock it off. You knew the deal. Stop it."

"Oh, I knew the deal? I knew the deal? Of course I knew the deal. But you are not going to sit up here and treat me as if I'm not shit. Like I'm not worthy of you," she yelled, throwing all kinds of items at me as Charice stood back and watched the festivities. "It was me that catapulted your career by allowing you to be my man back in the day, Chad. I was Iris the Model long before you were the fucking Prodigy! While you were in high school chasing after *homegirls* like her, I was gallivanting in Europe, Asia, and Africa, making a name for myself. I was a multimillionaire at the age of eighteen, you miserable piece of shit. I don't need nobody making me into a damn charity case." She screamed at me as the lamp whirled past my head and hit the floor. "Get the hell out of my hotel room," she screamed, her Barbadian accent shining through.

I hurriedly slid on my shorts and T-shirt as Charice stood there clapping.

Iris and I both turned and looked at her. "What?" we both said in unison.

"I was just thinking that this has finally come full circle. Not too long ago, it was me screaming and crying after you came running back to me when Iris left you for Tobias Tate. You know, back when I was the one thinking I meant more to you than what I really did. Back when it was *me* who was just the rebound sex. The goose has finally gotten its gander, both ways. Checkmate," she said and walked out of the room.

I ran out of the room after her. "Charice! Charice! Wait." I caught up with her. "Baby, you don't mean this. You can't. I've made mistakes, but we have a great life together. Don't I give you everything your heart needs and desires?"

"You have no clue what I need or what my heart desires. All you have ever been concerned with out of life is Ryan Chad Westmore—the Prodigy. Everyone and everything else always came second string to *your* heart's desires. I'm cool with that now. No hard feelings. I'm just not gonna deal with it any longer. This is the new Charice. Not the one you fell for in high school. I'm not even gonna make an apology for who I was because that person helped me form who I am today. I'm cool with both the old and the new me, but don't you dare think this decision had anything to do with you. I wouldn't give you the satisfaction. This decision had everything to do with me. *Charice*. It's about what I want and need for me. Do us both a favor. Sign the papers and do you." With that, she simply walked away.

I stood there and stared as Charice trotted down the hallway, looking at her until I could no longer see her. Gripping my keys and wallet in one hand and my divorce papers in the other, I slowly walked to the elevator, got on, and went to my car without even a backward glance toward Iris's room.

Once inside my car, I put the key in the ignition and opened the envelope. At the top in bold letters it read: *Dissolution of Marriage*. The plaintiff was listed as Charice Taylor Westmore, and the defendant was listed as Ryan Chad Westmore. I couldn't even read anymore and slid the papers back into the envelope.

I tried to suck it up. I swear to God I did, but soon, tears slid down my face. It felt as if someone had ripped my heart out of my chest. Finally, I drove off in silence and rode around for hours, going nowhere in particular. There was nothing on my mind except my failed marriage. I, Ryan Chad Westmore, had officially failed at something in my life.

It had to be after midnight when I pulled up to one of the sports bars to grab a drink or two. Then and there, I decided I wouldn't fight it. If this was what was going to make Charice happy, then I was going to give it to her. She deserved happiness. It was time.

"Fancy seeing you here all lit up." I heard a voice and a few laughs from behind me.

I turned to see Lincoln, Randy, and Rico all standing behind me, getting ready to leave. "I'm not in the mood," I said.

"What's the matter? Not getting enough from your wife?" Rico joked, garnering laughter from the others.

I jumped up and grabbed him. "Fuck you, muthafucka!"

Lincoln and Randy jumped between us. "Hey! Hey! Calm down!"

"You better not ever put your hands on me again," Rico shouted as he smoothed his shirt.

Turning to chug the last of my whiskey, I plopped back in my seat. "My bad. Any of you all got a pen?"

They looked at each other before Randy grabbed the one from the bar. "What's that, dude?" he asked after handing me the pen.

I lifted the papers out of the envelope. "Oh, these things? My divorce settlement. Charice hit me with it. Funny part is the terms are cool. I guess that shit was inevitable, and I'm not gonna prolong it any further."

Lincoln held up his hands. His face showed that he was completely taken off guard by the news. "Wait a minute. You two are getting a divorce?" Lincoln asked.

Squinting my eyes to see all of the appropriate areas to sign, I answered, "It was news to me, too. She must've been working on it for a minute behind my back. I guess I'll be pissed later. Right now, I just want to sign and drink my life away." I scribbled my signature.

"I'm sorry to hear that, bro," Randy said.

"Yeah, me too. Man, that's rough," Rico added.

"I'm sorry, too. I had no idea," Lincoln said sadly.

That was when the letterhead caught my attention. Berchman, Reynolds and Sims. The paperwork was signed by Mona Sims. Son of a bitch! I jumped up and grabbed Lincoln, punching him in his face.

"You set me up. You gave your little girlfriend my wife as a client!"

Lincoln punched me back. "What the fuck are you talking about? I have no idea who all Mona represents, especially not your wife."

"Read it!" I showed him the letterhead and Mona's signature, and his mouth dropped. "So, you knew nothing about this?" I asked.

"I swear to God, man. I didn't. I'm just as shocked as you," Lincoln said.

"Well, you better pray you're telling the truth." I stepped back from him. "'Cause if I find out you're lying, I'ma kill you." I shoved my chair back under the table and finished my shot of whiskey before I walked out.

Chapter 13

Charice

It so awesomely pays to make friends with the wives of other football players. I'd shied away from them at first because most of them were superficial. Eighty percent of them were actresses, athletes, models, or singers, so there was no being on their level, and the other nineteen percent of us were old high school or college flames. Last was what I called the lucky one percent, who were those females who just happened to be at the right place at the right time like Mona.

Felicia wasn't Don's college sweetheart, but they had been good friends in college. She was a cheerleader for the football team, and that slick chick decided to go "job hunting" in the same city as the NFL team that drafted him. She tried out for the cheer squad just so Don would know she was there, not necessarily to make the squad, which she didn't. She didn't have the squad, but what she did have was connections. After a couple of parties, she became a familiar face for Don, a "home-away-from-home" type of chick, and that did it. They'd been an item ever since, and now, her bachelor's degree in international studies that she earned was serving the purpose she'd intended—only for show.

I can't lie. With all that effort, she'd definitely earned Don, so I understood her stance on sticking with him through the storms. She'd invested in being his wife. Me, I just wanted a damn husband. I was the old-fashioned one believing and hoping in love. I would've married Ryan whether he was the Prodigy or the plumber. My feelings were genuine. Just as they were for Lincoln. I didn't give a damn that Lincoln was NFL material either. I would've loved him whether he was The Big Truck or drove trucks for a living. I just wanted someone to genuinely love me, no schemes, ploys, or ultimatums attached.

Ryan and Lincoln showed me ten times over that life didn't work that way. People got ahead by breaking backs, not with helping hands. If you didn't join them, then you got run over. Well, I had on my running shoes, and I was sprinting to the head of my game.

Give Felicia a few glasses of Merlot, and you could find out anything about anybody who ran in any major inner circle in New York. If Felicia didn't know about it, you were either wise enough not to trust her or any of her cronies with your business, or you weren't anyone who was on that radar. Plain and simple. I laughed, joked, and befriended her, but none of my business I dared to tell. I knew so much shit on everybody, even Felicia, that I could've been the fucking governor of New York by coercion alone.

Luckily, Don was the type of husband who told his wife everything except what he was doing, which Felicia always seemed to find out anyway. Imagine my surprise to find out that on my honeymoon vacation, a certain young housekeeper was servicing my husband in exchange for money. Felicia said Don swore by it. I shrugged it off, but the missing lump sum of money from Ryan's personal account that week made sense with their story.

Oh, please. Don't get anything twisted. I was up on mine. Ryan *thought* he had a secret account under his granddaddy's name that I didn't know about, but I did. I just didn't care. He was entitled to some "get out quick" funds in the event we didn't make it or he had IRS troubles. I let him have that. Hell, I had my own account, which I was sure he was aware of. I wanted him to be aware of it to keep him out of the portfolios and other personal savings of mine I knew he had no record of. That info would always remain at my momma's house in good ol' Atlanta, Georgia, with her name on the account. I may have been foolish in love, but your girl ain't never been foolish in money. Believe that.

Now, he did manage to fool me with the extra cell phone locked up in his study that he used to set up titty club hangouts and hoes. That was because I didn't disturb his study. I figured everyone needed privacy, so that's why I didn't know. He probably would've gotten away with his affair with Iris for that reason alone because he didn't even tell Don about his fling with her.

That mishap was at the hands of his mama. Instead of giving Ryan the confirmation of the room for Iris's stay in New York, she gave it to me, thinking it was work-related for some of Ryan's businesses. Creeping with family members around to meddle was a recipe for disaster. She bragged to me about how hard and late her son was working while I was at the hip-hop competition. Really? Then we must've had different calendars. My husband's calendar was free and clear, which was why he was supposed to be spending time with his mama, not creating another potential baby mama.

To verify the information that his mother had so unknowingly provided, I had to dispatch my guns. Mona was my attorney, right? Why not use her? I paid that broad a shit ton of money, so I was going to utilize all her services on the dime I paid her. It was a decision that paid off for both of us. Her little secret investigator got me photos and meeting times for Ryan and Iris's rendezvous while I was away and then for their second hookup. See, this last hookup, Ryan thought I was headed to an art auction to collect pieces for the dance studio when I was really biding my time to see him paint his artwork on Iris. In true fashion, he delivered.

It was so hard standing outside that hotel room listening to him tell her that her shit was creamy. To think, at first, I began to feel bad because he almost got a conscience and left. Then his ego took over, and he just had to tap it one last time. I hoped it was good. My divorce was inevitable regardless of his cheating ways, but knowing he cheated on me with the same bitch he tried to play me against made it so much easier to serve his ass.

Dissolution of Marriage were the sweetest words in my ear besides *child support, alimony*, and *lump sum payment.* The greatest part of all was that once Ryan signed the papers, it'd only take thirty days to be final. If Mona happened to get her britches in a knot about Lincoln and me, I had her ass, too. She'd broken a few laws to try to get next to this buttercream between my legs, so I was covered. No matter how anybody sliced it, I was the queen bitch.

"I'm so glad you decided to do this. I know this came at the right time," Mona said as I sat in her bathroom with the door shut. "I can't wait until Lincoln gets here. He's gonna be so shocked."

"Did you tell him?"

"No, I only told him that I had a surprise for him."
She giggled. "He thinks it's because he finally gets
to come to my house. He's gonna be shocked when
I make both of our ultimate fantasies come to life."
She squealed, and I cringed as she left to give me
a moment.

I was so glad she gave me my privacy. I was
locked up in the bathroom "preparing" for my first
orgy/lesbian experience with Mona and Lincoln,
but what I was really doing was trying my best to
keep up the nerve to put on this act. This bitch was
really feeling me. She'd gone all out and purchased
us matching negligees, scented candles to create
the ambiance and relax the mood, and so many
pleasure toys it was ridiculous. She wanted it to be
the ultimate experience for me. She thought she
was going to get her lifelong dream, a boyfriend
and a girlfriend. Shittin' me. Not on my watch.

"Are you okay in there, baby?" she whispered
through the door. "I know you're a little apprehensive, but I made us some cocktails to loosen up.
Lincoln just called, and he's on the way."

"I'm cool. Just fixing my hair." I gave myself the
once over. The negligee was sexy as hell, revealing
just enough cleavage and an extreme amount of
ass. On some level, I wished I would be boning
Lincoln when he got there. I felt hot as hell, and I
knew I looked the same way.

When I emerged, Mona's mouth dropped. Then she tossed her hair back and licked her lips, smiling sexily at me. If I was gay, I'd be attracted to Mona, too. No lie, she was working the shit out of her negligee. There was no question about it. As pissed as I was with the situation, I couldn't deny that she was an attractive woman.

She grabbed two glasses and approached me. Then she handed one glass to me. "Let's make a toast to closed books, new beginnings, and getting all of our hearts' desires," Mona said, touching glasses with me. "Oh my God. If Lincoln is cool with this, I will have the best of both worlds, a baby and a bae." She giggled as she took a big swig of her drink. "I've just decided that is my ultimate marriage."

"I believe that's called polygamy," I mumbled as I sipped my cocktail.

Mona sat beside me, placing a hand on my thigh. The gesture stirred my gaze in her direction. Her demeanor had changed from giddy and girlish to solemn and contemplative. The next words out of her mouth rocked me to my core because for the first time, I felt the seriousness of the matter for her. This was no game. This was real life. Her life. Lincoln's life. My life. But I couldn't fold now. I'd come too far, and Lincoln had to suffer the consequences of toying with my heart the same way that Ryan had. I only began to regret that Mona was stuck in the middle of a battle that had been brewing for years, one she knew nothing about. At the end of the day, she had been my friend and had a genuine interest in making me her lover.

"So, do you think you can handle a relationship with Lincoln and me? Do you think you could commit to getting along with Lincoln and having to share me? Having to share yourself? I mean, being with me means you'd have to be with him, too. Are you ready for that?"

Damn. I'd been so focused on my mission that I'd miscalculated Mona's intent. She wanted more than a good time. She wanted a life with me and with Lincoln. I couldn't tell her the truth, but I damn sure wouldn't lie to her.

"Mona, this is an encounter. If I don't like the encounter, I'm not sticking with Lincoln, but you and I can have what we have, and you and Lincoln can have what you have. I'm sure he'd like it better that way. I told you before, you care so much about both of us individually that you forget we might not feel the same for each other. Just go with the flow, and whichever way the wind blows, you'll still have me." I brushed her locks from the side of her face.

She looked at me nervously and hugged me. "This is why I want you so much. You're my friend, and I can't wait to make you official. If Lincoln isn't cool, he's just gonna have to understand that there is a part of me he can't have. The part that belongs to you."

That was the statement that brought this entire mission full circle to me. Lincoln had made this woman his girlfriend, even been down for the threesome or extra relationship or whatever the hell they had agreed on, while tossing me to the side. He'd made claims of consciousness, making me feel subpar for indulging in my acts of infidelity while literally plotting with Mona to have his cake and eat some more cake, too. He couldn't afford me—his ex-fiancée and baby's mother—the opportunity to get my life together for him, but Mona was good enough to fuck up his moral barometer. Fuck this. Fuck her. And fuck him.

I smiled devilishly. *Oh, trust me, my friend. Nothing about me belongs to you, and when I'm done, you would not want it to.*

The thought made me angry and anxious as we waited on the arrival of the great Lincoln Harper. The mere fact that she didn't know that her boyfriend was my baby's father or that he had slept with me just a couple of weeks ago added fuel to my growing inferno. Eyeing Mona in all her excited glory still caused a tinge of regret to pool in my belly for pulling Mona into the foolishness, but Lincoln was to blame for that. Had he been honest with her and with me, we wouldn't be in this predicament. I was sick of the games, sick of the back and forth, and sick of these men. I'd clipped Ryan's string this afternoon. Now, it was time for the last two puppets to go.

The doorbell rang, and Mona jumped up, running to the door. "It's Lincoln!"

Her excitement pained me once again at my deception in all of this. After everything blew over, I would have to send Mona some type of apology. After all, it wasn't her fault, but I couldn't focus on her hurt feelings now. It was string clipping time.

I went to the bathroom when I heard Mona leading Lincoln up the stairs. He kept trying to interrupt her with something as she went on and on about having a huge surprise for him.

"Baby, you look sexy. What is all of this?" he asked once in the bedroom.

"Part of my surprise. It's what I've been trying to tell you."

"I know, but I have just one question to ask. Please," he pleaded with her.

Hurry up with all these damn questions, you fucker, I thought impatiently as I stood in the bathroom.

"You helped with a divorce for one of my team members, Ryan Westmore. Were you representing his wife, Charice?" Lincoln asked her.

"I'm bound to strict legal confidentiality regarding those things, baby. Why?"

"He just tried to pummel me about it. He thinks I plotted to have you hook up with his wife to get the divorce."

Mona sighed. "That arrogant son of a bitch would think something like that. He was a pig, baby. He was doing all kinds of things. Cheating with his ex-girlfriend, that model Iris. He even cheated on her when they went on their honeymoon vacation. Who does that? Okay, yes, I represented Charice, and I'm only telling you that because I'm confident it's okay."

"Wait. Are you serious that he did those things to her? How do you know this?"

"Babe, I'm an attorney, and part of my job is to find out those things for my clients. That poor woman has been through the wringer with him. Even so, she made sure she carefully planned everything out and only asked for what she felt she was entitled to.

"I'll never forget almost three months ago when she came into my office. She was a wreck. She said she had to get the divorce not only for herself, but so that she could finally have her chance at true love," Mona confessed to Lincoln.

Yes, honey, butter me up, because now Lincoln really looked like an ass.

Lincoln breathed out long and hard. "Damn. She's been working on it that long? She really said those things?"

"Yes. She was so hopeful that soon all her dreams would come true, and she simply couldn't wait. I've never felt so liberated for a woman in all my life," Mona cooed. A beat passed before Mona asked, "What's with the sad face?"

"I just . . . damn . . . I can't believe . . . Mona, I have to tell you something, and I think this is the best time—"

She cut him off. "My surprise first. Serious talks later. Please."

He huffed and begrudgingly agreed. "Okay, your surprise first, then we really need to talk."

"Good. Now, remember how I explained to you about my bisexuality?"

"Yes."

"Well, you said if I have the urge, then you wanted to be included."

"Yes."

"Well, I met someone, and I really like her. If you give it a chance, I think you'll like her, too. This will be her first, well, I guess both of your first lesbian/ orgy experience. But trust me, she fits the bill, and you'll be pleased."

"What? Are you serious? I mean, I thought you were joking."

"No, I told you that I still desired women. We discussed this."

"I get that, but you just bring some random woman in here on us? Did you even consider my reputation or my status? Some things take plain finesse."

"Yes, I did, and that's why I know this won't be a problem. Listen, am I your girl?"

Lincoln sighed. "Yeah, you're my girl."

"So just know I got this. We're going to have a wonderful experience. Even if it's only once. Okay?"

Lincoln was quiet a moment, possibly considering the situation. Then, he let out a rough chortle. "I can't believe I'm doing this, but I trust you," he agreed, and I heard them kissing. Ugh! "So where is this vixen? Now that I'm all excited, I'm about to split bricks," he moaned.

"Just hold on," she told him.

I heard her ease to the door, and a gamut of emotions flooded my body. Instantly, I was hurt, sad, pissed, and bitter. I didn't know whether to laugh or cry or run. I forced my body not to tremble and to just go through with the plan. I didn't need Lincoln. I didn't love him. That's what I told myself repeatedly.

"Ready?" Mona smiled at me as she opened the door.

"Yes," I mumbled as we emerged out of the bathroom together.

"Surprise, baby!" Mona exclaimed as Lincoln turned to face me.

If I had a camera for the look on his face, I know without a shadow of a doubt I would've won the top cash prize for an *America's Funniest Home Videos* "after dark" edition. His mouth dropped, he gasped, grabbed his chest, swallowed hard, looked confused, sucked his lip, shifted his eyes, flared his nose, and then his face contorted. It was the weirdest shit I'd seen in my life.

"Baby? Are you all right?" Mona asked.

"Hell no! Are you all right?" Lincoln yelled.

"I know she's your teammate's soon-to-be ex-wife, but that's why she's perfect. She understands the sensitivity of the situation. She's on her way to a finalized divorce, and well, she is the finest woman I've ever laid eyes on. Additionally, she's my friend," Mona gushed.

"This is why you chose Mona as your attorney, huh?" Lincoln asked angrily.

I shook my head in disgust. "Don't play dumb. You already did the math, Lincoln. You know I chose her three months ago."

"I'm sorry. Do you know each other? I mean personally?" Mona asked, scratching her head.

Lincoln slapped his palms to his forehead. "Shit."

"Shit is right, Linc," I countered as he realized that I had been keeping my promise to him all along.

"I guess you do know each other," Mona said, flopping on the bed. "Do you all want to fill me in on what's going on?"

I snapped my fingers, facing her. "Of course, Mona. We sure can. Since Lincoln is your *man*— your *boyfriend*—I think he should do the honors."

Lincoln swallowed hard. "Please, Charice. Don't do this. Let me just talk to you and then talk to Mona in private."

Crossing my arms, I looked around. "Why? It's a party now."

Lincoln walked over to me and grabbed my hands. "I'm so sorry. I had no idea. I thought you were still holding on, and I didn't realize—"

I pulled one hand free and put it up to stop him. "Keep your explanations for your girlfriend. I'm just here to set the record straight. All of you athletes can go to hell. I'm leaving and taking my children somewhere away from all of this ruckus, and this time, you can watch *me* as I walk away." I stormed over to grab my keys and changing bag.

Mona stood up and walked over to Lincoln. "You wanna explain this to me?"

"Wait a minute! Hold up, Charice," Lincoln said, running toward me. "Have you forgotten that one of your children is actually mine, too?"

"What the fuck?" Mona shrieked.

"Here we go," I mumbled.

Mona hauled off and slapped him. "What do you mean you have a baby with Charice?" Mona screamed.

"It's a long story and—"

Mona slapped him again, thwarting his words, before she turned her rage to me. "And how the fuck could you not tell me something like that, Charice? You were supposed to be my friend!"

Tossing my hands in the air, I had my comeback prepared. "Hell, you didn't consult me before you went football player shopping. I could've forewarned you, but it's not like I knew. Plus, it wasn't my business to do so. You're the one who was dating Lincoln. Go ahead and ask him why he didn't tell you." I looked back and forth between the two of them.

Mona faced him with her arms crossed. "Lincoln, you know everything about me. My secrets, my pet peeves, my desires—everything. When you asked me for privacy regarding your baby's mother, I gave it to you out of respect that things were complicated, not because I thought you were hiding anything from me. Give me the same respect. Start from the beginning, the part where I come in, and don't skip a fucking beat," she said.

Her sternness was on full display that night. This wasn't the bubbly, friendly Mona Sims. This was Attorney Mona Sims. Time to watch the fireworks in action. I leaned against the door frame as a sense of accomplishment filled my soul. Checkmate, Charice.

Lincoln sighed and looked at both of us. "First off, let me apologize to the both of you—"

"Get on with the story, man," I cut him off.

Lincoln looked at Mona, who had tears streaming down her face. "I never meant to hurt you. I swear it. If I could take this back, I would. Back in the day, before Charice married Ryan, she was engaged to me. Ryan and she had been high school sweethearts, so when he found out about us, he framed me to get us to break up, and we did. Only Charice was pregnant with our daughter, Lexi. In her anger, she married Ryan. The thing is, I fought for Charice and convinced her to leave Ryan because we were meant to be together. She told me she would. I didn't believe her. I guess that's where you entered the picture for her. I'd given her an ultimatum. When I thought she wasn't adhering to it, I decided to go on the prowl. That's when I met you at the club. Since we've been together, I've not been around Charice except for our daughter because I was trying to start a new life with you. And that's all I can say."

"What you're saying to me is that I was a rebound chick because you thought you couldn't have the woman you really loved, who happens to be your *second* baby's mother, whom I knew nothing about, and rather than resolve that situation, you just strung me along," Mona said, wiping her tears.

"No, I didn't string you along. I'd given up hope on that situation, and I was honestly going to try to make it work with you," Lincoln confessed.

Mona rolled her eyes and then shot a glare over at me. "And you used me after you found out Lincoln was my man." Mona spewed the hot words at me.

Action time. I walked up to her. Time to fake my emotions. "No, sweetie. I didn't. I knew Lincoln was dogging me out. I was shocked to find out, but I wanted him to be honest with you. He owed you that, and me, too. I knew this was the only way he'd be truthful. I will admit that part of me came here tonight to bust him out, but for the most part, I was here for you. I wanted you to see that men aren't shit, and we don't need them."

"*What?*" Lincoln belted, confusion etched all over his face. He held a hand up to interrupt us and asked, "Are you switch-hitting now, Charice?"

"*Switch-hitting?*" I feigned disdain. "You're an insensitive bastard. She's a beautiful woman and the only person out of you or Ryan who was even concerned about my feelings."

Noticing my tears, however fake they were, Mona hugged me. "It's okay, baby. You're right. Men ain't shit, and we don't need them."

Lincoln eyed me in disbelief. "This cannot be real."

Rolling my eyes at him and pulling back to hold Mona's hands, I implemented the final part in my plan. "I have a confession to make to you, baby," I said, looking into Mona's eyes. "I have to prove

to you that Lincoln is not the man you thought he
was."

"Charice? What the hell are you talking about?
What is this even about?"

"Shut up!" Mona yelled at him. "Go ahead, baby."
She caressed my face.

"The real reason he doesn't want you to know
where he lives is because he lives three doors down
from my house. He moved there to try to break
up my marriage. He convinced me that I was the
one for him. I even had a weak moment for him,
Mona. Two weeks ago, he invited me to his family's
cookout, and I thought it was just to see Lexi, but
he caught me in a weak moment, and we had sex.
I wanted to tell you so badly. He's a dog. He told
me he was going back to you and treated me like
trash!"

"Now that is a lie!" Lincoln yelled.

"Oh, so now I'm a liar, Lincoln? You didn't fuck
me in your parents' bathroom in Queens two
weeks ago unprotected? I wasn't invited to the
family cookout?" I cried hysterically. "I thought I
meant something to you. I thought I could have a
family."

"Yes! No! Yes, I mean, damn it! That is not what
happened, and you know it," Lincoln argued.

His varied answers caused Mona to side with
me. "Did you or did you not fuck her while you
were supposed to be my man, Lincoln? Was she

invited and I wasn't? Were you supposed to be a family with her?" Mona shouted as she consoled me.

"Mona," he breathed out, exasperated.

"Tell the fucking truth!" she yelled.

Lincoln threw his hands up. "Yes! Okay. Yes, she was invited, and we did have sex, but—"

The next thing I knew, Mona cold clocked him with a swift punch. "Get the hell out of my house! I never want to see you again! Charice is right. You fucking ball players are all the same. She got rid of hers, and now I'm getting rid of my mine," Mona screamed. "Get out!" She plopped onto the bed, a heap of emotion.

Without another word, Lincoln glared at me while he gathered his things, walked downstairs, and out of Mona's house. I turned to face Mona, and we could only stare at each other and cry. Knowing that Mona was soft on me, I was going to ride this train to the end.

"I'm so sorry. Given the circumstances, I think it's better if I just go. I think it's best if we just remain friends, Mona. I've hurt you so much," I whimpered.

She fanned me off. "You were protecting me. I understand. But I think you're right. I think it is best. I can't deal with Lincoln, and knowing that you're his baby's mother, I can't risk having to see him." She stood and walked over to me. "I'm just sorry we never got our chance."

I smiled at her. "Me, too," I lied. "You be sweet, baby. One day you'll find the one."

She hugged me tightly. "Look me up when Lexi is eighteen."

"It's a deal." And with those words, I was gone.

Wow. I'd done it. I'd managed to flip the entire thing on Lincoln, end my fake-ass relationship with Mona, divorce Ryan, and leave Lincoln all at the same time. As I backed out of Mona's driveway, I was impressed with myself. Clip. Clip. Clip. Checkmate. Game over. Karma, bitches.

By the time I got to the light, I was in tears. It was the first time I fully realized I no longer had Lincoln in my life. For the first time, I allowed myself to feel it, and it hurt.

Chapter 14

Lincoln

After what had gone down at Mona's house, I drove around aimlessly. I was so fucking mad with Charice that I didn't know what to think or do. All those years of fucking with Ryan had truly made her just like him. Never in a million years would I have suspected that she'd be such a low-down schemer.

Truth be told, it wasn't losing Mona that pissed me off. I liked Mona, but I could survive without her. I hadn't attached myself like that to her. How could I? I was still fighting feelings for Charice. Besides, I didn't need a woman who was more concerned with it being the three of us than the two of us. The next thing she would've been asking for is another man in the picture, and that was not gonna go down. I might share my pussy with another piece of pussy and even let them swap pussies at the ladies' will, but I was not about to let another hairy-legged, thick-wood nigga jump in the bed with me while I was doing my action and trying to tap either one of my pussies; and he *for damn sure* wasn't gonna suck or stick shit in me. Hell to the muthafuckin' no. I wasn't against gay people, but I am a pure-bred, one thousand percent heterosexual alpha male, and that was the end of the fucking discussion. Period.

The thing that hurt was that Charice had set me up. She could've talked to me. If she had included me in her plans, I could've understood. That shit she pulled was sneaky and underhanded. There was no way I could love a woman who could go to such great lengths just to hurt me. Faking to be bisexual and purposefully screwing me just to get me caught up? It takes a sick individual to come up with some shit like that. It's like I didn't even know her anymore.

One thing I did know was that regardless of how she felt about me or Ryan, she wasn't going to take Lexi away from me without allowing me to be in my daughter's life. Crazy or not, she was gonna see straight fuckin' loco if she tried me with that bullshit. Even though I dreaded having to deal with her, I would just have to force myself to put up with her for the sake of Lexi. She was most important.

It still didn't stop me from being disappointed in Charice. She was more than what she'd allowed herself to become. This new Charice was immature and unattractive, and it turned me off. If she wasn't careful, she wasn't going to be able to make it work with any man, not just me or Ryan.

As I pulled up at my house, I saw Charice's garage door letting down. I had to see her. Confront her. I didn't give a damn if Ryan or the kids were there. I was gonna get everything off my chest and put down my ground rules about Lexi. All I wanted her to know was that she had better lawyer the fuck up.

Running full steam ahead to her front door, I rang the bell, and I mean I rang the fuck outta that bell for what had to be five minutes, and I still didn't get answer. I didn't want any of our neighbors calling the law, so I decided to leave and catch her in the morning. As I was leaving, I heard soft music and what sounded like crying coming from the back of the house.

I slowly walked around to her backyard and through the gate. I could see Charice sitting on the patio furniture, drinking liquor, crying, and listening to her iHome mini speaker system. I carefully undid the latch and walked to the back.

She jumped up. "What are you doing here?" she cried.

"We need to fucking talk! I can't believe you did that shit, and you are not going to keep Lexi away from me—" I stopped because tears filled Charice's eyes, and she fell to her knees, crying almost hysterically.

All the anger and hatred I felt took an immediate back seat to her meltdown. I ran to her and picked her up. "Okay, let's get you inside."

"No! No," she yelled, kicking and screaming. "Put me down! I don't need you. I don't want your sympathy. I hate you, Lincoln Harper. I hate you!"

"That may be so, but I'm taking you in this house so you can calm down." I took her inside to the family room and placed her on the sofa as she continued to cry. "Where is Ryan?"

She shrugged. "I don't know. I don't care. Probably with Iris or at his apartment on the Upper West Side."

"Where are the boys and Lexi?"

"Spending the night at Johanna's house," she whimpered. "Lincoln, if you came over here about Lexi, don't worry. I will not keep her from you. If I decide to move back to Atlanta or wherever, I will give you plenty of notice. Now you can leave," she said, wiping her tears with a Kleenex.

I wanted to scream at her. I wanted to yell. I wanted to put my fingers around her throat and choke the hell out of her, but standing there watching her vulnerability, her sensitivity, and her raw emotions made me see that this new Charice was the same person just dealing with years of old Charice hurts. That made me feel sad for her and angry with myself because, for the first time in a while, I realized I was to blame for some of this. That singular notion compelled me into sympathy for a woman who, just moments ago, I was set to send away fuck-off style into the oblivion of my former lovers.

"Why didn't you just tell me that you were getting a divorce from Ryan?"

She huffed. "What the fuck difference did it make to you? You were such a fucking spoiled-ass baby about the situation that you didn't give me time to handle my business before you went out there looking for my replacement. You found one, so go try to correct that situation. Mona is one hell of an attorney, but she's naïve in love, just like I used to be. If you sweet talk her enough, she'll take you back."

Hearing her confession hurt, and I paced the floor, trying to wrap my mind around everything that had transpired. "Charice, I pined away for you every day and night. Do you fucking know how hard it was to see you and my baby go up the street and live with Ryan instead of being a family with me?"

She stood up with fire in her eyes. "Yes, I do. It's the same way I felt when I discovered you'd been sleeping with Mona while I was doing all I could to get rid of Ryan."

"Well, you should've said something!"

With fluid steps, she walked over and spat, "You arrogant, self-centered son of a bitch! Don't you dare put that on me. You got your fucking panties in a bunch because you found out Ryan and I had sex on our honeymoon vacation. It had nothing to do with my failure to communicate. You couldn't lay claims to me, so you tried to own me through my pussy, and when you thought I was giving that away, you shut down from me. You never gave me a chance to explain what I was doing. You refused to answer my text messages, took me off your contact lists, wouldn't answer my calls, and refused to meet me if it wasn't about Lexi. You even took London out of my school so you wouldn't have to deal with me. If you had paused for one second to find out the truth instead of reacting like a bitch, this whole Mona situation wouldn't even exist."

"And what is the truth, Charice?"

"The truth is that I love you," she blurted out. "*Loved* you, I meant. I was there for you. All I needed was time. I had to build a case against Ryan because he's slick. I didn't want anything to jeopardize our relationship with Lexi, the boys, or my career. I just wanted to be free and clear of him. I tried to tell you, but you cut me off and refused to talk to me. The only reason I even fucked Ryan on the vacation was because I thought he'd take me unwillingly. He was so demanding, and he was forcing me. He knew my period wasn't on, and I couldn't risk telling him the truth for both of our safety and futures. So, I did it.

"Immediately after the vacation, I came home and shopped around until I found Mona. By the time you even met her, I was halfway done building my divorce case, but you wouldn't even talk to me to know it. Then I find out that you were with Mona. So, yes, I plotted on you, too. Fuck it. If you couldn't love me enough to wait, then screw you, too, Lincoln Harper. I don't need Ryan or you or anybody else!"

I thought back over all the times she had tried to talk to me, begged me for alone time, and sent me urgent text messages and emails. I thought she was just trying to ease back into my good graces. I never thought she was keeping her promise. She'd been stuck under Ryan's thumb for so long that I assumed she was using me as a pawn. I didn't realize that she was actually leaving him *for* me.

"And what about my parents' house? What was that?" I asked out of curiosity, since everything was being put on the line.

"Ammunition for tonight. I knew your girl was sweet on me. Hell, the moment my papers were ready to be signed, she was begging me to switch teams. You sure know how to pick 'em," she scoffed. "Mona loves women entirely too much to stick to any one man, but somehow, I think you knew that deep down. That's why you stayed with her. Too afraid to stick up for a real relationship, so you'd give into a companionship with sex on the side. Shit, if I wanted, I could've taken Mona from you. That's how bad she wanted me over you. I'm no switch-hitter. I love men, and there's only one man that I've ever loved completely, and as it turns out, he broke my heart, too. So, now, I'm done. I'm done being Ryan's doormat, faking being a switch-hitter, and most of all, Lincoln, I'm done completely loving you. In your words, all we have is Lexi," she said, then staggered to the back door and opened it. "This is your cue to leave."

I felt like a total and complete ass because right there at that moment, not only had Charice just handed me my ass on a platter, but I also realized I'd lost the opportunity that I'd waited on for months. I'd lost my one true love over bullshit.

It was the first time in a couple of months that I allowed my heart to accept what I'd been hiding from out of the fear that I would never have it. I loved Charice, and I loved her more now than I ever had in my life. I had never known heartache like this before. Tears came to my eyes as I struggled to hold everything in.

Charice looked away from me as her tears began to fall again, too. "Please leave, Lincoln."

I slowly walked to the door. Facing her, I attempted to hold her hands, but she snatched them away from me. "Baby, let's just go to my house

and talk about this. Please. We can work this out.
I'll do whatever it is you want. Let's just start over,
Charice. Please."

"What I want you to do for me is leave. You had
your chance. We both blew it. I'm tired of *trying*
to make *something* work. I want a relationship
that just is. A relationship without plots, demands,
complications, schemes, and outside interference.
Right now, I need time for Charice. I have to get
back to being happy with me. I'm no good to myself, my kids, or any man, and you are no good for
me. It ends tonight," Charice said sadly yet firmly.

I swallowed hard as tears slid down my face.
"I'm so sorry for all the hurt I've put you through. I
love you."

"Me, too," she said as she wiped her tears with
her hands. "Me, too."

I reached down and lifted her chin. I softly
kissed her lips as our tears meshed in the softest
kiss we'd ever shared. "Take care of yourself, baby."
I rubbed her tears away with my thumb.

"Goodbye, Lincoln." With that, she closed the
door in my face.

I walked back to my house, and everything in
me wanted to go back and fight for her. I wanted to
try to salvage something. Yet, I knew if I did, she'd
misconstrue it as either a ploy to get in her pants
or as weakness. Neither was the case. The case was
that I was the biggest ass in all of New York. I'd

plotted to move here from a team I could've very well benefitted from to follow Charice. I'd plotted to break up her marriage, and before I could see my plan come true, I fucked it up. Me. By myself. All because of my insecurities. Not only was I an ass, but I was also dumb as hell. Now my heart was heavy, and no one and nothing would ever be able to fill the void that Charice left.

Chapter 15

Lucinda

Every day I got a little bit stronger. I accepted my fate with Aldris and what we had become, or the lack thereof. I realized it was okay to acknowledge that I'd loved him and embrace that. It was only through that realization that I could heal and learn to love another. Some things in life just weren't meant to be, and the problem most people had was accepting that. That had been my issue, but it wasn't anymore. I'd always cherish what I had with Aldris. Always. He showed me what a real man could do for a woman. He built me up, put me on, and loved me and mine fiercely. He also showed me that even good men weren't perfect. I'd tried to make him perfect, and he wasn't. When he cheated on me, I felt that God himself had slapped me in the face. Now I realize it wasn't God at all. It was Aldris. The imperfect part of Aldris.

We all make mistakes. I got that now. However,
we all must pay for them in some form or fashion.
For Aldris and me, the payment was grave. We
couldn't be together. A love that started out so
pure and raw had been tainted by too much deceit,
lies, and harshness to ever look back. It was a
learning experience for both of us. I knew now that
I couldn't put immortal expectations on a human
being because I was not immortal myself. I learned
what I could tolerate and what I simply couldn't,
and I was able to lay that out on front street for the
next man.

After Raul, I'd been afraid to love, and when I
found Aldris, I loved hard. Now I could manage.
I could love hard, *real hard*, but my expectations
weren't unrealistic. I expected to have the same
level of respect and love, but I was wise enough to
realize that people made mistakes or that sometimes things just didn't work out. That was cool
because I could readjust myself, pick up the pieces,
and move on instead of being broken like I was
after Aldris.

In the weeks that followed, after I found out
about Aldris's engagement to Jennifer, I really
opened up to Mike. Freely. Not as a couple, but as
a friend. I let him inside in a way that only Aldris
had been let in before. In return, he let me in. We
shared our most intimate and personal secrets
with each other. We became each other's rock and

backbone, and naturally, without trying, infatuation followed. I knew that Mike was already in love with me, but for the first time, I allowed myself to be open to falling in love with him.

Something about our relationship was just different this time around. It was real and not forced. Though we were still growing, I loved our relationship. I had healed, and I'd done what I couldn't do before—let Aldris go.

Deep down, Mike and I both felt some level of guilt because of Mike's personal relationship with Aldris, but the heart couldn't help who it loved, and I was tired of making excuses and apologizing for it. What was done was done, so people could say whatever they wanted about how they felt about the situation. As long as I was happy with Mike and he was happy with me, then we were cool. We were the only ones who needed to be concerned with us, and that made our relationship flow a hell of a lot better.

Even though I felt I was over Aldris, I wondered how I'd feel if I ever saw him and Jennifer again. I was so devastated at the restaurant when I found out their news that it nearly ripped me in half. After the dust settled, I wanted to be able to look at them and feel like they didn't matter to me. To know that my heart had actually healed and my feelings for Mike were truly real and not based off of a broken heart.

I got my answer at Uniquely Tastes Cakes. I
wanted to laugh to myself when I walked up on
Aldris and Jennifer arguing over me, but I was
a lady, and that would've been so uncivilized. I
felt sad for Jennifer despite the hell she'd put me
through. She seemed to be hanging on to Aldris by
a thread, and not just because of me, but because
Aldris honestly didn't seem happy with her. I knew
him intimately and deeply, as deep as any woman
could know a man, and I could tell in his demeanor
and in his eyes that something inside of him was
missing toward Jennifer.

Now, I'm from the hood, and I'd issued many
ass whippings to females who disrespected me to
the level Jennifer had, but she'd come out of this
entire situation unscathed. So, I had to admit that
seeing her squirm in my presence because of Aldris
did pucker up my butt cheek a bit. Ha! It was one
of those moments where nothing needed to be said
or done because we both knew on some level, I'd
touched Aldris in a place that she was either not
welcomed or could no longer unlock, and that was
payback enough for me.

The best reward was that seeing them together,
wedding planning, didn't bother me. He'd chosen
Jennifer fair and square, and when I walked out of
the cake store, I wished them well, and I prayed
that Aldris could one day come to know with
Jennifer the happiness that I felt with Mike. I'd

done what I thought was virtually impossible for me to do. I felt liberated and free. Not that I wouldn't have wanted us to work out, but since we didn't, it felt good to be able to freely say I could move on. And I had.

Confession time. Since Aldris was obviously bothered by seeing me and Mike at Uniquely Tastes Cakes, I knew I was affecting him in the worst way. I had to admit that I did get a little pleasure in making him grovel, even if it was a misperception. Actually, I wasn't there for myself. I'd never go through that much extravaganza for a damn cake. Wal-Mart worked just fine for me. Five hundred dollars for a beautiful, sweet-as-hell, four-tiered wedding cake was good enough for me. Five grand for one was fucking ridiculous. Maybe if I was rolling in dough like Trinity or Charice, I might splurge on frivolous things like that, but my money was decent, not tall or long like theirs, and at the end of the day, I still had a mortgage to pay and a child to feed, so my day had to be special on a budget. I'd actually met LaMeka there for her cake tasting, and since Mike was with me when she'd asked me to come along, he came, too.

LaMeka had finished her appointment and left before Aldris and Jennifer came in, but Mike wanted to stay and try some more groom's cakes and wine, which was why we were still there when Aldris saw us. I was going to tell them the truth, but watching Aldris squirm and Jennifer fume put the icing on my cake, so I let them go at it and reveled at that moment. Oh, well. That much they deserved.

"Mom," Nadia called, breaking my thoughts. I was filling out my paperwork to enroll in classes for my master's degree.

"Yes, baby."

She fidgeted nervously as she stood at my bedroom door. "Jessica called me and um . . . I know that you and Mr. Aldris don't really talk, but we really want to see each other. She asked her daddy, and he said it was cool if you were okay with it. So, can I please go over to her house? Please," Nadia pleaded.

The girls had remained close friends, best friends even. I didn't stop them from talking on the phone, but between Aldris and me, we'd made up a thousand excuses to keep them from each other, so we didn't have to interact with each other. I realized that wasn't fair to them. We had introduced them, and because of our differences, we tried to separate them. Now that I had my new lease on life, it no longer bothered me. If the children wanted to interact with each other, I had no problems with that.

"Sure. Tell Jessica I'll bring you over to her dad's house within the hour."

She jumped up and down. "Are you serious?"

Her excited energy made me smile. "Yes, I'm serious."

She ran full steam ahead and hugged me. "I love you, Mamí! Gracías!"

I showered her with forehead kisses. "De nada, niña."

She whipped the cell phone from behind her back. "Did you hear that, Jessica? I'm coming over. I'll bring my doll head, and we can play Fortnite." She ran out of the room like a cannon.

Their joy lit up my world. I'd never seen two little girls so happy. They reminded me so much of Trinity and me. Just then, my cell phone rang.

"Hi, baby," Mike said.

"Hi, baby. How is work?"

"It's work," he answered. "A distraction from you."

I blushed. "Well, the day is halfway over. Soon, you'll be back in my waiting arms."

"That is refreshing and should pull me through the next four hours." He chuckled. "So, what are two of my favorite girls doing today?"

I refused to lie to Mike. There had been too much of that going on, and I wanted our relationship to be based on utter and complete honesty. "Actually, Jessica called and wants to see Nadia, so I'm getting ready to take her over to Aldris's house to play."

Dead silence. I mean *dead* silence.

"Hello?"

"What the fuck are you doing that for? I thought you said that Nadia would have to get used to not dealing with Jessica because of Aldris," Mike asked angrily.

"Baby, calm down." I exhaled and continued. "I thought about it. Aldris is no longer a factor in my life, but we brought the girls into each other's lives. They're best friends, and I figured we can't let our issues be a burden to them. I'm asking you to trust me."

"It's not you that I don't trust, Lu. Something tells me Dri still has it bad for you, and I don't want you around him."

"Why not? Because you don't trust me enough to turn him down if he does try something?" At this point, I was slightly irritated. "A man can only go as far as a woman allows him. You're my man, a hundred grand, and I'm done riding the Aldris gravy train. You know this. It's for the girls and only for the girls."

He huffed. "I guess you're right."

"Of course, I'm right. You're not gonna stop being friends with Rod because of the rift between you and Aldris, are you?"

"When you put it like that, no," he sulked.

"We're adults, and it's time we all acted like it. I could've gone and not told you, but I hope the fact that I did proves to you that you come first, and this relationship is what matters to me."

He paused briefly, then relented. "It does. You sure you didn't miss your calling as an attorney? You make a hell of an argument."

"Don't tempt me. The sky is the limit." I laughed.

"Well, Attorney Rojas, you win your case. I'm cool with it. Just do me a favor and try not to look *too* sexy."

Playing coyly with him, I said, "Honey, please. I exude sexiness no matter what I have on. I'm just that kinda gal. It's a fate you have to live with."

"Indeed, I do," he concurred. "Well, let me go so you can go. The sooner you get there, the faster you can leave. I'll see you when I get off."

I blew a kiss into the phone. "I'll see you later, baby."

I had planned on going out for drinks with Meka before Mike got off work, so I tried to put together an outfit that wasn't too sexy, as he put it. However, he knew my wardrobe was on point, and other than looking like I was straight hood'n it, I was gonna be sexy. I decided on a cream-colored, long-sleeved cashmere sweater, some fitted denim jeans, and my red leopard print knee-high stiletto boots.

"You look nice, Mama," Nadia said.

"You do, too, kiddo." I admired her choice of blue jeans, a long-sleeved red shirt, and UGG boots. "Got everything?"

"Yep," she said as she grabbed her coat.

I opened the door and allowed her to dash out. I shook my head at her joy as we headed to the car. Once in the car, I called Aldris to confirm that it was cool.

"Lucinda," he said, sounding a little too overzealous.

"Hi, Aldris. I was calling to confirm that it was cool that I brought Nadia over."

"Yes, I told Jessica that Nadia could come."

"Okay, well, we're en route, and I should be there in about ten or fifteen minutes."

"All right. Cool. Thanks for allowing Nadia to see Jessica," he said sincerely.

"You're welcome, and thank you for allowing the same."

"It's no problem at all."

A brief silence passed between us before we hung up.

As soon as we pulled up, Nadia jumped out and ran full steam ahead. I barely had a chance to get out of the car before Aldris had the door open, and she rushed inside, hugging him and Jessica.

"I guess she's excited," I said once I entered the house.

Aldris nodded with a chuckle. "Yes, they both are."

"Mrs. Lucinda!" Jessica screeched in exuberance as she hugged on me tightly. "Thank you so much. I love you!"

"Aww, sweetie. I love you, too, and you're welcome. Now you girls go on and play. You have about a good hour and a half before we have to go."

They barreled to the back of the house while Aldris and I looked uneasily at each other. To avoid the discomfort, I looked around. It'd been forever since I'd been inside of this house. My old house. His house. Nothing had changed except the occupants.

"Have a seat." Aldris gestured to the loveseat as he sat down, and I sat on the sofa. "You look nice today."

"Thank you." I set my purse down beside me. "Anything good on the tube?"

"Not much for a Saturday afternoon. I have movies, though. Would you like something to drink?"

"Nah, I'm good." There was another awkward silence before I posed a question. "So, where's your better half?"

"At her house. I'm keeping Jessica to give her a break."

I couldn't help the joke that popped into my head, so I teased him. "I guess Nadia is keeping Jessica busy to give you a break, huh?"

He laughed, raising his hands in the air. "Nah, she asked. I swear it."

"I believe you. Just jerking you around."

"So where is *your* better half?" he asked before he took a swig of his beer.

"At work. I just got off the phone with him actually."

"Oh, so he knows you're here?"

"Yes, of course. Why wouldn't he?"

"Just thought he'd trip."

My side-eye was strong. "He trusts me enough not to trip, Aldris."

"Good for him." His tone was curt.

I decided to ignore him because I didn't want to get into a tit for tat. To avoid any more stressful conversation, I got up and walked to the cabinets that contained the movies and decided to put on one of Katt Williams' comedy specials. It still made me laugh, and being in that tense-ass room with Aldris, I needed a laugh.

Halfway through the movie, we were both rolling in laughter. All that cackling made me thirsty, so I decided to get up and grab a bottle of water. When I closed the fridge and turned around, Aldris was in the kitchen.

"I tried to stop you. I was gonna ask you to bring me one, too. A bottle of water," he said, pointing at my hand. I handed him the one I had and grabbed another. "Thank you."

"Sorry," I said, recapping my water after taking a swig. "You're welcome."

He stood there sipping on his water and staring at me intently. I didn't want to walk out because it seemed as if something was on his mind. However, the moment felt like we were about to travel into murky waters.

Finally, he asked, "Can I ask you a question?"

"I figured a discussion loomed."

He put his hand up with a slick smile. "Just a question."

"Shoot."

I could tell his question was weighted by the deep exhale of his breath. "Are you and Mike really getting married, or were you just saying that?"

Now that caught me off guard. "Excuse me?"

"I know you, Lu. You were obviously hurt when Jennifer announced our engagement, and to be honest, I don't believe that you and Mike are getting married."

Giving him the strong side-eye, I posed the question he really wanted to ask. "You think I said that because of what Jennifer said?"

He hunched his shoulders and nodded. "Since we're being honest, more or less, yes."

I bit my bottom lip and leaned back against the kitchen counter, taken aback by what he'd said. Although there was truth in it, the audacity of him to verbalize it was what took me. This dude was really on his own sac right now.

"I mean, I probably would've said the same thing if I'd been stung like that. It's kind of funny actually. You and Mike *actually* getting married with *all* those kids he has. That's too much of a

ready-made family, even for you," he joked arrogantly. "You don't have to hide it anymore. We're
adults. You can tell me the truth."

In disbelief of his attitude, I could only shake
my head. He had the unmitigated gall to stand
there and patronize me because of his insecurities
and unhappiness. I didn't want to burst his bubble,
but now, it was time. He had pulled out the boxing
gloves, and this was about to be a one-round
heavyweight knockout punch.

"Well, Aldris, this is the truth. You're right.
When I first found out about you and Jennifer, it
hurt, and I lied to save face. I'm not ashamed of
that, and at this point in my life, I don't care if you
or she knows that. However, I have a little more
truth for you. That incident made me stronger. It
helped me become friends and then *real* lovers
with Mike. Our relationship is *real*. Our love is
real. Our engagement is *very real*." I showed him
the diamond dazzling on my ring finger that he'd
obviously ignored.

"I wasn't engaged that night, but I am now, and
I'm loving every second of it and every bit of Mike.
I am marrying Mike, and I look forward to being
Mrs. Michael Johnson. You need to look forward
to making Mrs. Jennifer Sharper happy because
Mike's holding me down. I'm *all* good. Me and my
ready-made family." I watched his jaw drop, and I
walked back into the living room.

"Nadia, you've got five minutes," I called out.

I needed to be away from him as quickly as possible. Even though it had only been a little over an hour, I couldn't stay there any longer. He'd pushed the right button with me, and I wanted to keep Hurricane Lucinda at bay.

"Lucinda, I'm sorry. I didn't realize—"

I put my hand up to stop him. "Save it. I know you get a kick out of watching my heartache, but I have none for you today, Aldris. My tears are gone, and my heart is healed. I'm sorry. You don't win." With that, I placed my purse on my shoulder and paced impatiently as I waited for Nadia.

Looking embarrassed, he mustered up the strength to say, "I can bring her home if you like."

"No, she came with me. She leaves with me."

Nadia and Jessica emerged from the back looking heartbroken, but the look on my face told them not to press their luck with begging for any time extensions.

"Can she come over again some other time?" Jessica asked shyly.

"Sure, honey. Next time, I'll make sure I have time to drop her off so you all can have more time," I said to Jessica as they hugged each other, excited to know that they would see each other again.

Sometimes being an adult meant being adult enough not to allow every mishap to tarnish you. It was easy for me to say hell no and not allow Nadia to ever see Jessica again, but that would only cause an issue with me and my daughter based off Aldris's immaturity, and I wasn't going to allow that to happen. I was determined to carry myself as an adult from this point forward.

Nadia and I walked out the door, and Aldris followed, closing the door behind him. I sent Nadia to get in the car, sensing Aldris had more to say.

"Lucinda, I'm truly sorry. I was being an ass. In a lot of ways, seeing you with Mike still hurts me, so I guess I just wanted to stroke my ego," he admitted.

"I'm sure it does, but that's neither my problem nor my concern anymore, and it shouldn't be for you either. You've cut Mike off as a friend, which is rightfully justified, but you've moved on to Jennifer. Miss me with the jealous love routine. If you're still jealous, then obviously the person who needs the pep talk about not getting married is you, not me." I glanced at the time on my cell. "I need to go." I turned to walk off but stopped short when I saw the plant.

"You kept it?" I pointed to the stunningly beautiful plant.

"Yeah, I cared for it. It reminds me of my mom and dad's plant." He paused. "Well, anyway, it was yours, and I figured if you ever wanted it, it'd be here for you."

"You know what? I do want it." I picked up the plant.

"It's yours. You can have it. I'm sure it'll blossom nicely at your house," he said as I began to walk off.

"Actually." I paused as I stuck it in my back seat. "I'm going to take it and trash it. It means nothing, and keeping it around only symbolizes that which has long since died. Have a good night, Aldris."

His saddened expression as I pulled off melted my heart a little bit, and I decided that I'd leave the plant at my mother's house when I dropped Nadia off on my way to meet Meka. It wasn't the plant's fault, after all.

"What's up, girl?" I greeted Meka with an irritated tone as I took my seat in the booth at the restaurant.

The look on her face matched my mood. "Too much," she said, sounding defeated. "But we can discuss me in a minute. I know you, chick. What's got you upset?" she asked, sliding me a mimosa.

I took a sip as I drummed my nails on the table. "Aldris."

Meka rolled her eyes. "Really? How in the hell did Aldris manage to piss you off? I thought everything was all good in the hood with you and your new fiancé, Mr. Mike."

"It is. Nadia asked me if she could see Jessica."

Meka sipped her drink and nodded. "Oh, so you finally broke down and let the child play with her best friend."

"Yes. I told you. Aldris is a non-factor for me, so I didn't see any issue with it. I even told Mike about it before I took her. He was a little ticked and uncomfortable, but after I explained the situation, he was cool with it."

Meka raised her eyebrow. "Wow. I'm impressed. Keep going."

"So, I'm there allowing Nadia to play as we watched a movie. An hour into the movie, his ego takes over, and he trips. He had the nerve to question me on whether my engagement was real. He totally blew my cover on the night I found out he was marrying Jennifer, but he was so arrogant and cocky about it, as if Mike and I could never actually get married. Had the nerve to tell me that we were adults, and I could tell him the truth. Who in the hell does he think he is? He was really on some king shit then. As if my world could not revolve unless he was the center of the revolution. Girl, who?"

Meka keeled over. "No, he didn't. Aldris is certifiable. I can't believe he actually formed his mouth to say that. Not after he got busted at Uniquely Tastes Cakes."

Throwing my hand in the air, I giggled. "Exactly. I believe that's exactly why he did it. He wanted to bring me down a notch because he was devastated that I'd really moved on. He moved on. Why can't I?"

Flailing her hand, Meka said, "Men are possessive and egotistical. He'll never be quite the same since you're with his ex-homeboy. Let's just keep it one hundred, Lu. I understand you and Mike honestly love each other, but you really can't expect Aldris to ever get over that. You were his fiancée, and Mike was his dude since sandboxes."

"Nope. I'm not going down that road. He left that doorway open for Mike, and all of us had our part in that. I'm over it, and whether he will ever be is not my concern. He cheated on me with his ex-fiancée and baby's mama, no less, because he was drunk, and now they're engaged. So, the shade spreads out further than just Mike and me."

"True that. So, what did you say to him?"

"I told the truth. I admitted that I lied at first, and then I slapped him with my engagement ring. He looked like the fool he was trying to act like. I even called him on his shit and told him that if my being with Mike was still bothering him even after he was claiming to want to wife-up Jennifer, then he was the one that needed to consider whether he should be getting married."

Meka chuckled and playfully slapped my hand. "That's the Lucinda I know and love, and I'm still shocked by you. I can't believe you told him that. Wait! Yes, I can."

"I didn't want to go there, but I had to. He claims to have this new lease on life all because of Jennifer, so why dwell on past hurts of Mike and me? I'm not dwelling on him."

Meka looked at me as if I were dumb. "Are you really asking that question? Anybody with half a brain and one good eye could see that Aldris is still in love with you, and he probably always will be. It's you who refuses to believe that."

"If he's so in love with me, then why did he go running to her and choose her as his wife? Come on now."

"Oh, I don't know. Maybe because you were with Mike," she said sarcastically.

The cynical expression on my face was evident. "So, he's gonna marry the chick because I'm with someone else. That makes a whole lot of sense right there."

"You have a point. I hate when you're right, but now that you mention it, the whole engagement thing with Jennifer just never has sat well with me. I don't know. It could be me, but I just feel there's so much more to this story than you know about."

I finished my drink and motioned for the waiter. "Well, forgive me if I don't want to hear any more about the story."

Meka pointed at me. "All right, but you know me and my sixth sense. I'm telling you. Where there is smoke, there is fire."

For a moment, we sat in silence as the waiter approached us. "So, Smokey Bear, what fires are blazing in your life then?" I joked after we had ordered some food and I ordered another mimosa from the waiter.

"Damn. You got me on that one."

"Some more water, ma'am?" the waiter asked Meka as he doubled back.

"Yes, please," she answered, still laughing at my comment.

"Mm-hmm. Seriously, have you talked to Gavin about what you've been feeling and about what Tony said?"

She exhaled deeply and put her head down. "No. It's been so good between us since that one week when he went flipping crazy. I mean, he's catering to me left and right, and we are making plans like crazy for this wedding. I totally think Tony was just being jealous of us like always, but deep down, I feel like something is off even though everything, for the most part, seems good."

"Talk about me with smoke and fire. At least I know where Aldris and I stand, and that's apart. You're talking about marrying Gavin with doubts."

She shook her head vehemently. "No, I have no doubts about him. He's meant to be my husband. This I know. Unlike some people."

I shot her the bird. "I know, too, heifer."

She fanned me off. "Whatever. Anyway, I am concerned about his family."

"So concerned you won't even ask the man."

"I'm trying to trust him on this. Give him the space and room that I didn't before. I don't want to mess this up, Lu. I have to learn to let him be a man about it and trust in that."

LaMeka's situation was sticky, to put it mildly. Yet, she shouldn't shortchange her position in Gavin's life to pacify his manhood. Her life, and from what we understood, her livelihood, was at stake. When it came to that, all bets were off. Besides, if one of Gavin's racist family members came for my friend, it would be the hood against the heritage. And the hood don't never lose.

Exhaling, I took a moment to tailor my next statement as softly as all my Lucinda glory knew how. "So, you just roll over and play obedient puppy? Girl, you're going to be his wife. *His wife,* Meka. You deserve to know the answers to any of your questions, especially concerning the welfare of you and your kids. I like Gavin, and out of all the muthafuckas we've all dated, present company included, I feel like he's the realest that you're gonna get. Hell, he's damn sure the realest I've seen thus far, but that doesn't make him exempt from simple questioning. I commend you for sticking by your man despite his modern-day KKK family, but at least stick by him with the whole truth and not with your eyes closed and blindfolded."

"You've got a point. Why is it that we have the best advice to give each other, but can't ever figure our own shit out?"

"Simple." I drank more of my mimosa. "Other people's problems are a hell of a lot easier to solve because they ain't your own."

Meka raised her glass. "Now, Lu, I'll drink to that!"

We sat there for another hour eating, and I downed a couple more mimosas. It was always good when we could meet up and chill together. We were the last two original crew members still standing in ol' ATL, so all we had was each other, especially when the family just wouldn't do.

After the conversation and sweet sparkling champagne, I felt like a weight was lifted off my shoulders, but I couldn't shake Meka's smoke and fire comment. It kept coming back to me, and the crazy part was that the feeling behind what she said was strong, too strong almost.

Chapter 16

Gavin

I'd downed my third dose of Pepto Bismol in six hours. My stomach was in damn knots. My countdown was almost up, and I wasn't any closer to a resolution today than I was twenty-seven days ago. Three days left until doomsday. I had tried to think of everything in my power to fight against my family, but nothing I could think of would work. My dad's reach, influence, and money were so long that it was virtually impossible to touch him.

A man with that much power and money must have had enemies, but even enemies wouldn't go to war without some kind of benefit for them, and I had nothing to offer. The risk of retaliation was too great to go on a suicide mission just for the hell of it. I was so desperate I'd even considered taking a hit out on him. Yes, that's some cold and heartless shit. Still, even I wasn't nasty enough to do that. He was still my dad.

I focused my energy on other things, like making Meka happy. It was the least I could do. I hated selling her false happiness, but I felt I owed it to her to make either the beginning or the end of our relationship the best she'd ever known. I tucked away my pity party act and prayed that God had mercy on me for my good deeds. I put it down in the bedroom on her any way she wanted. I showered her with gifts and did whatever she asked of me. I cooked, I cleaned, I shopped for groceries, I played with the boys and helped them with their work. I mean, I did it all. You name it. When she talked, I listened. Whatever she wanted to do in regard to the wedding planning, we did. Not that I wasn't doing any of these things before. I just made sure I went above and beyond with it. Each gesture was grand and sweeping. Before she put head to pillow each night, I bathed her, massaged her, made love to her, and even prayed with her, provided we didn't knock straight out from lovemaking. In return, I received a happy-go-lucky woman with a constant smile on her face. It gave me joy to see her joy, and at the same time, I felt like the biggest ass in the world for selling her an illusion. At this point in the game, illusions were all I had. I had to fake it until I could—well, break it.

As the time neared for me to let Meka go, I decided to start spending the night at my own house. I had to get used to it. I had made sure that I left her house the past two nights by eleven. I made up bullshit about giving her space for her studies so she could get some real rest. She protested, of course, but she knew how I was when my mind was made up. I guess because things were still going well, she really didn't put up much of a fight. In her mind, we'd have our time together when we were married. She didn't know that I was trying to get both of us used to being apart from each other.

I was happy to have the day off. I'd worked ten days straight, and I needed the time to rest, recuperate, and develop a strategy to try to salvage my relationship instead of breaking my baby's heart and mine. There was no way Meka could ever be just a jump-off to me. I'd never use her in that capacity. Either I could be all in with her, or we couldn't be together at all. Hell, the last thing on my mind was a jump-off. Who needed one, with a woman who filled me completely in every aspect of my life, including the bedroom? Definitely not me. I *was* all in with her, and all I needed was her as my wife.

As I washed my car, I saw Tony's truck pull up in front of my house. I knew what he was there for. He'd kept his promise and not leaked what he knew to LaMeka and not made waves for us, but now, he was interested in knowing what the outcome of our relationship was going to be. As he got out of his truck, I stopped washing my car so that we could step inside my house. I didn't need my business in the street.

He followed me just inside my doorway before he began his questioning. "What's up? You got a plan? 'Cause you and Meka been real cozy lately."

Without hesitation, I said, "I've got nothing."

He looked at me sideways. "You're joking, right?"

"Wish I was, dawg." I doubled down. "I've got nothing."

"Wait a minute. You mean to tell me that you two have been running around here planning a wedding and playing the world's best couple, and in three days you have to ditch her?"

Pinching the bridge of my nose, I agreed. "That's about what it boils down to."

"Are you fucking insane?" Tony practically yelled. "I've been holding back this secret for you, and you're going to break her heart? Damn! The least you could do is fall the fuck back."

"I love her! How the hell am I supposed to fall back? I'm trying to give her the best of me while I can. If I stop, I have to tell her the truth. At least this way, when she finds out, I will have ended it on the best note I possibly could."

"No, this way she's gonna end up hating you or killing you or possibly both. You are playing with fire, and I suggest that if you have nothing, you need to break it to her. Give her that much courtesy and respect not to just slap her with the news and bounce," Tony pleaded.

"You don't know my inner struggle and pain—"

"And I don't give a fuck about it either. I care about the effect it will have on Meka. What about her inner struggle and pain? If you love her, truly love her, end this shit now, because I can't keep pretending not to know."

I shook my head with my eyes closed. "I just don't know how to tell her."

"Tell me what?" LaMeka's voice asked.

My eyes flew open, and Tony spun around to see her standing in the doorway. "Baby," I called out, rushing to her side. "What are you doing here?"

She looked back and forth between Tony and me. "What the fuck are you doing here, Tony? And what the fuck were you two discussing?" she asked with tension in her voice.

I looked back at Tony and pleaded with my eyes not to say anything. He shuffled his feet and put his head down. "I was just here because . . . well . . . you ruined your surprise. Gavin and I called a truce, and I was giving him some information on the honeymoon spot my parents went to on their twenty-fifth anniversary," he lied.

She crossed her arms. "Really?" she asked suspiciously.

Clasping her about the waist, I tried to affirm the lie. "Yes, baby. It's the truth. I am trying to go all out for you."

She waved her hand between us, then folded her arms. "You're both standing here telling me that this conversation was about a honeymoon spot?" We both nodded in agreement.

She turned to face Tony. "'Cause it sure sounded like you told my fiancé to end things with me because you could no longer pretend not to know some type of information," she said matter-of-factly.

Tony laughed it off. "Man, you must've heard wrong."

LaMeka put her hand up to stop him. "Do not patronize me. I know what I heard. I'm not deaf, dumb, nor blind. Tony, you tell me right fucking now what secret of Gavin's you've been keeping, since my fiancé can't seem to tell me," she spewed out angrily as she snatched away from my grasp.

Tony rubbed his head. "This shit is wild. I'm not in this."

She rushed up to Tony and pushed him. "Not in it my ass. You tell me. Tell me right now, damn it!" she yelled at him on the brink of a breakdown.

I came up behind her and pulled her back. "Don't do that to him, Meka. He's right. It's not his place," I whispered.

Tony took a deep breath and shook his head. "Meka, I'm sorry. I really am." He looked at me. "I can't do it, dude. You've got to tell her."

LaMeka turned to me, and I swear that shit was in slow motion. Instantly, her eyes glazed over with tears, and she began to tremble slightly. "Gavin, I came over here because our wedding coordinator needs the money to lock down the venue for the wedding reception. It's a grand. Give me the money, so I can take it to her," she said as tears rolled down her face.

This part was called denial. I saw it all through her. She knew tragedy loomed, and even in the darkest hour, she couldn't bring herself to face the heartbreaking truth. I knew the feeling well. I'd been in the state all month. However, her denial made me realize that I'd made things so much worse for her. My heart broke as I struggled to fight back my own tears. I knew I was on the verge of not only hurting LaMeka, but also ending our relationship.

Reaching out, I clasped her hands. "Baby, I need you to listen to me."

She snatched her hands away. "No! I need the money, Gavin. We have a wedding to plan, and I need the money for the reception. Now, go get the money or give me a check, and I'll be out. Okay? Please," she begged, cutting me off.

I forced the lump that had formed in my throat to go down. "Meka, there's something I have to tell you, and you have to listen to me."

She began to tremble more, and the floodgates opened. "We're getting married, Gavin. You promised me forever. I'm going to be your wife, and we're going to live happily with our babies. Whatever it is, it's not important."

I grabbed her hands and kissed them. "Baby, I am so sorry." The emotion inside of me caused my voice to tremble.

"Why are you apologizing?"

"I should've told you this a while ago. I fucked up so bad. I truly did. I thought I could make this work for us, and I can't."

She pulled away from me, continuing to cry. "No. I'm not listening to this. Not at all. Not from you."

"You have to. Please."

She wiped her tears and sucked in as much air as she could. "Are we getting married, Gavin?" she asked slowly. I couldn't even open my mouth to answer her question. I just stood there like a bump on a log, staring at her. "Are we getting married, Gavin!" she seethed.

"Meka, I have to tell you—"

"Answer the question," she said with so much force it almost sounded demonic.

I shook my head. "We can't, Meka. My father . . . he found a way to stop us. He gave me thirty days to dump you, or he'd strip the funding from the hospital, and they would fire us. He also told me that I had to pay back all the interest I'd lived off, and lastly, that he'd have the biggest sponsor of the autism program to pull funding as well. I've tried everything I can to stop him—"

"How long have you known this?" she asked, and I could feel her devastation.

"He told me the night I proposed. After you accepted," I confessed.

"And you went on with this, knowing that you were selling me a pipe dream?"

"I was trying to find a way to stop him so that our dream could be real." I defended myself.

"And you knew about this?" she asked, looking over at Tony.

"I came over here to confront him, and I heard his father give him the ultimatum. But he wanted to try to find a way to make you his wife, Meka. He really did."

I was shocked. For once, Tony was being a stand-up man. He was the last person who I expected to have my back. Oddly enough, his vouching for me seemed like the only leg I had to stand on. When she turned back to face me, my breath hitched as I silently prayed that she would forgive me.

"All this time you've let me believe in this so-called engagement, and you knew your family was going to stop it. You *knew* it," she shouted.

"Baby, I'm so sorry," I apologized as more of my own tears fell.

"No, no. I refuse to believe this. Give me the money to pay for the reception, Gavin."

"I can't do that. Your welfare comes first. I can't marry you, Meka, and I'm so very sorry."

Her face contorted, and she fell back against the door frame as if someone had knocked the wind straight out of her chest. She began heaving, and I rushed to her side. She pushed me away from her with so much force it nearly knocked me on my ass.

"I can't believe you did this to me. Why, Gavin? Why? What did I ever do to you? You chased me. You begged me to be with you. You made me fall in love with you. Even when I left you alone, you begged me back. You asked me to marry you, and I accepted because you gave me your word, and I trusted that. Why didn't you just let me be? Why? Did you get a kick out of playing Captain Save-a-Ho to the poor, lonely black chick? Hmm? Why bring me this far with you if you knew you'd only walk away?" she shot at me, her voice lined with teary emotions.

"No, I want to marry you. I wanted all those things with you. I just didn't know how to tell you when I couldn't deliver on my promise."

She looked at Tony, who was quietly shaking his head. "You can have your laugh now. You were right, and I was wrong."

"Never that. I'd never get a kick out of your pain," Tony said solemnly.

She looked back at me, and this was my first true testament of the strength of a black woman. She squared her shoulders, wiped her tears, and slid her engagement ring off her finger. "You, your daddy, your brother, and your whole gawd-damned family can kiss my black ass. I hope all you sons of bitches rot in hell!" She flung the ring at me as she turned to leave.

My floodgates burst open as I ran up to her and caught her arm. "I'm sorry, Meka. Please don't hate me. I love you. I swear to God, I do. I messed up because I couldn't save us. I failed. I'm sorry."

She pulled her arm away. "Don't apologize anymore. Don't. I don't care anymore, Gavin. I simply do not care. I never want to see you again. Do you hear me? *Never*. Do not call me. Do not come by my house. When you see me, act as if you never knew me. That would be to your benefit. To you, I don't exist, because you don't exist to me," she with pure hatred and conviction in her tone. With that, she turned and walked down the steps.

I went to follow her, but Tony held me back. "Let her go, man. For real. This will end badly if you chase her."

We stood on the porch, watching her stride to her SUV.

Once inside, she let down her window. "Oh, and just so you know, and you can give this message to your family, too, I'm pregnant, muthafucka. But don't worry. I won't be for long. This is one less half-breed baby the world will have to worry about," she yelled as she flung the pregnancy test out of the window and sped off.

Tony and I ran down the steps, and I grabbed the test off the ground. It said that she was positively carrying my seed. I grabbed my chest and fell to one knee as I realized what had just happened. In my effort to hide the truth from her, I didn't remember that I'd already paid for the wedding reception venue last week. She'd really come over to tell me that I was gonna be a daddy.

With that, I let out a scream that rocked all of Atlanta, and all I could see was red. I promised that karma was about to unleash the greatest payback. *Everybody* in my way was about to feel the wrath of Gavin Randall.

Chapter 17

LaMeka

I looked at the black alarm clock, and the red digits displaying 6:00 p.m. stared back. It had been a full twenty-four hours and some change since Gavin had broken the news to me about our future. I'd been in the same spot, except for using the restroom, in room 423 at the Holiday Inn.

I had called my mother once I sped off from Gavin's house. The only thing I remember telling her was to watch the kids for a couple of days because I wouldn't be at home and I needed time to myself. After that, I powered off my phone. I remember stopping at the convenience store and buying a box of Little Debbie's Oatmeal Crème pies, some bottles of water, some Kleenex, and Tylenol before ending up here.

I hadn't eaten, hadn't really slept, and had barely drunk anything since I'd gotten here. I just sat on the bed with the television on, rubbing

my pregnant belly. The funny thing was I was so
in tune with my body and Gavin that I knew the
moment he had planted the seed in me. I felt
the connection as we made love. It was the first
night he came to my house after his week of tripping. *Now* I know why he was *really* tripping. Oh
my God! That night, we made love so fiercely we
couldn't do anything but create a life. I don't mean
like rough and nasty. I mean like our souls and
hearts made love. It was beyond physical. It was
spiritual. Our love had transcended, and I knew
that loving that man had to be ordained by God
himself. That's the kind of powerful lovemaking it
was. When we were done, we were speechless and
forever connected.

In the back of my mind, I felt I was pregnant,
and when I'd missed my cycle, I took one of those
pregnancy tests that could read results up to six
days before a missed period. It said yes, and so
did the blood test that my doctor ran to confirm
it. I'd saved the test for Gavin. It was going to be
our souvenir. I couldn't wait to tell him that he was
gonna be a daddy. I never thought I'd hear that I
was looking at being a single mother again.

Three kids, no husband. It wasn't going down
like that a third time. I'd played a fool for Tony
and been made a fool by Gavin. It was time out for
being foolish. I wasn't going to take care of another
child by myself. Besides, the thought of carrying

Gavin's baby after what he'd done to me made me sick to my stomach. Here I was, so proud to become Mrs. Gavin Randall, so proud to carry my soon-to-be husband's baby, not realizing that soon I wouldn't even have a man, let alone a husband.

I blamed myself to a certain extent. I should've asked the hard questions. I didn't because I wanted to believe so badly that Gavin could and would deliver to protect our relationship from his family. He'd failed me and our family, and I refused to allow him to hurt me any further. I had to rid myself of all reminders of my life with him. That included his seed.

Yet, as I sat here a day after having my life shattered and rubbing my belly, my sense of motherhood overcame me. I loved my kids, even the seed I was carrying. Despite my situation with Gavin, this was my child, too. Hell, I loved Gavin and hated him with the same intensity. How was that even possible? Anyway, now I struggled between aborting this baby and having this baby. Tears fell from my eyes as I sat there crying over what could've been and what may not be.

I hugged myself about the stomach. "Oh, God. What am I going to do?"

I'd been in the same clothes for a full day. I knew I looked like a wreck. I felt like a wreck. I got up and looked in the mirror. My eyes were bloodshot red. My hair was unkempt. My clothes were wrinkled. My face was puffy, and my lips were chapped and parched. I felt weak from the lack of nourishment and hydration. If I could stay there and waste away, I probably would have. I couldn't believe my life had come to this. The one man I truly loved had broken me down further than I ever thought imaginable, and the thought brought me to tears once more.

"Why did you do this to me, Gavin? Why?" I cried aloud to the four walls. "I loved you so much." I flopped back down on the bed.

Suddenly, a wave of sickness rushed through me, and I jumped up from the bed, moving by leaps and bounds, heading for the porcelain savior. The combination of the pregnancy and my depressed state of mind all came rushing out in liquid form over and over again as I held onto the toilet for dear life. Afterward, I sat down on the cool tile and leaned against the wall. The coolness of the floor and the wall felt refreshing to my skin. After a few moments, I slowly got up and turned on the water for a shower. I needed one in the worst way, and perhaps after that, I'd have a clear head and a final decision.

I stepped in and pondered my life, and it hit me that I'd let this control me. I hadn't seen my boys. I hadn't been to class. I hadn't been to work. I had to pull myself together because my life didn't stop just because it changed, no matter how drastic the change was. As I washed my body, my silent tears fell. It was like watching my worries roll down the drain with the water. I had to keep pushing no matter what. I had to, if for no other reason than for my children. I stepped out of the shower, dried off, and put my T-shirt back on. Then I grabbed my cell phone and climbed back into the bed.

Once I turned my cell phone on, it immediately bombarded me with text messages and voicemail alerts. Damn! There were so many alerts I thought my phone would explode from the dinging and buzzing. The messages were from everyone: Gavin, my mom, my sister, Lucinda, Tony, my instructor, and people at the job. Everybody.

I called Lucinda first to assess the situation.

"LaMeka Shantel Roberts! Where in the fuck are you?" she said as soon as she answered.

"I'm at a hotel. I'm fine, Lu. What's the news on the streets?"

"Oh, you couldn't tell me you were knocked up, but you wanna know the news on the streets? Why don't you come out of hiding and find out?" she asked harshly.

I knew Lu meant well. She always reacted with anger when she was the most concerned. That was just her way. Besides, she'd given me enough information to let me know that everybody knew the deal.

"I'm sorry I didn't tell you. I was going to, but I wanted to tell . . . to tell . . . Gavin that he . . . uh . . . was gonna be a daddy." I stumbled over the words, getting choked up again.

Lucinda's sighs indicated her sorrow for my situation. A beat passed before she responded. This time, her tone was soft and concerned. "Sweetie, I'm so sorry about what's happened. I am. But you have to come out of hiding. Your boys are hysterical. Your mom is about to lose her mind. Your sister is ready to go shoot 'em up—well, and me, too. Tony has been at your house trying to hold everybody down since Gavin came over and broke down the news. Your mama and Misha nearly broke down in tears."

"I don't want to hear anything about that rotten bastard."

"I understand, but Meka, he is going off the deep end, claiming he was going to do in his family and shit. He's driven everywhere from Fulton, Decatur, Dekalb, and Gwinnett Counties looking for you and asking us to beg you not to kill his seed. He's out riding now. That man might end up in Athens before too long."

"Why should I want his seed? He doesn't want me and my seeds," I asked nonchalantly as I snacked on a Little Debbie.

"Look, honey. Come home. Let's all sit down and discuss this. Your head is not in the right place, and I don't want you to do anything that you might regret," Lucinda begged.

I knew that was her way of telling me that nobody wanted me to have an abortion, but that was not their decision. It was mine. Whatever I chose, it was done. However, I would give her some peace of mind when it came to my hiding out.

"Listen, I hear you, Lu. I just needed some time for me," I said around a sigh. "Call my mom and tell her I'm fine and that I'm coming home in the morning. I need a peaceful night's rest before I can deal with all of this. Needless to say, I haven't slept since I left Gavin's house. I love you, chica."

"I love you, too, mamacita."

After I hung up with Lucinda, I got in my car to go grab some real food and some more water. I took that time to make the call that I felt I needed to make. I was an adult, so I was going to handle it as one.

"Meka! Shit! Where the fuck are you? I've been driving around like a fool for an entire day looking for you," Gavin said worriedly.

"Don't worry about where I am. I'm good. We don't need you. I'm only calling you to let you know that I'm all right. I don't want you locked up or hurt on my account. There's nothing you can do for me anymore. I want you to stay out of my life."

There was a pregnant pause on the line, and I could tell he was emotional. I knew him. He wanted to protest, but he knew it was best not to. "Did you kill my baby?" he managed to ask, his emotions spilling over.

Taking a deep breath, I forced the truthful answer. "No, I didn't."

He breathed a sigh of relief. "Thank you, baby. Thank you."

It was no use withholding information. Hearing his voice only helped me make my final decision. I was going through with the plans I'd made earlier that day. "Gavin, my appointment is tomorrow. I'm not keeping this baby, and that's final. I just thought you should know," I said, then hung up and powered my cell phone back off.

"Can I get a two-piece snack with an extra biscuit?" I ordered through the Popeye's drive through.

Fuck Gavin Randall and anything to do with him.

Chapter 18

Terrence

The heart wants what the heart wants. I had been so fuckin' pissed with Trinity for agreeing to a deal with Pooch behind my back that I did send Thomas out to stalk her. I knew it was fucked up, but he wasn't going to do anything to her except scare her and let her know that the family wasn't pleased with her dealings with Pooch. That's it. Also, I had to find out if Trinity was being real with me. That was my harsh truth. As much as I loved Trinity, my trust in her was as shaky as a nigga waiting on a paternity test. The facts were that Trinity loved Pooch and had his baby, and there was a point in her life when her loyalty to him even overshadowed me. I had to be sure she wasn't playing both sides of the field.

I wanted to trust and believe in Trinity, but I also knew that I wasn't Trinity's only love, regardless of whether I was her first. Even though I never viewed Pooch as a threat or thought that he even mattered regarding my relationship with Trinity, I had to remind myself that he wasn't just a jump-off for her. He, just like me, was her baby's daddy, a man she used to love. Add to that my insecurities about my leg and not being a hundred percent, and it was a recipe for disastrous thoughts.

After Thomas, Trinity, and the DA all confirmed Trinity's recanted statement, I knew it was an honest mistake, a bad decision made from fear of the unknown. I hated that she'd been put in a position to ever feel like I couldn't protect her. However, how could I blame her? My own cousin baited me and infiltrated us with the help of Pooch, and I couldn't stop it then. More than anything, that fucked with my manhood. I knew if that had never happened, then Trinity would've never agreed to those foolish terms. Then again, if that had never happened, Pooch would've never gotten out and would've still been somewhere in west hell doing his original bid. I blamed Aaron and faulted myself. I'd been careless and sloppy. I'd gotten too comfortable, and I didn't pay attention to the warning signs. I had to get back to my original self, the man that always stayed one step ahead of the game. Now that I'd put Pooch on notice, I knew I had to be on point. That bastard would try to get at me if for no other reason than to see me in a fuckin' box.

I started by making it up to Trinity. She knew I'd sent Thomas to trail her. Hell, I did very little to hide that fact, and I was surprised that Thomas didn't leak that information the moment he saw her. His ass was so far gone on a mission to get revenge on Pooch that he immediately hated anyone or anything affiliated with him. He'd been the one out of us three who doubted Trinity's ability to be loyal to me when we first plotted to take Pooch down and get my lady back. Her actions only added fuel to his already burning inferno. Now, he loathed Trinity, even though she hadn't followed through. He said it was the mere fact that she agreed that was the ultimate betrayal.

Now, I could understand his point if it were regarding me, but Trinity owed no loyalty to him and especially not to Aaron. Putting myself in her shoes, I'd hate Aaron and anything or anyone affiliated with him, so from her standpoint, I couldn't be angry. Hell, as much love as I had for Aaron, I can't help but understand. The muthafucka tried to kill me, his own cousin. His own blood. To me, the lines of loyalty had been blurred long before Trinity's impaired decision. At the least, I could say she felt her decision was in some way going to protect our family, not kill us, like Aaron had planned.

At any rate, like a true ride or die chick, she forgave me and told me she understood. She apol-

ogized for even considering the deal and especially
for accepting without first consulting me. But I still
had to make it up to her. It wasn't in my nature to
throw out "I'm sorries" and expect my lady to be
cool with it, so I loaded up with pain killers to keep
my leg right, left the babies with their grandma,
and flew her to Manhattan for a shopping spree.
Manolos, Christian Dior, Hermes, Prada, and
Dereon—hell, anything she wanted—went on my
Black Card. We stayed at the finest hotel in the
penthouse honeymoon suite, ate at the best restau-
rants, caught a comedy show, and even chilled in
VIP at the 40/40 Club. By the time we got back, we
were just as tired as we were relaxed, and my Black
Card was smoking with a $200,000 bill to pay. But
my lady was happy as hell, and in return, she put
in some major work in the bedroom.

My stroke might've still been off because of my
leg, but my head game was on point. It made me
swell with pride to see her damn near climbing the
walls like she used to, and when we climaxed, we
reunited—Dreads and li'l mama together again. I
had my wifey back, and more importantly, she had
her husband back.

However, I'd created a monster in Thomas.
Letting him in on the fact that Trinity had copped
a deal to be a material witness for Pooch refueled
him. He was back on a mission and paranoid as
hell about anybody who got down with Vernon

Pooch Smalls. All that nigga could see was revenge
and red, and neither one of them was good by itself,
let alone combined. He felt Trinity was playing me
for a fool. I felt he was letting the situation play
him. Either way, I knew there'd come a time when
I'd have to choose between him and Trinity. What I
didn't realize was that time was now.

"You sure you don't want nothing to eat, fam?" I
asked Thomas as we sat in my breakfast area while
I ate. "You know how Trinity gets down."

Thomas laughed slightly as he hissed away the
after taste of his beer. "Yeah, I know *exactly* how
she gets down."

I wiped my hands on my dinner napkin, popped
a pain pill, and sat back. "We're back on this again?
She's my wife, Thomas. She fucked up, but we all
have. I know she's faithful and loyal."

"Faithful and loyal?" Thomas asked sarcastically.
"Does the pussy have you that fucked up?"

I put my hands together, interlocking my fingers
to keep me from popping him square in the jaw.
"On the real, you are my fam, but that's my wife,
and what you ain't gonna do is disrespect her in my
face in her home."

"You muthafuckas are so blind. All the shit that
all of you are in is on account of her ass. Pooch is
locked up 'cause her pussy got him off his game.
You done got locked up trying to make ways for
her and got shot at and shot up trying to defend

her honor. And my brother, well, he's resting in eternal damnation because the pussy drove him crazy. Don't you find it strange that all of you have dug out the same bitch and ended up getting hurt, or in Aaron's case, dead over her?" he asked, trying to reason with me.

No, this muthafucka didn't. Granted, when it was put like that, it sounded fucked up, but he acted like us three grown men didn't have a hand in that shit. We all had a hand in our crazy situation, and we all could've handled things differently.

"Bitch! Let me tell you something. Just because Trinity has been the common denominator doesn't make her the problem. Your anger is misplaced. Try it like this. I got locked up for slangin'. Me. She told me to stop, but I chose to slang. The muthafucka who set me up was Pooch. The same muthafucka was after my woman. He sweet-talked her while I was locked away after I *chose* to break up with her. She was gon' do the bid wit' me, but I bounced her ass. I opened the door for Pooch. She was out here broke with two of my muthafuckin' kids. What was she supposed to do? The nigga put her on, and she fell for him. I wanted Trinity back because I knew Pooch set us up to break up, and I knew that nigga wasn't no good for her or my kids. We—yes, *we*—me, you, and Aaron set up a foolproof plan to get her back and take his bitch ass down.

"Trinity didn't even know y'all was my fam. You got her out here like she on some ho shit, and the only niggas she ever fucked was us three. And Aaron's ass coulda said no. Hell, he shoulda said no. His mission was to help out his fam and earn a collar, not fuck my babies' mother. She fucked him 'cause she was hurt and drunk, and she didn't even remember the shit, so *hell*, it really don't count. If Pooch and I can say one thing we have in common, it's when we laid it down, she remembered it. So, nigga, we were the ones creating the common denominator because all three of us wanted the same thing—Trinity. But she belongs with me, and that's where the fuck she's gonna stay. If you don't like it, then fuck you, too." I stood up, bracing myself on the table and leaning in his face.

He stood up and pushed me down, but I missed the chair and hit the floor. "You disrespectful, crippled, limped-legged summa bitch. You gon' dog me out over her ass? Why you think I never come around when she here? I'm tryna protect you 'cause she smell foul, and you gon' ride for *her*? You know what, fam? Fuck you. Whatever happens to your ass on account of that bitch happens. I'ma piss on your grave, you rotten bastard. I hope to God Pooch deadens both y'all asses. And when he does, I'ma dead him. But not for y'all, for Aaron and for the Terrence I used to have love for," Thomas yelled.

Just then, Trinity ran in the breakfast room. "Oh my God. Dreads," she screamed as she helped me up. "The fuck is wrong with you, Thomas?" she screamed at him as I got my balance back.

He grabbed her by the arm and pulled her toward him. "You tell us right muthafuckin' now who you ridin' for. Us or Pooch?"

My pride was hurt because of this bum leg. Thomas had threatened me and laid hands on me in my own house. The fact that I wasn't a hundred percent was the only thing that kept me at bay, until he put his hands on Trinity. I limped over there to break his grasp from her, and he pushed me back.

"Go over there and pop another pill, you fuckin' prescription pain pill junkie," Thomas popped off.

Trinity gasped at Thomas's remark as she struggled to free herself from his grasp. "Thomas, you're drunk. You know I love Dreads, and I'm his family. We all are. I'd never intentionally hurt any of you. The thing with Pooch was a mistake. I thought I was protecting us," she explained as tears began to fall from her face. "Let go of my arms. You're hurting me!"

It was at that time that I made the decision to man the fuck up. He was right. Trinity had been right. Eric, my trainer, had been right. I was using the pills as a crutch, and my addiction to them was slowly increasing. It's funny how certain incidents in life make you have the best epiphany in the world. As pissed as I was with Thomas right now, I was gonna force this leg to act right if I had to break the muthafucka off to do it, 'cause Thomas had broken all the rules. Nobody disrespected my house, my woman, or my manhood.

I charged toward Thomas with full force to make him let go of Trinity. Trinity flew back as she stumbled to keep her balance. "I've got your junkie, muthafucka," I hollered as we began a slugfest from the breakfast room to the kitchen.

I felt all my frustrations and anger rise as I stung him with several one-two combinations. I alternated tagging his face and his body. He snuck a couple of shots in, and the dirty bastard even tried to go for my leg, but I didn't feel shit. All I felt was adrenaline rush through me as I continued to deliver devastating blows.

"Dreads, stop! You're gonna kill him," Trinity yelled as I delivered my message over and over again.

I punched Thomas so hard he flew back a few feet and landed in my family room. He could barely move. His face looked like I'd taken a meat tenderizer to it, and my hands were cut up and bloody from the multiple shots to his face. I picked up his limp body as Trinity continued to scream for me to stop. I was just about to punch him again.

"Think about our kids!" she yelled. "Please, Dreads. Stop."

I thought about my kids and how I didn't want to go to prison again. I pulled Thomas to me by the collar. He could barely focus on me as blood oozed out of the sides of his mouth and face.

"Do you want to know what loyalty is, muthafucka? Loyalty is my wife saving your life. I've always rode hard for you and Aaron. You and that fat, grimy muthafucka pay me back by disrespecting me, my woman, my manhood, and trying to kill me. Where is the loyalty in that? There is none. I'll tell you what I'm gonna do. I'm gonna ride for Trinity hard. You and Aaron can go to hell. Piss on that, bitch." I dropped him back to the floor. I couldn't help it. I kicked him in the stomach so hard blood flew out of his mouth. "Get the fuck outta my house and stop bleeding all over my floors and shit." With his blood on my hands and shirt, I walked to the sofa and plopped down.

Trinity ran over to Thomas and helped him up. "I'm so sorry. Are you okay?"

Thomas stumbled up and waved her off. "I'm fine." He could barely mumble. "Fuck you, T," he grumbled as he staggered toward the front door, but it came out sounding all jumbled because of his injuries.

I shrugged. "Be out, nigga." I pointed to the door with my back toward him from the sofa. "And don't come back."

Trinity walked to me. "That's your fam. He's just going through it because of Aaron."

"And I'm going through it because of what they put us through. Just be with me on this," I fumed, putting up my hand to end the conversation.

Leaning forward, she hugged me tightly. "I'm with you. We're all we need," she said as I embraced her back. Her concession was a breath of fresh air to my wounded soul.

Thomas exited and slammed the door. A few seconds later and out of nowhere, we heard gunshots.

"Oh, shit!" Trinity screamed.

"Get the fuck down!"

I crawled to my entertainment system and grabbed my chrome-plated .45 that I kept hidden in a small compartment. I rushed to the door, opened it, and slowly peered out. I figured I was gonna have to exchange gunfire with Thomas, but the sight before me caused the air to catch in my chest. Thomas was lying face down on the ground with blood all around him. He hadn't been doing the shooting. He was the one shot.

"Oh, shit! Thomas is hit!" I turned on the security lights and wobbled out the door, looking for suspects. All I saw were the taillights of some car turning the corner at the end of the long street.

Trinity ran to the doorway, screaming and crying.

"No!" I stopped her in her tracks. "Go back in the house. Dial 911. Get some help!"

She nodded and quickly turned and grabbed her cell phone as she stood by the window, peering out. I could hear her frantically speaking with the 911 operator.

I turned Thomas over and started doing CPR. "Come on, muthafucka. Don't you die on me!" I yelled. "Come on!"

His breathing was shallow, and I could hear the blood gurgling in his throat. "Shit!" I yelled as my neighbors screamed in horror as they began to gather. "Come on, Thomas. I'm so sorry, dude. Come on." I continued the CPR.

Soon, the ambulance pulled up in my driveway and prepared to carry him off to the hospital.

"You can follow us, sir," the paramedic informed me.

I went in the house, and Trinity already had her purse and keys ready. I slipped my gun in her purse. "Keep that on you. We might need it."

"Who could've done this?" Trinity asked through her tears.

"Only one person would be ballsy enough to bring it to my house like that. As soon as I finish up business at this hospital, I'ma see that nigga," I said as we got in her Mercedes.

She drove, following the ambulance, and looked over at me. "Pooch."

I nodded slowly. "Now I'ma give that nigga something he'll *always* remember. It's curtains for that bitch. I'm done playing."

Chapter 19

Pooch

I felt my cell phone buzz as I threw the laundry in the big bin. I rolled the bin to the side where the others were and quickly pulled out my cell. It was a text message from Flava.

The grass has been watered.

I smiled to myself and texted back. Tell the kids thanks for taking care of their chores. Make sure they get a good allowance.

I'll do that. Love you, babe.

Love you, too, always.

I put my cell phone away and finished up with my duty detail. The whole time, I could barely contain my smile. After all this time, I'd finally touched that nigga. Muthafuckas need to be more appreciative when you spare them. I guess that nigga forgot who I was since I was on lockdown. It was time to send him and everybody else in the game from the suburbs to the hoods a reminder that I was still a force to be reckoned with. I had to send a message to make all them muthafuckas remember *that shit*. Especially Terrence and Trinity.

That bitch was lucky that Princess was my baby, or it would've been her ass on the chopping block, too. I guess it's true what they say. Kids do change you. My sister had enough children to tend to, and my mom ain't been right in the head since Pops got killed. With me and the majority of all her brothers and nephews doing federal time, she wasn't fit for shit. She would be no good to raise Princess. By default, Trinity was spared. That bitch had more lives than a cat.

It didn't matter, though, because I got my point across. That was the shit that happened when you crossed Pooch. That was the shit that happened when you didn't follow through. Prison and near-death had made me soft-hearted. Weakened me. I'd been so focused on getting out that I'd let too much shit slide, and I'd let my love and loyalty to Trinity outweigh the shit that needed to be done. It only took one thing to make a man snap, and that was when another man tried his manhood. I knew Terrence was doing the manly thing by confronting me about trying to make a deal with Trinity. That was what he was supposed to do. I woulda done the same thing if the roles were reversed, but once you showed your cards, you had to be ready to play your hand. I was ready. He wasn't.

I would never tell a soul, but I did feel a twinge of guilt about the situation. Even though my love had run out for Trinity and my loyalty to her was now only because of my seed, I knew that taking that nigga away from her might just kill her on the inside, and I worried about Princess, Terry, and Brittany. I might not have been the best father and stepfather to them, but even through all of this, I loved them and cared about their wellbeing. Hell, I even thought about the baby from time to time, even though he wasn't mine. A part of me still wished he were, and if I'm honest, a part of me still felt as if he was. I know that Trinity's mom would step in and be there for the kids if Trinity ever couldn't, so that twinge of guilt was short lived. I hated to be the one to break their hearts, but their daddy asked for it, so I delivered it. The moral of the story was: be careful what you ask for, because you just might get it.

The oddest thing came over me after I finished my detail. I felt the urge to pray. Therefore, I said a silent one. *God, Father, Jesus, and Christ . . . all y'all. Look, I fucked up. Yep, I know it. It ain't even in me to apologize for it because I knew exactly what I was doing. I don't know how not to be the way I am. It's how I'm built. Forgive me for being who I am. It ain't right, but I can't help it. I guess at least send his soul to Heaven, please. I can at least pray for that. I tried. All right then. I guess that's it. Amen.*

I went into the recreational room for the first time in a long time and sat at one of the tables closest to the television then got in on a game of Spades with a couple of dudes in my cell block.

Suddenly, I heard one of the other cats shout out, "Yo, cut that up," and we all turned around to see the news.

"In another late-breaking story today, tragedy has rocked a suburban community in Evanston, Illinois this afternoon with what appears to be an apparent drive-by shooting. Witnesses say they heard what sounded like fireworks going off at the residence on Asbury Lane only to find out that it was actually gunfire. They say nothing like that has ever happened in this community, and they are appalled that such incidents have found their way into their neighborhood. Investigators tell us that the shooting victim, twenty-six-year-old Thomas Marsh, was shot twice in the front yard of a residence on Asbury Lane. Currently, he is in critical condition. Thomas Marsh is the brother of recently slain police officer Detective Aaron Marsh, who was killed as result of a sordid love triangle. Police are not releasing any further details about the investigation at this time, and there are no reports that this incident is related to the previous shooting of Detective Marsh. At this time, no suspects have been identified. We will be following this story closely as it unfolds," the news anchor reported.

"Damn, Pooch, your people are back on the news again," one of the dudes at the table said. "You sure you ain't got nothing to do with that?"

I sucked my teeth. "Nigga, I'm locked up. I ain't fuckin' wit' none of them cats. Play your fuckin' hand and quit tryna add time to my muthafuckin' bid."

I played that hand and the next until it was time to go to Bible study. I took my Bible in there and turned to the book of Hebrews just as the good reverend said. Then I slipped my cell phone in front of me, hidden by the Bible, and texted Flava.

They watered the wrong fuckin' grass.

I heard I'm on it. The kids are gonna go back out and finish their chores.

No. It's too late. The sun's out. Take the allowance back and wait until I can find another chore for them to do. And next time get it right.

They are very sorry. We all are.

Yeah, I know.

I powered the phone off and slid it back in my pocket.

"Vernon, would you like to read the verse aloud tonight?" the reverend asked me.

I looked up at him. "Huh? My fault. I didn't hear the chapter and verse."

"Could you read for us Hebrews chapter eleven verse one?"

I nodded. "Sure, Rev." I flipped to the verse. "For faith is the substance of things hoped for, the evidence of things unseen."

"Let's talk tonight about faith, gentlemen."

I sat back and pondered that. Yep, let's talk about faith. Faith was the only thing I had for whenever I finally did get to touch Terrence for real. I had faith that I could do it. I had faith that I had the right team in place to do it, but the evidence that it had been done was still not there.

My patience was running thin. Somebody had to start doing something right this time around because in this game, mistakes were costly, and that one was a greater cost than anyone could dream. I knew by this time Terrence had already pointed his finger at me. Even if I wasn't the one who'd set up the hit, I knew I'd be the first person he'd accuse. Now, I ain't no scared-ass cat by any means, but there were three advantages that Terrence had over me: the freedom to make moves, the money to make shit happen, and the heart to do it. Don't get it twisted. I knew people viewed Terrence as this easygoing, smart cat who got caught up in the game, but that nigga was a beast. A smart, cold, calculating ghetto beast. He had the balls to make the moves, and he was efficient enough not to have it traced back to him even if he did it himself.

Real recognized real, and for those who didn't really know Terrence, that nigga was *real*. I don't even think Trinity knew how really real he was 'cause he was one way in front of his family and a completely different way in the streets. Now these idiots made me a sitting target, and my only prayer was that while Thomas's bitch ass was laid up in that hospital, it kept Terrence at bay long enough to give me the opportunity to make my next move. Otherwise, the next time I might see the inside of a chapel was during my eulogy. And Terrence had enough money, power, and front businesses to pull it off.

Chapter 20

Ryan

"Ryan, is it true that you were having an affair with your ex-girlfriend, supermodel Iris?" a reporter shouted at me as I exited the courtroom, starting the flurry of questions.

"Ryan, did you have an affair while on vacation in the Grand Cayman Islands? Is it true that you frequented strip clubs and adult after-hours spots with other fellow teammates? How do you feel now that your divorce is final? Will you go back to Iris? Will you remain single?"

"My client has no comment at this time. Please respect his privacy," my attorney announced as we pushed past the crowds of people and the sea of reporters.

I jumped into the back of the limo with my attorney, unbuttoned my long pea coat, and took off my leather cap and gloves. My attorney handed me a glass of brandy, and I swallowed it in damn

near one gulp. He looked at me with sorrowful
eyes as I leaned my head back against the headrest.
Tears found their way into my eyes, and I rubbed
my hand across my face to keep them from falling.

It was officially over now. My marriage. With
my celebrity status, it was only a matter of time
before news of my divorce hit every media outlet
in America. When it did hit, those pesky, meddling,
ruthless reporters managed to dig up every detail
that wasn't even mentioned in the filing of the case.
The friends I thought I had blabbed all they knew
about my partying antics at the titty bars and the
after-hours spots. Of course, Iris's big payback was
to confirm that we'd been intimate with each other
during my marriage. I'd lost a couple of endorsement deals that were family-oriented and a movie
role because my recent immoral acts tainted my
image. The people I thought were on my side were
nowhere to be found during my darkest hour. The
public slaughtered me because of my mistreatment
of Charice after the death of our daughter. Even my
parents, who stood by me in public, showed very
little support in private. My mom was infuriated
with me, and my dad was disappointed.

I couldn't even look Charice in the eyes, but
what bothered me the worst was the hurt in my
boys' eyes and hearts. They suffered the most because of my indiscretions, and that broke me down.
Ray was like his mom, so while he hurt, he still

wanted to hold on to me as his daddy, but Ryan Jr. was a different story. He not only looked like me, but he was also cut from the same cloth. He rode hard for his mom just like I would've for mine, and he made it clear that he wanted nothing to do with me. I prayed that time would heal his wounds and that if I kept pressing, he'd let me back in. I'd just gotten them in my life, and after the loss of Charity, I deeply regretted never having been there from the start. Maybe if I had, he would still want to be around me despite the hurt of the divorce.

You'd think that it was some high-profile criminal case or a nasty divorce settlement the way the media and the crowds gathered, but it was only a meeting in front of the judge to finalize the agreement and terms of our divorce. No arguments, no battles, no drama. Just short and simple. In a twist that shocked me, Charice had withdrawn her request for alimony, but just to let her know I didn't harbor any bad feelings I had insisted that she keep it. She was shocked. She walked away with everything she wanted, and I walked away with nothing I wanted.

What did I want? Just one thing. My family. I'd plotted and schemed my way in and out of my wife's life, and if I could take it all back, I would, and not just starting at the marriage. I would take it back to the day she told me she was pregnant with the triplets. I'd hug her and tell her we'd get through it together. I'd enlist my parents' help to make sure her pregnancy went well. I would've been there for her and the triplets. I would've married her the moment I got drafted, and I would've been faithful. But that was hindsight. In the present reality, there was no room for shoulda, coulda, or woulda. I had made my bed, and I was lying knee-deep in all the shit I'd stirred up since high school.

A single, bloated tear fell from my eye as my attorney handed me another glass of brandy.

"Are you going to be okay, Ryan?"

I nodded slowly. "Yeah. I have no choice but to be," I said as I drank a swig of the liquor.

As we rolled past a park where Charice and I used to stroll through late nights, I saw her standing by one of our favorite spots. "Driver! Stop the car and pull over," I demanded.

"Is everything all right, Ryan?" my attorney asked.

"Yes. I'll be back." I opened the car door and got out. I buttoned my jacket and approached Charice.

"I'm shocked to see you here," I said.

She turned to face me with tears in her eyes. "Yeah. I just needed to clear my head. That's all."

I walked over to her, clasping her face between my hands, then wiped her tears with my thumbs. "Don't cry."

Gazing up at me, she offered a tepid smile. "I can't believe it's actually over. I mean, this is what I wanted and needed, but I never got married with the intent of getting a divorce. I've loved you for so long that it seems almost surreal to let you go. Like I should be with you even if I hate you."

My hands slipped from her face, and my brow lifted at her candid comment. This new Charice was damn sure a spitfire if nothing else. I couldn't help but chuckle. "Wow. Well, I'm glad you left before it came to that."

"I'm just saying. I didn't mean it like that."

"I understand." I put my hand up, showing I didn't take offense.

Looking at me intently, she released a slow, deep breath. "Where do we go from here?"

"We go one day at a time. I have to rebuild my relationship with Junior and keep nurturing my relationship with Ray."

"Junior loves you. He's just hurt by all of this. He'll come around. But how fast he does depends on you. Don't let them down this time, Ryan. Please."

Ashamed, I held my head down as I explained, "I won't. I never should've let them or you down the first time. But you live and you learn."

Charice released breath from the pit of her belly. "Ain't that the truth?"

Without notice, the tears I'd been holding back silently fell from my eyes, and I grabbed her hands and caressed them. "You know, it took me all the way to our divorce to realize what I had in you. From the beginning to the end, you were my rock, and I failed you, Charice. If you never believe anything else I say, believe this: I love you from the bottom of my heart, and for every hurt and hell I put you through, I'm so sorry. I wish you nothing but the very best, and I pray you find the love you deserve."

Charice's lip began to quiver, and she held her hand to her mouth as tears streamed down her face. After a few moments, she was able to gather herself enough to let out a shaky response. "Ryan, I needed that like I need air. Thank you. I accept that, and I forgive you. I really do." She cried as we embraced each other.

"No, thank you."

She pulled back and looked away. "I have a confession to make."

"What is that?" I asked her, placing the curl of my index finger at her chin and forcing her to look into my eyes.

Nervously, she confessed, "I hope you can forgive me, but I had an affair, too. I cheated with Lincoln."

Her confession caused me to turn away, and I swallowed hard.

"Ryan, I'm sorry. That's why I wanted to give the alimony payments back. We can still readjust it if you want."

"I already knew, Charice."

"Huh?" she asked, stunned and confused.

Facing her again, I explained, "I didn't have proof, but I felt it. Deep down. I knew you and he were closer than you let on. What confirmed it for me was when you asked to stop the alimony payments. I know you better than you think. I knew that if you were willing to give something up after all I'd put you through, that you were guilty of something, too. And I know the only person who could ever come between us was Lincoln. Instantly, it made sense. Mona being your attorney, your closeness with Lincoln after the proceedings with Lexi, him never having a lady friend, you never giving me any sex, and even the sudden stop in communication between you two a few months back. It hit me in the courtroom."

Her eyes danced with bewilderment. "Yet, you gave me the alimony payments?"

"After all the hell I put you both through, I had it coming to me. Can't hate the players, gotta hate the game. I've been playing you since high school, Charice, so what goes around comes around. Can't do nothing but charge it to the game. It's the price you pay when you play. I knew eventually karma would pay me back."

She looked shocked. "I'm speechless. I don't know what to say." She looked at me intently. "And you're not mad? Not going to kill Lincoln or come back at me?"

It saddened me that my past behavior had left such a damning impact on her. She'd won and didn't even realize she had the victory. This entire debacle I'd made of my life had changed me. I, Ryan Chad Westmore, the man who never failed, had failed and fallen from grace. This entire clusterfuck that I'd created was a sobering experience. Losing my family was a humbling one. Charice had finally humbled me.

"Shit gets old. Lincoln and I played each other. In the end, neither one of us ended up with you. What's to fight for? We were just two grimy muthafuckas out here doing dirt, and the only thing it got me was bad publicity and a broken home. It's time out for that shit. Time to work on being a better man and a better father, and then I can work on rebuilding my image. I don't know, maybe somewhere down the road I can get a steady girlfriend." I chuckled.

She laughed and playfully punched me. "You've been divorced all of one hour and already you're talking about getting a girlfriend. Next hour, it'll be talks of marriage."

I put my hands up as I laughed. "I said *down the road,* and I'm not doing the marriage thing again.

Only one person deserved my hand in marriage, and that was you, so I'm gonna bachelor this thing out until the end."

"Well, if you ever change your mind and decide to get married again, just make sure you're ready and that she's worthy of you."

I closed the space between us and lifted her chin so she could look into my eyes. "Only if that woman is you."

She blushed and shook her head. "Thank you, but it just wasn't meant to be. I think we both know that."

"All I know is that I made some foul decisions and that if I'd spent my time making the right ones, you'd still be Mrs. Ryan Westmore."

She shrugged. "That's true, but that's not the hand that we played, so we have to deal with the life we chose. I appreciate even the things that I regret because without them, I wouldn't be the person I am today, and neither would you. We made three beautiful children and shared a great love story. And for all the things you did wrong and right, it helped make me stronger, and I'm cool with that."

"I can live with that."

She looked at her watch and back up at me. "I better get going. I have to get the boys in an hour or so, and I need to wind down and get some 'me time' before I have to deal with schoolwork and dinner and stuff."

"If you need me to get them, I'd be glad to," I offered.

"If you don't mind, I'd rather be with them today. I need them right now just as much as they need me. Not saying you don't or anything . . . it's just—"

When she paused, the unspoken understanding regarding Ryan Jr. was understood. "I get it." I nodded my head. "Well, you better get going. Don't want you to miss out on that '*me* time.' I know how rare it is."

"Yeah." She sighed. We stared at each other briefly and then embraced again. "Take care of yourself. Goodbye, Ryan."

"You too, baby," I said as we pulled away from each other. As she walked away, my heart filled with regret for what could've been. "I love you, Charice. I always will," I whispered aloud and headed toward the limo.

"You good?" my attorney asked as we pulled off, headed toward my condo.

As I settled into my seat, I pondered his question for a moment. "Yeah. Actually, I am," I answered as I thought back over my life with Charice.

I was sad that my future had just walked away from me, but there was nothing that could be done about it now. I'd lost her forever. There was nothing left to do besides move on and pick up the pieces. Picking up and adapting was what I did best. I was Ryan Chad Westmore after all. Yet, for the first time in my life, I wanted that name to be more than just a brand. I wanted it to be what so many had tried to instill in me before. I wanted it to be a representation of the man in me. I would use this loss to start a new lease on the man, Ryan Chad Westmore, not the Prodigy. Smiling once again, I had Charice to thank for that. Her decision to divorce me was not only the best decision for her, but for me as well. It was our chance to get ourselves right.

I raised my glass to my attorney. "To Charice."

My attorney shook his head in confusion but still touched glasses with me and repeated, "To . . . Charice."

Chapter 21

Lincoln

"My client has no comment at this time. Please respect his privacy," I heard Ryan's attorney say before I grabbed the remote and turned the television off.

Well, it's done now. Charice Westmore was officially Charice Taylor again. She looked stunning and flawless on the television as she entered the courtroom. You couldn't tell she was there for a divorce. She'd always found a way to be poised and gracious even when she was going through the worst of times. That's one of the many things that made me fall in love with her. The public had deemed her the heroine when all of Ryan's immoral acts, including his infidelity, surfaced. They even went as far back as when he was in college. The media that he loved so much had nailed him to the sacrificial cross. The team's management and coaching staff stuck beside him, and believe it or not, players Ryan didn't hang with stuck beside him. He learned the hard way that choosing friends wisely worked to his advantage.

Amazingly, my affair and child with Charice never surfaced during any of this. Charice and I both understood it paid to keep your dirt to yourself. Besides, the select few people who knew of our affair had too much to lose by talking. The best thing in the world that we had ever decided to do was to seal the court records regarding Lexi's paternity. During this situation, it would've been a media frenzy just on that story alone, and there was no way that either one of us would've allowed the media to drag Lexi into that mess because of our mistakes. Thank God for small favors.

After the whole incident at Mona's house, Mona had contacted me once. She was still hurt by how I handled the situation. I apologized to her, and she accepted that. Then she hit me with the news that the situation helped her realize that her heart would always belong to a woman. Ironically, the person she missed the most was Charice. Wow. She'd never had sex with her and never kissed her, but Charice had been a friend to her and understood her in a way that a man never could. Even though she realized she couldn't have Charice, she was going to put her efforts into finding the right woman for her.

Damn. I'd managed to turn a bisexual woman completely lesbian, or maybe Charice had. I don't know, but whatever floated her boat worked for me. I liked a freak in the bedroom, but in hindsight, that was just a little too much freaky shit even for me. I would never agree to the threesome long term the way Mona wanted. One-time deal, perhaps, before the fiasco with Charice. Nowadays, I wasn't even into the whole jump-off thing anymore. I'd jumped off too many women during my career. It had gotten old. Just as much as I used them, they used me. While sex had been my old end game, they used me for the clout, the chance to make their own moves, to trap me with a baby or a ring—most times both—and for my money. When you're young and enjoying the single life, it doesn't matter. When you're thirty years old and have two children and no wife, it matters.

I hadn't said much to Ryan in the days leading up to his divorce. I stayed at a distance and kept our conversation strictly about football. I think he respected that from me. It already bruised him to be publicly ridiculed. He didn't need his wife's ex starting in on him, too, or asking questions. I was man enough to be a man about the situation. I realized when I needed to walk away and let shit go, and it was definitely that time. I think the whole thing had matured Ryan. He'd demonstrated some hellacious growth over the past month. They always say there's something that will break a man down. Losing Charice must've been it for him. Ironically, losing her was it for me, too.

If I could do it all over again, I would've told Charice immediately about Ryan's plan to break us up. Jumping into an affair with her went against what both of us stood for, and in the end, the game we tried to play swallowed us whole. I took a risk with a woman I truly loved, and I fucked over her and myself. Karma was definitely that bitch.

I wanted to be there for her throughout the process, but she refused. Besides her mom, she depended on Mona, Felicia, and her girl Lucinda. Her mom had flown to New York to help her out with the kids for a while, but Charice asked her to leave before the actual court date. She wanted to be by herself. I had convinced her to let my mom keep Lexi for a few days. I felt like right now, she and the boys needed their time to bond together. Not that Lexi was a distraction, but Lexi had me, and she wasn't losing anything. The boys were, and they were old enough to feel the pain behind it. I wanted to do all I could to make that transition easier for all of them. It was the least I could do.

At about ten o'clock that night, I couldn't stand it anymore. I grabbed a bottle of Riesling and walked down to Charice's house. I had to see how she was doing. I figured I'd find her in the backyard, and that's exactly where she was. I opened her gate.

Without looking up, she spoke to me. "You know, Lincoln, I could have you arrested for trespassing one day."

"Well, call them now. I'm not running." I walked over beside her and set the bottle of wine down on the table, then sat in the chair next to her. "Are the boys asleep?"

"They asked to spend the night at Johanna's house with her son. I let them. It's been a lot for them today." She sighed. "How's Lexi?"

"I can't even imagine. And Lexi is fine. You know my parents are spoiling her rotten. Don't worry about her. We've got her," I informed her. "Back to the boys. Did they do their homework?"

She shook her head. "Thank you. I'm grateful that the boys' teachers gave them a week homework pass considering all the publicity of the divorce. I cooked for them, and they played until Johanna took them with her. I can honestly say I needed the break. Not from them, just from this day. The reporters and fans were crazy, and I needed space to process that I am officially a single woman yet again," she said, lifting her bare ring finger in the air.

I looked over at her for the first time since I had sat down. "How are you feeling about that?"

She looked at me and smiled. "Good, actually. Believe it or not, Ryan and I had a nice, cleansing, mature talk today. I'm sad about the divorce, but for the first time in a long time, I'm really, *really* good . . . you know . . . with myself. I think Ryan is finally learning how to grow up and be good with himself." She drank the last sip of the wine she'd been drinking, and then her eyes rolled over to me. "I have a confession to make."

I heaved a sigh, knowing what she was about to confess. "You told him about us, didn't you?"

Her eyebrows knitted together. "How'd you know?"

"What else is there for you to confess?" I asked, shrugging. "What'd he say?"

"He charged it to the game. He said he owed it to us to let it go," she said with a slight chuckle. "Shocking, but true."

"Man, oh man. After all this time, it ends civilly," I said, shocked by the outcome. I pondered that thought for a moment before my concern turned to her. "Have you eaten?"

"Yes, with the boys. I ate some grilled chicken with a salad."

I picked up the bottle of wine that I'd brought. "Have a glass with me?"

She stood up. "Sure."

Together, we walked inside her house and into the kitchen. She pulled down two wine glasses as I popped the top then poured us both a glass.

"I'd like to make a toast," I declared, and we raised our glasses. "To the return of Charice Taylor."

"Here, here. I'll drink to that." We touched glasses and took a sip.

I set down my glass. "Can I ask you a question?"

She nodded her agreement, holding her glass in her hand.

"After your talk—with Ryan, I mean—do you think you'll ever get back together? I mean, are you still in love with him?"

She set down her glass and leaned against the counter. "I'll always love Ryan. He was my first love. My first lover. My children's father. My first husband. For all those reasons, I'll always, always love him. Still, he was also the first man to break my heart, kill my spirit, abandon my children and me, and lie to me. For those reasons, I could never be with him again, even though those things also had a hand in shaping my being. To answer your other question, I stopped being in love with Ryan a long time ago. I think I was in love with the idea of being in love more than anything else," she said, took another sip of her wine, and then looked at me. "So, why don't you ask me what you really want to ask me?"

Shit. She knows me. The abruptness rattled me and forced me to take another swig of my wine. Then, I nervously looked up at her and asked, "Do you still have any love for me?"

She let out a scoff behind her smirk and crossed her arms. "That's not what you want to ask me."

She was right. It wasn't. I wanted Charice back. I'd waited patiently, and the entire time, I'd longed for her. I wanted to give her all the things she needed and wanted in a man. I wanted to be free to love her and show her what a real relationship with me would be like. I wanted to make her my wife.

I walked over to her, placed my hands on the counter, and leaned close to her. "Okay then. I'll ask. Are you still in love with me? Because I'm still in love with you. I love you, Charice, with everything inside of me, and I'm ready. I want to love you with no holds barred. I messed up with Mona, but I did that out of spite because I didn't want to be hurt by you. I realize now that I couldn't have been more wrong. I should've trusted you, and I've regretted that decision. I can't change it, but I'm asking you to forgive me, Charice. Forgive me and let's start over. We're good together, and we're meant to be together. I'm asking you to let me love you, please."

She held my face in her hands, leaned down, and kissed me. I damn near melted from her touch. She had me hook, line, and sinker, and she knew it. She pulled back and looked me in the eyes.

"I do love you, Lincoln. You're the only man I've ever loved so completely. I forgive you about Mona because I understand. You were hurt and protecting your feelings, and in hindsight, it makes sense, but I can't be with you. I have a life to rebuild. My boys need me now."

I bit my lip. "But I can help you. We can rebuild together."

She smiled at me, and it ripped through my heart. God, I loved this woman.

"You're sweet. I love you because of that, but that won't work. This is something I have to do by myself for myself. As much as I appreciate what you're offering me, I respectfully decline," she said as she continued to hold my face in her hands. "I hope that you understand."

"No, I don't understand, but I can accept it. If that's the way you want it, I fully respect it."

"Thank you."

"You're welcome." This time, it was me who pecked her on the lips. "I better get going. It's only so long I can be around you knowing I can't have you."

"Then I don't want to make it hard for you." She grabbed my hand and walked me to the door and opened it.

"Goodbye, Charice."

"Goodnight, Lincoln."

I stepped outside, and she shut the door. I walked in sadness and was halfway to my house before I realized one thing. *She didn't say goodbye. She said goodnight.* I smiled to myself. There was hope for us.

Chapter 22

Aldris

Jennifer snuggled up closer to me, and I slid away from her. Peering at the clock, I saw that it was 2:41 a.m. I'd been up ever since we had sex. That was one shower and three hours ago. Something on the inside just wasn't right. In my gut, I felt it. It was the primary reason I hadn't been having sex with her and didn't want to tonight, but Jennifer had insisted. She even wanted me to go in raw. Hell no. Condoms it was until we made it down that damn aisle, just in case we didn't make it down that damn aisle. I had one child out of wedlock, and that was one enough.

What wasn't right? Everything. It had all started when Jennifer forgave me for calling her Lucinda at Uniquely Tastes Cakes. Not that I was not glad about it, but it was just—I don't know— too soon. I must have been crazy to have a woman who didn't trip and then think it was crazy when she didn't trip, but there was something about the way she didn't trip. It just didn't sit well with me.

The day Lucinda had come over with Nadia was the day that Jennifer forgave me about the incident. It had been an entire week. Now, the funny thing about it was that this was the first time that either of us had reached out to the other that entire week. I wanted to give her a chance to cool off. So, when I showed up at her house, I totally expected to go through the fire, hail, and brimstone with her. To my surprise, she listened to my apology, then calmly explained that I did hurt her, but she could move on from it. Then she hugged me, kissed me, and acted as if the entire incident had never happened. I took Jessica to my house for the weekend as a way to make up to her so she could have some alone time. Also, I needed time away from her to process how in the hell she had gone from slapping me and leaving me at the store to accepting my apology without so much as one residual stitch of anger. She'd been acting that way ever since.

Don't get me wrong, I am all for no drama, but sometimes, drama was a good thing. At least enough drama to let me know that she wasn't a sociopath. What black woman in America can be called an ex-girlfriend's name during an apology in the middle of wedding planning and just be cool with that without a real conversation? Exactly.

Jennifer was on that survivor island all by herself because I don't know a woman—black, white, Hispanic, Asian, purple, blue, or orange—who would be *all right* with that. Either something was up, or I was sleeping with the fucking enemy. I wasn't about to go to sleep in her house and end up buck naked on a pool table with a stick shoved up my ass like ol' dude in the movie *In Too Deep*. Hell no.

I decided I needed to have a talk with her. Granted, it was damn near three o'clock in the morning, but I needed my talk now. If we were gonna do this thing and get married, there had to be some clear air between us. I had to get to the place where I felt comfortable in this relationship because if not, getting down the aisle was going to be on permanent hold. Lucinda was right. I had to get back to my happiness. If I couldn't get to that with Jennifer, then I'd rather stay single. I could be miserable all by myself. I didn't need or want any company for that.

"Jennifer," I called quietly. "Jennifer."

"Hmm," she said and rolled over.

"Jennifer," I said a bit louder. "Damn."

She was dead to the world. Mandingo had knocked her the fuck out. Good job for my manhood, but bad for her mental state. Instead, I decided to get up and grab a bottle of water. I made my way into the kitchen and drank a long swig.

Easing down the hallway, I peeped in on Jessica. My angel was sleeping, nicely tucked away in her bed. I missed peeping in on Nadia the same way. Hearing her and Jessica play at my house last week had brought back so many fond memories. Both of my daughters under one roof again. Damn. I still considered Nadia my daughter. Truth be told, I always would. She still held my heart, and I was glad that, despite my breakup with her mom, I still had a place in hers.

Since I couldn't sleep and couldn't wake Jennifer, I opted to go into the room Jennifer had designated for Jessica to do homework or where she could catch up on her own work when necessary. I liked that room. It was a nice, quiet getaway from the rest of the house. You could read a book, surf the net, or just chill, and I thought it was a great idea to have it in the house.

When I went to power up the computer, I noticed it was in hibernation mode, and when I shook the mouse, it awakened to Jennifer's email inbox. I was about to log out of her email, but that gut feeling came over me, and I thought about my mother's words: *women have female intuition, and men have gut instinct. Trust it.*

I knew I was wrong, and I would've been pissed if Jennifer did it to me, but I began to scroll down her inbox. There was nothing really, just a bunch of advertisement emails for Nordstrom, Frederick's of Hollywood, Wal-Mart, and some wedding places. It looked like a few work-related emails and email jokes between her and some of her friends.

You're just paranoid and wrong.

I was just about to log out when I noticed an email folder labeled M. Now, that was strange. She had folders labeled for bank statements, cell phone bill receipts, light bill receipts, so on and so forth, but this one was simply labeled *M.*

What the fuck is M? My name begins with an A, hers and Jessica's begin with J. What or who in the hell is M?

I got up and peeped in Jennifer's bedroom to find she was still in a deep sleep. Good. I had to find out what the hell that folder was. I hurriedly went back into the computer room and clicked on *M.*

"What the fuck?" I asked aloud to myself. There were different emails going back and forth between her and *Mike?*

I clicked on the most recent one, dated a couple of days after we saw him and Lucinda at Uniquely Tastes Cakes. I started reading the thread from the bottom.

> mzjennifer@net.com:
> Mike,
> I don't know what to do. I know that it was all my idea, but I'm getting tired of this. It

seems like Aldris will never shake his feelings for Lucinda. No matter how hard I try, it's like I'm always competing with her for his heart, even when she's not even in the fucking picture. After you all left the cake store today, do you know he called me Lucinda? How embarrassing is that? He's my fiancé and calling me his ex-fiancée's name. I'm thinking about just letting him go. I'm not happy like I thought I'd be, and holding on to him just for the sake of holding on is getting old. I love him, but it's so hard trying to get him to love me back. My only fear of letting go is that if I do, he'll run right back to Lucinda. You say she's over him, but I don't know. If I were you, I'd keep my guard up. Those two got closer than we thought, and I don't trust your girlfriend as far as I can throw her, and you shouldn't either. I'm at a crossroads here. I'm just letting you know where my head is at. Hit me back.

Jenn

bigmikej@awl.com:
I don't know what you need to do, but I know you better not let him go. You dragged me into this mess. I wasn't even gonna go through with it, but I did for you. Now you gotta do this for me. Lucinda finally loves me

the way I love her, and we're good. I don't
need Aldris distracting her. Give me time to
at least get her down the fucking aisle. Damn
your crossroads. You signed up for this shit.
Suck it up. You knew the deal. I suggest you
forgive the man and be cool. Aldris will suck
up to you and make up. So, make the fuck up,
remain engaged, and get the fuck married.
You owe me.

mzjennifer@net.com:
Kiss my ass, Mike! I don't owe you shit.
You decided to be with Lucinda on your
own. You could've said no. The only thing
I asked you to do was be with her when the
opportunity presented itself. You chose to
betray your friendship with Aldris and break
the code. You could've walked away. So, I
don't owe you a damn thing, but you do owe
me. If it wasn't for me continuing to infiltrate
so that I could get next to Aldris, you never
would've had a REAL shot at her heart. It was
me who kept Aldris away from your precious
little mamacita, so don't get it twisted. Let's
not forget, it was me who chose to accept
this engagement sooner than I planned at
your request so you could set up that whole
restaurant thing. Remember that? Now that
you're on top, you wanna forget who helped

put you there. Do me a favor and keep your
Latin lover away from my man, or I just
might have to mess up her pretty little face
or deflate that overly humungous ass of hers.

bigmikej@awl.com:
If you touch Lucinda, it's me and you. For
real. I may owe you, but no matter how far
away I keep Lucinda from Aldris, you remember this: she ain't the one with the feelings. He
is. So put your big girl drawers on and handle
your business with your man. You wanted
him. You have him. It's your job to hold on
to him. Not mine. I did my part, and I'm still
doing it. Maybe you should take some lessons
from Lu and get a routine and a nickname.
That might just keep your man focused on
your ass instead of Lu's. Don't contact me by
this email anymore. You know Lu uses my PC
to do some of her work sometimes. Hit me on
my work cell or messenger.

I couldn't believe what I'd just read. I had to
reread the shit again just to be sure of what exactly
I was reading. *Gut instincts. Trust them.* Instantly,
I became enraged. This whole fucking time Lu
and I were being played by Mike and Jennifer?
They played on the problems in our relationship
so that we could remain separated, and we both

fell right into their traps. In all my life, I'd never known that Mike could be this grimy. To think, I was in fact sleeping with the muthafucking enemy. The mother of my child could actually do this to me. Wow. Lu and I had said and done some harsh shit to each other, but at least we kept it real with each other. Always. No matter what. But this shit here. This was on some next-level shit. I didn't even know these two people anymore, nor did I want to. They were in for a rude awakening because the only thing keeping me from wringing Jennifer's neck was Jessica, and now, that's all we had between us. Fuck that bitch and the horse she rode in on.

I was so glad we had one of those silent printers as I quickly printed out the email trail between Mike and Jennifer. I made sure to leave her inbox just how she had left it, and I put the computer back in hibernation mode. I tiptoed back into her bedroom, slipped my clothes back on, and scribbled a note that I had to leave early for a work-related emergency.

I didn't give a damn that it was after three in the morning. I had to talk to Lucinda. I had to show her what I'd found. I only prayed that she was at her condo alone because I didn't want a confrontation with Mike. I knew I'd kill his punk ass on sight if I did see him. I needed to calm down before I slapped him and Jennifer with the truth. First, I had to inform Lucinda about who her man and my woman really were—partners in muthafucking crime.

I drove through Lu's condo parking lot twice, looking for Mike's car, but I didn't see it. I decided to be safe and call her cell phone. She didn't answer on the first try, so I tried again.

"Come on, Lu. Pick up." I willed her to answer.

"Hello?" she said groggily.

"Lucinda! Wake up."

"Huh?" she asked, confused.

"Is Mike in the house with you?" I asked.

"Wait a minute. Who is this?" she asked sleepily.

"It's Aldris. Is Mike with you?"

"No. Wait. Aldris?" she said as she began waking up. I could hear her movement in the bed. "What time . . . what time is it? Three forty-one! In the morning? Are you fucking crazy? You do realize the hour?"

"Yes, but I had to tell you this tonight."

"What? Oh my God! Nothing is wrong with your mama or anything? Jessica?" she asked frantically.

At her concern, my heart melted. Damn. It was in that very moment that I allowed the realization that I'd been avoiding to sink in. My anger toward her had overshadowed my feelings for her. They were feelings I had buried when I tried to allow Jennifer to replace the woman I honestly and truly loved, Lucinda. I couldn't move on because I wasn't supposed to. I was built and meant to love Lucinda. And boy, did I ever love her. I really loved this woman. It was time to stop fooling myself.

"No, nothing like that, but I thank you for asking."

"Thank me for asking? Aldris, if you don't start explaining why the hell we're up in the middle of the night on the phone, I'm hanging up. Ain't nobody up this time of night, in the middle of a work week no less, but freaks and Jesus."

Taking her threat seriously, I moved on to the reason for my early morning intrusion. "Open your door. I have some important news to show you, and it can't wait. You know I'd never be over here like this if it were not extremely important. Trust me on this. Open the door and just see for yourself."

She paused for a moment. "Let me get decent. Give me two minutes."

I parked my car and walked to her door. In two minutes, she opened the door and motioned me inside. We walked to her living room and sat on the sofa beside each other.

"Okay, so what in the hell was so important that you had to barge over to my house in the middle of the week at this time of morning? I swear, if this is some bullshit, I'ma kick your ass myself," Lucinda warned me.

There she was, my little hurricane. Call me crazy, but even Category 5 attitude turned me on. Damn. I had missed her. As I eyed her, I also couldn't help

but admire her beauty. Lucinda was hot-natured
and never slept in anything longer than a pair of
shorts. So even with her wifebeater, short shorts,
plush flip flop slippers, and robe, she looked sexy.
It was the kind of hood-girl sexy where you just
wanted to tear that ass up. Her curly hair was a bit
disheveled from sleeping, the way I remembered
it being when we lived together, but it was always
sexy to me. It reminded me of the way it looked
after we made love. God, how I used to love to run
my fingers through those curly locks. Her skin was
smoother than a baby's ass, and speaking of asses,
I wished I'd gotten a look at hers as we walked in.
That rotund mound was nothing less than sheer
perfection.

"Earth to Aldris," Lucinda said, running her
hand in front of my face.

I snapped out of it. "My bad."

She threw her head back and rolled her eyes.
"Why did I even let you in? I don't have time for
this. You're interrupting my rest." She stood up.

I grabbed her by the hand. "Please. I'm sorry. Sit
down. I promise it's important."

She looked down at my hand and bit her lip. She
sat down and then slowly we let go of each other's
hands. "Okay, so what's up?"

I leaned forward. "Have you ever wondered
about your relationship with Mike? Like how you
all got to the point you're at?"

"Oh God! No. No. No. I know damn well you did not come over here tonight to criticize, critique, or contest my relationship with Mike. Please tell me you didn't. This is becoming insane, Aldris. I can't live in your insanity anymore. I get that you're pissed about us, but it's time for you to focus on Jennifer. That's who *you* chose."

"And I probably wouldn't have chosen her if it wasn't for your man and her plotting against us."

My words caused her mouth snap open, and I took a beat to gather my bearings.

"I'm sorry to raise my voice. I know Nadia's sleeping."

Lucinda stared blankly at me for a moment. "Aldris, what the hell are you talking about?"

I wanted to show her the proof, but I just had to know if deep down, she felt like I did at some point.

"Lucinda, haven't you had an inclination that something about the way you and Mike kept ending up together wasn't right? Not because of my friendship with him, but just because it seems like more than just happenstance. Think about it. Every time we went through drama or doubted our feelings for each other, here comes Mike to the rescue. Tell me it seemed odd to you. At least once. Please."

She bit her bottom lip and finally nodded. "Okay. Okay. Sometimes I get the feeling that there was something more to Mike's agenda. At times, it does feel like there's something odd that I can't put my finger on. But why?"

I pulled out the two pages of emails and gave them to her. "I pulled this from Jennifer's email tonight. I think both of us should see this so that we can make an informed decision."

She took the papers from me and began reading. As she read, her facial expressions told it all. She went from shock to sheer anger in a matter of minutes. She set down the papers, picked them up again, and reread them.

"Is this for real?" she asked me, her voice quivering with anger.

"As real as I am sitting here in front of you. I was going to confront Jennifer because I felt like she forgave me too fast for calling her your name at Uniquely Tastes Cakes. I just felt like something wasn't right, but she wouldn't wake up, so I decided to surf the net. Her email inbox was up. I started to log out, but I had this gut feeling that I needed to look for something, and this is what I found. They've been playing us both like a fiddle for God knows how long."

"Wait a minute. So, you called Jennifer by my name?"

In my haste to tell her the story, I'd spilled the beans on information she hadn't been privy to. I swallowed hard. "Yes. After you and Mike left your cake tasting."

Lucinda sat back and folded her arms and began shaking her leg. Suddenly, tears fell from her eyes. Then she grabbed her ring finger and slung the ring off and unleashed a tirade of emotions and questions. "I trusted that bastardo. I can't believe I let my guard down. All this time, he's been playing me. Plotting with that crazy-ass heifer to keep me away from you. Why does this keep happening to me? Why? Every time I think I've found the one, it's always so messed up. And now, to find out that Mike was plotting against me." She put her head in her hands.

I eased next to her and put my hand on her thigh. "I know how you feel. Jennifer did the same thing to me. They both did it to us. I know you're hurting, and I'm sorry to have to be the one to tell you this."

She threw her hands up. "Fuck being hurt. I'm pissed off. At least you kept your guard up. You weren't even happy with her, Aldris. I let Mike in," she fussed as tears streamed down her face.

I forced her to look at me and wiped her tears away. "Don't beat yourself up. We both let them in at one point or another. If we both think about it, I only let Jennifer in when I thought you truly wanted Mike, and I'm guessing you only let Mike in after you felt that I truly wanted Jennifer. At the time, we both thought we did want them. If I'm honest with myself, I've never truly fallen in love with Jennifer. I just allowed myself to think that she was the better choice."

"But you know me, Aldris. It takes a lot for me to love a man. It took even more for me to open myself in that way to Mike. I can't believe I didn't see through his bullshit. I can't believe I loved him."

Lifting her chin, I forced her to look at me again. "But you could never love him how you loved me."

"Oh, not now." She waved me off. "I'm not venturing down this path again."

I stood up and walked to her table. "Oh, no? Why in the hell do you have the plant that we grew together as a symbol of our love sitting in your house when you claimed you were gonna trash it? Seems like you never left that path. You simply detoured, like me."

She stood up. "Because . . . because . . ."

I walked up to her and pulled her into my arms. "Because deep down inside, no matter how happy Mike made you feel, no matter how much you thought you loved him, it's always been me who had your heart. I captured your heart the first time we ever ate lunch at the Varsity, and I've had it ever since. I know because no matter how many lies I told myself, I've loved you since that same moment, and I have never, ever stopped."

Without warning, I kissed her passionately for a few minutes before we pulled back from each other. For the first time in months, my heart sang.

This was where my happiness was, and it was as if that kiss had unlocked a hidden treasure that had been buried for centuries.

"Lucinda, I love you. Fuck what I've done and you've done. We're meant to be. Me and you. If you just trust me one last time, I promise to God above that I'll never take it for granted again. I'll give you the lifetime of love and commitment that you deserve," I begged, holding her face in my hands.

She shook her head. "But we've done so many things to each other. Bad things. And there's Jennifer and Mike."

My eyebrows knitted and my mouth grew into a grimace. "Are you saying that you're going to stay with Mike after this?"

Shaking her head vehemently, she clarified, "Hell no. I would never. We both need time to rectify our situations with Jennifer and Mike. We have to figure out so many things between us."

I shook my head and kissed her to shut her up. "Do you love me?" I stared into her eyes.

"Aldris—"

"Lucinda, I'm begging you to be honest with yourself. For the first time in forever, I am being honest with myself. I love you. I love you, and I don't give a damn about the technicalities. We'll make it work. Me and you. I just need you. *All* I need is you. *I love you*. Do you love me?"

She searched my eyes for what seemed like an eternity. Her face contorted as if she were going through a gamut of emotions. Then her face relaxed into what looked like a realization before she spoke.

"Oh my God. You really mean that. I can see it in your eyes. You really do love me," she said, accepting my words for the first time.

I put her hand on my chest. "Feel it with my heart. Only you have my heart. I've been trying to breathe for so long. Let me exhale. I can only exhale with you. I love you, Lu. Tell me you love me. Please." I kissed her about the forehead, nose, and mouth.

She looked me in the eyes as a single tear fell from her face. She looked as if she were in deep contemplation, then she exhaled and smiled slightly with a nod. "Yes. Yes, I do love you. I was just so scared. When you chose Jennifer, I was so hurt. I just want to know that I'm the only one with your heart."

I hugged her close to me. "You are. I'm sorry, Lu. I'm sorry I took you for granted. I'm sorry I let you down, but I swear on my life, I will never do it again. You are my heart, and I need you in my life as my lady. We'll take as much time as we need to nurture our love into healing. Just as long as you're with me and you're willing to give it a real try."

Minutes seemed like hours before she agreed. "I want to try. I want to take our time and do this right."

Pulling her into an embrace, I sealed our deal. "Then that's exactly what we'll do."

After a few minutes of holding each other in a cleansing embrace, she gently pulled away, and there was fire in her eyes. "But first, before we move forward, we've got some exes to bury. This time, when we get rid of them, it's for fucking good. I'm not playing with their asses anymore. They've fucked with the wrong bitch this time."

"Hurricane Lucinda is back," I sang.

"And with a muthafucking vengeance."

"Well, Holyfield, before you go throwing punches and blows, get some rest tonight. We'll figure out how to deal with Batman and Robin after some sleep," I said as I gently leaned my forehead against hers.

She nodded. "Okay. I'll try to rest."

Realizing the hour, I leaned forward and delivered a soft peck to her lips. "I better get going. It's after four in the morning, and we both need some sleep."

Stepping back, I gave her one last smile and headed toward the door, so that I could rest and figure out how we would address our two Judases.

"Aldris," Lucinda called out just as I turned the doorknob. "It's late. Why don't you stay here?"

I turned around, my eyes questioning and long-
ing at the same time. "You sure?"

Offering a mischievous smile, she turned to
walk to her bedroom. "It *is* four in the morning,
after all."

I put my hands together to thank God and
hauled ass to the bedroom behind her. If I had
anything to do with it, I wouldn't be getting any
sleep. I had some making up and rekindling to
do. Me and Mandingo. And fuck it, if she let me, I
was diving in raw because I knew exactly who
I was going down the aisle with. I finally had my
Lucinda back, and she wasn't going anywhere. And
neither was I.

Chapter 23

Gavin

It was the day after Meka was supposed to send my seed to Heaven. She wouldn't answer her phone. No one would answer her door or house phone. Lucinda wouldn't give up any information, and Tony was unreachable. I was out there on my own without my woman and without my first child. So there I sat, drinking myself into a drunken stupor.

I called into work and took off a full week, stating personal reasons. I was going to head out of town to my father and brother's company, Randall Enterprises. I'd plead for leniency on the life of my child, but if they refused, they'd suffer dire consequences. If my child had to go to Heaven, then I was gonna send their racist, homewrecking asses straight to Hell. I'd been plotting how I could take them out for a couple of days. At first, I came up with an elaborate scheme so I wouldn't get caught, and then I realized I didn't give a fuck if I got caught. The people I loved most in life had been ripped away from me. I didn't have my mom, LaMeka was gone, and she'd aborted my baby, so what the fuck did I have to live for? So what if I had to spend a lifetime behind bars? Losing Meka already felt like a death sentence.

I finished off my beer. It was time to either win my family back, go to prison, or go straight to Hell trying. I had nothing to lose. Before I left, I decided to go to God in prayer. I owed Him a conversation about my intentions. Hopefully, He'd have mercy on me. I got down on my knees and put my hands together.

"Lord, I'ma make it short and sweet. I've tried to wait on you, and I'm sorry. I'm taking vengeance into my own hands. Please forgive me, for I know exactly what I'm about to do. Amen." I got up, heading to my back bedroom.

I went into the closet and pulled out my gun from the gun safe and reached up to grab the box of bullets to load it. When I grabbed the box, another small black lockbox fell and clattered on the floor. The top sprang open, and some of the contents slipped out of the box. I cursed myself for my clumsiness. I knew exactly what was in that box. Special mementos from my mother that she'd willed to me, which were given to me after her death. I'd never gone through it because it either didn't seem like the right time, or when the right times had come, it was too hard to deal with.

Placing the gun and bullets down, I squatted to retrieve the items to place them back in the box. The last thing I needed was my mother's spirit thwarting my intended plans. As I picked them up, pictures of the past caught my eye, and my chest tightened at the memories. Just like that, my heartstrings had been tugged into relishing the memories of yesteryear. As much as I wanted to place this rabbit hole of mementos back in the box, I felt an energy forcing me to indulge. I slid down against the wall onto the floor and began sifting through the fallen items.

There were a bunch of pictures of me as a kid with my mother and brother, some memories that I'd long since forgotten. I couldn't help but laugh at some of them. It felt good to remember the good days back when my mom was our hero and my brother was, well, my brother. There was her favorite locket, my grandma's engagement ring, photos of her and my dad, and a picture of my grandma and some man.

Who in the hell is the man in the photo? I flipped the picture over. Jerry and Lois Jennings. *My grandfather?* I'd never known who my grandfather was. He'd died long before Gary and I were born, and my grandmother died when Gary and I were very young. I couldn't put my finger on it, but something looked odd about the photo. I kept digging until I found what I hoped was in the box, my mom's birth certificate.

Child: *Diana Laurie Jennings* **Mother:** *Lois Zimmer Jennings.* **Race:** *White.* **Father:** *Jerry Lee Jennings.* **Race: Negro**.

What the fuck? Hell no! It couldn't be. I looked back at the photo, and sure enough, my grandfather was a light complexion, but he wasn't white.

Hot damn! My mom was fucking biracial. That meant Gary and I were one quarter black.

My mom had inherited all my grandmother's features, from her blue eyes to her strawberry blond hair. You would've never been able to tell in a million fucking years that she was the product of an interracial couple, a black man and a white woman. This gave me a whole new meaning to the movie *Imitation of Life*. At the bottom of the box, I found an envelope addressed to me. I opened it.

My dearest Gavin,

If you are reading this, I assume that you saw the birth certificate and the only picture I have of my father. I know you may find it hard to believe, but I want to confirm it for you that yes, I am a bi-racial child. I know this comes as a complete shock to you.

I wasn't ashamed of my heritage and never intended on hiding it from you all, but after I met your father and became pregnant with Gary, I learned of his asinine views of interracial dating. There was no way I could ever tell you all or him the truth about who I was. I loved him, and I didn't want him to hate me or take it out on you boys because of something that none of us could control. But as we got deeper into our relationship, I realized I'd never known the true Gerald Randall. When his viewpoints went beyond mixing races to all out racism against minorities, it all became too much. I'd procreated with one of the vilest men I'd ever known

You should probably know that his viewpoints forced me into the arms of another man. I began a relationship with a black man named Robert. He was the true love of my life, and I had plans to leave your father, but he found out before I could leave him. He not only ran Robert away, but completely destroyed his life. I can't and won't tell you the hell that your father put that man through. That's how bad it truly was. Robert was so far broken that he couldn't see me again because it hurt too badly. After that, I knew I had to leave your father. We weren't married, and there was no use staying around and exposing you all to that foolishness. So, I took you boys and left without the money or the support. I was determined to never look back, and I didn't.

After your father expressed interest in wanting to raise you all, I hid you for as many years as I could, moving from residence to residence just to keep him from pinpointing exactly where we were. But he finally caught up with us, and you know the rest of the story. He got to Gary, and it was downhill from there.

Gary still doesn't know my true identity. After he sided with your father, I couldn't trust him. I never told you because I know you allow your temper to overcome you at times, and I didn't want you to reveal anything that could hurt you or Gary out of anger.

I apologize for just now telling you my true identity and, in essence, yours. I hope that you forgive me for keeping it from you. Please know that everything I did, I did for the best interests of you and your brother. I love you, Gavin. And even though Gary doesn't think so, I love him, too.

Love, Mom

The paper slipped from my hands as I processed the news that I'd just learned. Floored. I was absolutely floored. My father was so concerned about us marrying into other races, and he didn't even realize that his own kids, his own flesh and blood, were part black.

This changed everything. I knew exactly how to get him now. If he didn't want this information leaked to his country club buddies or business associates, he would leave LaMcka and her family alone and stand out of my way as I fought to get my wifey back.

I looked toward the heavens. "Lord, I'm so sorry. Please find it in your heart to forgive me for my thoughts and the acts I was ready to commit. I should've trusted you. You are always on time, and from now on out, I promise to keep my faith in you."

Instead of driving, I booked a flight to leave that day. Just as I finished packing so that I could make my scheduled flight to Virginia, I heard my doorbell. When I got to the door, to my surprise, I saw Misha standing there.

"Misha?" I let her in.

"Surprised, right?" she asked.

"Yeah. Everybody has been following Meka's strict orders to avoid me at all costs."

"Yeah, well, if she knew I were here, she'd probably kick me out and ban me from her will."

I folded my arms. "So, why are you here?"

She released a pregnant sigh. "To tell you that Meka needs you. She's driving us insane with her depression over you," Misha said. "And I know what she says, but my sister is in love with you. There's no two ways about that. All I want is for her to be happy. That's it. And I know that deep down, that happiness is only with you. I'm begging you to find a way to make this work despite your family issues."

"What if I told you I have a way to ensure I can keep my family away from you all and out of my relationship with Meka?"

"I'd probably drive you to Meka's house myself and take the full blame for it."

I smiled at her. "I have a way to do just that."

Misha jumped up and down. "Are you for real this time? Are you serious?"

I nodded. "As a heart attack."

"Oh my God! Gavin!" she shrieked, hugging me.

After we disengaged from the hug, I said somberly, "Even though Meka got rid of my seed, I can forgive her. I just need her in my life. We can work on another baby after we get down the aisle."

Misha cringed. "Well, she's gonna kill me anyway once she finds out I talked to you, so I may as well tell you the truth."

I frowned. "The truth?"

Misha nodded. "Yep. The truth is she's still pregnant."

"What? But she said—"

"When she got to the appointment, she couldn't go through with it. Your seed isn't dead. There is a living, growing baby inside of her belly, just waiting to meet his or her father." She smiled at me.

Instantly, my eyes watered. I'd done more crying over Meka than I had my entire life, and now that I had a baby on the way, I was sure I was just at the beginning of discovering my inner emotions. But I wasn't sad. I was abundantly happy. LaMeka hadn't killed our baby, and that was all the encouragement I needed to make my family whole again. Whether she knew it or not, she was gonna be Mrs. Gavin Randall, and that I meant.

Misha hugged me. "I know you're happy. You're still gonna be a daddy. So, let's get over to Meka's house and tell her the good news so you two can get back to being a couple."

"Actually, I have to catch a flight. I have to settle this thing with my family once and for all. I'd love to go with you to Meka's, but unless I have some concrete proof that I can deliver on my word this time, Meka ain't gonna hear nothing I have to say. I'll only make it worse for myself if she believes that I'm just giving her false promises. I let her down once. I refuse to do that again. More importantly, she refuses to let me. Just keep our conversation to yourself. I want to be the one to give her the good news."

Misha nodded. "Fair enough. What is this fool-proof plan? You never told me."

"If I told you, there's no way you'd keep it to yourself. Let's just say we have more in common than you know."

Misha shrugged. "I don't know what the hell that means, but I'm sure I'll find out whenever you get back. You be safe and stay out of trouble. My new niece or nephew needs you, and so does my sister."

"I promise, and that is one promise I know I can keep," I said, walking her out.

I watched her get in her car and then ran into the house to make sure I'd packed everything. I only needed one carry-on. This was going to be one very nice and very short meeting with Gerald and Gary Randall. Armed with the letter, birth certificate, and the picture of my grandparents all in my inside jacket pocket, I made my way to the airport and boarded the plane.

I was so wired that I couldn't even take a nap. I was on edge, and I wanted to make sure that nothing mysteriously happened to my proof while I was on the plane. Call me cautious, paranoid, hell even crazy, but I would be all those things to get back to LaMeka.

I jumped out of the cab and walked into Randall Enterprises, and an amazing sense of calm and happiness washed over me. I knew in that very instant that everything was going to be all right. Better than all right. It was time to set the record straight. In the words of my favorite comedian, Kevin Hart, it was about to go down.

The receptionist looked at me and smiled as I got off the elevator on the tenth floor, the executives' floor. "Why, hello. How may I help you today?" she said in a voice that was a little overly friendly.

Although highly inappropriate, I saw it as a definite advantage. I showed her my pearly whites and put on the best fake smile I could muster.

"Hi," I said, looking down at her nameplate. "Lindsey, how are you?"

She blushed and pushed her hair behind her ear on one side. "I am doing very well, and yourself?"

"I've never felt better. Thank you for asking," I said sweetly.

"You're welcome." She gazed up at me starry eyed. Suddenly, she remembered that she was at work, so she did her job. "How may I assist you, Mr. . . . Uh?"

"Gavin."

"Mr. Gavin, how may I assist you?"

"I'm here to see Mr. Gerald and Gary Randall."

Her face instantly flushed as if she were caught off guard. She started looking down at what I already knew was her appointment calendar.

"I'm . . . uh . . . sorry. Did you have an appointment with them? Usually, they don't take appointments after three, and I don't have your name down on the calendar," she said almost frantically as she continued to search.

I leaned over the desk. "Lindsey, I'm actually not on the calendar, but it is imperative that I speak with them right away. If there is anything that you could do to make that happen for me, I'd greatly appreciate it," I said, pouring my charm on extra thick. "Greatly."

She damn near melted in her chair, and I could bet money she creamed herself. She twirled her pen around and shrugged. "I'd love to help you out, Mr. Gavin, but both Mr. Randalls are very strict about appointments," she said nervously.

"I understand and, trust me, I respect that this is your job, which you do very nicely, might I add; however, what I need to see them about simply can't wait. Can't you please make an exception for me?"

"Umm, I can at least try. Can you tell me the nature of your business?"

"I have some important information to give them."

She playfully tapped my hand. "Now, Mr. Gavin, you're going to have to be just a teensy bit more specific than that."

"Okay then. Tell them my last name is Randall, and that the prodigal son and the ungrateful brother has come to visit."

She looked confused. "I'm sure they'd know if they had a family member coming to visit them."

I pulled out my identification. "I'm Gavin Randall, youngest son to Gerald Randall and baby brother to Gary Randall. It's a *surprise* visit."

She gasped. "Oh, my goodness! I didn't even pick up on the similarities. I'm so sorry, Mr. Gavin—I mean Randall," she stammered, jumping up. "Please. Follow me." She led me to the door of the conference room where they were located. "Just give me a moment."

I placed my hand on her shoulder. "Do me a favor and don't tell them who it is if you possibly can. Remember, it's a surprise visit."

She looked back at me and smiled. "For you, I'd try to pull any strings I could. I mean, sure I will try," she said, covering her face in embarrassment.

I winked at her. "Don't be ashamed. I'm not like my father or brother."

She smiled. "I can see and surely tell," she said as she took a deep breath and knocked on the door.

"Yes." I heard my dad answer.

"Mr. Randall, may I come in? It's extremely important."

"Come in."

She opened the door. "I know that you do not accept open appointments, but I have a man out here who urgently needs to see both you and Mr. Gary," she said nervously.

"Lindsey, you know we do not allow anyone without an appointment, and it's after three. Or did you forget the time?" my father chastised her smugly.

She took a beat before she continued. "I understand that sir, and no, I have not forgotten the hour. However, this man is stating it is imperative that he sees the both of you, and I think it's best if you acknowledge him."

"Lindsey, you are interrupting our daily day-end review session with this nonsense." My father began to fuss.

"Father, let it go. We can entertain whoever this is for five minutes. Obviously, if he was annoying enough to have Lindsey interrupt our session, then we should at least see who it is and find out what it is they want," Gary stated matter-of-factly.

My father huffed. "All right, we'll meet with him. He's got *two* minutes. Send him in," he stated arrogantly.

Lindsey closed the door, turned, and winked at me. "If you're free after five, perhaps you could hang around for drinks and dinner on me," she whispered.

"You're sweet, but I'm afraid I'll have to pass on that. I'm only in town for a little while, and then I have to get home to my fiancée."

She looked flushed and disappointed. "I'm sorry to hear that, but I can respect it. You are *definitely* not like your father and brother. Go on inside. They're waiting," she said sweetly.

I walked in the door, and both my father and brother stood up.

"Gavin, what a surprise," my father said.

Gary stared at the bag. "I hope you don't have any assault weapons in that bag."

I laughed. "Oh, dear brother, I could only wish. You know Randall security is airtight. It's my carry-on. I came here personally to visit you guys to tell you the news."

My father waved for me to take a seat. "I take that comment to mean you've gotten rid of her. Trust me, son, it's for your own good. I hope you see that since you can't beat us, you can join us. There's always an open spot for you here at Randall. It is your company, too, after all."

"As *unflattering* as that offer sounds, I'll have to pass."

"The term is *flattering*," Gary corrected.

"No, I said the term that I was looking for."

"You're bitter. Understandable. So, why are you here?" Gary asked.

"I'm glad you asked," I said, pulling out copies of the letter and the birth certificate, as well as the picture. "I've prayed and prayed and asked God to deliver me from this bind that you two had me in, and I have finally received my answer."

My father laughed. "How is that, son, when I pull all the strings?"

"But you don't hold all the cards," I said bluntly. "I have here in my possession a birth certificate for my mother—correction, *our* mother, Gary—along with a picture of our mother's parents, *our* grandparents, and a letter from *our* mother. I want you both to look at this." I handed it to them.

Gary took it and walked over to our dad. "Jerry and Lois Jennings," he read on the back of the picture. They both shrugged. "Okay, and?" he said, putting it down on the table. I picked it up as he looked at the next document. He read the names on the birth certificate out loud, but again, he and my father shrugged.

"Gavin, have you lost it? We know our grandparents' names. It's the first time I've seen the picture of Granddad, but what does this prove?" Gary asked.

"You were never the one to get all the facts. I guess you get that from your father. Too busy trying to rule the world instead of getting to know it. Read the race sections. It'll shed more light."

My father read out loud. "Mother, white. Father, Negro. *Negro*?" He yelled. "It can't be. There's no way in hell your mother is half jig. No way!"

Gary's mouth dropped, and he fell back in one of the chairs. "How can you be so sure, Dad? Did you investigate that, too? Take a blood test for her?"

"She's white! Strawberry blond hair and blue eyes are character traits of white people, not fucking blacks," my dad damn near screamed.

"You're right. She looks just like her mother. A white woman. But her father, Jerry Lee Jennings—*our* grandfather—is one hundred percent black. You had two sons by a biracial woman, Father. Gary and I are one-quarter black, or *Negro,* as the certificate says."

Gary snatched the picture out of my hands and stared it before he let it slip back on the conference table. I retrieved it, and Gary put his head on the conference room table.

"Oh my God. It's true. I could see it in the picture. He has a light complexion, but he's black," he said.

"Read the letter," I told Gary.

Gary lifted his head, then slowly picked up the letter and read it silently as my dad paced the floor, looking like he was on the edge of insanity. By the time Gary finished, his eyes were filled with tears.

"What does it say?" my father yelled at Gary.

"Here. Read it for yourself," Gary said, choking back tears.

"No! You read it aloud," my father demanded.

Gary sighed, cleared his throat, and read the letter aloud for all of us to hear.

"Bullshit! This is a complete fabrication. Damned mendacity," my father yelled as he knocked over one of the chairs. "You probably made this up to try to clear your ass. These are copies. None of it is original."

"The picture is the original, *Father*, but I figured that General Custer would try to take his last stand, so I came prepared." I pulled out the original letter and birth certificate and placed them on the table. I held it firmly so neither of them could pick it up and destroy it. "See for yourself."

He and Gary peered at the original documents, and it looked as if my father's heart was about to stop beating right then and there. He grabbed his chest and fell into a chair. Then he jumped up and opened one of the hidden panels in the wall and poured himself a shot, swallowing it in one gulp. He poured another and pulled a cigar from his stash and sat back down.

"How long have you known?" Gary managed to ask.

"Just today. Do you think I would've hesitated one moment to spring this on you two over all these years? Mom gave me a box of mementos, and fate decided that I should go through it today."

My father jumped up. "You fucking bastard! You would do this just to try to bring me down? After all I've done for your . . . your—"

"*Black* ass?" I asked, finishing his sentence. "Well, Father, you no longer have to worry about my black ass anymore. Take my portion of the shares back, and we'll call it even, but what you are not going to do is bother LaMeka, any member of her family, me, or my unborn child. I'm going to marry her, and you're not going to interfere with that ever in life. Not unless you want your business associates, your buddies at the country club, and the rest of the Randall family to know that you fucked up your pure white bloodline by screwing and having babies with a biracial woman. I mean, the choice is yours. Hell, why not make it public? Forget TMZ and Twitter. Let's just take it straight to CNN."

"No. No," my father said, puffing on his cigar. "Fine. You win. Don't release this information," he said, sounding defeated as I folded the originals and placed them back inside my jacket pocket. "But that still doesn't mean I can't require you to pay me back, you fucker. I'll have your ass in so much financial debt that you couldn't provide a decent life for your new wife and family. You'll be nothing more than a bunch of ghetto birds living and hanging in the ghetto projects where you belong."

"Go ahead. I'll pay you back in installments. As for my financial situation, it doesn't matter because I trust that God will make a way for us. He made a way out of *this* after all."

My father was about to speak when Gary put up his hand and cut him off. He turned to face him. "You are truly one stone-cold-hearted bastard. Do you know that?"

"Gary?" my father asked in shock.

And he wasn't the only one who was shocked. During our entire exchange, Gary had been in silent contemplation as he observed me and Gerald interacting. I thought he'd been too stunned and outdone to speak, but apparently, he'd developed a few choice words for dear old Dad.

"If you could *still* feel that way about Gavin, *your baby son*, because of the news that we both have another ethnicity in our blood, then what do you think of me?" Gary asked.

Gerald's mouth dropped, and he coughed anxiously. "You're still *you*. I mean, you're *Gary*. I won't even think that way about you. You're a Randall. You're cut from my cloth," he stammered.

Gary stood and popped his suit jacket before he buttoned it. Slowly, he rounded the table and stood in Gerald's space, staring him eye to eye. "And every day, you'll grow to resent me because of the black blood that runs through my veins. I can hear it in your voice. You've already started to resent me. You already hate Gavin for accepting the truth."

The flinch in Gerald's eyes and the scowl on his face said all we needed to know. "What are you saying?" he asked tensely.

Gary's stare matched his. "For so long, I've admired you and stood by you, even when I knew you were wrong, because you were my father, and I wanted so much to be accepted by you. I allowed you to rip me from my mother and my brother for the promise of riches and power, believing your lie that she chose a life of poverty rather than the truth that she simply wanted us to grow up as wholesome humans. But knowing how you truly treated my mother and hearing you prove it in the way you just spoke to Gavin did something to me. It gave me an epiphany.

"I'm tired of being the devil's advocate. You are right about one thing. We are who we are, and that is Randall men. But we also have the blood of both a white and black man running through us. That doesn't change us. It never will. It shouldn't change your perception of us either. To love me is to love all of me, and for first time, I realize that the only people who have ever and would ever love me unconditionally are my mother and Gavin."

Gerald stepped more into his space, with his finger boldly pointed in his face. "Now, you listen to me. I've afforded you more privileges, power, money, and opportunities than ninety-nine percent of America will ever see. You will not speak to me in that manner, and what you will do is *shut up and sit your black ass down*," he screamed at Gary.

Gary scoffed and stepped back, wagging his finger. "And there it is. My black ass." Gary laughed. "Well, let me show you what my black ass is going to do." Gary walked over to me, placing a hand on my shoulder. "Gavin, I'm so sorry. I hope that one day you can forgive me. You've been more of a brother to me than I ever realized."

I hugged him, and he embraced me back. "I forgive you, and I love you. You'll always be my brother."

He pulled back and patted me on the shoulders. "And I'm going to be a brother to you starting right now," he said and then faced our father. "Gavin doesn't have to worry about paying you back."

Gerald stared menacingly at Gary. "Who in the hell gave you the authority to make that decision?"

"No one," he said, pulling his checkbook out of his back pocket. He wrote a check for $500,000 and put in the memo section: *On behalf of Gavin Randall, repayment to Gerald Randall.*

"Here. This is your payment from Gavin." He handed him the check.

"You can't do that," my father said in disbelief.

"Yes, I can, and I will. It's my money, and if you don't accept it, I have a carbon copy that proves he tried to repay you, and you wouldn't accept it, therefore declaring him free and clear of any legal obligation of repayment to you," Gary said to him.

My father swallowed hard. "Gary, how could you do this to me? I was there for you."

"Oh, please. Your loyalty is to your name, power, and money. I was nothing more than a pawn to carry on your legacy. I see that now."

My father stood up and buttoned his suit jacket. "Fine then. If you want to side with your brother in this foolishness, I have no choice but to cut you off, too. The consequences are grave for disloyalty, son, and I'm about to teach you a lesson. You're both cut out of my will. Also, Gary, you're fired, and you have to repay me every cent of the profit you've spent off of your shares, too."

Gary laughed and winked at me. "Watch me work." He turned back to our father. "As for your will, well, I couldn't care less about that. That doesn't matter. But here's what does, *Father*. You can't fire me. Last year, you agreed to the CEO position as an overseer. As acting CEO and President, *I* have the authority in the company. While I don't exercise my power because I still allow you to make the decisions, I would like to politely remind you that on paper and in the court of law, I am the man."

He waved off Gary. "I'll just get my lawyers to say it was coercion or something so that it won't stand up in court."

"And I will just turn over your financials to the courts, too. Your *real* records. The ones that you signed off on as overseer that do not contain my signature. The ones that can implicate you in certain instances of insider trading and trading from your personal offshore account to lower the stock price of certain companies who refused to help Randall out during its financial crisis four years ago. I do believe that both are a direct violation of the Securities Exchange Act. Federal time. If you want to go to war with me, Father, we can do that. The difference between you and me is that I will bring this company to its knees before I ever allow you to win, and you would never risk losing your name, stature, and position to follow through with this little game. Sorry to bitch slap you, old man, but who's your daddy now?" Gary said snidely to him.

Damn! Gary was more on point than I thought. To hell with Randall. That was that Jennings blood shining through, and I couldn't do anything but have major love for it. It was the first time in my life that I even had a little fear of Gary. All this time I had thought he was just being our father's bitch, but in essence, he was creating one—our father. I don't think it was ever his intent to play his cards this way, but rather, he stacked his deck just in case he ever had to. Who knew it would come to fruition?

"You sneaky, conniving little son of a bitch," Gerald said in disbelief.

Gary walked over and patted him on the arm. "Don't get mad, Father. I'm just being the best Randall man that you trained me to be. Sit back and enjoy the fruits of your labor," Gary said, picking up a cigar. "Our business will continue as usual, but you will leave Gavin and LaMeka alone. Besides, we have a new addition to the family to welcome in a few months."

After what seemed like an hour-long pause, our father looked at us and laughed. "The goose finally gets his gander. Ahh. I truly hate the both of you," he said. "But my name and reputation mean more to me than a long-time war with either of you. Gavin, go ahead and be with that woman. Just don't ever expect me to be a part of that *tribe*."

"Oh, Father, not only would I not expect you to be a part of my family, but I also don't want you to. My child will not grow up to hate him or herself on account of you. However, what I will need is a statement in writing from both you and Gary, acknowledging your agreement. Sorry, bro, but business is still business. As a Randall man, you do understand, right?" I asked, looking at Gary.

"Indeed. I'll type up the statement right now," he said, going to sit at his laptop.

Soon, the statement was typed and printed, and both Gary and my father signed, albeit my father did it begrudgingly. My father stared out of the window as Gary walked me out of the conference room.

Concerned for Gary, I asked, "Are you sure you're going to be all right? He's a shark, and he's just aiming to attack you."

"He trained me to be better than him. I'm always ten steps and twenty ideas ahead of him, even when he thinks I'm not. I hate to admit it, but when it comes to this, I am truly cut from his cloth. Right now, he's probably trying to think of some other groups who have voting rights in the company, but all the ones who do are the children of the parents that he was friends with. They have their loyalties to me for saving their asses. You know, getting a DUI charge dropped here or getting the old man to provide them with insider trading information there. I'm a Randall. What can I say?"

"Nah, man. You're a Jennings."

He laughed. "True," he said and bumped my shoulder. "I can never make it up to you about all the awful things I've said and done to you and

LaMeka, but there is something I want to do that I feel is only right."

"What's that?"

"Mom left me a quarter million–dollar life insurance policy that I never cashed. I never wanted to because I turned my back on her so long ago. I felt guilty for ever taking money from her in her death. I'm going to sign it over to you and LaMeka. Consider it an early wedding present or college fund from me."

"You don't have to do that."

He put his hand up. "I know I don't have to, but I want to. Let me have this moment, please."

For a moment, I considered what he was truly asking of me. It was his way of making up for all the hell he'd not only put me through, but our mother. He needed redemption. If his soul felt this was how to make it right, then who was I stand in the way?

"Well, far be it from me to turn down free-with-no-strings-attached money."

"Good. I'll have the paperwork over to you in a few days. So, how long are you here for?"

"Another hour. I have to get going so I can hail a cab to the airport. I have a flight to catch."

"Our limo service will take you," he said. "I'll have Lindsey call them. You have a safe flight back, and hopefully one day, I might get to see my niece or nephew." He hugged me again.

"My door is always open. You decide when you want to come through it."

He had Lindsey get the limo, and by the time I got downstairs, they were waiting to take me to the airport. I couldn't wait to board the plane and get back to LaMeka. I had so much to share with her.

The few times on the plane that I nodded off, I jumped up feeling for the proof and the statement, which were still tucked away in my inside jacket pocket. I wasn't going to sleep until I did two things: show LaMeka the good news and put this good news in my safe deposit box at the bank. There was no way I was going to allow this information to stay at my house for it to magically disappear. I was a Randall man, too, and I knew my father was not above setting up a break-in just to get back at me. He just wasn't smart enough to realize that I thought like him.

The moment I landed at the airport and got my car, I headed straight to LaMeka's house. It took everything in me to obey the traffic laws. I didn't need anything getting in my way of getting to her. I was tired and completely drained, but I pushed all of that to the back of my mind because a bigger issue was at hand. It was time to get my family back.

As I walked up the steps, I said a silent prayer and rang the doorbell. Misha answered.

"I figured it'd be you," she said. "Come in."

"Where is she?" I asked.

"In the family room, watching television with Mom and the boys," Misha answered. "I must warn you that it's not going to be easy. She's still highly pissed and extremely hurt. Do you have what you need?"

"Yes." I patted my jacket. "Right here. In fact, I'd like you and your mother to stay while I speak with Meka. You all need to hear this, and I need all the help I can get."

Misha sighed. "No truer words have ever been spoken. Come on." She led the way.

"Meka, you have a visitor," Misha called out as I entered the room.

She looked back at me and turned back. "I don't know that man. Since you let him in, you can get him out of my house *now*."

Misha looked at me. "I told you."

I looked at her mom. "Hi, Ms. Barbara."

She smiled at me. "Hey, Gavin," she said as the boys ran over to me and hugged me.

"Gavin!" they yelled.

"Hey, boys," I hugged them tightly. "I've missed you guys so much."

"Boys!" Meka yelled. "Go to your room."

Without hesitation, they headed out, stalking to their bedroom.

"Was that really necessary?" Ms. Barbara said to Meka.

"They don't need to reattach themselves to someone who is no longer in our lives. Do I have to remind you that you're my mother, not his?" Meka said angrily.

Ms. Barbara threw up her hands. "Gavin, do you need some privacy with her?" she asked with an attitude.

"No, he needs to be gone," Meka yelled.

"You all have a baby together, Meka, damn!" her mother yelled and covered her mouth. "I'm sorry."

Meka shrugged. "It doesn't matter if he knows or not. He's a non-muthafucking-factor now." She glared angrily at me.

"Meka, that is my child, too. I want to be a part of his or her life—both of y'all's lives. All of y'all's lives."

"Really? So, um, how do you suppose we do that? Live under a rock? I'm not putting my family at risk for your emotions, and you damn sure can't protect us."

"That's why I'm here. I can."

She threw her hands up and stormed up to me, pushing and hitting me. "*Get out! Get out!* I've heard enough lies outta you. There's nothing you can do. You are a liar, Gavin Randall, and I do not have time for your fake-ass promises. Get out before I fuck you up," she screamed as her mom and sister pulled her back.

I put my hand up. "It's okay. That much I deserved."

"Ugh! Why are you here?" Meka yelled so loud it shook the pictures. Then she grabbed her stomach. "Ow! Ugh!" She winced, and I ran to her aid.

"Baby, stop this. You're going to make you and the baby sick."

"She's been so depressed lately that the doctor has already put her on strict bed rest for six weeks," her mother said. "Meka, calm down before you cause harm to this child!"

"Thank you, Mother, for telling *all* of my business," Meka said sarcastically as she sat back on the sofa and took deep breaths.

I sat down beside her. "Baby, even if you don't accept me back, don't put your health or the baby's at risk over this. All I'm asking is that you just listen to what I have to say. Please. You can hate me later if you choose. Just don't do this to yourself or the baby."

She exhaled, exhausted from the flurry of action. "I don't even have the energy to argue with you. Make it quick, Gavin," she said as Misha brought her a bottle of water. She took a sip and looked at me. "Seriously, I can't be calm while you're here, so be quick about this so you can leave."

I took her hand, and surprisingly, she didn't snatch away from me. "I apologize for not telling you the truth about my dad's plans before. I always thought I would come up with some way to get out of his scheme without losing you. I'm sorry that it made you feel that I was selling you a fake dream. I just wanted to spend as much time with you as I could while I could." I caressed her hand.

She looked away from me. "Get on with it."

"But I'm free and clear of my father for good, and I have the proof. There's something that you all need to know about me that I just found out this morning," I said as I pulled out the picture, birth certificate, letter, and statement. "You remember the box of mementos that you always told me that I should go through?"

"The ones your mother left you?" Meka asked me. I nodded. "Yeah. What does that have to do with anything?"

"Everything. Baby, I should've listened to you long ago. The box fell as I was preparing to do something very stupid, and when I looked, I found something that halted my crazy decision."

LaMeka eyed me in disbelief. "Do not tell me you went for that gun?"

My face was a stone. "Do you see me laughing right now? Woman, do you not know how much I love you? I am prepared to do whatever it takes for you, to have you, to protect you, and to love you. You and my seed." I rubbed my hand across her stomach.

Tears dropped from her eyes, and she wiped them quickly. "Umm, go ahead with your story," she said, getting emotional.

"Anyway, I found this," I showed her the picture.

"Who is this?" she asked as her mom and Misha looked on.

"That is Jerry and Lois Jennings. My grandparents. My mother's parents."

She shrugged. "Okay. You finally have a picture of your grandfather."

"Then there's this. Pay attention the names and the boxes right beside the names." I handed her the birth certificate. "Go ahead. Read it aloud."

Reluctantly taking the paper out of my hand, she rolled her eyes in aggravation. "Certificate of Live Birth. Child: Diana Laurie Jennings. That's your mother. Okay, so this is her birth certificate," she said aloud.

I nodded. "Just keep reading."

She huffed, then continued. "Mother: Lois Zimmer Jennings, and the box beside it says the ethnicity is white. Okay, moving on to the father, it says Jerry Lee Jennings, and the ethnicity box says he is Negro." She stopped and looked at me. Then she looked back at the birth certificate. "Wait a minute!"

"He's black?" Meka, Misha, and her mother said together as they all looked back at the photo of my grandfather.

"Yep, he's got a light complexion, but he's black."

"Wait a minute. So your mother, the blond-head and blue-eyed lady you have in your wallet is biracial?" Meka asked.

I nodded. "Yep. She is. She took all of my grandmother's features."

"So that means you're one-quarter black?" Misha asked, though it came off as more of a statement. "Damn it, man. I knew you had some black in you somewhere."

"That's not all. Here's a letter that my mom wrote to me." I gave it to Meka, and she read the letter aloud.

She gasped and covered her mouth. "Oh my God! So, you never knew this, and neither did your brother or father?"

"Nope. Not at all."

Misha snapped her fingers. "That's why you left. To tell them," she blurted as LaMeka looked over at her. "I mean, I'm guessing you told them," she stammered.

"Mm-hmm. Whatever. I know you can't hold water, Misha. Save it. You and Gavin have always been two peas in a pod," LaMeka said.

"I simply can't believe this. Talk about family secrets. Oh my gosh, Gavin. So, did you tell your father and brother?" Ms. Barbara asked.

"Did I? In fact, I have a statement that my brother personally typed up, stating that they will not interfere with our relationship or bring unjust harm either physically, mentally, or financially to me or Meka and our family. They both signed it," I said, giving Meka the statement. "Apparently, it's better for my father to keep up his reputation than to interfere with us."

Meka gasped. "Gavin, is this for real? Like, seriously for real?"

"Yes. Not only is it for real. It gets better. My brother turned on my dad today after he found out how my dad truly treated my mother, and well, of course, after finding out he was part of a black man himself. I couldn't have dreamt up a better ending. I only wish you had been there to see it all unfold."

Shaking her head with confusion, she flailed her hands. "So, how do things stand with you, your dad, and your brother?" Meka asked me.

"Gerald is caught between a rock and hard place. He still doesn't care for our arrangement, but he has no choice, and Gary has him in a bind with the business so he can't retaliate. Surprisingly, Gary and I were able to talk for a minute, and he apologized to me and you," I explained, and then I whispered in her ear so that no one could hear. "He even turned over his life insurance policy my mom left him. He said it's for our wedding or a college fund for the baby."

Meka simply nodded to let me know that she'd heard me, and then laughed. "This is surreal."

"It feels that way, but I promise you, it is very real."

Ms. Barbara hit Misha. "This is our cue. Let's give these two some alone time." They both hugged me and walked out to give us a moment.

I knew this was my time to shine. It was now or never in order to win Meka's heart back. It was all good sharing the news, but it was all for nothing if I couldn't have my lady back in my life. I'd never been more nervous in my life when I turned to face her. Yet, by the grace of God, I found the courage to try.

I looked at Meka and held her hands. "You know I'd never do anything to intentionally hurt you. When you found out, a part of me died, and when I thought you killed our baby, I was ready to die. Meka, without you in my life, I'm just a shell of a man moving from one day to the next, existing but not living. I want to live, and I want to live with you. Hell, I feel like I need you to live. You, the boys, our baby, you all are my life. I just want my life back. I love you."

Meka shed the tears she had tried so hard to hide.

"Don't cry, baby," I said, wiping her tears away.

We sat in our emotions for a long time. I didn't rush her or push her. I wanted to be fair and give her the time to process her thoughts, her feelings, and her answer, even if a part of me slowly died on the inside.

"It's just that I love you, too, Gavin. I know that you went through all this trouble to get this proof and settle this, but I'm so afraid still. Who's to say that your father won't think of some way to get back at us? Then I don't know if I believe in you to protect us the way you say you can. I've heard this before, and I still ended up without you."

"No, you can choose to end up with me. If you had never found out—"

"We would still be in the same position. You would've left me."

"And I would've went off the deep end to plot against my family, read the mementos, and we would still be here in the same place—me with proof that they will leave us alone and you choosing whether or not to give me one last chance. Don't you see that no matter what happens, we always end up back together?

"We pray every day, go to church, and believe in God. Where is your faith, Meka? Don't put it in me. Put it in God that He'll take care of us. I have. He's brought us this far. What further proof do you need?" I was shocked by my own words. I'd never intended to say those things, but it was as if God Himself took over my mouth, and out it flowed. I prayed it would be enough.

She stood up and walked to the bay window and sat down on the ledge. She stared out of it for a few moments, and then I got up and walked over to her. There was nothing else left to say. I'd put it all out there on the line. The ball was in her court. Whatever she decided was what would be. I wouldn't force the issue anymore if she chose not to be with me because after putting it out on the line like that, I'd finally come to terms that I could make peace with whatever decision she made. I'd take care of her and my child regardless. That was my word.

She looked back at me and stood up. "I never thought that I would say this to you, especially after you didn't tell me about your father's threats, but you are right. I pray every day, and yet I still haven't learned where to put my faith. I thank you for reminding me of that. I *needed* to hear that. You see, I've been praying for guidance, answers, and understanding, and I didn't realize that God would send all of that through you. The choice is clear, and I choose to trust God," she said as she walked up to me and held my hands. "I'm going to trust God that you are meant to be my husband, but you have to put forth the effort to get there."

I smiled at her and gently pulled her to me by the waist. "What does that mean?"

She wrapped her arms around my neck and stared me directly in the eyes. "It means that you have a lot of making up to do. You are at my every beck and call. I figure that you can start with nightly body massages, which means you'd have to stay here every night, and since I'm starting to have cravings, it means two a.m. runs for some Ben and Jerry's. Perhaps a little girls' vacation weekend paid for by you for me, Lucinda, Misha, and my mother is in order, too."

"Wow. All of that, huh?" I chuckled.

"Yep. All of that. And there's *plenty* more where that came from."

"Am I doing all of this as your baby's daddy, or as your man?"

"Neither."

I furrowed my brow. "Neither?"

She nodded her head. "Yes. I said neither. You are doing all of that as my fiancé."

I smiled and hugged her tightly. "I love you so much, baby."

She pulled back. "I love you, too, but you're not my fiancé yet."

"Huh? But you just said—"

"I need the ring back first. Then, it'll be official."

"Oh, don't think I didn't come prepared. I've carried this thing with me everywhere I went, just waiting for this moment to happen." I pulled the ring out of my inside jacket pocket and kneeled on one knee. "LaMeka Roberts, will you do me the honor of becoming my wife?"

She rubbed her thumb across my cheek. "I'd love nothing more than to be Mrs. Gavin Randall."

I slipped the ring back on her finger. "It's right where it belongs." I stood up and passionately kissed my future bride.

In the background, we heard a thunderous applause and yelps. LaMeka and I began laughing.

"Oh, come on in and celebrate with us, you nosy heifers," LaMeka yelled to her mom and sister.

"This calls for a drink," her mom said in excitement. "Well, at least for Gavin and me. Misha is underage, and Meka is with child."

I put my hand up. "Actually, Momma, you can have the drink by yourself. I'm cutting that out. It's time to make some changes in my life. I have to set a better example for my sons and my baby." I rubbed Meka's belly.

Ms. Barbara smiled. "Well, all right then. That'll be a glass of Riesling for me, some Sprite for you and Misha, and some good old-fashioned H2O for Meka coming right up."

Misha hugged me. "Welcome back, bro-in-law."

"Good to be back," I said as I kneeled and kissed Meka's belly. "And Daddy's not going anywhere anymore."

Meka held the back of my head and smiled down at me. "That's right, baby. He's definitely not," she confirmed.

I hugged her about her waist and silently thanked God for my answered prayers. I could finally rest easy because I, Gavin Randall, had my family back. Nothing could ever feel better than that.

Chapter 24

Mike

That's right. That nigga Babyface was crooning. *Yes. As soon as I get home from work, I'll make Lucinda's dinner, pay the mortgage, and buy her clothes, and anything else she wants. Hell yeah,* I thought as I cruised down the crowded Atlanta streets. I could feel the hell outta this song and thousands of others like it. When you have a good woman on your side that loves you, you'd do anything to keep her.

I was in a great mood. I had my lady, and we were a family. What could be any greater than that? Sure. I'd done some dirt to ensure that I got to that point, but all was fair in love and war. That was my motto. I'd created a war for Lucinda because of my love for her, and I'd won. Plain and simple. I had to laugh to myself at times. Aldris was completely insane to let her slip through his fingers. Once Lucinda opened to me, it was a whole new world between us, and when she told me she loved me, I knew it was "adios Aldris" for good.

Being in love with Lucinda and having her love me back was just like experiencing my first kiss again. It was magical. We were magic together. I'd never thought I'd be in this place in my life. In love. Sure, I had love for my babies' mother, but there was never a time when I was in love with her. Hell, the love I had for her now was solely because of my kids. I respected their mother because she gave me the greatest gift in the world, a legacy. Other than that, she could've kicked rocks with all the hell she put me through. There was only one woman who was ever worth any of my time, aggravation, headaches, and heartaches, and that was Ms. Rojas.

I was so ready to be with this woman that I was committed to 24/7 Lucinda. I swear, I'd tried a billion times to get her to sell her place and move in with me. She wouldn't do it until after the wedding, which was officially four months away. Our wedding invitations were going to be sent out that day. Then I could breathe a little easier because it would be official to everyone we knew, and there would be no turning back from there. If she didn't have a dream of walking down the aisle, I would have taken her to the courthouse and done the damn thang that day. In fact, I would've done it the day I proposed. I was *that* ready.

Ah! Just the thought of her brightened my day. I had a picture of her on the dash of my SUV, in my wallet, and as my wallpaper on my cell phone. Everywhere I went, she was with me. It eased the pain of not being able to physically have her with me at work or when she stayed at her own condo. It also eased the pain of having to share her with her parents, siblings, and LaMeka. Like now. She was out trying to help Meka cope with the situation about Gavin, but it didn't matter because in a half hour, I was meeting her at a Chinese restaurant to share lunch with her. Then it would be my time.

It was also perfect timing. It gave me time to meet up with Jennifer before Lucinda got there. I needed to find out what in the hell she wanted with me. I'd already told her that Aldris was her responsibility. How many more memos did she need before she got that? But at any rate, I was gonna meet up with her, feed her some bullshit to keep her off my back, and have her kick rocks so I could have lunch with the future Mrs. Michael Johnson.

I walked into the restaurant and spotted Jennifer. Before I walked over, I decided to call Lucinda. I needed to make sure she was still far enough away to keep her from bumping into Jennifer and me. I could never be too careful.

"Hey, baby," I sang as she answered her cell.

"Hey, you."

"Um, so are we still on for lunch?"

"But of course," she answered.

"Are you still with Meka?"

"Yeah. I should be at the restaurant in another fifteen minutes, so if you beat me there, just grab a seat, and I'll be on my way in a little bit."

"All right, baby. I'll do that. I'll see you in a bit."

"All right. See you in about fifteen."

"I love you."

"Love you, too."

Good. Now I can give this broad five minutes of my time and get rid of her before my lady gets here. By the time Lu arrives, she should be long gone.

I approached Jennifer. She looked irritated when I walked up.

"You finally made it. What took you so damn long?" she snapped.

"I'm only a couple of minutes late."

"Five minutes to be exact, and if you give someone a damn time to meet you, the least you can do is be on time."

I looked at her as if she were crazy. "Me? You're the one who texted me and asked me to meet you here."

She laughed. "You must be losing it, or does that Spanish pussy have you going loco? *You* texted *me* and told me to meet you here."

I pulled out my phone. This bitch was going crazy. I pulled up her text message and showed it to her. "Is this not your damn phone number? And your text?"

She looked confused. "It is, but—"

"Thank you." I cut her off.

"No. I'm saying it's my phone number, but I didn't send that to you." She pulled out her cell phone. "See. Look." She showed me a text from my cell phone, asking her to meet me at the same time, place, and date to finish our email discussion about Lu and Aldris.

I shook my head. "That's not possible because I never sent that to you."

She looked at me. "Well, if I didn't send it to you and you didn't send it to me, who in the hell sent these messages?"

Before we had a chance to comprehend what was going on, Aldris and Lucinda appeared next to us from somewhere straight out of the cut. What the fuck was going on?

"Fancy seeing you two here together," Lucinda said snidely.

Aldris looked at her. "Actually, Lu, it's not being that we sent the text messages, right?"

Lucinda snapped her fingers. "Oh, yeah. That's right. We did, didn't we?"

"What the fuck is going on?" Jennifer asked.

"We would ask you two the same fucking question, but we already know," Aldris answered as Lucinda pulled out some paper.

"Should I do the honors, or do you want to?" Lucinda asked Aldris.

"You do it, baby," Aldris said.

"Okay then." She giggled. "I love it when you call me baby," she said as she set the papers on the table in front of Jennifer and me.

We both peered down at them because frankly, I was so shocked I didn't know what the fuck else to do. Immediately, my heart sank. It was a copy of the emails that Jennifer and I had recently sent back and forth to each other. Jennifer's face looked like a bomb had just exploded, and she gasped for air.

"Aldris, I can explain—"

"No need. You're nothing but a scandalous bitch, and that pretty much sums it up. I just want you to know that I know, and now that I know, I feel so much better because I'm secure in my decision not to be with you anymore. Something didn't feel right about us, and now I know what it was besides the fact that I don't even love you," Aldris spewed. Jennifer threw her face in her hands and cried.

Lucinda crossed her arms as she peered at me with disgust. I stood up and tried to grab her hands. She snatched away from me. "Baby, please let me explain. You know I never would've agreed to it. I

really didn't do anything. It was all Jennifer's idea,"
I rambled, throwing Jennifer under the bus.

Lucinda put her hand up to stop me from
talking. "You are so tired. You truly disgust me. I
can't believe I allowed myself to get suckered by
you. So, how long have you plotting this? Hmm?
Since Nadia's party? Or maybe ever since you saw
me in the grocery store? The sad part about it is
that it doesn't even matter. You could've had me
without the games. You chose to play them, and
you played yourself."

My world was falling apart. I couldn't believe
what was happening. I loved her. We were going to
get married. I couldn't lose her now.

Begging was my only option at this point, so I
fell to one knee. "Please, Lu. Don't give up on us. I
know how it looks, and I'm so sorry that I allowed
myself to get sucked into this game, but how we
feel about each other is real. I love you, and I know
you love me. Don't throw that away. I'll spend the
rest of my life making it up to you. Just don't leave
me."

Out of nowhere, Jennifer followed suit. She
got down on her knees beside me. "Aldris, I'm so
sorry. I am. I just loved you so much. Mike has
Lu, and you have me. He's right. This is the way
it's supposed to be. Please, let's move on, and I'll
spend the rest of my life making it up to you," she
begged.

"Damn. You two are *really* partners in mutha-fucking crime until the end." Aldris chuckled. "You can save it, Jennifer. I'm already done with you. You can keep the ring as a consolation gift, and you, Mike, I must admit I like seeing you grovel like the grimy muthafucka you are, but this is too much even for you..I've known you all my life. You were my brother, but it only goes to show that you ain't shit but another nigga," he spewed as Jennifer got up and ran out of the restaurant in tears.

"Fuck you, Aldris," I said, my focus still on Lucinda. "Baby, please. I'm begging you. Please."

Lucinda reached in her pocket and placed my ring on the table. "Go to hell. Since your loyalty was to Jennifer, give her this piece-of-shit ring and kiss my ass. At least when Aldris was wrong, I could count on him to be one hundred percent *real* about it. So, I have some realness for you. My head is clear, and so is my heart, and I'm giving it back to Aldris where it belongs. And this time, it's for good. Besides, all is fair in love and war, isn't that *your* motto?" she said with an attitude as she took Aldris's hand, interlocked fingers with him, and turned and walked away.

"Lucinda!" I continued to call out for her despite the fact that the people in the restaurant stared at me as if I were crazy. "Lucinda, please. I'm sorry!"

It was no use. They kept walking right out of the restaurant.

I plopped back down in the booth, staring at the ring, and rubbed my head, not believing what had just happened. I was so in shock that I didn't even realize tears were rolling down my face until I saw the droplets hitting the table. Lucinda was gone. Karma had come back to slap both me and Jennifer in the face. What was I supposed to do now?

Just then, my cell phone buzzed, and I clicked on the screen.

It was a text from Aldris. It didn't have any words, but once I opened it up, it played the song "The Big Payback" by James Brown. I slammed my phone down on the table as the waitress walked over to me.

"You buy buffet?" the Chinese lady asked, smiling.

"Kiss my ass," I said, storming out of the restaurant.

Chapter 25

Terrence

For three days, I'd been sitting in the same chair, in the same room in the hospital, waiting for Thomas to wake up. His dried blood still stained my shirt and pants. He'd survived two emergency surgeries for complications due to hemorrhaging. Amazingly, he was in serious yet stable condition.

I couldn't help but feel like it was my fault. I should've let him do Pooch in like he wanted. Or maybe if I had found another way to deescalate our situation, he would've never been outside to take those shots, which I knew were meant for me. Nobody rolls up to your house and shoots a guest. That's not even logical. That fucking Pooch tried to deliver on his promise to take me out, and I swore on my cousin's life that he would not get a second chance.

I'd had a couple of my friends on the police force escort Trinity back to the house the first night

Thomas was in the hospital. I asked her to gather as many things as she could for her and the kids so they could move into our condo. There was no way I could stay at the hospital knowing that killers knew where my house was and could possibly come back. I even had her move her mother into the condo with them. I couldn't be too careful. Surely, if they knew my main residence, they knew, or at the very least, had tried to locate Trinity's mother's residence. I had security surrounding my family as they traveled to school or to the art gallery. Hell, even to the grocery store. As long as my family was safe, I could be contained. Yes, I said *contained*, not *content*.

Personally, I didn't have to worry about protection. There was a twenty-four-hour surveillance team set up outside of Thomas's room. Good. He needed it. Besides protection for Thomas and me, it kept me from leaving the hospital room, going to that prison, and firing off a round dead in Pooch's cranium. Like I said, it kept me *contained*. Still, even containment couldn't stop me from pondering everything I'd been put through because of Pooch. Not only me, but Trinity and my kids. The more I mulled over the situation, the more I wondered why I hadn't killed that muthafucka from the jump. He'd been walking around on a ticking time clock, and the way I felt, it was just about time for that muthafucka to expire.

"Any change?" I heard Trinity's voice as she broke my thoughts. I didn't even realize she'd come into the room.

I looked up at her. "No."

She sat down beside me and rubbed slow circles on my back. "Baby, this isn't healthy. You need to go home. You need to go take a shower, change out of these three-day-old clothes, and rest. You're not going to be any good for Thomas like this. You're exhausted."

"I have to make sure he wakes up. It's my fault he's in here. When he wakes up, I'll rest." I clasped my hands together and rocked back and forth.

She grabbed my chin and forced me to look at her. "Listen to me. This is not your fault. The person who pulled the trigger and the person who ordered the hit are the people to blame for this. I will not let you carry this burden on your shoulders. I will not let you do that to yourself."

"No. It's my fault. If I hadn't kicked him out, then he wouldn't be here. I'd already kicked his ass. I should've made sure he was okay." I put my head down, feeling defeated.

"Dreads, baby, listen to me. What good would've come of that? The people probably would've stormed the house with us and the kids in the house. What potentially could've happened then? I'm not saying that anybody should've gotten shot. I definitely don't want Thomas laying up in here like this despite his feelings about me, but I'm just telling you that it could've been worse. I know it seems harsh to say, but we must look at the blessing in the storm. Focus on that. That will pull you through this, and it will give you the hope to help pull him through."

Before I could respond to her, we heard a commotion outside the door. I immediately jumped up and pushed Trinity behind me. "Get down."

"I'm going inside," we heard a female's voice say. Soon, Charice walked through the door. "You better get this police officer out here, Terrence. He better recognize who I am," she said with an attitude.

I breathed a sigh of relief. "Officer Dunn, she's cool, man. She's our cousin."

He looked at me sternly. "You know we need to keep traffic to a minimum until we find out who Thomas's shooter is."

My temper flared slightly at his attitude. "I *said* she's cool. She came all the way from New York."

"You should've informed me."

Charice stomped her foot and directed her tirade to the officer. "Do I really look like I'm packing? Seriously. The man just told you I'm family. Besides, I didn't tell them I was coming, I just came. That's what real family does. Or do you not know that?"

Trinity walked over to her and hugged her. "Thank you so much for coming. I need you so bad. We both do," she said, her voice quivering from emotion.

Charice hugged her tightly. "I need you, too, honey, and after everything that's going on down here, there's no way I could stay away."

I looked at Officer Dunn. "See? Besides, she's Ryan Westmore's wife." I threw that out there just because I knew he'd leave her alone after hearing that.

Despite their breakup, The Prodigy was still one of every football fan's favorite players.

"Ex-wife," Charice corrected me.

Officer Dunn smiled. "Oh. I'm sorry, Mrs. Westmore. I didn't realize—"

Charice gave him the evil eye because she knew he was only being nice now that he knew she'd been married to Ryan. "It's Taylor now, and I know you didn't realize. Can you give us some space and privacy, please?"

He put his hands up, backing out of the room. "Sure. Not a problem."

Charice walked over to me. "Damn asshole 'bout to make me bring all the hood outta my black ass. How are you holding up, T?"

"I'm holding. Just waiting for Thomas to wake up. Since when did you get slick at the mouth?"

"Being married to Ryan and dealing with the foolishness I've endured over the last couple of years changes you. Believe that. I ain't the same Charice I used to be."

"I see." I shook my head in disbelief.

"I'm trying to get my husband to go home for a little while," Trinity said, coming to sit beside me again.

Charice looked me up and down. "And I certainly agree. Terrence, you need to leave this place at least for a little while."

"I don't want to miss—"

Charice put her hand up. "Listen to me. You are going to stress yourself out. Now, my cousin needs you. She's been through enough this year just trying to nurse you back to health, so do this for her. If anything changes, we will call you immediately. Besides, we have Deputy Do Right guarding the door. We'll be fine."

"All right. You two are gonna browbeat me. I'll leave and get cleaned up, but I'm coming right back."

Trinity hugged me. "That's fine. I just need for you to take a break, baby. You're not going to be any good to any of us running on E."

As I drove to my condo, my mind ran a million miles a minute. Everything that had gone wrong in my life since my bid was either directly or indirectly a result of the bullshit Pooch did to me and my family. I'd done federal time, lost Trinity, lost my cousin, was in danger of losing another one, and damn near lost my own life on account of his sick, twisted behavior. All those things just kept running through my mind as if the devil himself were sitting on my shoulders, whispering in my ear.

I tried to be a good dude. I was raised right. Yeah, I hustled, but a real man does whatever he has to do to make sure his family eats. It was never my intention to get tied up in that street-life bullshit, but with Trinity being in high school and having not one but two of my seeds, what the hell else was I supposed to do? Let them struggle? Hell no. I'd always done a little something on the side, small-time shit. I didn't want Fed time, but once Trinity told me she was pregnant again, shit had to change. Then to find out I was having a daughter made me that much hungrier. I already had Trinity and my son struggling, and I'd be damned if I was gonna let another one of my seeds come into this world struggling, especially not my *little girl*. Damn that. My only mission once I jumped full-fledged into hustling was to make enough to bounce. I was gonna breeze in, hustle hard, and breeze out. Be smart.

It's funny that hustling was the one thing that made me a direct target for Pooch because it gave him leverage to get to Trinity. Back when I was working on cars—you know, robbing Peter to pay Paul—Trinity and I were good. We were happy. Drama free. Once I got into hustling, that street life bullshit that comes with it followed me, even with me being out of the game. Even though my family didn't have shit to worry about financially, I was miserable. I guess the old adage was true: Mo' money, mo' problems. I'd gladly trade in all my riches just to have peace of mind and a normal marriage with Trinity. Just like back in the day, when we were just li'l mama and Dreads from the block.

Armed with my 9 mm Beretta, I roamed through every room and closet in my house to make sure I didn't have any surprises. Once everything was clear, I went into the closet in the bedroom and found some new clothes. I laid out a pair of khaki casual pants and a gray crew neck T-shirt on the bed and grabbed my gray Jordans. Then I peeled off the clothes I had on and put them in a trash bag as I waited for the water to heat up for my shower.

As I set down the trash bag, all the pain I had endured washed over me, and tears slid down my face. Thomas looked up to me as a big brother. Even if he was on some bullshit, I never wished anything like this on him. The more I thought about it, the more my blood boiled.

If it weren't for Trinity and my kids, I would walk straight in that muthafuckin' prison and put that bitch-ass nigga straight outta his fuckin' misery. I swear to God I would, I thought. Nothing would give me greater pleasure than to be the one to do it. Nothing.

After I'd washed away the physical reminders of the last three days, I leaned my forehead against the cool shower tile and let the water relax my tired muscles. I lifted my head when I thought I heard my phone ring. I opened the shower door to hear my phone buzzing across the counter, so I hurriedly wrapped a towel around my waist and answered it right before it ended.

"'Sup baby? What's wrong?" I asked Trinity in a panic.

"Nothing. Everything is going to be just fine. Thomas woke up. He's asking for you," she said excitedly.

Joy spread from the bottom of my heart across my body so fast it felt like fire. "Yes! Tell him I'll be right there. I swear I will. Give me twenty minutes."

"I will, baby. God is good. I told you it would work out," Trinity said.

"You did. I love you."

"I love you, too. See you soon."

We disconnected the line, and I got dressed quickly. I broke God only knows how many traffic laws trying to get back to the hospital. The moment my feet touched the ICU floor; I made a mad dash to his room.

"Thomas," I called out as I entered.

He tried to sit up, but the doctor and nurse stopped him. "Take it easy there," the doctor said as he turned to face me.

"I want to make it as brief as possible. We have to run some tests to make sure he doesn't have any long-term effects, but for now, he's stable and safe," the doctor said to me. He patted me on the back, and then he walked out with the nurse.

"We'll give you two some space," Trinity said, hugging me, then she and Charice also exited.

I pulled my chair close to Thomas's bed and grabbed his hand. "I'm here for you, man." A tear streaked down my face, and I let it.

"They told me you never left my side until a few minutes ago," he struggled to say.

"Yep. I could never leave your side. Regardless of anything, we are family. Always will be."

He formed a half-smile and swallowed. "I'm so sorry about Trinity," he said, and I could tell he was getting choked up.

I put my hand up. "Forget it. I understand. You're gonna always be fam."

"I love you, man."

"Back at you," I said to him. "I know who did this and—"

"Pooch did it. I know he was gunning for you. But don't," Thomas mumbled.

"Don't what?" I asked, leaning close as his words became shallow.

"Don't get revenge. The cycle stops here. I'm not dying at twenty-six, and I ain't burying you before you turn thirty. This game stops with me." He was struggling to speak.

I just patted his shoulder and nodded. "Okay. Don't force yourself to do too much. Just stop talking."

"I'm serious. Don't you go after him."

"Okay. I hear you. Get your rest. You need it to gather strength. We'll talk later," I said as I stood up. He didn't say anymore, but instead closed his eyes.

I walked up to Charice and Trinity in the waiting area, and they stood up. I faced Charice. "Thank you, Charice, for coming down. Trinity really needed this. We both appreciate you to the fullest."

"You know I had to be here. We're family."

"Always will be," I said and then turned to Trinity. "Baby, you and Charice stay up here a little while longer with Thomas. He's resting now."

Trinity looked at me with a questionable expression. "Where are you going?"

I shook my head. "Nowhere. I just need to clear my head. I'll grab us some food on my way back. How's that?"

She eyed me suspiciously, then nodded. "Sounds good," she said and pulled me close. "Don't do any stupid stuff. I can't lose you," she whispered.

I pulled back. "I give you and Thomas my word that I'm not doing anything."

She smiled and looked a little relieved. "Okay. See you when you get back, baby."

I walked to my truck and got in. Once I was safely out of the hospital parking lot, I picked up my cell phone.

"Hey, are you in town?" I asked.

"Yep. We're just waiting on you to get to the spot with our package," she said and then got serious. "Again, I'm sorry about your cousin. Has there been any change?"

Ignoring her questions about Thomas, I kept my focus on the business at hand. "I'll be there in like fifteen minutes. You ladies just hold tight and grab yourselves some drinks. This is a celebration after all."

She laughed. "Yep, it sure is. We love reuniting with old friends."

"Yeah, I'm sure you do, Danielle. This will be a reunion that you and Lisa will never forget." With that, I hung up.

I opened my glove box and felt for the brown envelope. One hundred grand in unmarked bills. Check. What? I told the truth. I told Thomas and Trinity that *I* wasn't doing anything to Pooch, and I was not. He had enough other enemies to handle that for me. I never intended to do a thing to Pooch. My threats were merely meant to keep him away from my family, but I always kept an ace in the hole. Always. As much as Pooch would like to think that he could touch me, he forgot that he also wasn't untouchable. If there was one thing I'd learned, it was that you can only get away with screwing people over for so long. Sooner or later, you get screwed right back, and Pooch was about to be screwed raw with no protection.

My camp had gotten word from this nigga named Wolf about what went down when Aaron got Pooch out. In return for his generous information, I set aside a nice investment for him for when he won his appeal. Very legal and very untraceable, of course. Lisa and Danielle had been in my back pocket ever since. I didn't show my cards, and I didn't play them until absolutely necessary. Now it was necessary.

For three days, I'd sat by Thomas, and for three days, I'd made the necessary connections to get to this point. My only regret was that I would not be the one to see this plan through. Oh, well. Clean hands can't get accused of dirt. And for Pooch, the situation was about to get real dirty.

Chapter 26

Pooch

Pins and fucking needles were what I had been on ever since I heard the news that Thomas had made it. Flava and Adrienne had done me the hugest favor and rode up to the neighborhood, pretending to be interested in purchasing a home, so they could scope out the situation. From what they had gathered, Terrence and Trinity weren't even living at the house anymore. Slick-ass mutha-fuckas. I couldn't bring any more heat around their home without it looking like a hit versus some random act of violence. As of now, the dumb-ass police detectives kept teetering between two explanations for the shooting. The good news was that it had not been linked back to me. At least not yet. The bad news was that I had no clue as to where Terrence was.

On the real, it didn't even fuckin' matter what the police thought or didn't think. Terrence was smart enough to know it was me. He didn't need proof to see the writing on the wall. Now, the gangsta part of me didn't give a fuck if he knew or not, but the locked-up part of me knew better. In this street game, if you lived by the sword, you were more than likely to die by it, too. That didn't scare me anymore, but I wanted to go out on my terms in my own way. The streets owed me that much.

"Mail call," Flex said, then he called out my name.

We called him Flex because he was always flexin' like he was the number one man in this joint when he was truly just a pet nigga for Warden Sims and the COs. I bet they took his ass out in the yard and threw the Frisbee to him like a dog. These dudes were a trip, acting like these damn police cared about them. Hell, if they cared that much, they'd let their asses out of this dump. Niggas fell for anything. Don't sell me no fuckin' pipe dreams. If you love me, you have to prove that shit for real. Let me the hell out, hook me up with some cash flow and a great piece of pussy. That's *real* love. Shit.

"Thanks, man," I said as I grabbed my letter and sat on my bunk.

I looked at it. It had no return address, and I wondered who in the hell was writing me. Flava and Adrienne never wrote anymore. Stein's letters would've at least had his firm's address on it, so I knew it wasn't him either. I was interested in finding out who in the hell wanted to hit me up. If it was some ol' pen pal shit, I was gonna be mad as hell. These damn loser-ass broads were always trying to write a brother on lockdown. There were some lonely-ass women in the world to be doing that shit. Or maybe it was just that all the niggas were getting locked the fuck up, so these broads figured they'd catch one on the way out so they could say they had a man.

I opened the letter and leaned back on my bed. My eyes bucked when I read the signature. It was from Wolf.

'Sup, Pooch

I bet you never thought you'd hear from me again. And I must admit, I shared the same sentiment. Then I found out you got locked back up. I still don't know the whole story, but I know that cop that got you off is dead now, and you're the reason why. Damn, dude. Do you have loyalty for anybody?

Ah well. I'm just writing you because I wanted you to know that despite what you did to me, I forgive you. I may have slipped up with Cock Diesel in the heat of my own personal moment, but I was loyal to you, and I never betrayed you. I hope you remember that. I hope that one day you see the error of your ways and that when you do, you'll be man enough to ask for forgiveness from everyone you betrayed. I'm just letting you know upfront that you don't have to ask me because it's already done. My mind is at ease.

I'm getting my appeal, and I hope to get out soon. I'm gonna get out and relax and chill for the rest of my life. No more street hustlin' or street life.

I'm flying straight and hopefully, I'll be sitting on some beach sippin' on a Heineken. I wish you could join me, but I have a feeling that this time your lockdown is gonna be a permanent stay instead of a temporary visit. But if it ain't, it's all good. I'm positive this time you won't take freedom for granted. And if you do get free, make amends with God for the things you did because at this point in your life, only God can help you.

Peace, Wolf

I ripped the letter up. Man, fuck Wolf. I didn't give a damn about his newfound religion or his pleas to get me to ask for redemption. Whatever. My confessions and my testimonies were for me and God to handle. I didn't need no undercover faggot–ass summa bitch who was in the same situation as me to tell me what to do. Talkin' 'bout he forgive me. What the fuck ever. If he was in my predicament, he would've stuck my ass, too. He was just mad 'cause I stuck his ass first. And Big Cal or Detective Marsh, whoever he was, wasn't nothin' but self-defense. I told him we were straight, but that stupid bastard turned rogue, so he got dealt with street style. I didn't want to kill that bastard, but he had left me no choice. None. In a battle between your life and the next nigga, who would *you* choose? Exactly.

The thing that was really pissin' me off above all else, though, was the fact that Wolf had an appeal, and he felt confident that he was gonna get out. Freedom. The one thing I longed for the most was this bastard's lot in life and not my own. Call it jealousy or what you wanted. He had what I desperately wanted, and it was time to focus on that. Stein, Flava, and Adrienne needed to get their asses in gear because I was not gonna spend the rest of my life locked up like some gawd-damned caged monkey! Hell to the muthafuckin' no!

"Smalls," CO Smith called out to me.

I sat up. "What's up?"

"You have a visitor. I think it's your attorney."

"What the fuck is Stein doing here?" *He must've gotten some news about my case.* "A'ight." I stood up and walked to the cell door to get suited and booted, as I called it.

"You might be outta here soon, huh?" CO Smith asked as we walked down the corridor.

"Shit. That's the fuckin' plan."

"Damn. I forgot my walkie-talkie. I have to get it," he said as he looked to the side where the other cell blocks were. "Come with me." We walked to another area. "Just stay here. I'm gonna get another CO to take you."

Soon, this big dude with a cap and some shades came over and began walking with me.

"Damn. You didn't even warm up to me first," I said. "I'm Smalls. And you are?"

The dude just smirked and kept walking with me. Crazy muthafucka. He thought he was a bad ass. *I'm glad he's not on my cell block.*

"Hey, dude. Where are you going? Smith said I had a visitor. We ain't going that direction," I said.

"Pit stop," he mumbled.

When we came up to the infirmary, my heart got a little heavy. I remembered at my old facility going to the infirmary and visiting Lisa all the time. I missed her ass. I wished she could've understood the situation that I was in, but she didn't. That's because she wasn't built for street life, and she wasn't built to have a thug nigga like me. I was too much of a bad boy for her to handle.

The CO opened the door, and we went inside. He shut the door and forced me into the seat. I thought it was strange that there wasn't but one nurse on duty that day, but hell, stranger things had happened. I was just ready for this CO to get whatever he needed so I could get to the visitor's area.

"Hello, Mr. Smalls," a female's voice floated through the air. The shit startled me as I looked up and realized the nurse was Lisa.

"Lisa?" I gasped.

She smiled. "Yep." The next thing I knew, I felt handcuffs slap around my ankles, locking me to the chair.

"What the fuck?"

The CO stood up and pulled off the shades and the cap. It was muthafuckin' Danielle. CO Brown. That damn big bull!

"How the fuck did you two bitches get in here? Where is Smith? What the fuck are y'all doing to me?"

"He always did have too much mouth, didn't he?" Danielle asked Lisa, who nodded and laughed. "Well, we're gonna have to fix that." She pulled out some duct tape and taped it across my mouth.

"You have questions, Pooch. I'm gonna answer them," Lisa said as she slipped on some gloves, filled a syringe with some clear liquid, and thumped the needle. She walked over to me. "I loved you, Pooch. I told you to leave that Flava bitch alone, but you just couldn't do it. I was the one who had your back. I could've been your bottom bitch. Me. How the hell do you think you got the chance to actually run drugs in and out of a prison without being caught? How do you think the hits you performed on inmates never got linked back to you? How do you really think you got the chance to be the kingpin of that prison?

"I'ma let you in on a little secret, a secret that only me, Danielle, and the warden know. The warden of the old facility . . . he's my father. He didn't want me to work there, but I wanted to. All my boyfriends from high school to college were nothing but dope boys. I don't know. I guess I'm addicted to the life. Why wouldn't I want the number one bad boy of them all, Mr. Vernon Pooch Smalls?" she said as my eyes bucked.

"Are you surprised that I was really a wolf in sheep's clothing? I made your business flow from behind the scenes. Hell, I could've even chopped it up and cooked it for a much better potency if I felt I could trust you, but I knew I couldn't. You're selfish. Always had to be in control and never wanted to give anything for another person. I let you think you were in charge. You and your whole little clique. You should've stuck with me. I could've had you out by now, but you just couldn't wait. You had to have it your way. Oh, well. That's the way you played the game, and you lost," she said as she and Danielle began to laugh.

"Tell him what this is really about," Danielle snickered.

"Do you want to know what this is about?" she asked. Danielle nodded my head yes for me. "It's about payback. This is for everyone you've fucked over. Me, Danielle, all the gangstas and hustlas, but most importantly, this is for your *ex-cellmate, your one true love, and her one true love*," she said. "For you, you can look at it as redemption. We're gonna relieve you of all of your sins."

My eyes bucked, realizing this shit was a part of an even bigger set up. Wolf, Trinity, and Terrence. My whole day flashed before my eyes. My cellmate, Johnson, had been out of the cell for a long time. Smith and the walkie-talkie, Danielle the CO, and Lisa the nurse. All these muthafuckas had been paid off. All of 'em!

Danielle held my arms as I bucked and struggled to get free. It wasn't going down like this. Not at all. Taken out by two bitches on account of Terrence? Hell no!

"Stop struggling, Pooch. It's no use," Danielle said.

Lisa sat down right in front of me and smiled. "Just think of this as a cough drop. One last big cough, and you'll be all better," Lisa said as she brought the needle close to my arm. "Oh, um, do you have any last-minute confessions for God?"

I thought about Wolf's letter. That bastard was sending me a warning. Fuck him and everybody else.

"Confession is good for the soul," Danielle said, looking down at me.

I glared at both of them. There comes a point in your life when you have to deal with the decisions you've made. I could've opted to plead for the miserable life I led, but I wasn't about to. Not Pooch Smalls. I came in this world a boy, but I was gonna leave out of it a man. So instead of giving them their satisfaction, I said fuck it. If I was gonna go out like this, I was gonna go out as Vernon—that muthafuckin' nigga—Pooch Smalls. I sat back, squared my shoulders, and gave them the best I-don't-give-a-fuck attitude I could.

Lisa shook her head. "Even in your last moments, you refuse to show remorse. I hope you rot in hell, you bastard," she said.

"Take off the duct tape," she demanded of Danielle. "Say something," she demanded of me.

I laughed sinisterly. "Fuck you. Fuck all of you. I will live forever, you bitch."

"Go to hell," Lisa seethed.

"Don't worry, baby. You'll join me soon enough."

"No last wishes?" Danielle asked as Lisa pierced my vein with the needle.

I thought of my last days with Trinity and Princess. No matter what my fate in life was, it always came back to my two favorite girls. It was then that I realized that the only person I had ever truly loved in life would always be Trinity. Even if I had to die over her, it was all right with me because my soul had died the day she left with my daughter. Death would only be a sweet relief.

"Tell my daughter that her daddy loves her, and tell Trinity I'll always love her," I said.

"Yeah, I'll do that." Danielle rolled her eyes.

"Oh, and T told me to deliver a message to you," Lisa said to me. "He said, 'Karma is a bitch.' Now, remember that shit," she said as I began to slump over in the chair.

I felt the burning fluid rushing through my veins. It gripped me into a peaceful stillness. Everything surrounding me seemed close but so far away. As I began to fade in and out of consciousness, a sense of calm came over my body. This was freedom. CO Smith was right. I wasn't gonna spend the rest of my life there. I was gonna be free. Finally, I was gonna be free.

As my heartbeat began to slow to a few steady beats, I looked up and saw Big Cal, Pops, and a bunch of niggas I knew who had died in the streets, and on the other side, I saw my grandma.

"Confess, Poochie, before it's too late," she whispered.

I smiled at her. "I'm sorry. Sorry I couldn't be the son you raised. I love you. But it's up to the Almighty. He knows my heart," I said faintly, and suddenly, everything faded to black.

Chapter 27

Trinity

Life is funny. One day, you're on a path and you think everything was okay, then everything goes awry. Your life is suddenly turned upside down for no apparent reason, and you are left to gather the pieces. People have changed. Circumstances have changed, and then you're left wondering what it all really means. Where do I go from here?

When I was a little girl, I imagined my life being much simpler. I didn't plan for complications. Now, every time I turned around, that was all that life ever presented me with—complicated situations. I didn't know what to do when I lost Dreads to the system, so I had settled with Pooch. When God gave me Dreads back, I'd hoped that my life would be the simple and easy life I'd prayed for, but I never imagined all the drama that would follow. All the drama, the lies, the hatred, and everything had become unbearable. All I wanted was for it to be over. But never, ever like this.

I couldn't knock everything about my life with Pooch. It wasn't all bad, and even through the bad times came life lessons that I will never forget. I mean, how could you ever learn how to survive if you've never gone through the struggle? On the good side of Pooch, he had picked me up during a time I didn't know how I was gonna make it with two babies. It was true that he had caused it, but he didn't treat me as if I were some cut buddy or chick on the side. He took us in as his family. I chose to remember the brighter side of that instead of the negative.

Despite his attitude and behavior, a part of me would always feel that the good side of Pooch truly loved me. Not to mention that our bond brought forth a beautiful baby girl. My life would be incomplete without my Princess, just as it would without Terry, Brittany, and Tyson. I just never thought I'd have to reflect on all of this as I was doing today.

I leaned over and hugged Dreads tight. Then I stood up and smoothed out my black skirt, dabbed my eyes, and walked to the front of the church with grace and elegance. My black hat slightly shaded my eyes, which I was happy about. It hid the few tears that threatened to fall. I looked out over the sea of people in the congregation. My eyes landed on Attorney Stein, Sonja, and Adrienne, who were drenched in tears. Sonja's eyes were so sorrowful yet jealous because she knew, like everyone else, that no matter what they did for Pooch, I was the one who had his heart.

My whole crew was there: LaMeka, Charice, and Lucinda. Even Aldris, Gavin, and of course, both Lincoln and Ryan had showed up. I gazed over at Thomas and Dreads sitting there with our children, and my focus landed on Princess. She was so young that she didn't even realize what was truly going on. That's where my true sadness lay for our daughter. She was going to grow up never having truly known her dad.

I looked over at the big portrait of Pooch's and ran my hand across the closed casket as I took my spot at the podium. "As I stand here today and listen to all the things being said about Vernon, I have to admit that it's wonderful, but those of us who knew him best knew him as Pooch or Poochie, as his grandmother used to call him," I said, and people let out small chuckles. I looked over at Pooch's picture and smiled. "Out of all the people who knew him, I probably knew him best. There are many things that I could say about Pooch, but what I want to leave you with the most are the things that truly defined him. He was strong willed and took no nonsense. To most people, he seldom showed emotion, but it was in our private moments that the measure of his heart was known, even if only briefly, to me. That is the man I will always remember. Take your rest now, Pooch, and may God grant you the peace that you never found on Earth." I kissed my fingertips and placed my hand back on the casket. Everyone said their "Amens" as I whispered to him that I loved him before I sat back down next to Dreads.

"Are you okay?" Dreads asked me.

My head dipped low in sorrow. "I never wanted it to come to this. I will always have love for him, ya know."

"Yeah, I know," Dreads said quietly.

"But you will always have my heart," I said, looking over at him as he held Princess.

He turned to face me as the choir began their rendition of "For Every Mountain."

"Yeah, I know that too," he said and kissed me on the forehead.

Chapter 28

One Year Later . . .

"I'm on my way down now," Lucinda said as she hung up her cell phone and stepped onto the elevator.

She was thankful that it was empty. She'd finally gotten a few moments of peace to herself, so she could just clear her mind and meditate. The hum of the elevator combined with the soothing music was therapeutic to her ears, mind, and soul. The joy in the simple things could bring the greatest of comfort, and she'd learned to appreciate that more and more every day.

Heaving a sigh, she stepped off the elevator to prepare for the chaos once again. She was ready for this to be over so things could go back to normal.

Making her way down the corridor, she bumped into a man and nearly choked as their eyes connected. It had been over a year, but she'd recognize that face and that scent anywhere. Every emotion humanly possible ran through her veins as her mind notated exactly who was standing in front of her. On the inside, she laughed because she'd always wondered how she'd feel or what she'd do if she ever came face to face with him again. Amazingly, the only emotion that lingered was pity.

"Lucinda?" Mike asked as if he were trying to confirm that the vision before him was real.

She nodded slowly. "Mike."

She was surprised to see him there, but not at the same time. After their breakup, Rod and Alize had explained that Mike decided to move out of the state of Georgia for a fresh start. According to them, he was living in Richmond, Virginia, so she was positive his visit today was for his children.

"Unbelievable. You look amazing." He admired her. "It's good to see you."

She smiled. "Thanks. Well, I have to get going."

"Wait! It's been a long time, Lu. A year. I knew better than to contact you at first, and even when I did try, your number was disconnected. I promise I won't hold you. I just have something to say. I've wanted to tell you this for a few months now."

Even though she was uncomfortable and her momentary moments of relaxation were fading fast, she decided that she had to hear this. But she wasn't buying anything he was selling if this was a sales pitch.

"What is it?" she asked

Sensing her apprehension, he decided to spill it—straight up, no chaser. "I'm sorry. I am truly sorry," he said sincerely. "I swear to you on my children's lives that I never intended for what I did to happen. It just kind of snowballed into this big ball of deception. I loved you, but it was misguided by fear. Fear that I would lose you to Aldris. Now I realize that what was going to be, was going to be, and what wasn't meant to be, simply wasn't. For the first time in my life, I'm okay with that. I just hope that you and Aldris can one day forgive me."

Lucinda exhaled. Truth be told, she'd forgiven Mike a long time ago, partly because she blamed herself to a certain extent for his destructive path. The basis of the relationship was wrong from beginning to end, so how else did either of them expect it to turn out?

But Aldris was a different story. He'd made it clear that while he was willing to move past what Mike did, he'd never forget, and Mike was declared a blackballed discussion.

"Mike, I'm glad that you've moved on, and I accept your apology. In essence, we both had some blame, but as far as forgiveness, I forgave you a long time ago because it was impossible for me to move on without doing so. My heart couldn't be open to love if I was holding on to anger and hurt. However, I thank you for that. It means a lot."

Mike was intrigued by her statement and excited at the same time. "So, who is your heart open to? Whoever it is must not be in Atlanta," he said, hoping that meant she was no longer with Aldris and hoping that finding her in a hotel meant she no longer lived here.

Lucinda sensed the glimmer of hope in his tone. Even a year later, she knew he'd take her back in a New York minute if she'd give him the okay. Lucinda smiled and removed her light jacket. Mike's mouth dropped.

"I didn't leave, if that's what you're wondering. I'm still an Atlanta native," she confirmed, revealing her ensemble—a T-shirt embroidered with *Mrs. Sharper* on the front and sweatpants. "I'm marrying Aldris tomorrow, Mike. If you'll excuse me, I'm running late for my bachelorette party. It was good seeing you again, though. Have a good one," she said as she walked away, leaving Mike to stare at the embroidery on the seat of her pants: *The Bride*.

"What took you so long?" Trinity asked Lucinda as she walked to the back after greeting her guests.

"You'll never believe who I ran into on the way in here," Lucinda said.

"I hope it wasn't Aldris," Charice joked. "Tell that man you'll see him on the other side of the church tomorrow. My goodness," she joked about Aldris's clingy behavior ever since the wedding weekend had gotten underway.

Lucinda laughed. "He's just excited. I am, too. This has been a long time coming."

"Who are you telling? I was scared to buy my dress," Trinity joked. Lucinda playfully pushed her. "I'm just saying. You two love to break up and date other people and shit, so I wasn't gonna get too cozy with the idea that you'd actually get to this day."

"Well, I can assure you, chica, that my baby and I are definitely doing the damn thing this time. No one or nothing can hold us back. Not even Mike." She laughed.

"Bitch, no!" Charice laughed, damn near spitting out her champagne. "Tell me that's not who you saw!"

Lucinda nodded. "Uh-huh."

"What did you say to him? What did he say to you?" they asked in unison.

"He actually apologized for what he did, and I told him I forgave him. He seemed sincere," Lucinda said. "Up until he thought I was hinting that I was trying to be back with him, to which I promptly showed him my ensemble," she said, turning around slowly. "No, papi. Clearly, he misunderstood. This shit here is Aldris's all damn day long." She laughed but was interrupted by LaMeka ending a phone call.

"I love you too, baby," LaMeka said, hanging up her cell phone as she approached the ladies sitting at the table. "Sorry. I had to take that."

Lucinda laughed. "It wasn't nobody but your husband. Tell Gavin you're all good. This is my time. After tomorrow night, he's got you all to himself again."

"So, how does it feel to join the ranks of married women?" Trinity asked, toasting with LaMeka.

"Great! You know, Gavin is just amazing. I told him he didn't have to stay home with the baby. He could've gone out with the fellas for Aldris's bachelor party," LaMeka said, sipping on her sparkling water. "But you know him. Besides, he loves spending time with his little girl."

"I'm still upset about that non-wedding you had. I wanted my opportunity to be the maid of honor," Charice said, rolling her eyes at LaMeka and referring to their decision to elope during Meka's second month of pregnancy. "But anyway, how is my goddaughter doing?"

Trinity laughed. "Yes, please change that subject. We've been hearing that for a year."

"And I've been apologizing to her for a year about it, too," LaMeka said nonchalantly. "But anyway, Gabriela is wonderful. She's the perfect little one. Never gives us a moment's trouble," she said about her three-month-old daughter.

Charice smiled. "That's my Gabby." She giggled. "I guess I can't be too upset. You did bless the baby with *my* name. Gabriela Charice Randall," she said to rub it in.

"Oh, what*ever*." Lucinda and Trinity laughed.

"And let's not forget, mamí, that her full name is Gabriela *Diana* Charice Randall." Lucinda poked fun at Charice.

"Well, my name is still up in there, though. I don't mind making room for Gavin's mother. That is who birthed him after all, *mamí*," Charice shot back. "You just get down this damn aisle tomorrow and have some twins, so you can name them after me and Trinity." They laughed.

"Shiiiit. I want a boy when we do decide to have children. Two girls living in our household are enough for me," Lucinda said.

"How is Jessica adjusting to that?" Trinity asked.

"We have good days and bad days, but I'm happy that she accepts and loves Nadia and me. It makes it much easier," Lucinda said sadly.

"I just don't understand that. How can a mother just abandon her child like that? Just because she's torn up over a man. I don't give a damn how much my kids look like their father. They are still mine," Charice declared. Trinity and LaMeka agreed.

"I think losing Aldris for a second time was just too much for her. She's welcome to be in Jessica's life when she's ready, as long as Jessica is okay with it. Neither Aldris nor I are going to put her through anything she doesn't want. She's been through enough," Lucinda said.

"Enough of this talk. It's reminding me of Pooch." Trinity sighed, and they all got quiet.

"I can't believe it's been a year," Lucinda said.

"Me either. Princess barely remembers him, and I suppose in a lot of ways that's good on my end. I don't have to deal with what you go through." She looked over at Lucinda. "Besides, Terrence is as great a father to all of them as he is an excellent husband, so at the end of the day, I'm blessed, and so is she. I just feel so bad for her. I never knew my dad, and despite all the hell Pooch put us through, I guess I always felt that he'd get it together and be the dad she needed even if it was only from prison."

There was calm amongst the ladies as an air of sadness washed over them. Each of them reflected on the mistakes and blessings they'd endured over the past two years. They'd lost loves, loved ones, and even themselves, but finally, everything had come full circle. Almost at the same time, they reflected on all the goodness they'd achieved and come to know as they leaned on each other and smiled.

"Enough of this. Raise your glasses. I'd like to make a toast," Trinity said. "Well, we'll raise our champagne glasses, and you raise your sparkling water, First Lady Randall," she said. They all burst into laughter.

"Reverend Randall is still in training. I'll take a sip if I want." LaMeka laughed.

"Not on my watch, because so are you." Trinity giggled. "To Lucinda and Aldris. May you have a long and happy life together!"

"And you ain't lying 'cause never again . . . no more am I going through this again." Lucinda laughed.

"Me either," the rest said in unison.

"Never say never." LaMeka pointed at Charice. "You might be married again one day. 'Cause you know what goes around tends to come back around again," she joked.

"No more babies and marriage for this chick," Charice shouted. "I am so loving my freedom."

"You say that now, but you'll get tired of the game soon enough," Lucinda said.

Just then, four men walked in, dressed in cowboy hats and leather stirrups, asking where the bride was. The women went crazy.

"Over here." Charice pointed. "But stop here first!" she screamed as she moved toward the dance floor where the men were.

"Lincoln is gonna kill her," LaMeka said, shielding her eyes from all the ass and ding-a-ling popping around.

Lucinda fanned off LaMeka's comment. "Girl, please. They're only discussing possibly dating each other again. She's a single parent and a divorcee. She deserves to have a little fun. Besides, she ain't his wife."

"*Yet*," LaMeka quipped smartly with a giggle.

Lucinda shrugged.

"And I ain't Aldris's wife *yet* either," she joked, running onto the floor with Charice.

Trinity and LaMeka looked at each other and shrugged. "What the hell?" they said in unison.

"You think we'll still have husbands in the morning?" LaMeka joked.

"Hell yeah, 'cause Terrence and Gavin are stuck with us," Trinity joked, and they hugged. "Besides . . ."

"What happens at the Marriott stays at the Marriott," they said in unison as they joined their girls on the dance floor.

Epilogue

The Cost of Loyalty

It was a scorching hot day. It was so hot that it seemed the sun's rays were beaming up from the ground like fire rising from a grill. It was definitely the day and age to get your life right because God had the heat on hell, and if this was any indication of what hell might be like, no one needed to find out the truth.

The constant hum of the AC was just as soothing as the air blowing from it. Whoever the muthafucka was that came up with this invention needed to get royalties off every unit made and sold throughout the world. It's actually funny that God's punishment to non-believers was to burn. It was the one thing that black and white folks had in common: white folks didn't like that they turned black when they died, and black folks couldn't stand heat, so roasting our asses in eternal damnation should be enough for both races to get their lives together.

At the sound of the car pulling up, I couldn't help but smile. It was time. I picked up my hand-kerchief and wiped the sweat from my brow as I opened the door.

"Come inside!" I shouted.

Soon, I was joined, and the door quickly shut.

"It's hotter than the devil's ass out there."

"I know. That's why I'm in here," I said.

"You just had to move out here in the desert."

"Don't judge my place of peace. Besides, it's a win-win for everyone."

"Yeah, I guess you're right." He pulled out the duffel bag. "I've brought my money machine."

"Honestly, I trust you, but we can count it just to be sure," I said. "I can't really argue with you anyway. I owe you my life and for getting my life back."

"Yeah, and the sooner I get out of this Mojave Desert and back to my family, the better," Terrence said.

I had tried to tell Danielle and Lisa that Pooch would live on forever. On the real, I thought I was dead when Lisa pushed that poison into my veins. At first, when I woke up in that deserted-ass hotel, I vowed that Terrence would wish that he had killed me because I was dead set to get at him. But then that bastard made me an offer I couldn't refuse, literally. Freedom and cash in exchange for our lives back. No one but us could ever know, since they'd reported me as deceased and held a funeral service for me. I couldn't go after Wolf, Danielle, or Lisa, and no more messing with him, Trinity, or any of his family. Lastly, I had to allow him to be the father to Princess. Wasn't that a bitch?

The freedom, money, and leaving everybody alone was a no-brainer, but I hated letting Princess go. Yet, I had to because this time, that mutha-fucka had me by the balls. If I showed up on the East Coast, I'd be back in prison so fucking fast the ink wouldn't have time to dry on my fake-ass death certificate. I had no choice. As I said, that muthafucka was smart and slick as hell. It was my payback for all the bad Karma I had put out into the universe.

I took the initial one hundred grand and dipped to a location undisclosed to everybody but me and Terrence. He told me to give him a year to move some money around and he'd give me a million dollars free and clear in exchange for what he was offering me. I couldn't knock that shit. The mutha-fucka was paying me back every penny he stole and then some. On another note, at least this way, I got to live my life and maybe one day have a chance to build a real relationship with my daughter.

As the money machine finally counted out the last set of thousands to equal one million dollars, Terrence handed me a beer. We touched bottles and drank. Then we both began to laugh.

"It feels good to be back in business." I stood up and stretched.

Terrence stood. "Just remember the terms of our deal."

"Always. Just remember my terms," I said.

He reached in his pocket and handed me a recent photo of my daughter, and a drawing that Princess had done of me and her. A tear came to my eye, and I wiped it quickly. "She's gotten so big. She gets more beautiful every year."

"Text me a forwarding address and you'll get a new picture every time we take one," Terrence said.

"Will do." I kissed her picture and placed it in my wallet beside my previous picture of her and Trinity, and across from my picture of Lucia.

"Are you gonna stay out here in the desert?" Terrence asked.

"Nah, I don't want to pop up on the grid. I met a cute little Mexican named Lucia, and her cousin is hooked up with all kinds of shit. I got a new passport and ID. Cabo San Lucas ain't sounding too bad right now. My new name is Virgil Simmons."

"Just keep your ass out of Tijuana and it's all good," Terrence joked as he walked to the door to leave. "Well, take care of yourself, *Virgil*."

"Take care of my daughter," I said as we shook hands to our agreement. "Now, get out of the desert, city boy," I said.

Terrence bounded for the rental SUV and took off down the dusty road.

I shut the door and fell back onto the bed across all my cash. Pooch—I mean Virgil Simmons— had a new lease on life, and it was time to cross the border to do just that. I laughed to myself as I sat up and pulled out the kilo of cocaine under my bed. That shit was the purest fire I'd ever sniffed. Within thirty seconds, my face felt like I had a hundred ccs of morphine coursing through my veins. I wasn't crazy. I wasn't going to, nor did I want to live in Tijuana, but that didn't mean I wasn't going into business there. What can I say? A real hustler's game was never over. These Mexican muthafuckas weren't gon' know what hit 'em. I was back!

Notes